Holly Hepburn has wanted to ~~write books~~ for as long she can remember but she was ~~too scared~~ to try. One day she decided to be brave and dipped a toe into the bubble bath of romantic fiction with her first novella, *Cupidity*, and she's never looked back. She often tries to be funny, except for when faced with traffic wardens and border control staff. Her favourite things are making people smile and Aidan Turner.

She's tried many jobs over the years, from barmaid to market researcher and she even had a brief flirtation with modelling. These days she is mostly found writing.

She lives near London with her grey tabby cat, Portia. They both have an unhealthy obsession with Marmite.

Follow Holly on Twitter @HollyH_Author.

Praise for the *Star and Sixpence* series:

'A fresh new voice, brings wit and warmth to this charming tale of two sisters' Rowan Coleman

'You'll fall in love with this fantastic new series from a new star of women's fiction, Holly Hepburn. Filled to the brim with captivating characters and fantastic storylines in a gorgeous setting, *Snowdrops at the Star and Sixpence* is simply wonderful. I want to read more!' Miranda Dickinson

'The Star and Sixpence sparkles with fun, romance, mystery, and a hunky blacksmith. It's a real delight' Julie Cohen

GREENWICH LIBRARIES

3 8028 02077588 5

A Year at the Star and Sixpence

holly hepburn

**SIMON &
SCHUSTER**

London · New York · Sydney · Toronto · New Delhi

A CBS COMPANY

First published as *Snowdrops at the Star and Sixpence, Valentine's Day at the Star and Sixpence, Summer at the Star and Sixpence, Autumn at the Star and Sixpence* and *Christmas at the Star and Sixpence* in ebook in Great Britain by Simon & Schuster UK Ltd, 2015 and 2016
A CBS COMPANY

3 5 7 9 10 8 6 4 2

Simon & Schuster UK Ltd
1st Floor
222 Gray's Inn Road
London WC1X 8HB

www.simonandschuster.co.uk

Simon & Schuster Australia, Sydney
Simon & Schuster India, New Delhi

A CIP catalogue record for this book is available from the British Library

Paperback ISBN: 978-1-4711-6314-2
eBook ISBN: 978-1-4711-6315-9

Typeset in the UK by M Rules
Printed and bound by CPI Group (UK) Ltd, Croydon, CR0 4YY

Simon & Schuster UK Ltd are committed to sourcing paper that is made from wood grown in sustainable forests and support the Forest Stewardship Council, the leading international forest certification organisation. Our books displaying the FSC logo are printed on FSC certified paper.

To Pauline and Francis,
because I don't think I ever thanked you

Snowdrops at the Star and Sixpence

Mrs Vanessa Blake
23 Westmoreland Avenue
Godalming
Surrey
GU7 8PB

20th August 2015

Dear Mrs Blake

I write in connection to the estate of your father, the late Andrew Chapman, Esq. As executor of his Will, it is my duty to inform you that you and your sister, Miss Samantha Chapman, are the sole beneficiaries of Mr Chapman's estate, comprising the property known as the Star and Sixpence Public House, Sixpence Lane, Little Monkham, Shropshire, SY6 2XY.

I should be grateful if you would contact me at your earliest convenience to indicate your acceptance of the inheritance and to complete the necessary paperwork thereafter.

Yours faithfully,
Quentin Harris
Harris and Taylor Solicitors

Chapter One

Nessie peered through the windscreen at the night, staring into the darkness that even her full-beam headlights were doing little to disperse. 'Are you sure it's the next left?'

There was a short sigh from the passenger seat beside her. 'That's what the sat nav says, although we're so far from bloody civilisation that it's probably as lost as we are.' Samantha gave the sat nav an experimental tap and stared at the screen again. 'Left turn in fifty yards.'

Nessie pressed her foot against the brake, gazing in vain for a break in the inky trees. 'Only I don't think there's a road.'

'You're the one who's been here before,' Sam fired back. 'I thought you knew the way?'

I did, Nessie wanted to explain, *but it was daylight last time and I had a solicitor's assistant to guide me, instead of a sister who thinks I'm directionally challenged and zooms from calm to cross in four seconds flat.* She didn't say any of that, however. She also didn't point out that if Sam had been ready when she was meant to be, they wouldn't be driving in the dark. Instead, Nessie concentrated on locating the turn Sam insisted was coming up.

After a few more seconds, she saw it: a gap that was more of a dirt track than a road, with a five-bar gate across it and a heavy chain holding it shut. She slowed the car to a halt. 'I'm pretty sure this isn't right.'

With a huff of irritation, Sam wrenched the sat nav device from its holder on the windscreen. 'For God's sake, the postcode must be wrong,' she snapped, stabbing at the screen. 'Did you check it before you put it in?'

Nessie knew she had; she'd read the solicitor's papers over and over to make sure she had exactly the right address details, to reassure herself that she hadn't in fact dreamed up the whole inheritance. But faced with Sam's flash of anger, she felt her certainty drain away. She stared down at her hands, tight and jittery on the wheel. 'I thought I did. Maybe I typed it wrong.'

Sam let out a long slow breath. 'No, I'm sorry. I didn't mean to lose it, it's just been a rough few weeks, you know . . .' Her mouth twisted into a crooked smile and she held up the device. 'There's no signal out here anyway. We could be nearer Luxembourg than Little Monking for all this thing knows.'

Nessie smiled back in spite of her anxiety. 'It's Monkham, not Monking. As featured in the Domesday Book, no less.'

'It's the arse end of nowhere, that's what it is,' Sam muttered, dropping the sat nav into her lap. 'So, now what? Does anything look familiar?'

Nessie gazed around, trying to picture the road in daylight. *Think*, she told herself. *What came after the humpback bridge? A crossroads? A roundabout?* 'There might be a junction around the next bend,' she said slowly, hoping her memory wasn't playing tricks on her. 'I think we went left.'

Sam sat back in her seat. 'Let's find out.'

Taking a deep breath, Nessie put the car in gear and set off once again. 'So, what's this place like?' Sam asked. 'Are we completely mental?'

Nessie pictured the Star and Sixpence, sitting at the top of Little Monkham's immaculate village green, its black and white timber frame bright in the winter sunlight. 'Like I told you, it's old, built around 1600, I think.'

A pained look crossed Sam's face. 'Ugh, old. Tell me there's a shower, at least, and central heating?' She shuddered as she glanced at the sat nav again. 'And Wi-Fi?'

Nessie thought of the dripping showerhead over the chipped enamel bath in the flat upstairs and the vast stone fireplace that dominated the middle of the pub's wood-beamed lounge. She nodded. 'There's a shower and heating, although they could both do with some TLC – the whole place could, to be honest. I'd be amazed if there's Wi-Fi but that's easily fixable if we want it.' She hesitated for a fraction of a second, then plunged on. 'I thought you might want a bit of a break from the internet, to be honest.'

Sam was silent as they rounded the bend and, not for the first time Nessie wondered what would have happened if the father they hadn't spoken to for over twenty years hadn't left them this pub. For her, probably nothing – she'd still be with Patrick, caught up in the inertia of a marriage that had run its course. But Sam was different; she'd been in more pressing need of a way out and help had come from a source neither of them could have predicted.

A signpost loomed into view at the side of the road. 'Little Monkham, one mile,' Sam said triumphantly. 'Who needs technology?'

Nessie didn't know whether she meant the sat nav or the internet or both but it was another reminder that at least part of the reason they were going to Little Monkham was to hide away. Then again, where better to lick your wounds than a place nobody could find?

'Exactly,' Nessie replied, pointing the car along the road that led to the village. 'Maybe there's something to be said for being lost after all.'

The village green was bathed in amber from the streetlamps as they drove into Little Monkham. A man was walking his dog past the war memorial and stopped to tip his hat as they drove by. Nessie raised a self-conscious hand to wave while Sam simply stared back.

'We've gone back to the 1950s, haven't we?' Sam said. 'There's an old blue phone box over there or is it the Tardis?'

'I expect it's a phone box,' Nessie replied mildly. 'Not everyone has a mobile.'

Sam raised her eyebrows. 'But they do have landlines? They don't all queue up to use the public phone?'

Nessie laughed. 'Maybe. Look, there's the pub.'

The Star and Sixpence stood at the head of the green and was lit by a lone old-fashioned streetlamp just outside its door. A sign hung from a wooden pole, a painted silver sixpence next to a bright star, swaying gently in the wind. The windows were inky holes in the white paintwork and the roof sagged above as though tired from its battle with gravity. Sam shivered. 'It doesn't look very welcoming.'

Nessie pulled into the car park and hauled on the hand-brake. 'It will once we get the lights on. Come on.'

It wasn't until they got inside and flicked the light switch that Nessie thought to wonder whether the electricity was still connected. 'Oh,' she said, feeling like an idiot. 'I suppose it's been cut off.'

Sam tapped on the torch on her phone. 'Maybe the power has tripped. That used to happen sometimes at the flat. Where's the fuse box, do you think?'

Nessie thought back to her whistle-stop tour at the hands of the thirteen-year-old assistant. 'I don't know. There's a cellar. Down there, maybe?'

Her sister's nose wrinkled in distaste. 'Marvellous. How do I get to this cellar?'

The windows were small and let in little light from the solitary streetlamp. Sam's phone illuminated her face and the floor when she pointed it downwards, but not much else. There were shadows and pools of darkness every-where. 'Um . . . behind the bar, I think,' Nessie said, trying to ignore the prickling unease between her shoulder blades. 'There's a door and some stairs. Hang on, I'll show you.'

But Sam was already moving, the light from her phone bobbing in the dark. 'Don't worry, I'll find it.'

'Be careful!' Nessie called. From what she remembered, the cellar steps were worn and narrow – easy to fall down in the blackness. Nessie waited, feeling in her pocket for her own phone, the pay-as-you-go one she'd bought when she'd left Patrick. It was cheap and plasticky and definitely didn't have a light. It didn't even go online. But it was okay for keeping in touch with Sam when she needed to. Who would she have called anyway? Her friends had turned out to be *his* friends, which she'd discovered made it easier to cut all ties and start again.

The silence stretched. The darkness felt heavy and Nessie's mind began to race. In an unfamiliar place, at night ... wasn't that the start of a million horror movies? There was no one else there but even so, she couldn't stop her imagination. *You're thirty-five years old*, she told herself, *not five – too old to be afraid of the dark*. It made absolutely no difference. She was about to go in search of Sam when there was a flash of light through the window at the entrance of the pub. The door clattered open, silhouetting a hulking figure that almost filled the frame.

Nessie swallowed a scream. 'Who's there?' she called, taking a step backwards and hating the vibration in her voice. Her legs bumped against something hard and she gripped it for support: a table, she decided, not exactly something she could throw.

Torchlight swept over her face, temporarily blinding her, and then turned upwards to reveal a man's face with a shock of black curls above it. 'Hello,' he said. 'You must be the new owner.'

Nessie's fingers tightened their grip on the table. *Stupid, stupid, he's not a crazed psychopath.* Her heart thudded and thundered in her chest all the same. 'That's right,' she said, as evenly as she could. 'I'm Nessie Blake. Who are you?'

'Owen Rhys,' he said and Nessie noticed his lilting accent. 'From the forge next door. Pleased to meet you.'

Her shoulders relaxed a fraction as she cast her mind back to her visit a few weeks earlier – there'd been a solid-looking building next door, with a yard and a picture-postcard cottage off to one side. So that was a forge, was it?

'I would have been here to meet you, only we thought you were arriving much earlier,' Owen went on. Nessie was relieved to see that he hadn't moved from the doorway and seemed to be waiting for some kind of invitation before he came any closer.

'We . . . we were held up,' she explained. 'Sorry if you were waiting around.'

'No problem,' the man said easily. 'I live in the cottage beside the forge. My boy, Luke, has been keeping an eye out for you since it got dark.'

Nessie nodded, then realised he wouldn't be able to see the movement. 'Right.'

Silence hung between them. 'So, shall I come in and put the lights on? I expect the switch has tripped; the electrics are older than they should be and it doesn't take much of a surge to knock them out.'

'Actually—' Nessie began but she was interrupted by a triumphant shout. Suddenly the room was filled with sickly yellow light. 'My sister, Sam,' Nessie said, squinting. 'It looks like she found the fuse box.'

She blinked as her eyes adjusted. Owen Rhys was around six feet tall, with jet-black curls that tumbled haphazardly across his forehead and dark eyes that were fixed on her. He looked like a blacksmith, she decided, although she wasn't sure how she knew that, since he was the first she'd ever met. He stood in the doorway, slightly stooped under the thick wooden lintel, the torch in one hand and a basket covered with blue and white gingham in the other.

'You look like your father,' Owen said, clicking off his torch. 'You have the same eyes. I'm sorry for your loss, by the way. He was a big part of village life, was Andrew.'

Nessie swallowed an involuntary snort of derision and turned it into a cough. Green eyes were the only thing she and Sam had in common with their father and she knew Sam had gone through a phase of disguising hers with blue contact lenses, her way of distancing herself from him. It was difficult to imagine him being a valued member of any community. But then Nessie remembered where she was and felt the tiniest bit guilty. Whatever Andrew Chapman's other failings, and there'd been plenty, he'd given his daughters somewhere to go when they'd needed it. 'Thank you,' Nessie said, unable to think of anything else to say.

They stood for a moment, watching each other, and Nessie felt more of her tension drain away. For a big man, Owen was curiously unthreatening, perhaps because he'd kept his distance. She gave herself a mental shake, tried a smile. 'Would you like to—'

Owen started to speak at exactly the same moment. 'Do you need me to—'

They stopped and another small silence formed. 'After you,' Owen said politely.

Nessie took a breath. 'I was going to say, would you like to come in?'

He nodded. 'And I was going to ask if you need me to help you with anything, bring any bags or boxes in?' His gaze flickered to the fireplace, which was cold and blackened. 'I can get the fire going if you like? It warms the place up lovely once it's burning.'

Nessie dared to take her eyes off him then and looked around the pub, taking in the dusty, unmatched tables and the worn carpet. The brasses over the bar were dull, the wood in front of the beer pumps was stained and unpolished, the beamed ceiling was yellowed with age and old nicotine. More than half the bulbs in the hideous 1970s wall lamps were blown. Everywhere she looked, she saw the signs of neglect. It needed a lot of work. Then again, what else did she and Sam have to do?

She dragged her gaze back to Owen. 'I think we'll be okay. Thanks, though.'

'You wouldn't believe how filthy it is down there,' Sam

said, bursting into the room from behind the bar. 'There's a spider the size of Shelob – oh!'

She stopped when she saw Owen, her eyes widening.

'This is Owen, from the forge next door,' Nessie said. 'He's a blacksmith.'

'I bet he is,' Sam said as she looked him up and down. 'A real life blacksmith. Good Lord, I feel like I've walked into a BBC period drama. I'm Sam, by the way.'

Owen nodded a greeting and took a step forward. He lifted the basket and held it out. 'This is for you, just a few things we thought you might need.'

We, Nessie noted. He must mean his wife, of course. Hadn't he mentioned a son too?

Sam pushed past her, taking the basket. 'Brilliant,' she said, lowering it to a table and pulling off the gingham. 'Is there a bottle of wine in here?'

Owen's eyes crinkled as he smiled. 'No, just milk, cake, bread, that kind of thing. I didn't think you'd need wine, this being a pub and all.'

'Good point.' Sam glanced around and seemed to take in her surroundings for the first time. She stared at a large oil painting, a rough seascape full of broiling waves and angry sky, hanging on one of the bare brick walls. 'Bloody hell, that has got to go.'

Wait until she discovers the ship inside the bottle, Nessie thought, recalling the minimalist calm of Sam's London flat. *She'll want a skip to clear this lot out.*

'That's Henry Fitzsimmons' work. I dare say he'll take it back if it's not to your tastes,' Owen said. His tone was mild

12

but Nessie thought she detected an undercurrent of disapproval.

'We're not making any snap decisions about what stays and what goes,' she said hurriedly, giving her sister a meaningful look. 'Thanks for the supplies, though. It's very thoughtful of you.'

Owen's gaze lingered on her for a moment but he took the dismissal with no obvious sign of offence. 'A pleasure. Like I said, I'm just next door if you need anything. All you have to do is shout.'

He nodded first at Sam, then at Nessie and ducked under the doorway, disappearing into the night as fast as he had arrived. 'Well,' Sam said, grinning at Nessie with undisguised approval. 'You didn't waste any time.'

'Sam—' Nessie began.

'What?' Sam replied with raised eyebrows. 'You could have charged half the National Grid from the electricity I felt when I walked in on you, that's all I'm saying.'

Nessie felt her cheeks growing hot. 'Really, you do talk rubbish sometimes. He's married.'

Her sister cocked her head. 'Maybe not him, then, but I bet there's someone else here who'll help you get back on the horse.'

'Sam!' Nessie protested, blushing even more. 'Stop.'

'It's okay, Ness. Getting divorced doesn't have to mean game over, you know.'

It must seem so straightforward to Sam, Nessie thought, feeling a surge of emotion and willing herself not to cry. She couldn't know what it was like to walk away from fifteen years of marriage; although she hadn't got as far as divorce – not yet. *One step at a time*, Nessie told herself.

Sam's voice broke into her thoughts again. 'It's time you moved on, that's all I'm saying. Now, where do you suppose our father left the wine? Or do you think he drank it all before he died?'

Chapter Two

An insistent rumbling whine woke Sam early the next day. Clamping the pillow around her ears, she closed her eyes but it was like trying to sleep through roadworks. She stared at the bumpy, unfamiliar ceiling for a while, summoning the courage to poke her toes out of the covers and into the chill morning air. It was a long way from her life as a PR golden girl with a chic little flat in Kensington, she thought with a rueful sigh. She and Nessie hadn't been able to get the central heating working the night before so the only source of warmth in the bedroom was an electric heater that glowed radioactively in one corner and looked like it might spontaneously combust as she slept. Deciding to brave the cold, Sam had unplugged it.

The bed, which looked as though it had been hijacked from *Antiques Roadshow*, had proved unexpectedly comfortable and once she'd adjusted to the peal of church bells marking the hour, she'd slept well. Until now. It was probably a good thing she hadn't been able to find a single drop of alcohol in the pub or she'd have had a hangover to contend with as well as London withdrawal. But either someone had done an excellent job of hiding the booze or Andrew Chapman really had drunk the place dry.

The rumbling finally drove Sam out of bed. She winced as her feet connected with the thinly carpeted bedroom floor – she'd have to invest in some heavy duty slippers or possibly some snow boots for these early winter mornings: her fat-burning flip-flops were going to be no use here. Shivering, she tugged on some clothes and crossed the creaking floorboards to the window. It was hidden behind thick wooden shutters but she could see a crack of brilliance around the edges, suggesting sunshine outside, and the illusion of warmth. Tentatively, she pulled the shutters open, half-expecting an avalanche of spiders but the doors came open easily, with no nasty surprises. They revealed blurry leaded diamonds and beyond them, a sea of emerald grass: the village green bathed in the bright December sun.

Sam blinked and took a step back. 'Coffee,' she croaked, rubbing her arms to get the blood flowing. 'That's what I need. A vat load of coffee.'

The upstairs rooms of the pub were even more in need of TLC than downstairs, Sam thought, as she negotiated the narrow landing that led from the bedrooms. Technically, it was a duplex, with a living room, bathroom, kitchen and two bedrooms on the first floor, and three more bedrooms in the attics above, but not even the most optimistic estate agent would have described it that way. Sam and Nessie had taken one look at the dark and crooked stairs to the attic and agreed to leave exploring up there until they'd settled in a little more. Or possibly a lot more. They had explored the tiny kitchen, which boasted an assortment of scruffy wall units, a fridge-freezer that leaned alarmingly to one side and a sink that seemed to have been used as a tea-urn. A small round table and two wobbly chairs took up the rest of the space. The living room held two mismatched sofas, an empty bookshelf and a boxy old TV.

'Let's get the beds made,' Nessie had suggested, trying to stifle a yawn. 'It'll look better in the morning.'

Sam found Nessie downstairs, doing battle with the kind of vacuum cleaner that looked like it had come out of the seventies. It had a gigantic, heavy-looking plastic base and a blue bag ballooned above it. Nessie was using both her hands to push it around the floor. She'd grouped all the tables at one end, piled the chairs on top in a precarious-looking pile, and there was a bucket of dirty water next to the much-cleaner fireplace. *What time did she get up?* Sam wondered. *Had she even been to bed?*

'Ness!' she called, over the thunder of the cleaner. 'Nessie!'

Her sister's head jerked up, like a startled meerkat. She relaxed when she saw Sam and reached for the off switch. 'Morning. How did you sleep?'

'Pretty well,' Sam admitted. 'How about you?'

'Not bad.' Nessie glanced away and Sam knew it was a lie. She wondered exactly how many times her sister had got up to check the door was bolted shut, or to investigate a noise she couldn't identify. The pub was an old building, full of creaks and groans, and Nessie could be anxious at the best of times. She'd probably been awake all night.

'Fancy a coffee?' she asked.

Nessie pulled a face. 'No coffee. Sorry, I thought I'd brought some.'

'No problem, I'll go and get a jar. There must be a shop somewhere here.'

'I think the Post Office sells groceries,' Nessie said. 'You'll probably get some in there.'

'Excellent,' Sam said, her mouth watering at the thought of a deliciously dark roasted blend. 'I'll see what I can find.'

The Post Office was on Star Lane, which ran along one side of the green. Sam grinned as she passed the phone box, half-expecting an eccentrically dressed stranger to leap out waving a sonic screwdriver but it was empty, unused. The war memorial held a handful of names, villagers who'd gone to fight for their country and never returned. Just like every other village in England, Sam thought, decimated by a war they thought would be over by Christmas.

The shop was split between a glass-fronted, unattended Post Office counter at the back and another counter nearer the front, with a woman stood behind it. She was thin and grey-haired and her eyes gleamed when Sam walked in. She peered over the top of her wire-rimmed glasses. 'Hello. Now let me see . . . you must be Samantha Chapman.'

Sam blinked. 'Uh, yes, I'm Sam. Hello.'

The woman held out a paper-skinned hand. 'I'm Franny Forster, postmistress and Chair of the Little Monkham Preservation Society. How are you and Vanessa feeling after your long drive from London?'

'We're okay,' Sam said cautiously. Was this how everyone behaved in a village, acting like they knew all about you even though you'd only just met? Maybe Nessie had run into her when she'd visited the pub originally, although she'd never mentioned it. 'I've come in search of coffee.'

'Of course you have,' Franny said, bustling out from behind the counter. 'You arrived so late last night that I expect you need a bit of caffeine to boost your energy levels. Of course, you've got a lot of work ahead of you if you want to get the pub back up and running in time for the grand re-opening.'

She plucked a blue-lidded jar from a shelf and handed it to Sam.

'Grand re-opening?' Sam echoed. 'I don't think we'd got as far as planning—'

'Oh yes, you must have a re-opening party,' Franny said, returning to her position behind the counter and stabbing at the till. 'The Star and Sixpence has been part of village life here for over four centuries. It's never been closed, not even through the wars, until your father's unfortunate demise. So we thought Boxing Day for the re-opening, if that suits you?'

Sam felt her mouth drop open. 'Boxing Day? But that's less than a month away. Three weeks, in fact. And it's Christmas first.'

Franny's eyes gleamed. 'That is how it usually works, yes. So I expect you'll want to get back there, won't you? To get on with things?'

'Yes,' Sam said faintly, feeling more in need of coffee than ever. 'Yes, I suppose I will.'

'That'll be three pounds ninety-nine, then,' Franny said with a satisfied nod, holding out her hand. 'For the coffee.'

'Fucking hell!' Sam burst out, glancing at the cheap-looking jar in her hand. Franny sniffed, as though she didn't approve of such language and took the note Sam gave her.

Sam decided two things on her way back to the Star and Sixpence: life in Little Monkham was going to take a *lot* of getting used to, and they needed to find somewhere else to shop.

There was a man peering through the windows of the pub. He was bent low, one hand shading his eyes as he stared inside. Sam felt a stab of alarm and broke into a run.

'Hey!' she shouted the moment she was near enough. 'What do you think you're doing?'

He straightened up at the sound of her voice and turned around, just as Sam skidded to a halt in front of him. 'I was looking for the new owner. I guess that might be you?'

He was taller than her, maybe a year or two younger, she guessed, which made him late twenties. He was fair-haired with a slightly untidy beard and bright blue eyes that were fixed on her with undisguised interest. His waxed jacket had seen better days and his jeans were faded but when he

smiled, his eyes twinkled with warmth and Sam realised he
was quite attractive, in spite of the beard. He didn't look like
trouble but she wasn't about to lower her guard, not yet.
Ignoring his outstretched hand, she narrowed her eyes.
'Who wants to know?'

His smile faded. 'Joss Felstead. I came about the job.'

'Job?' she echoed. 'What job?'

'I used to be cellarman here, for Andrew, and I reckon
you're going to need my help to get the place ready for the
re-opening. It's only—'

'—three weeks away,' Sam interrupted. 'Yes, so I've been
told.'

She stared at him and he met her gaze, relaxed and apparently confident that she wasn't about to turn his offer down.
Sam upgraded her opinion from attractive to good looking.
He was nothing like the immaculately groomed men she
encountered in London PR circles but cleaner – fresher –
somehow, and more appealing. The confidence was familiar,
though, the in-built awareness of his own charm that so
many men seemed to have; arrogance, almost. She bet he
was a real heart-breaker among the village's female
population.

'What makes you so sure we need your help?' she asked,
raising an eyebrow.

Joss shrugged. 'I worked here for eleven years; I know the
cellars like the back of my hand. I know what beers do well,
which ones need a cool corner, which ones won't settle on
the uneven bit of floor. I know how to flush the pipes and

21

clean the lines and you'll forgive me for saying this, but you don't look like you know much about any of that.'

Sam let out a small huff of disbelief. What had the residents done, issued a newsletter with their names and photographs before she and Nessie had arrived? It was weird, that's what it was. And where did he get off, telling her what she did and didn't know? 'I might,' she said, haughtily. 'I might know everything there is to know about beer and . . . and pipelines.'

He smiled. 'If that's the case, then I suppose you don't need me after all. Sorry to have bothered you.'

He turned and began to walk away. Sam knew – just *knew* – he was waiting for her to call him back, to admit she didn't know the first thing about ridiculously named beers like *Badger's Arse* and *Rusty Ferret*. He was probably counting to ten, a smug, self-satisfied grin hovering around his beardy mouth. She wouldn't give in, she wouldn't, *she wouldn't* . . . except that the entire village was expecting the pub to re-open on Boxing Day; they'd practically thrown down a gauntlet challenging the two sisters and Sam wasn't one to refuse a challenge. More than that, she wasn't one to *fail* a challenge. And the trick to always winning was knowing when to accept help.

'Wait!' she called, despising herself a little bit for doing so. 'Wait. Are you any good with spiders?'

'Nessie?' Sam called, pushing open the door and walking into the pub. 'There's someone here I think you should meet.'

Her sister popped her head above the bar, rubber gloves on her hands and a dripping sponge clenched between her fingers. 'What?'

Sam led Joss forward, hoping he hadn't seen the wary look Nessie aimed his way. 'This is Joss. He used to look after the cellars before the pub closed.'

'Hi,' Joss said, and flashed an easy smile. Sam decided it was something he did a lot, a weapon he used to get his own way. And then she thought of all the times she'd done exactly the same thing back in London, to swing an important deal or charm a big client.

'Joss wondered if we could use his help to get things ready to re-open.'

Nessie frowned uncertainly and lowered the sponge to the bar. 'Oh. Well, yes, I expect we will do, when the time comes but there's a lot to do before then.'

'That's the other thing I need to tell you,' Sam said. 'Apparently, we're having a grand re-opening. In about three weeks' time.'

'Three weeks?' Nessie squeaked, her nervousness about Joss vanishing. 'Says who?'

'Says Franny Forster, chairwoman of the village Preservation Society,' Joss said gravely. 'And trust me, Franny is not someone you want to be on the wrong side of, especially if you are trying to run a business in Little Monkham.' He lowered his voice to a conspiratorial whisper. 'The last shopkeeper to cross her ended up closing down and moving four hundred miles away.'

'That's ridic—' Sam began, but then she thought of the way Franny had known who she was and where she'd come from before she'd even stepped over the threshold and she shivered. A woman like that in charge of the village Post Office might know an awful lot about people. Maybe it wasn't so ridiculous that she wielded a lot of power in Little Monkham. Sam looked at Joss and found him already watching her. 'Right,' she said, swallowing a rueful sigh. 'When can you start?'

Chapter Three

The clean-up began in earnest after that. Sam set up an office on the kitchen table and spent most of the morning on the phone, speaking to the breweries and builders, arranging for deliveries and getting quotes for skips.

'It's a good thing I did my licensee course and all the legal stuff before we came,' Nessie said, reading through the paperwork from the local council. 'We'll just have to hope the premises licence comes through in time, although Christmas is going to be a problem. Everything shuts down for the holidays.'

'It'll come through in time,' Joss said, as he came up the cellar stairs with an armful of mouldy cardboard. 'Franny will make sure of that. She'll sort your builders out too. You won't have any problems, as long as you do what she wants.'

'I'm a little bit scared of Franny,' Sam said.

Joss shook his head solemnly. 'Don't underestimate her. She's basically Darth Vader in a dress, but she gets things done.'

Nessie wasn't sure what to make of Joss yet but she had to admit he worked hard; the cellar had been cleared of spiders and debris, and he'd shifted all the tarnished old kegs to make way for the incoming fresh ones. She'd been horrified to discover her father had been paying him in cash for as long as he'd worked there and Joss had been less than enthusiastic about setting things straight; in fact, he'd brazenly negotiated a pay rise to cover the tax he'd have to pay once they added him officially to the payroll. Nessie didn't like the way he looked at Sam, either; his gaze lingered a fraction too long when he spoke to her and his smile became just a little bit more charming. He was making an effort. Sam might be too busy to have noticed yet but Nessie knew her sister well; it was only a matter of time before she started to pick up on Joss's interest and then Nessie would have to remind her that she was technically his employer – fooling around would only complicate things. At least Joss hadn't tried to flirt with *her* – then again, she knew she lacked her sister's sparkle. Sam was only four years younger but she turned heads, not because she was classically beautiful but because she shone. Nessie had never been able to compete; she had learned long ago not to try, so it was no surprise that Joss had barely looked her way. She was actually glad of her invisibility – she'd forgotten more than she ever knew about flirting but the havoc she'd seen Sam wreak was enough to put her off for life. Nessie preferred to busy herself cleaning the tables and chairs, doing her best to match them up and fit them into the pub's nooks and cubby holes. Once she'd finished those, she began polishing the brass until it gleamed. By the time she was done, the pub looked reasonable, if a bit haphazard.

'Hey, it doesn't look half-bad. Nothing that a bit of paint and some decent lighting won't fix,' Sam declared, when she came downstairs from the cramped kitchen. She peered around the back of the terrible oil painting she'd pointed out the night before. 'And it'll be even better once I get rid of this.'

Nessie hesitated. The painting *was* awful. 'Don't damage it.'

Sam unhooked the mock-gilt frame and lifted it off the wall. 'I'm not sure I could. And the others are even worse.'

She waved a hand at the other paintings on the walls, all with the same frame, all less than brilliant. Nessie counted three seascapes, a still life and a nude that made her wince. A snippet of conversation from the night before floated through her head: Owen had mentioned the name of the artist, hadn't he? Frowning, she tried to remember who it was. 'It was someone from the village. We should try to find out where they live, give the paintings back.'

'You want Henry,' Joss called across the bar. 'World War Two veteran and pillar of the Little Monkham community. Can't paint much but it doesn't stop him trying.'

'See?' Sam demanded, glancing at Nessie. 'No one likes them. I don't know why they're even here.'

'Henry and Andrew had an agreement,' Joss said as he unscrewed one of the empty optics and lifted it carefully down to soak. 'The paintings were displayed here and when someone bought one, they split the money.'

'Like a gallery,' Nessie said.

'Yeah,' Joss replied. 'There aren't any around here so this was a way for Henry to show off his handiwork.'

'And how many did he sell?' Sam asked.

Joss looked up at the ceiling thoughtfully. 'Let's see now, I worked here for eleven years and I reckon, in all that time, they must have sold . . .' he paused to count on his fingers, then nodded. 'None. They never sold a single one.'

'That settles it,' Sam said firmly. 'They're gone.'

It didn't matter how much Nessie argued with her, Sam's mind was made up. She had a vision of how the revamped interior of the Star and Sixpence was going to look and it most certainly did not involve any dodgy art by local residents. Nor did it include any ships in bottles, although none of them knew who that belonged to so she'd agreed to stash it in one of the unused bedrooms upstairs for now. The paintings she'd loaded into the back of the car and driven round to the address Joss had given her for Henry Fitzsimmons.

She'd found Mulberry Cottage opposite the square steeple of St Mary's Church. The garden was immaculate, the flowers lining the path standing to stiff attention and the grass mowed with military precision. When no one answered her three sharp raps on the door, she knocked again. Silence.

'Now what?' she muttered, glancing around. There was no sign of anyone, no obliging neighbour pottering in the garden she could leave the paintings with. She knocked at the cottage next door just to be safe – no one in there either.

'Henry is at the village council meeting,' a helpful voice called.

Sam looked up to see a man in a dog collar standing at the gate of the churchyard, watching her. 'He'll be a little while yet, I expect. The meetings are usually lengthy affairs.'

'Oh,' Sam said grumpily. 'Thanks.'

'No problem,' the vicar said, his face splitting into a cheerful smile. He turned and walked up the shallow hill to the church and disappeared behind its wooden doors.

Sam began to get back into the car, then paused and looked up at the sky. It was cold but dry, and still light. Surely if she left the paintings on Henry's doorstep, he'd find them when he got back from his meeting and take them inside. Then he would have his precious art back, and Sam wouldn't have to hand them over face to face. It was a win–win.

Checking the vicar hadn't reappeared, she took the paintings out of the car one at a time and stacked them carefully underneath the pointed porch of the cottage, leaning them against one wall. Then she got into the car and drove away, without looking back.

Chapter Four

It was early evening when Nessie knocked at the cottage beside the forge. An elegantly carved sign declared it was Snowdrop Cottage, with a delicate pair of white flowers painted beside the name. Nessie touched it, smiling gently; snowdrops had been her favourite flower as a child. Glancing up, she saw a blackened iron horseshoe above the door – wasn't there an old superstition about iron keeping witches at bay? Her smile deepened; it was hard to imagine solidly built Owen believing such things, but he was a blacksmith and the job did have a touch of ancient magic about it.

The smile faded as she braced herself to lift the door knocker; she would have preferred not to bother the Rhys family at all, would rather have waited until she ran into Owen in the village to thank him and his wife for the welcome basket they had put together, but when cleaning out the enormous metal grate in the fireplace of the pub, she'd discovered a jagged hole in its middle. Which meant she needed to order a new one and it seemed rude not to ask the village blacksmith, especially when he lived right next door.

The door opened wide and a petite, dark-haired woman gazed enquiringly out. 'Hello, how can I help?' Then her brown eyes lit up. 'Oh, you must be Nessie, from the pub. Owen told me all about you last night; how lovely to meet you. I'm Kathryn.'

Nessie smiled, noticing the woman's identical Welsh accent. Childhood sweethearts, she decided. 'Hi Kathryn. Thanks so much for the things you sent us. I'll bring the basket back over later.'

'Whenever you're ready,' the woman said easily. 'No rush. So are you after Owen for something or can I tempt you in for tea?'

Nessie hesitated. There was something charming about the undisguised interest on Kathryn's face, an uncomplicated curiosity that was so refreshing that Nessie was almost tempted to accept. But there was a mountain of work waiting for her at the pub. 'Another time,' she promised. 'What I really need is a new grate for the big fireplace. If I tell you what I need, could you pass the message on to Owen, please?'

Kathryn shook her head. 'Not on your life, I'd only get it wrong. I'll tell you what, he's working in the forge. Why don't you pop in and tell him yourself?'

She pointed at the wooden door opposite the cottage.

'Oh, I don't want to bother him,' Nessie said. 'I can always come back later if he's busy.'

'Owen is always busy,' Kathryn said, snorting. 'Go and interrupt him. He might stop work at a reasonable hour then and come home in time to read his son a bedtime story.'

There wasn't a trace of malice around the words, just affection and good-humoured resignation, and Nessie felt a stab of envy. It had been a long time since she and Patrick had been that way; for the last few years they'd almost lived separate lives. This fleeting glimpse of Kathryn and Owen's warmth made her suddenly realise how lonely she'd been.

She forced a smile. 'All right.'

'No need to knock, just pop these on and walk right in,' Kathryn urged. She held out a pair of plastic safety goggles. 'And I'll hold you to that promise of tea, okay? Little Monkham is fine once you get used to it but it scared me half to death when I first moved here. You need to know we're not all power-crazed slave drivers.'

With another friendly smile, she closed the door, leaving Nessie with no alternative but to cross the yard to the forge.

She wasn't prepared for what she found inside. The forge was hot, so hot that her clothes stuck to her skin the moment the door closed behind her. Red-hot coals blazed under a vast steel hood against the far wall and there were heavy metal tools ranged everywhere she looked. A round metal barrel filled with water stood in front of the fire. But the most striking sight of all was Owen himself. He stood with his back to her, bending over a low anvil with a hammer in one hand and tongs gripping a piece of glowing orange metal in the other. The white t-shirt he wore stretched across his muscles as he raised an arm and brought the hammer down hard on the anvil. Sparks flew out as metal struck metal and he lifted his arm again.

Nessie stood mesmerised, watching him work. The heat was stifling and sweat began to bead on her forehead but she couldn't take her eyes from him. Eventually, she managed to look away and coughed as loudly as she dared. Instantly, he stopped hammering and turned around.

His eyes widened behind the goggles. 'Nessie. What brings you in here?'

She took a step backwards, then got hold of herself and moved closer. 'Kathryn sent me over here. I need a new grate for the fireplace, is that something you could do? I could probably get one online but it seemed silly with you being right next door.'

The words tumbled out before she could stop them. Now that she was closer, she could see streaks of dirt on his face, mixing with sweat. The flames danced and flared and the air was rich with sulphur. Owen nodded, turning away to plunge both the metal and the tongs into the barrel of water. It hissed and bubbled into a cloud of steam. 'Sure, I could do that,' he said, straightening up. 'I think I've still got the measurements for it, somewhere. Do you want me to do a quote for you, drop it over?'

Nessie shifted uneasily. She wasn't sure she wanted another man in the pub and especially not one who looked like Owen. Not when he made her feel so strange and not when his wife was less than a hundred yards away looking after their son. 'Oh no, we'll pay whatever it costs. Just let me know how much.'

'Right,' Owen said. 'How are you settling in? Is there anything you need?'

'No, I don't think so,' Nessie said, puffing a few strands of hair from her damp forehead. 'We've taken on Joss Felstead to look after the cellar. And apparently we're opening again on Boxing Day.'

Owen smiled. 'You've had your orders from Franny, I see. If you think it's too soon then say so.'

'Does anyone say no to Franny?' she asked. 'I mean, I've heard some pretty fearful things about her.'

He laughed, a deep throaty rumble that Nessie was surprised to discover she liked. 'Don't let her bully you,' he said. If there's anything I can help with though, just let me know.'

'Thanks,' Nessie said.

She was about to ask what he'd been hammering on the anvil when the door flew back and a boy of around eight or nine tumbled in. He skidded to a halt when he saw her, regarding her seriously with deep blue eyes from underneath a floppy white-gold fringe. 'Hello,' he said. 'You must be our new neighbour. Have you met Elijah Blackheart yet? He's the ghostly highwayman who haunts the building. Did he try to murder you in your bed while you slept?'

'Luke!' Owen warned, his eyebrows beetling together forbiddingly.

The boy turned an injured gaze upon him. 'What? There *is*

a ghost, Andrew said there was. It roams the corridors of the pub at night, waiting to kill the unwary.'

Owen sighed and glanced at Nessie. 'This is my son, Luke. He has quite an imagination, as you can see.'

Nessie smiled. 'Hi Luke, I'm Nessie. I'm afraid I haven't met Elijah yet but we've only been there one night. Maybe he's waiting until we've settled in before he murders us.'

Luke regarded her gravely. 'I expect that's it.' He turned to Owen again. 'I came to say supper's ready. And then I need you to help me with my English homework. I have to say three things I liked about the book I've just read and I can only think of two.'

Nessie studied them, marvelling at how different they were: blond and dark, blue eyes and brown. Luke was a sunny day and Owen was midnight. But there were similarities too – the same shaped mouth, the same jaw. He might be all legs and freckles now but Luke Rhys was definitely cut from the same cloth as his father. 'I should be getting back,' she said, suddenly aware she was staring. 'Sam wants to look at carpet samples this evening.'

Owen nodded. 'I'll pop in to measure up for the grate and get it done as soon as I can.'

'Thank you,' Nessie said. She smiled at Luke again. 'It was lovely to meet you. If you hear screaming in the night, it probably means the ghost has shown up.'

'Awesome!' Luke said, his eyes gleaming.

Nessie laughed and handed over her goggles. She risked a final look at Owen, standing in the glow of the fire. 'See you later,' she said, reaching for the door handle.

Outside, it was cool and fresh but she still fanned her too-hot cheeks as she hurried back to the pub. Really, it had been unbearable in the forge but she knew Sam wouldn't believe that was all there was to it. Nessie paused under the lamppost, letting the night air soothe away the worst of the heat. The last thing she needed was a guilty-looking flush to feed her sister's imagination.

Chapter Five

When the door thundered and rattled in its frame around seven o'clock that evening, both women froze. They were sitting at a battered wooden table in the cramped kitchen upstairs but the sound still freed a sprinkling of dust from the ceiling to dance beneath the bare yellow light bulb. Nessie lowered her knife and fork with a frown.

Sam pushed back her chair. 'I'll get it, shall I? It's probably that sexy blacksmith, come to show you his red hot poker.'

It wouldn't be Owen, Nessie thought as the hammering began again. His knock would be more respectful – whoever this was, they were bullish and determined . . . and angry. But if it wasn't Owen, who was it?

'Maybe it's Franny, coming to check how we're getting on with the refurbishment,' she said, doing her best to match her sister's lightness of tone.

'Or Sotheby's, wanting to value the carpet in the bar.' Sam paused and looked at Nessie. 'Shall we find out?'

If it had been up to Nessie, she'd have pulled the door open carefully to peer through the crack. Not Sam, though: she snapped back the bolts so that they cracked and hauled the door wide to stand defiant and imperious. 'Yes?'

An old man with a short white moustache and reddened, thread-veined cheeks scowled back. 'Was it you who dumped my paintings on the doorstep of my house?'

Nessie stepped forward in dismay. 'Oh Sam, you didn't?'

Her sister folded her arms. 'I knocked and no one answered. What was I supposed to do? We're modernising the pub and the paintings don't fit in with the new look. Sorry.'

The trouble was she didn't sound the least bit sorry, Nessie thought, and Henry Fitzsimmons obviously agreed. 'This pub has been here for centuries,' he growled, his bushy old-man eyebrows bristling. 'She's an old lady, a local in every sense – the heart of our community, cared for by people who recognised her importance. You've got no right to modernise her. I don't know who you think you are—'

'The owners,' Sam interrupted in a silky smooth tone, clearly unimpressed by Henry's lyrical comparisons. 'So we have every right to do whatever we like. Look around you – have you ever seen a place more in need of modernisation? If this pub is a woman, she deserves a facelift.'

'And I suppose you've no place for art in this *modern* pub you're planning?' Henry snapped.

Nessie heard a low-level buzzing in her ears as the argument escalated. 'Sam, maybe we should think about—'

'No, we should not,' Sam said firmly. 'We don't want the

paintings. Now Mr Fitzsimmons here can find a new home for them. Preferably somewhere dark.'

She spun and crossed the room without a single backward look, leaving Nessie to try and minimise the damage.

'Look, Mr Fitzsimmons, I'm sorry Sam didn't take more care with your paintings.'

Henry stared at her through narrowed eyes for a moment, then his lip curled in disgust. 'Your father often said his daughters were nothing like him. I see exactly what he meant now.'

He turned on his heel and stalked away, the light from the streetlamp turning his hair to silver. Nessie closed the door with a sigh and pushed the bolts home.

'Moron,' Sam called irritably, as Nessie trudged back upstairs. 'I wouldn't mind if he'd been any good but you saw the paintings. That spider in the cellar had more artistic talent.'

Nessie closed her eyes briefly, picturing the incensed look on Henry Fitzsimmons' face. 'You didn't have to be so rude. At some point we're going to need customers and it's going to be a real struggle if you've insulted half the village.'

'One old man is hardly half the village,' Sam scoffed.

Perhaps not, Nessie thought as she sat down to finish her now cold dinner. But Henry hadn't struck her as the type to bear his grievances quietly. And word spread fast in small communities. The last thing they needed was a mob with flaming pitchforks at their door.

★   ★   ★

Nessie lay awake long after they'd gone to bed that night. It wasn't the sound of the freezing rain hammering against the leaded windows that troubled her, or the whistle of the wind through the gaps between the walls and the frames. It wasn't even the thought of Luke's murderous ghost, grinning evilly outside her door, blood-stained sword in hand, although that image made her burrow under the covers a little deeper. The argument with Henry whirled around and around in her head, especially his parting shot about how unlike their father they were. Afterwards, Sam had declared that could only be a good thing – who wanted to be a degenerate, alcoholic loser anyway? At the time, Nessie had agreed but now in the dark half-silence, she knew that wasn't what Henry had meant. She got the sense Andrew Chapman hadn't been a loser in Little Monkham. Owen's tone had been respectful when he'd spoken of their father, although he had been offering his condolences at the time. Joss seemed genuinely fond of his former employer and the anecdotes he'd shared as he worked that afternoon had been wryly affectionate. And she'd yet to meet the formidable Franny but she didn't sound like the kind of person who would tolerate an incompetent drunk to run something as important as – what had Henry Fitzsimmons called it? – the *heart* of their community. No, whatever she and Sam remembered of their father, the residents of Little Monkham clearly knew him as someone else. Someone they'd liked and respected. And some of that goodwill had been inherited by his daughters, along with the Star and Sixpence, but it would soon evaporate if Sam treated everyone the way she'd treated Henry.

Nessie heard the clock strike two and turned over in the vast iron-framed bed. Maybe she'd find out from Joss what the old man liked to drink and send him a bottle or two over by way of an apology. It wouldn't do much to unpick the hurt Sam had caused but it was a start. And it might just calm Henry's wounded pride enough for Nessie to show him they were worthy custodians of the Little Monkham's heart after all.

Nessie's eyes were gritty and sore the next morning. She lay in the dark for a few moments, blinking up at the dark-beamed ceiling, before accepting that going back to sleep was not an option and levering herself out of bed. Sam had arranged for the local paper to send a photographer to cover the story of the pub's renovation and had told Nessie in no uncertain terms that she would need to fly the flag.

'Can't you do it?' Nessie had asked in dismay, casting an envious glance at her sister's sleek blonde bob. 'The camera loves you.'

'It's too risky,' Sam said. 'I know it's only a local paper but if the wrong person picks up on it then I'm in trouble. Besides, there's nothing wrong with you that a decent concealer and a haircut wouldn't fix.'

Her hair was in need of a cut, Nessie conceded as she splashed cold water on her face in the freezing bathroom. And her concealer was so old it had cracked in its plastic tube – it had been a long time since she'd felt like making an effort. She studied her image in the age-spotted mirror over the sink, noting the downturned curve of her lips and faint purple smudges under her eyes. Maybe it was time she started to take some pride in her appearance again, for the benefit of her battered self-esteem. And if she was completely honest, perhaps a tiny bit for the *Cotswold Chronicle* photographer.

The milkman had left two bottles at the door. Nessie took a deep breath of sharp morning air as she stooped to collect them and glanced across the green as she did so. The grass was covered in a blanket of frost, turning it an enticing silvery green. Beyond it, she could see thatched roofs and whitewashed walls nestling beneath a peach and lemon-streaked sunrise. As views went it wasn't half bad, she decided, straightening up. Sam thought Little Monkham was twee, an overblown caricature of the stereotypical English village, but Nessie liked its Christmas card perfection.

A movement to her right caught her eye. Luke tumbled out of Snowdrop Cottage, a woolly hat jammed snugly over his ears and a scarf trailing behind him as he half ran, half skidded across the yard.

Kathryn appeared in the door frame. 'I told you not to run, it's too icy!'

Grinning, Luke slid the rest of the way to the old Land Rover and thudded his gloved hands onto the bonnet. 'I can't slide properly if I don't run.'

Nessie watched Kathryn pick her way across the treacherous yard. When she reached the car, she snaked out an arm to pull Luke close. 'Where's my morning kiss?'

'Urgh, get off!' the boy replied but Nessie noticed he didn't wriggle away. Instead, his arms encircled Kathryn and he returned the hug. They stood like that for a second or two before Kathryn dropped a kiss onto his forehead and released him.

'Now, get in the car and let's take our chances on the roads.'

The fear of imminent death didn't appear to bother Luke. He slithered around to the passenger side, catching sight of Nessie as he did so. A flicker of something crossed his face – curiosity? Disappointment that the ghost hadn't finished her off yet? – then he raised an arm to wave at her. Kathryn looked up too, ice scraper in hand. 'Morning!' she called. 'Brisk today, isn't it?'

Nessie nodded, suddenly aware of the goosebumps on her arms. She wrapped her dressing gown around herself a little more tightly. 'Morning. Yes, it's freezing.'

'Wait until January, we'll need a blowtorch to defrost the windscreen then.' Kathryn's expression brightened. 'Hey, are you free later for a cuppa?'

Nessie thought of the morning ahead: the plumber was coming to look at the antiquated heating system, the carpet fitter was due to measure up and of course there was the dreaded interview to deal with. It would be nice to have something to look forward to, she thought. 'I'd like that.'

'Great,' Kathryn said, smiling. 'I'll be back around four if that suits you? Just knock when you see the car.'

'Okay,' Nessie said, returning her smile. 'See you later.'

Luke rolled down the window and fixed her with an intense stare. 'Unless you see Elijah first.'

Nessie laughed and stepped back into the pub. The Land Rover swung around and Kathryn cracked her window down a fraction. 'Four o'clock, then. Bring cake!'

Nessie nodded and waved as they drove away. She shut the door with a sigh and trudged back to the stairs. Soon she'd have to start the epic task of making herself presentable for the camera but not before she'd had tea and a bacon sandwich. Everything would feel easier then.

'So is it fair to say you and your sister are novices in the hospitality business?'

Joe Poole of the *Cotswold Chronicle* had a charming smile and an easy-going manner but Nessie couldn't shake the worry that every question he asked had a double meaning. Sam had given strict instructions on how much information Nessie could reveal. 'Stick to the pub and the story of how we got it but don't get drawn into our family history,' she'd said, when Nessie had presented herself for inspection. 'Talk about how we envisage making the Star and Sixpence the centre of Little Monkham life, in symbiosis with the village. And try not to mention my name if you can help it.'

'How am I supposed to do that?' Nessie had asked, her

head spinning with all the dos and don'ts. 'He's bound to ask about you.'

'Give me your surname, then,' Sam replied promptly. 'No one is going to be searching the internet for Sam Blake.'

'It might look that way on the surface but I managed a bookshop for years and a lot of the skills are transferable,' Nessie told Joe, smiling. 'There may be some things that are new to us but we're fast learners and we've got some expert help from Joss Felstead, who used to run the cellar for our father. The villagers have been great too. Running the Star and Sixpence is going to be a real community project.'

She hid her crossed fingers in the pocket of her chunky cardigan and pushed the image of Henry Fitzsimmons firmly out of her mind. Joe glanced down at his notes. 'Great. Well, I think I've got all I need, except for your full names and ages.'

He smiled again and Nessie decided it wasn't charming at all; there was something of the wolf about it, too many teeth. She didn't smile back as she told him how old they were, adding a year each for good measure.

'And your names? I know you're Vanessa but I don't think I caught your surname.'

She hesitated for a second, wondering how to keep Sam out of things, and realised that she couldn't. 'Chapman,' she said at last. 'I'm Vanessa Chapman and my sister is Sam Blake.'

It wasn't much, Nessie knew, and Google would make the link anyway but if anyone was looking for Sam, it might buy her a little more time. 'Okay,' Joe said, snapping his notebook shut. 'The story should hit next week's edition, just in time for Christmas. We thought outside for the photo, if it's not too cold for you?'

'Fine,' Nessie said, reaching for her coat.

Chapter Six

Sam was huddled at the bottom of the cellar steps, straining to hear the lower tones of male voices. Shivering, she wished for about the hundredth time she'd worn a thicker jumper – the cellar was cold. It smelled strange too: yeasty and damp, although Joss was meticulous about cleanliness so there wasn't a speck of dirt. She wrapped her arms around herself and shifted from one foot to the other. What was taking Nessie so long? It was supposed to be a quick chat about their plans to drag the Star and Sixpence into the twenty-first century, not *Newsnight*. Surely they must have finished by now?

The door at the top of the steps opened and a bulky figure loomed into view. Sam shrank back, peering upwards warily, then let out a silent sigh of relief when she realised it was Joss.

'Hello,' he said from halfway down the wooden stairs, spotting her skulking between two steel beer kegs. 'What brings you down here? Come to check on the Goblin's Grail?'

'Maybe,' she said, glancing sideways at the Best Before label on the top of one of the kegs. She had no idea if Goblin's Grail was a proper beer name or one he'd just made up. 'I'm just checking everything is in order.'

He studied her then, his blue-eyed gaze dancing with amusement. 'Right. And is it?'

She folded her arms and reminded herself that this was her pub; she had every right to be in the cellar if she wanted to be. 'Seems to be.'

Joss crossed the flagstones and checked the digital thermometer on the wall. 'Good,' he said solemnly. 'I'm glad we got that sorted out. Anything else I can help you with?'

'No. Just pretend I'm not here,' she said, listening again for the tell-tale murmur of conversation from upstairs.

His lips quirked but he didn't say anything and began checking the lines leading from each of the kegs. Sam watched with half an eye. Now that the cellar was almost operational, she was glad all over again that they'd taken Joss back on to take care of things; quite apart from the muscle required to manhandle the full and empty kegs, there was no way either she or Nessie had time to fathom the maze of tubes leading out of each barrel and up to the mass of copper pipes and narrow cylinders filled with amber liquid. And Nessie might be horrified at Joss's relaxed approach to paying tax but neither sister could fault his methodical approach in the cellar.

He had his back to Sam, drawing samples from each of the kegs and examining them closely. As far as she could tell, he'd taken her at her word and seemed to have forgotten she was there, which allowed her the opportunity to study him. Today, he was wearing a faded charcoal t-shirt with an almost illegible list of concert dates on the back and comfortable black jeans. His fair hair needed a trim; it was starting to curl against the freckled skin of his neck. Clearly he wasn't the type to visit the barber every two weeks, although she'd noticed his beard had been trimmed. He tilted his head, holding a beer sample up to the light, and gave her the chance to examine his profile. He had a good nose, she decided objectively, and decent, kissable lips; not pencil thin and hard-looking, like her last one-nighter. Now *he'd* been a poor kisser . . . a poor everything, really, but she hadn't expected more. He'd simply been in the right place at the right time when she'd needed a distraction. She'd left before it was light the following morning, promising to hook up again soon. They hadn't.

'You should just admit it, you know.' Joss broke into her thoughts without turning around.

Sam blinked. 'Admit what?'

'Well, I assume from the fact that you can't keep your eyes off me that you fancy me,' Joss said. 'But you don't want to admit it because you're my boss and you think it would make things awkward. It wouldn't.'

Sam's mouth fell open. She'd known he was cocky, but this? He ought to be working in the City with brass like his. 'Really? Is that what you think?'

He turned towards her. 'It's okay. You wouldn't be the first woman to find me irresistible and I dare say you won't be the last.'

She couldn't help herself: she laughed. 'So you're Little Monkham's answer to Casanova, are you?'

'I do all right,' he said easily. 'I'm no Owen Rhys, mind you.'

Sam felt her forehead furrow. 'What's that supposed to mean?'

'Haven't you noticed? Half the women in the village are pining away for Owen,' Joss said. 'A tragic past equals gold with the ladies. Not that he does anything about it.' He shook his head. 'Such a waste.'

Interesting, Sam thought, and she stored the information away for future consideration. 'Sounds like he's got some morals. Unlike you.'

Joss didn't look in the least bit offended. 'I don't lead anyone on and everyone has a good time.'

Until the woman wants to get serious, then I bet you're off like a hare. Sam threw him a cool look. 'Even if I did fancy you, Joss, and I'm not saying I do, there isn't the smallest chance I'd do anything about it. Firstly, I'm your employer and secondly, I am far too busy to help you add another notch to your over-loaded bedpost.'

Joss shrugged. 'Fair enough,' he said, turning back to the kegs. 'I'm a patient man.'

She wanted to wipe the smug arrogance from his face, to tell him how ridiculous he sounded. She'd met his type before, the kind who thought they were too good to pass up, and she knew how to deal with them. The trouble was that she couldn't afford to be too scathing – Joss was a good cellarman and they needed him. So she fought the urge to take him down a peg and contented herself with a sub-zero smile. 'You'll be waiting a long time.'

'Sam?' Nessie's voice floated faintly down the stairs. 'Where are you? The coast is clear.'

Joss glanced over, one eyebrow raised. 'Hiding from something?'

Summoning up a withering glare, Sam hurried upstairs. Apart from anything else she was freezing and the way things were going she wouldn't put it past Joss to offer her a warming hug.

'How did it go?' she asked when she reached the ground floor, taking the cup of coffee Nessie was holding out. 'When are they running the article?'

'Next week, they said.' Nessie frowned at the cellar door. 'Did I hear you talking to Joss down there?'

Sam pulled a face. 'Yeah. We're going to have to keep an eye on him. He's convinced I fancy him.'

Nessie folded her arms. 'You do. There might as well be a flashing sign on your head, it's so obvious. Just keep your mind on the job and don't encourage him.'

Sam scowled, stung at her sister's lack of faith. 'I wasn't planning to jump him across the bar. Honestly, Ness, credit me with some sense. You're a fine one to talk, anyway – what about you flirting with Mr Hotstuff next door?'

'We've spoken twice – that's hardly flirting,' Nessie said dismissively but her cheeks reddened all the same. 'Besides, he's married.'

Sam shook her head. 'It doesn't matter how often you've spoken – what matters is what was said. And according to Joss he's got a tragic past.'

Nessie stared at her. 'What does that mean?'

'He didn't say,' Sam said. 'Why don't you ask Kathryn?'

'I can't,' Nessie replied, looking scandalised. 'What will she think?'

'That you're a nosy neighbour,' Sam said promptly.

Nessie shuddered. 'That I'm sniffing round her husband, more like. No thanks.'

She made an excuse then, something about checking the brewery paperwork, but Sam knew her sister was running away before the conversation got any more difficult. She hadn't intended to embarrass Nessie; she'd only wanted to steer things away from her and Joss. Because deep down, Sam knew she hadn't been completely honest: she did fancy him a bit. And being told over and over he was off-limits wasn't going to do that little spark of attraction any good at all.

'Good morning,' Franny said, her eyes gleaming over her glasses as Sam walked into the Post Office just before lunchtime. 'How are things going with the refurbishment?'

Sam peeled off her gloves and reached for a packet of loo rolls. She'd wanted to wait until they had time to do a supermarket shop in Gloucester but there were some things they couldn't manage without.

'Fine,' she told Franny. 'Providing the toilets get finished and the electrician can get the new fridges then we should be good to re-open on Boxing Day.'

Franny nodded in evident approval. 'Good. Let me know if he needs a shove in the right direction. These traders need a firm hand sometimes, especially around the holidays.'

'I'm sure it won't come to that,' Sam said with a polite smile. 'I'm used to getting things done too.'

Franny sniffed, as though she found that hard to believe. 'You've managed to upset old Henry Fitzsimmons already, I see. He was in here first thing this morning, complaining about the way you'd treated him.' She gazed over her glasses at Sam. 'I told him you were bound to want to shake things up a bit, the young always do, but he wasn't having any of it, I'm afraid.'

Sam frowned. Was there an undercurrent of disapproval behind Franny's words? 'I did apologise to him. Unfortunately, he's not as good as he thinks he is.'

'We're all guilty of that, though, aren't we?' Franny said. 'He's got a real bee in his bonnet about it, says he's going to start a petition to get you shut down.'

Sam laughed. 'The daft old goat. Like that's even possible!'

Franny didn't laugh. She simply stared at Sam until her laughter died a nervous death. Sam shifted uneasily. 'Er – it's not possible, is it?'

'No,' Franny replied, in a way that made Sam think she meant the exact opposite. 'Not without the full backing of the village council, anyway.'

She smiled but it didn't quite reach her eyes. Sam narrowed

her gaze, all too aware of a lot of things that were hanging in the air unspoken. It almost felt as though Franny was threatening her . . .

'You don't get much post, do you?' Franny said, changing tack suddenly. 'I see lots for Vanessa but nothing for you.'

Sam blinked. What was she getting at now? That she had no friends? Or something else? 'It goes to my flat. In London.'

'Oh, I just wondered if you needed any help setting up a mail redirect,' Franny said but Sam noticed her gaze was calculating. 'I wouldn't want you to miss out on anything important. You haven't put your old place up for sale yet, have you?'

How could she possibly know that? Sam wondered in disbelief. Technically, she supposed it was possible to work it out by cross-referencing the Electoral Roll with the local estate agency websites, but who had the time or the inclination to do that? Franny, obviously. The government should whip her into MI5, Sam decided faintly; who needed a Snooper's Charter when they had a nosy old bat like her to deploy? 'Not yet.'

'I suppose your young man is looking after things for you,' Franny went on. 'Or are you separated like Vanessa?'

Sam shut her mouth with a snap, irritation rising like a cobra. It didn't matter how much they needed to keep Franny sweet, she wasn't answering questions like this for anyone, especially not when it suited her to keep her footprint in Little Monkham as low as possible. In fact, the village mentality of access-all-areas was really starting to grate. At least in

London people had the grace to dress their curiosity with manners, but here? It was almost as though Franny felt she had the right to know every last detail of her neighbours' lives and Sam would be damned if she was giving her the satisfaction. Placing the packet of toilet rolls onto the counter with exaggerated care, she plastered a bland expression across her face. 'Just these, please.'

Franny's lips tightened but she didn't push Sam any further. She handed her change over without a word and waited until she had almost reached the door before speaking again. 'Let me know if you need any help with those tradesmen.'

Sam managed a brittle smile. 'Will do.'

Lifting the old-fashioned handle, she swept from the shop, fighting the urge to bang the door in its frame. She hurried across the grass, seething at the old woman's nosiness. Nessie would no doubt remind her that they needed friends, not enemies in Little Monkham, but Nessie had yet to encounter Franny; she couldn't know what it was like to be cross-examined under that gimlet-eyed gaze. Scowling, Sam crossed the green, certain Franny was watching her. She needed to get out of Little Monkham before she did something Nessie would really get her knickers in a twist about.

Chapter Seven

Nessie needed a break. It felt like days – weeks – since she'd thought of anything other than the pub and since the plumbers had started work on the toilets, there was a strong and pervasive smell of stale urine in the air that made her eyes water. Sam had escaped to the shops in Gloucester so Nessie left Joss in charge and went for a lunchtime walk.

The graveyard was frozen despite the afternoon sunlight. Nessie spent half an hour wandering among the headstones, bending to read the faded inscriptions and spotting the names Forster and Fitzsimmons going back several generations. And then, tucked away in a quiet corner, she found her father's grave.

The headstone was simple – just his name and dates. Nessie stared down, aware that an unexpected lump was forming in her throat. It wasn't that she missed him; too much of her life had been spent without him for that. But she was saddened by a life cut short, its fire dimmed by drink.

Once, Andrew Chapman had been young and full of potential. He'd been bright and funny and smart enough to ensnare her mother at university, who herself had been whip sharp. But it had all gone wrong and now he was buried in this tiny village graveyard, leaving two daughters who didn't mourn his passing much.

But someone else clearly did, Nessie realised, blinking away the dampness that had cooled on her lashes. The grass around the base of the headstone was neatly trimmed and there were fresh flowers in the pot sunk into the ground below it. Someone had brought a mixture of roses and geraniums, had trimmed them and slipped them one by one into the holes so that they sat prettily, and they had done it within the last few days. It wouldn't have been Sam, Nessie was sure; they must have known Andrew would be buried in the churchyard but neither had mentioned seeking out his grave. It must have been someone in the village or the surrounding area, someone Nessie and Sam had yet to encounter. Once again, Nessie was reminded that there must have been more to her father than booze.

The clock struck two. Aware she could no longer feel her toes, Nessie headed home. She stopped at the bakery on the green, remembering Kathryn's instructions to get cake to have with their coffee later. Maybe she'd pick up some bread too – if all else failed, she could use it to plug her nose with.

The woman behind the counter was plump and dressed entirely in white. Her hair was caught up in a net attached to her hat. Her name badge declared she was Martha and Nessie decided she looked like she'd stepped straight from a bread advert, the kind that harkened nostalgically back to a bygone time when life was simpler and bread was *bread*. There was one other customer in the shop, a striking woman in a deep red coat with hair to match. She wore seamed stockings that led into gorgeously impractical high heels. She had her back to Nessie so she couldn't tell her age but everything about her screamed glamour, the kind that felt totally out of place in a quiet village bakery. The conversation between her and Martha suggested the woman in red was a regular, though; they were discussing Mrs Carruthers' ex-husband in a way that left no doubt he was someone they both knew. Nessie focused on the cakes underneath the glass counter, trying not to listen, and so it took a moment for her to notice the expectant silence that had settled over the shop. She looked up to see both women gazing at her.

'Sorry,' she said, feeling embarrassment flood her face. 'Were you talking to me?'

Martha smiled, her pink cheeks becoming even plumper. 'Ruby here was just saying how like Andrew you are.'

It caught Nessie out every time someone made a reference to her father. She and Sam had spent so many years never mentioning his name, trying to pretend he didn't exist, that it was a real shock to be confronted by him practically everywhere she turned in Little Monkham. Summoning up a careful smile, she turned to look at the red-haired woman.

Her make-up was immaculate; smoky black eyes, impossibly long lashes and perfectly arched brows over glossy red lips.

She wasn't young – Nessie guessed maybe mid-fifties – and her beauty had dimmed a little with age but she oozed sophistication. Sam would be amazed that such a woman lived in the village, Nessie thought, and she summoned up a polite smile. 'Do you think so? I think I'm more like my mother.' She held out a hand. 'I'm Nessie Blake.'

The woman shook her hand, a wry smile playing around her scarlet mouth. 'I know. My name is Ruby Cabernet and I've heard a lot about you.'

Franny, Nessie thought with a mild stab of annoyance. The gossip network in Little Monkham was something both she and Sam were struggling with – didn't these people have anything better to talk about? The name intrigued her though; it couldn't be real. 'Have you?' she said.

Some of her irritation must have carried to her voice because Ruby's smile cooled a little. 'From your father. He and I . . . well, how should I put it?' She paused thoughtfully. 'He and I were lovers.'

Nessie felt her mouth drop open. Her father and *Ruby* had been lovers? It didn't seem likely; from what she remembered of him Andrew Chapman had scarcely been able to stand upright most of the time, let alone manage to – well, it didn't seem possible. Maybe he'd found a way to stop drinking. She knew he'd tried over the years but had always fallen off the wagon, sometimes within hours of promising he'd never drink again. 'Oh,' Nessie said stiffly. 'I didn't know.'

'No reason you should,' Ruby said, with an elegant shrug. 'You weren't close. He was always very sad about that. He told me once that his biggest regret was losing you and your sister.'

Nessie didn't know what to say. Her stomach squirmed with a mixture of bewilderment and distress; she was already raw from her discovery in the churchyard and the last thing she'd expected at the bakery was to run into someone who could stir up her long-buried emotions even more. 'Look—' she began but Ruby cut across her.

'I didn't mean to make you uncomfortable,' she said, picking up her wrapped loaf. 'I'm sorry. But if you ever have any questions about him you'll find me at Weir Cottage. Or perhaps I'll see you in the pub, when it opens again.'

She nodded to the baker and swept past Nessie in a cloud of Chanel. 'I recommend the mince pie crumbles, just divine with a dash of Grand Marnier,' she called over one shoulder.

The door closed with a cheery jangle, leaving a small silence. Nessie stared at the glass counter and her eyes came to focus on a row of glistening mini crumbles, each decorated with a sugar-crusted red berry. 'Six of those, please,' she said, rousing herself to point at the cakes. 'And one of the snowman meringues.'

Rummaging around in her bag, she dug out her purse. She was an idiot not to have expected this really – of course he'd had friends and even a girlfriend in the village. He'd lived there for years and years, for heaven's sake. At least the mystery of the flowers was solved.

Outside in the chilly December air, she could see Ruby in the distance, picking her way along Sixpence Street. She started towards the pub, filled with the uneasy feeling that she was going to be seeing a lot more of her father's girlfriend. And as much as the Star and Sixpence needed customers, Nessie wasn't sure either she or Sam would be glad to see Ruby.

Kathryn greeted Nessie warmly when she knocked on the door of Snowdrop Cottage.

'Come in,' she said, beckoning her into the kitchen. Her gaze settled on the cake box in Nessie's hands. 'I see you've discovered Little Monkham's best kept secret. I'm terrified Martha will apply to go on one of these bakery shows on TV and we'll lose her to Mary Berry.'

Nessie handed over the cakes. 'I got Luke something too, I hope that's all right.'

'Fine,' Kathryn nodded. 'It'll take more than a puff of meringue to put that boy off his dinner. Luke! There's cake here, come and get it.'

Footsteps thudded overhead, followed by a thundering on the stairs. A moment later, Luke burst into the kitchen, a thick dinosaur book under one arm. He glanced at Nessie and then his attention was caught by the frosty confection Kathryn was scooping onto a plate. 'Awesome. Thank you!'

He flashed Nessie a grateful look and vanished back upstairs. Kathryn carried the teapot over to the pine table. 'Come and have a seat,' she said, waving to one of the matching pine chairs. Her dark eyes sparkled with mischief. 'Now, be honest – how many times have you considered leaving Little Monkham since you arrived? Ten? Twenty?'

Nessie couldn't help grinning. 'Sam's had it worse than me. But I did just meet someone unexpected in the bakery.'

Kathryn listened as Nessie gave her an edited version of events. 'Don't mind Ruby,' she said, once Nessie had finished. 'She's got a taste for the dramatic, comes from her acting days.'

'Oh,' Nessie said. 'That explains the name at least. TV or film?'

'Stage, mostly,' Kathryn replied, pouring the tea. 'I think she was quite the star back in the day. She spills all kinds of stories about Richard Burton and the like if she's had enough gin.'

If she's had enough gin . . . The words echoed in Nessie's head and things started falling into place. She'd wondered what her father and Ruby could possibly have had in common, apart from Little Monkham. 'Does she like a drink, then?'

Kathryn shrugged. 'Don't we all? But there were some nights she needed a helping hand getting home from the pub. I reckon that's how they got together, her and your dad. It was easier for Ruby than going home.' She stopped then and seemed to realise what she was implying. 'Not that I'm suggesting she didn't love him or anything.'

Nessie remembered the flowers on the grave, neatly trimmed and arranged with care, and Ruby's quiet dignity in the bakery. Andrew was definitely still in his lover's thoughts. 'No,' Nessie said. 'I got the impression they were quite close.'

Kathryn took a long sip of her tea and eyed her sideways.

'Tell me to bugger off if you like, but Andrew lived in Little Monkham for nearly ten years and you never came to visit. So I'm just wondering how much you knew about his life here?'

Nessie looked at her sharply. 'I know he drank.'

'Well, he was always very open about that,' Kathryn said quietly. 'You'd be surprised how many drinkers end up running pubs. And it wasn't much of a problem at first.' She glanced at Nessie, her expression uncharacteristically serious. 'Towards the end, it got worse. We worried he'd forget to settle the fire before bed, or that he'd take a tumble down the cellar steps one night. We took it in turns to check on him, pretending it was on Franny's orders but I think he knew the truth.'

Nessie took a gulp of too hot tea and swallowed. She'd guessed her father must have had some help but not that he'd been barely capable of looking after himself. Shame seared across her skin and made her want to shrivel away.

'Joss was brilliant with him,' Kathryn went on. She pulled a wry face. 'I know he comes across a bit brash but he's got a good heart. Most of us do, even though it might seem like the Village of the Damned here sometimes.'

'Thank you,' Nessie said, doing her best to smile. 'I – well, I'm sorry he was such a burden.'

Kathryn's eyes widened. 'He wasn't. Goodness no, he was a great man, always pleased to see you and so clever.' She paused and shook her head. 'We looked out for him because we cared, Nessie, that's what I'm trying to say. I don't want you to think we're all like Franny, because we're not.'

'I'm beginning to see that,' Nessie said and this time her smile wasn't forced. 'There's a lot to like about living here.'

Kathryn reached for the cake box. 'You'd better believe it. Wait until you try Martha's mince pies. You'll never want to leave.'

Chapter Eight

Nessie read the article in the *Cotswold Chronicle* three times but it didn't make her feel any less sick. The huge photo of her looking hopelessly mumsy in front of the pub was bad enough but the words beside it were so much worse. Instead of the upbeat puff piece Sam had been expecting, the article on page five had led with the headline *CHAMPAGNE SUPERNOWHERE?* and seemed to be slyly suggesting the two sisters were inexperienced, incompetent and heading for disaster. She folded the paper up and gazed blindly at the kitchen table. Where had she gone wrong? She'd said all the things Sam had told her to say but it maybe it had all sounded as wooden and as unconvincing as it had felt. Joe Poole clearly didn't believe she and Sam had what it took to run the pub.

Franny was going to have a field day when she saw the article. And Sam . . . Nessie dreaded to think what Sam was going to do when she got back from collecting the new flyers at the printer's. Arrange for Joe Poole to meet with an unfortunate PR accident, probably.

Hearing a knock at the door, Nessie shoved the paper underneath some magazines and went to answer. It was probably Joss, come to check the cellar before they opened at midday. His behaviour around Sam might set her teeth on edge but she had to admit he was superb at his job.

She unbolted the door and pulled it back. 'Morning, Joss—' she began but the words died in her throat. It wasn't Joss on the doorstep. It was an older woman, with a tight grey bun and an expression to match. Under one arm was a folded copy of a newspaper. Her eyes burned over her wire-rimmed glasses as she stared at Nessie.

'Vanessa, I presume?'

With a sinking heart, Nessie guessed who this must be. She took a deep breath and summoned up a smile. 'That's right. And you must be Franny.'

The woman nodded curtly. 'I won't take up too much of your time,' she said, unfurling the paper and holding it up so that Nessie could see the humiliating headline. 'This kind of thing won't do. We have high standards in Little Monkham and negative publicity like this won't be tolerated.'

Nessie went still. *Won't be tolerated?* What was that supposed to mean? 'I can assure you that we're just as disappointed as you, Ms Forster, and this article couldn't be further from the truth.'

Franny looked anything but convinced. Inside the pub, the telephone began to ring, its faint warble floating out through the open door. Nessie swallowed a heartfelt sigh of relief. 'Will you excuse me?' she said, smiling politely. 'I probably need to get that. Lovely to meet you at last.'

With a nod, she stepped back and shut the door in Franny's face. Closing her eyes, she leaned against the wood and breathed in and out, willing her thumping heart to slow. Then she hurried towards the phone. 'Hello, the Star and Sixpence, how can I help?'

Silence. 'Hello?' Nessie repeated. 'Who is this?'

Another one of those stupid cold-calling machines, she guessed, the ones that dialled a dozen numbers and then only connected one. Sighing, she was just about to hang up when she heard a faint sound, as though someone on the other end had cleared their throat. 'Is someone there?' she asked sharply.

There was a click and then the dialling tone filled her ear. Nessie replaced the handset and stood for a moment, deep in thought. It must have been a wrong number, she decided, pushing it out of her mind.

Sam took the article better than Nessie had been expecting.

'Well, it's not quite what I was expecting but at least we got a decent amount of coverage.' Sam studied the newspaper again. 'Page five, too. Not bad.'

'You're not angry?' Nessie asked in confusion. 'Isn't it bad publicity?'

Sam smiled. 'No such thing. I would have preferred a glowing write-up, obviously, but this is almost as good.' She held the page up for Nessie to see. 'It would have cost at least a couple of hundred pounds for a half-page advert like this. He mentions the Boxing Day re-opening twice and it'll get people talking, if nothing else. We might even get a few gawkers coming to see how badly we're doing.'

Nessie pursed her lips. 'Speaking of gawkers, I had a visit from Franny.'

She filled her sister in on Franny's displeasure.

'See?' Sam said, looking delighted. 'It's working already. Franny won't be able to resist coming to look and we'll charm the pants off her.'

Nessie shuddered. 'I'm not sure either of us has enough charm for that.'

'Rubbish,' Sam said, her eyes gleaming at the challenge. 'They're going to be falling over themselves to get through the door on Boxing Day. Just you wait and see.'

As Christmas drew nearer, the days blurred into a never-ending flow of builders, tradesmen and deliveries. The cellar was stacked high with crates, leaving the narrowest of alleys between them. By the time Christmas Eve arrived, the mismatched tables and chairs were no more, the brickwork walls inside the pub had been repointed and the nicotine yellow ceiling had been replastered. At Sam's insistence, it now boasted a galaxy of dimmable downlights between its dark wooden beams. They made Nessie want to reach for her sunglasses and she was certain the locals would hate it but Sam assured her the lights would never be that bright. 'The floor and table lamps I've ordered will be here next week,' her sister said, waving away her concerns. 'They'll soften everything up, don't worry.'

Nessie was amazed to get a call from the plumber just after midday, telling her he'd be round in an hour to fit the new boiler. Both she and Sam had resigned themselves to a cold Christmas Day with hot water that worked when it wanted to. .

'It's the Franny Effect,' Joss said, when Nessie expressed her surprise the plumber was working on Christmas Eve. 'I told you, when she wants something done, it gets done.'

By late afternoon, heat was pouring from the newly bled radiators. Sam waited until Joss had clocked off before heading purposefully for the stairs.

'It's like Santa looked into my heart and knew exactly what I wanted,' she said. 'If I'm not out of the tub in an hour, send in a frogman.'

The pub door was ajar, left that way by the departing plumber. Nessie was clearing up the empty cups he'd left dotted around the bar when Owen poked his head through the gap.

'Hello, Nessie,' he called. 'I've got your grate out here. Shall I bring it in?'

Nessie noticed he stayed at the door, waiting to be invited in. 'Of course, please do. Although I'm not sure we'll need a fire, given how much heat the radiators give off now they're working properly.'

Owen disappeared for a moment, then pushed back the door and swung into the room, a vast iron grate in his arms.

Nessie knew it must be heavy but there was no sign of it on his face as he carried it over to the fireplace and lowered it into place. His arms bulged under his shirt, though; *a smith's muscles*, Nessie thought, remembering him bent over the anvil, striking sparks from the fiery metal. Her cheeks grew a touch warmer at the memory.

'There you go,' Owen said, surveying the fireplace with a critical gaze. 'That should do the trick.'

Nessie crossed the room for a closer look. The basket where the fire would sit was unremarkable – a grid of dull black iron, practical and sturdy – but the casing around it was a work of art. Along the front, ten tall prongs had been bent into graceful curls and on either side stood an elegantly twisted thicker pole topped by a proud *fleur-de-lis*. The grate might be a no-nonsense object, destined to be covered by flames and soot, but she could see beauty in the quality of the workmanship. 'It's almost too good to spoil with a fire,' she said, with a wry shake of her head. 'Thank you.'

'My pleasure,' Owen replied, looking pleased. 'I don't often do things like this nowadays, not when you can get them machine-made so easily but it was lovely to do something other than gates.'

'We should have a ceremonial lighting at the re-opening, although I suppose it'll need to be lit before everyone arrives,' Nessie said. 'You are coming, aren't you? You and Kathryn?'

He nodded. 'Of course. Although Kath might have her own plans for Boxing Day, mind you. She's in a folk band and sometimes they have gigs in the evenings. I'll ask her.'

'A band?' Nessie said. 'What does she play?'

Owen pulled a face. 'The violin. I'm surprised you haven't heard it squawking.' He chuckled. 'Ah, but I'm being unfair – she's pretty good, if I'm honest.'

'Don't you ever go to see her play?' Nessie asked curiously.

'I have done, in the past,' Owen said. 'But I don't like to leave Luke too often and – well, I'm not sure she'd want me there all the time. I might get in the way.'

Nessie frowned. 'In the way? How?'

He grinned. 'She'll never admit it but I reckon she's got a huge crush on the lead singer. One of these days she might do something about it and I'd hate her to feel embarrassed in front of me.'

Nessie felt her stomach twist. 'But . . . but . . . wouldn't you mind?'

'Why would I mind?' Owen said, raising his eyebrows quizzically. 'She's old enough to – oh . . .' He trailed off and gazed at Nessie with a solemn expression. 'You think Kathryn and me are—'

'A couple,' Nessie finished, dying inside but unable to look away. 'Aren't you?'

He laughed, the rumbling throaty sound smoothing the edges of her embarrassment. 'No. Kathryn is my sister and Luke's aunt. His mother . . . well, his mother died a few years back.'

Nessie closed her eyes briefly. That would be what Joss meant by his tragic past. Now she felt even worse – clumsy and stupid and bloody insensitive. 'I'm sorry,' she managed. 'I didn't know.'

Owen shook his head. 'No need to apologise,' he said, smoothing over her embarrassment with kindly ease. 'It's common enough knowledge around the village – I'm surprised no one told you.'

Joss tried to, Nessie thought, *only I was too much of a coward to follow it up*. She was grateful Sam was out of earshot – she'd probably expect Nessie to launch a flirt offensive there and then. The idea made Nessie want to shudder – what kind of person followed up the revelation of a dead wife with an invitation to dinner? 'We've been pretty busy,' she said, seizing the chance to steer the conversation into less mortifying waters. 'What do you think of the place?'

'It looks great,' Owen said, glancing around. 'The same old place but newer. Better.'

'Let's hope everyone else agrees,' Nessie replied, taking a ridiculous amount of pleasure from his praise.

Owen nodded in encouragement. 'I'm sure they will. The problem will be getting rid of them, I expect. But I'll do my best to pop in too.'

'Good,' Nessie said, and she was surprised to discover quite how much she meant it. It had nothing to do with the discovery that he was single, she told herself as he said goodbye and headed for the door. Nothing at all.

Having forced herself to put the grand re-opening out of her mind, for one day at least, Nessie was looking forward to

Christmas dinner. She'd barely left the pub for days and was sure that if she saw another ready-meal she would explode. Sam had managed to squeeze in one last visit to the supermarket so the cupboards in the tiny kitchen upstairs were stocked with tempting treats, and the village butcher had supplied some glorious-looking sausages and a turkey crown for Christmas Day. Kathryn had tried to persuade Nessie to come to Snowdrop Cottage for dinner but she'd refused. 'Christmas is family time,' she'd said, when Kathryn found out they would be spending the day on their own in the pub.

'It's for family and *friends*,' Kathryn had replied. 'We're friends now, right?'

Nessie hadn't known how to answer that because she liked Kathryn immensely, especially her sly observations of Little Monkham life. Nessie liked Owen too, although not in the way Sam insisted she did, and Luke seemed lovably boyish. But she didn't know any of them very well and she knew Sam wouldn't be able to resist a spot of matchmaking over the Christmas crackers, not now she knew Owen was single. No, the thought of intruding on the Rhys family for Christmas dinner felt like too much. Besides, there was still plenty to do ahead of the re-opening on Boxing Day, although Sam had made her promise to take the whole of Christmas Day off.

It wasn't until Nessie twisted the oven dial to cook the turkey at nine o'clock on Christmas morning that she discovered the flaw with their plan: the oven had died. Sam was still in bed, having polished off the best part of a bottle of Moët the night before, and Nessie had been up since seven peeling potatoes, slicing vegetables and crushing cranberries. Now as she stared into the depths of the cold black oven, she wanted to cry. Why hadn't she thought to check it worked before now? she asked herself. The hob was fine, so she could cook the vegetables and probably the sausages too but there was no way she could cook the turkey or roast the potatoes. It was a disaster.

With a heavy sigh, she got up and wandered into the living room. A tiny artificial Christmas tree listed to one side in the corner, with a modest cluster of presents beneath it. Neither she nor Patrick had made much of an effort at Christmas, swapping token gifts and making sure they were surrounded by family and friends so that the silences didn't become too glaring. Even so, the contrast between Christmases gone by and now was so stark that Nessie couldn't help the small sigh that escaped her.

Sam appeared at her elbow. 'Happy Christmas,' she said, thrusting a tall glass of tomato juice at her. 'It's a Bloody Mary. Hair of the dog.'

'You're the only one who got bitten.' Nessie took a sip, grimacing as the Tabasco sauce and vodka burned her throat. 'Happy Christmas, though.'

'Shall we do presents now or after lunch?' Sam asked. She gave a little laugh. 'This is weird, isn't it, spending Christmas together again. Do you remember how strict Mum was? One present in the morning and no more until after the Queen's speech.'

Nessie nodded. 'Yeah. And then Dad would come back from the pub and they'd argue.'

Sam was silent for a moment. 'Remember the year he fell into the tree and crushed all the presents underneath?'

Once again, Nessie nodded, suddenly ten years old again. 'He broke the snow globe Mum had bought me from Paris.'

'And my Barbie Fairytale Carriage,' Sam said. She shuddered. 'God, no wonder I've always hated this time of year. What time's lunch?'

Nessie sighed. 'I've got some bad news about that . . .'

They made do with fried bacon, sausage and mash, doing their best to laugh it off with paper hats and bad jokes. After they'd eaten, they swapped gifts: Nessie had bought Sam a charm bracelet with a glittering star and a silver sixpence attached and Sam gave Nessie some eye-wateringly expensive lingerie, 'For when you make a move on Owen,' she'd said with an encouraging wink. Then Sam had produced a bottle of tawny port Joss had found in the cellar and they'd sipped from generous glasses as they watched a film. By ten o'clock in the evening both sisters were ready to call it a day.

'Still sober on Christmas night,' Sam marvelled, hugging Nessie goodnight. 'Dad would have disowned us.'

'Still, at least we won't have hangovers tomorrow,' Nessie said, pulling a face. 'Remind me whose idea it was to hold the grand re-opening on Boxing Day again?'

'Not mine,' Sam grumbled. 'Christmas is about pigging

out and relaxing, not worrying about whether you've stuffed enough vol-au-vents with prawn cocktail for the punters.'

'Next year will be different,' Nessie said soothingly. 'I promise.'

Sam nodded in agreement. 'Bloody right. Next year, we'll already be open, you'll be banging Mr Blacksmith and we can blast the sodding turkey on the forge.'

As she closed the shutters on her bedroom window, Nessie paused to glance into the shadowy yard of the forge below. The lamp over the door of Snowdrop Cottage glowed white, sending a pool of light cascading over the doorstep. She could see two empty milk bottles neatly lined up on one side and the silvery shimmer of an upturned wheelbarrow on the other. Closing her eyes, Nessie tried to picture the family inside the cottage: Luke should be asleep by now, although from what she knew of him, probably not. They might be playing a festive game, the kind no one ever won, or watching a film. Or perhaps Owen was raising a quiet glass to his wife and remembering Christmases past. Nessie had no way of knowing.

When the door cracked suddenly open, it made her jump. A figure appeared beneath the light: Owen. His breath formed clouds in the air as he glanced upwards. Nessie stepped hurriedly back – she didn't want him to think she was stalking him. Peering around the shutter, she watched as he turned the wheelbarrow the right way and wheeled it into the darkness. A minute later, he was back and the barrow was loaded with logs. He parked it by the cottage door and began to take the wood inside. When he'd finished, he tipped the wheelbarrow upside down and leaned it against the wall, then fired a swift glance at the pub again before disappearing inside once more.

Nessie sighed as he closed the door and leaned her head against the cool wood of the shutter. Her feelings were so jumbled and she suspected the tawny port was only partly to blame. In the silence, she could admit what she had strenuously denied to Sam – that a little flame of hope had flickered into life when she'd discovered Owen was single. But wasn't it too soon for another relationship? She hadn't even started looking into the divorce process yet and that was assuming Owen was even interested – as Joss had pointed out, he wasn't short of admirers among the village women. Why would he be interested in her?

He wouldn't be, of course. Closing the shutters, Nessie crossed to the bed and scooped up the lingerie Sam had given her. She held it for a moment, rubbing a thumb over its satin softness, then shook her head and buried it at the bottom of her underwear drawer. *Out of sight, out of mind,* she told herself, and slipped into bed.

Chapter Nine

The fire was burning low. Sam selected the heaviest log she could find from the burnished copper bucket and dropped it carefully among the glowing embers, flinching slightly at the flurry of sparks. Once the yellow flames began licking the dried wood, she straightened up and her eyes were drawn for what felt like the hundredth time to the oversized vintage clock on the wall, subtly lit by one of the downlights. She glanced over at Nessie, who was standing behind the bar looking every bit as anxious as Sam felt. 'We did say seven o'clock, didn't we? On the posters and flyers, I mean.'

Nessie's eyes strayed to the clock too: it was eight-twenty. She sighed. 'We did. I suppose that is the right time, is it?'

Joss checked his phone. 'Yep. Spot on.'

'I don't get it,' Sam said, frustration bubbling in her voice. 'What are they waiting for? A red carpet and a limo?'

'Search me,' Joss said, shrugging. He waved a hand at the trays of rapidly curling sandwiches on one of the long tables. 'Want me to cover them up? No sense in letting them dry out.'

Sam was about to agree when she heard the tread of heavy feet on the gravel outside. 'Finally,' she said.

When the door opened, Sam almost groaned at the sight of Owen. It wasn't that she wasn't pleased to see him – far from it – but she had been hoping for rather more than one potential customer. 'Hello,' she said, peering out into the night. 'You haven't got half the village behind you, have you?'

Owen stepped inside, shaking droplets of rain from his wax-covered coat. 'No, but it's a filthy night out there.' His roving gaze took in the subtle lighting, the untouched buffet and the empty bar. 'Am I the first?'

'The first and quite possibly the last,' Nessie said with a wry grimace, although Sam noticed her eyes lingering on his face. 'What can we get you?'

Owen hung his coat on the stand by the door. 'I'll have the Thirsty Bishop, please.'

Joss had given both sisters lessons in pulling the perfect pint, to give exactly the right amount of froth to beer ratio in the glass. He'd made it look so easy that Sam was annoyed with herself when she didn't get a flawless pint immediately. But Joss had turned out to be a surprisingly patient teacher and it wasn't long before they'd got the hang of the pumps.

Frowning in concentration, Nessie placed a foaming pint on the bar. 'This one's on the house,' she said, when Owen tried to pay. 'A thank you for making our grate so – er – great.'

Owen looked reluctant to accept but lifted the pint to his mouth and took a long sip. 'I can't tell you how much I've missed this, Joss,' he said at last, smacking his lips in appreciation. 'Bottled beer just isn't the same.'

Joss nodded and once again, Sam was grateful for his expertise. It wouldn't count for much if they didn't have more custom, however. 'Is there another grand re-opening tonight?' she asked Owen. 'Is that where everyone is?'

He took another drink, then placed it carefully on the bar. 'I did wonder if this might happen.'

'What?' Sam demanded.

Owen's dark-eyed gaze met hers. 'What you have to understand is that they're a funny lot in Little Monkham, a bit . . . set in their ways. They like things to stay mostly the same and – well, you've shaken things up a bit with all the changes here.'

Sam couldn't believe what she was hearing. 'Seriously? They expected us just to carry on with things the way they were?' She stared at him incredulously. 'The men's toilets flooded every time they were flushed.'

'I know,' Owen said reasonably. 'I'm all in favour of what you've done. But the truth is, you've ruffled a few feathers along the way too, on birds that take a lot of smoothing down once they've been disturbed.'

'You mean Henry Fitzsimmons,' Nessie said, turning a resigned gaze towards Sam. 'I told you we should have kept the paintings.'

'Oh please,' Sam snapped. 'That old goat needs to get over himself.'

'I heard you had a little run-in with Franny too,' Owen said, raising his eyebrows.

Sam folded her arms defensively. 'It was hardly a run-in. She started asking a lot of personal questions and I wouldn't tell her what she wanted to know, that's all.'

'I'm surprised she let you out of the shop,' Joss said, grinning. 'Parcel tape is almost as good as duct tape for interrogation purposes, I hear.'

'I know she can be a bit nosy but most of us have learned to humour her,' Owen said. 'The trouble is, she's got a lot of influence among the villagers. I wouldn't be surprised if she's the reason no one's here tonight – her and Henry.'

'But that's ridiculous!' Sam burst out. 'She's the one who gave us this crazy deadline. And now she's thrown her toys out of the pram because I didn't spill my guts the moment she asked?'

Owen took another sip of his beer. 'Looks that way.'

'And everyone else has gone along with it?' Sam went on, feeling an incandescent bubble of rage growing bigger and bigger. 'God, it's like that TV show where the whole village of weirdos was played by the same three people.'

'Never mind that now,' Nessie said. 'What can we do to fix things?'

He thought for a moment. 'Leave it with me and I'll see what I can find out. I might be barking up the wrong tree completely.'

Sam turned to Joss. 'What about you? Have you heard anything?'

'They'd hardly tell me, would they?' he said in a reasonable tone. 'Besides, I'm not exactly Franny's favourite person. She doesn't approve of me.'

Doesn't approve of your love life, you mean, Sam thought, but she didn't say it. To his credit, Joss didn't seem in the least bit troubled by Franny's condemnation. 'A couple of the village women have asked about you, though,' he added. 'There's a small chance they might be a little jealous.'

Sam glared at him. 'I hope you told them there's nothing to be jealous of?'

He spread his hands and threw her an innocent look. 'Of course. I'm not sure they believed me, mind. They've seen you.'

The look that accompanied his last few words was so openly suggestive that Sam almost blushed. Gritting her teeth, she refused to meet his gaze.

Nessie's shoulders slumped in defeat. 'What a mess. Joss, you might as well go home. I'm sure you've better things to do than hang around an empty pub.'

Joss glanced over at Sam and she thought for a moment he might argue. Then he laid the towel he'd been using to dry the coffee cups down and nodded. Owen drained his glass. 'I'll have to go too, I'm afraid,' he said apologetically. 'Kathryn has a gig, her last one of the year since their New Year's Eve booking got cancelled, so I need to get home to Luke. She's sorry she can't be here.'

Nessie offered a strained smile. 'Say hi to her for me.'

'Take some sandwiches, both of you,' Sam said, waving

towards the laden table. 'We'll be eating it for breakfast, lunch and dinner tomorrow otherwise.'

An uncomfortable silence descended once they'd gone. Sam sat next to the fire, prodding the coals moodily with a poker. 'Go on, you can say it,' she told her sister after a few minutes had gone by. 'This is all my fault.'

Nessie left the bar and sat opposite her. 'Don't be silly, of course it's not. We just need to find a way to win them back, that's all.' She smiled in encouragement. 'Luckily, we have a PR genius on the team who knows every trick when it comes to rebranding.'

Sam shook her head. She felt mentally exhausted, worn out by all the work they'd already done. She wasn't sure she had the strength to regroup and launch a PR offensive on Little Monkham's ungrateful population. 'I don't know, Ness, maybe we're not—'

The door swung back, interrupting Sam. Both sisters turned in some surprise and Sam saw a red-headed woman wearing a fur coat and thigh-high boots standing in the doorway.

'Hell's teeth, it's deader than Oliver Reed in here,' the woman announced. 'What did you do, threaten them all with a makeover?'

Sam couldn't help herself: she laughed. 'Something like that,' she said, getting to her feet. 'Welcome to the Star and Sixpence. What can I get you?'

The woman tottered forward and perched on a bar stool. 'I don't mind, darling, just make it a double.' She waited until

Sam was behind the bar and stared intently. 'You have his dimples.'

'Whose?' Sam said, her bewildered gaze flickering towards Nessie. *What the hell . . . ?*

Nessie hurried forwards. 'Let me introduce you to Ruby Cabernet – Dad's girlfriend.'

'A boycott?' Nessie yelped, staring in horror across the bar at Owen the next day. 'Is she trying to close the Star and Sixpence permanently?'

Owen shook his head. 'I doubt it. She's just showing you – or more correctly, Sam – who's boss. Franny doesn't like to be crossed and this is her way of making sure you don't do it again.'

'I'll show *her* who's boss,' Sam muttered, her stomach twisting with pent-up fury. 'Who does she think she is – Don Corleone?'

'Stop, Sam,' Nessie said. 'We talked about this, remember? There's no point in confronting Franny head on. We need to go around her and appeal to the villagers' curiosity.'

'How are you going to do that?' Owen asked.

Sam took a deep breath and forced herself to calm down. Nessie was right, of course – the best way to make Franny irrelevant was to break her stranglehold on them and the only way to do that was to tempt customers into the pub. She was fairly sure she could count on Ruby's help; once her astonishment that her father had ever managed to pull such a woman had worn off, she'd begun to admire Ruby's humour and quick-wit, not to mention her elegance. That admiration was only slightly tempered by the amount of gin she'd seen Ruby put away, but since the money Ruby paid for her drinks was the only income they'd taken that night, Sam wasn't complaining. 'This isn't anything new but we'll have a Happy Hour – buy one, get one free on house wines, beers and spirits, starting tonight. That should tempt some of them. And it's really short notice but on Tuesday night, I've called in a huge favour with a celebrity friend and we're hosting an "Evening With" event.'

'Anyone I know?' Ruby asked, her eyes dancing.

'I'd be very surprised if you didn't,' Sam said, grinning. 'And on New Year's Eve, we're pulling out all the stops and throwing a good old-fashioned party. I've even got one of London's top cocktail-makers designing us a signature drink.'

Nessie leaned forwards. 'We wondered if Kathryn's band might like to play – you said their gig got cancelled. What do you think?'

Owen smiled. 'I'm sure they'd love to. I'll bring Luke along too, if that's okay?'

'Absolutely, the more the merrier,' Nessie said. 'He can sleep in the spare room if he gets tired.'

'Ha, no chance of that,' Owen replied. 'He'll still be going when the rest of us are going to bed.'

Sam watched her sister closely. There was no sign now of the reticence she'd shown around Owen when she'd first met him. She was completely relaxed in his company and although it would be a stretch to call what either of them was doing as flirting, there was definite potential. Worth fanning the flames a little, Sam decided with satisfaction. He'd make a good starter boyfriend for Nessie, someone to restore her confidence. And maybe if things went well, Owen Rhys might turn out to be more. Time would tell.

'We're going to need to hit the ground running,' she explained, dragging her thoughts back to the plan she and Nessie had put together the night before. 'We'll get some flyers printed off tomorrow and hand-deliver them around the village. What we really need to do is generate some killer word of mouth buzz, though.'

'I get the feeling you've done this before,' Owen said.

'Close,' Sam admitted. 'Now, here's where you come in . . .'

Chapter Ten

Nessie had to hand it to Sam: she was as good as her word. The following morning, she went on a charm offensive, stopping people in the street, knocking on doors and calling into every business in the village apart from the Post Office.

'Happy Hour is between six and seven p.m. every evening until Twelfth Night,' she said, brandishing the flyers she'd printed. 'And you won't want to miss tomorrow night – it's a Star and Sixpence exclusive. Trust me, you cannot get this experience anywhere else.'

'*An Evening with Nick Borrowdale*,' Martha read, gazing down at the flyer Sam had pressed into her hand. '*The* Nick Borrowdale? The one from *Smugglers' Inn*?'

'The same,' Sam replied cheerfully. 'And you could meet him if you come to the Star and Sixpence tomorrow night.'

Martha looked tempted. 'But . . .'

'But what?' Sam said. She leaned forward. 'Worried what Franny will say? Look at it this way – can she give you access to Nick Borrowdale in all his smouldersome, dark-eyed glory? Can she bring him close enough to almost touch?'

Martha's eyes were like dinner plates. 'Really?' she breathed. 'That close?'

Sam nodded. 'And I hear he's single at the moment,' she said, knowing perfectly well that Martha wasn't. 'Did you notice the complimentary champagne cocktail, by the way?'

'Oh!' Martha squeaked. 'I'll be there. Definitely.'

'Great,' Sam said, smiling. 'Be sure to tell your friends and family, too.'

Martha nodded absently, her gaze fixed on the flyer. 'Yeah, of course. Friends and family . . .'

Sam smiled at Nessie and pointed towards the butchers. 'How about there next?'

Nessie gazed at her doubtfully. She didn't imagine Nick's photo and the offer of a Kir Royale would have quite the same effect on the burly brothers who supplied the village's meat but you never could tell. 'Are you sure Nick will be able to make it?' Nessie asked. 'What if he already has plans? He must be awfully busy.'

'Way ahead of you, Ness,' Sam replied. She glanced over her shoulder and lowered her voice. 'I've booked a look-alike to come in his place.'

Nessie felt her mouth drop open. 'What? But – but—'

Sam took one look at her horrified expression and laughed. 'I'm kidding. Actually, I've already spoken to Nick. It's all sorted. He's arriving around six o'clock tomorrow.'

'I hope this works,' Nessie said, biting her lip. She hadn't mentioned anything to Sam but between the expensive renovations and the new stock they'd ordered, their savings were starting to run alarmingly low. In fact, if trade didn't start to pick up soon, they'd have to dip into the emergency fund. And once that was gone . . .

'Of course it'll work,' Sam replied confidently. 'And once they see how amazing the pub looks, they won't be able to resist coming back for more on New Year's Eve. Trust me, we're going to be turning them away.'

Nessie was on her way back from coffee with Kathryn that afternoon when she saw the first snowdrops. They were nestled under a tree on the edge of the cottage garden and looked like tiny white bells among the lush green leaves. She stopped for a closer look, admiring the delicate blooms lit by the late afternoon sun, and saw that these were the first of many: tell-tale green shoots were poking out all across the dull mud around the edge of the grass, with plenty more along the stone wall that formed the boundary between the cottage and the pub. There might even be some in the neglected beer garden itself if she looked.

She picked her way over to the wall and leaned over, searching for more snowdrops. Sure enough, there were plenty; not quite in bloom but a forest of unopened buds and sturdy green spikes under the trees at the back. They'd make a carpet of white once the flowers were out. An unaccustomed sense of peace flowed into Nessie and she rested her head on her arms. It was less than a month since she and Sam had arrived – how things had changed from that dark December night. The nights were still dark, of course but here was a sign that spring was on its way. It seemed as though the pub was waking up after a long winter too – shedding its old skin and starting afresh. It was starting to feel like they belonged, although Sam hadn't had much alternative and Nessie knew she missed the excitement and sparkle of her old life. Even so, her sister had mellowed a bit from when they'd first arrived and Nessie was confident she was settling down. All they needed now were the customers.

'Lovely, aren't they?'

Nessie jumped at the sound of Owen's voice – she'd been so wrapped up in her own thoughts that she hadn't heard him approach. She let her thudding heartbeat slow before half-turning to smile in welcome. 'Beautiful,' she agreed. 'Yours are better, though.'

'They're early this year,' Owen said. 'We don't normally see them before February, although I think they've been out at the end of December once or twice.'

'I'm glad they're up early,' Nessie said. 'They make me think of new beginnings.'

Owen's dark eyes rested solemnly on her face. 'There's a lot to be said for those.'

She returned his gaze, enjoying the chance to look at him. He was as solid as ever, easy-going and uncomplicated, but Nessie wasn't fooled; Owen Rhys had depths. But there were shadows too, the loss of his wife had left its mark. Reaching the decision to leave Patrick had been hard but it had been her choice. Owen had been given no choice at all and she wondered if there was any way to begin again after something like that. Surely he would always feel the gap where his lost love should be.

'You've had your hair done,' Owen said, gazing at her neatly trimmed, expensively highlighted head. 'It looks lovely.'

Nessie felt the start of a blush and dug her fingernails into her palm. 'Thank you,' she said. 'It needed attention so badly that Sam said she wouldn't admit to Nick we were related if I didn't do something to fix it before tomorrow night. Are you coming?'

Owen shook his head. 'Kathryn is. She told me in no uncertain terms that she couldn't babysit Luke because she was meeting her future husband.'

Nessie grinned. Was there a woman alive who didn't fancy Nick Borrowdale? Actually, he reminded her a lot of Owen – the same brooding Celtic looks and smouldering dark eyes, although she guessed Owen was nearer forty than thirty. 'She might have to join the queue. Judging from the flurry of ticket orders, half the village is coming.'

'Good,' Owen said. 'And the New Year's Eve party should be fantastic.'

'I hope so,' Nessie sighed. 'We'll push the tickets for that tomorrow and hope it's not a repeat of Boxing Day. I don't think I could bear it if no one came again.'

His eyes softened. 'They'll come. A new year means a new beginning, remember?'

It would be a fresh start in more ways than one, Nessie decided once she was back inside the Star and Sixpence. Her sister was right – it was time to put the past behind her and start living again. Whether Sam was prepared to heed her own advice was another matter entirely.

Chapter Eleven

'Joss, I think the Grail's gone again,' Sam called, puffing a strand of hair away from her clammy forehead and releasing the sputtering beer pump. 'Can you change the barrel?'

The bar was elbow to elbow with customers, all waiting to be served. To say Nick's appearance had been a success was the understatement of the year – Sam couldn't imagine the Star and Sixpence *ever* being so full. And it seemed that sighing over handsome Irishmen was a thirsty business – once the complimentary cocktails had been drunk, the crowds had turned their attention to Nessie's carefully balanced wine and cocktail list with gusto. The audience wasn't predominantly female either – there were a surprising number of men in the audience. Husbands and boyfriends, Sam decided, come to make sure Nick didn't take a shine to their women. They were thirsty too.

'On it,' Joss called and vanished down the stairs to the cellar.

'Sorry,' Sam said, smiling at Father Goodluck. 'It'll be back on in a moment.'

'No problem,' the vicar said, smiling. 'You have a good crowd here tonight.'

Sam nodded, gazing past him at the throng. Ruby was there, of course, swapping star-studded stories with Nick and earning some sharp looks from the women around her. Martha was there too; she'd been sat in the front row during Nick's talk and had gazed in rapt adoration throughout. Kathryn couldn't take her eyes off him either and Sam made a mental note to introduce her. There was no sign of Franny, or Henry, and a couple of other villagers were missing but Sam hadn't really expected the stalwarts of the Little Monkham Preservation Society to give in so easily. She was confident they wouldn't be able to resist the New Year's Eve party, especially when she played her trump card.

She returned her gaze to the vicar and favoured him with a warm smile. 'It's amazing what a sprinkling of stardust will do.'

'And a glimmer of genius,' Father Goodluck said. 'But don't let me keep you. See to your other patrons.'

Sam threw him a grateful look and moved on to the next customer. A few minutes later Joss reappeared. 'All done,' he said, brushing past her closer than was strictly necessary in the narrow space behind the bar. She shook her head in wry amusement. Nessie was right, she was going to have to do something about him before long. But not tonight – tonight was all about congratulating themselves on a job well done.

By eleven o'clock, the crowd had thinned and Nick was trying not to yawn. Sam reached for the old-fashioned brass bell that hung over the bar and rang it briskly. 'Time, please, ladies and gentlemen. Thank you for your custom and goodnight.'

She and Nessie made their way round the tables, collecting up the empty glasses. When Sam reached Nick and Ruby, she stopped. 'Listen to you two luvvies,' she said, grinning. 'You're supposed to be working the crowd, Nick, not talking shop.'

Nick raised an eyebrow. 'You can take the girl out of PR,' he said to Ruby with a sigh. 'I've dished out more than my fair share of charm tonight, thank you.'

'He has,' Ruby confirmed. 'I'm sure I saw him sweet-talking Percy Miller at one point and he's an insufferable old bore. If that isn't above and beyond the call of duty I don't know what is.'

Sam reached out and squeezed Nick's arm. 'Thank you,' she said sincerely. 'I know how busy you are. Nessie and I really appreciate you doing this.'

He smiled. 'It's the least I can do. When are you coming back to London, anyway? I miss you.'

Sam laughed. 'I'm sure you do, Mr *Glitz* Magazine's Most Sexy.'

He regarded her seriously, his dark eyes concerned. 'I mean it. You should come back. Face up to whatever drove you here.'

Sam hesitated, acutely aware of Ruby listening in. The truth was, she missed London; she missed the energy and

95

excitement of the city. And she missed her social life. It had been hard to cut herself off in the middle of nowhere, much harder than it had been for Nessie, especially when everything in Little Monkham felt so claustrophobic. It didn't help that she wasn't used to hiding – the opposite, in fact. 'It's complicated,' she said, choosing her words with care. 'And Ness needs me. You understand, don't you?'

He reached out and enveloped her in a hug. 'Are you kidding? Of course I do. I'm all in favour of getting away from it all every now and then. But not forever.'

Sam leaned into him, closing her eyes. 'I'll come back when I can.'

He released her and stepped back. 'Okay. The great and the good of London need you. I need you.'

There were one or two people who definitely *didn't* need her, Sam thought, but she kept that sentiment to herself. 'Are you sure I can't tempt you to stay here tonight?' she said, noticing Nessie watching from behind the bar with slightly narrowed eyes. 'It's a long drive home and I'd definitely be public enemy number one if you fell asleep at the wheel.'

Nick shook his head. 'I've got an Italian TV interview in Rome, sadly, or I'd take you up on that offer. But let's have dinner when I'm back. If nothing else I can remind you what you're missing.'

To the casual observer it sounded as though Nick meant her old lifestyle but Sam knew it was a sneaky reference to the no-strings nights they'd spent together a number of times. She glanced sideways at Ruby, who was looking back and forth between her and Nick with amusement. 'Don't mind me, Sam,' the older woman said, with an expressive shrug. 'I'd be all over him myself if I was ten years younger. But you might want to pay some attention to Joss. If he gets any greener he'll burst into leaf.'

Frowning, Sam followed her gaze to where Joss stood glowering at Nick, his expression thunderous. She swore under her breath. It looked as though she was going to have to initiate that conversation sooner than she had planned.

Sam waited until Nick had set off home and Nessie had gone to bed before she tackled Joss. 'Good work tonight,' she said, opening the till to remove the drawer pleasingly stuffed with notes.

He didn't look up. Instead, he carried on unscrewing the sparklers from the pumps. 'I suppose.'

She stepped nearer, trying to catch his eye. 'I mean it. Thank you for everything you've done to help us. We're very grateful.'

Joss grunted. 'I'd like to see your boyfriend lumping barrels around the cellar. Acting's not exactly a manly job, is it?'

Sam bit her lip; she knew for a fact that Nick worked out every single day and had abs you could strike a match on. The social media spike during the episode of *Smugglers' Inn* where he'd stripped down to his breeches had almost crashed Twitter. But perhaps now wasn't the best time to mention that. 'Nick isn't my boyfriend.'

Joss's lips tightened. 'Whatever.'

She took a deep breath. 'Look, Joss, I think we need to get something straight. I'm your boss, you're my employee. Which means my relationship with Nick or anyone else I might fancy is nothing to do with you.'

'So you do fancy him then?' Joss said.

'It's none of your business,' Sam replied, fighting to keep her tone even. 'Just like it's none of mine who you fancy.'

'Except it is,' he said and looked up. 'It's your business if the person I fancy is you, right?'

'Nothing is going to happen, Joss,' she said quietly. 'Stop it now before you get hurt.'

He continued to gaze at her, his eyes a deep and stormy blue. If the circumstances had been different, Sam wouldn't have thought twice about taking things further – she might even have seen him more than once. He wasn't her usual type but there was something in him that caught her attention and held it; not the way he looked, not the way he acted, something she couldn't quite identify. Something that sent her good intentions about nipping things in the bud flying out of the window.

He seemed to read her mind. Sam wasn't sure whether he stepped forwards or she did but suddenly he was a lot nearer. Without breaking eye contact, he reached out and brushed her cheek with the back of his fingers. 'I think it's worth the risk.'

Her skin tingled at his touch. She gazed upwards, lost in the sea of blue. *He's going to kiss me*, she thought, and her flutter of panic was drowned in a flood of anticipation. But he didn't. Instead, he backed off and busied himself loading the last of the glasses into the dishwasher, leaving Sam staring after him. *What just happened?* she wondered, forcing her breathing to slow. *How did I get from saying I didn't fancy him to wanting him to kiss me? And how the hell am I going to stop it from happening again?*

Chapter Twelve

The phone rang just as Sam was passing. Juggling three jumbo bags of party poppers and an armful of candle holders, she snatched up the handset. 'Hello, Star and Sixpence?'

Seconds later, she banged it down, just as Nessie appeared from the bar. 'Another cold caller?' she asked sympathetically.

'Third one since yesterday,' Sam sighed, rearranging the party poppers before they tumbled to the ground. 'It's driving me nuts.'

Nessie hesitated. 'You don't think . . . ?'

'What?' Sam said, wondering if her sister was thinking the same thing she'd been thinking – that the calls were more than just random coincidences.

'Nothing,' Nessie said and she flashed a smile of reassurance. 'Anyway, I came to tell you that Henry's in the bar. Whatever you said to him, it worked.'

'Good,' Sam said, pushing the silent call out of her mind.

She hurried out into the bar and summoned up her brightest smile. 'Hello, Henry. Thank you so much for coming . . .'

Joss walked into the public lounge and stopped dead.

'Have you lost your mind?' he asked, staring at the painting Sam was hanging on the wall.

'Don't worry, it's for one night only,' Sam said, standing back to stare at the seascape and then straightening it. 'I had to eat a monster slice of humble pie and offer a regular Art Night but it was the only way I could think of to get around Henry. Never let it be said that I don't admit when I'm wrong.'

Joss's lips quirked but he kept whatever thought he'd had to himself and gazed around instead. 'And whose is that one?'

Sam glanced across at the still life watercolour. 'No idea. One of Henry's friends', I assume. Think of it as an added bonus for tonight's party – start the New Year with some new art, kind of thing. An unmissable opportunity to pick up some undiscovered talent before the artist goes stratospheric.'

Joss threw her an incredulous look. 'And you're expecting people to buy that?'

'Maybe,' Sam shrugged. 'People make odd choices when they've had a drink or two. It could work in Henry's favour.'

'I suppose it could work,' he conceded. 'Well played, boss.'

Sam only detected the faintest hint of mockery behind the last word. He'd kept a professional distance between them since the night before, which Sam refused to admit bothered her. His feelings might have been hurt but it was all for the best, she decided. Especially since it didn't appear she could trust herself around him.

'Thank you,' she said, lifting the last painting and carrying it to another wall. 'Let's hope the beer goggles do their job tonight.'

At five minutes to seven, Sam and Nessie stood behind the bar, gazing at the empty pub. The afternoon had been frantic, a whirl of preparation and last-minute tasks. The fridge was full of party food, the playlist was loaded with crowd-pleasing tunes to set the mood before Kathryn's band took centre-stage, and the champagne was on ice. This was the calm before the storm, Sam thought. At least she hoped it was.

'Are we ready, then?' she asked, with a glance at the locked door.

Her sister nodded. 'I think so. Time to open up and see if the residents of Little Monkham have forgiven us.'

She moved towards the door but Nessie caught her arm. 'Listen, Sam, I just wanted to say thanks for everything you've done here. I know it wasn't your choice to come to Little Monkham and it's been harder for you than it has for me.' She took a deep breath. 'So thank you.'

Sam smiled. 'Hey, we make a good team. And it's been fun.' She reviewed her last sentence and pulled a wry face. 'Well, not fun exactly, but interesting. And don't worry about me, I'm fine. Getting used to it, anyway.'

Nessie paused. 'There's something else I wanted to say,' she said slowly. 'I know I said we had to be careful as employers but I think I might have let the responsibility go to my head a bit. This is your new beginning too and I need to start trusting you more.'

Sam blinked. This was the last thing she'd been expecting Nessie to say. 'O–kay. What brought this on?'

'Something Owen said,' Nessie replied. 'And I don't want to stand in the way of you being happy here, so if you want to take things further with Joss then you should. I know you're not into commitment but really, not all men are like Dad. They don't all leave.'

Sam was silent. Was that the reason she'd never let herself get involved with anyone beyond a couple of dates? So that they never got the chance to leave her? Nick was different – they both knew it was purely fun, with no strings attached – but there'd been others, too many whose numbers she'd blocked when they'd tried to get in touch again. She'd told herself it was a freedom thing but had she really been insulating herself against the pain of being abandoned all over again?

Nessie cleared her throat. 'And if things don't work out – well, cellarmen are easier to replace than sisters.'

Sam understood then; Nessie had seen how restless she'd become and was holding out a lifeline, a way to encourage her to put down roots for the first time in her life. 'I'll bear that in mind,' she said carefully. 'Thanks.'

'Okay,' Nessie said, smiling. 'Shall we do this?'

Reaching out to pull her sister into a tight hug, Sam smiled too. 'Yes. Let's do it.'

By ten o'clock, the party was in full swing. Sonic Folk had just begun their set with a cracking Mumford and Sons cover, and there was plenty of toe-tapping that Sam was sure would turn into dancing before long. Several of Henry's seascapes had been sold. Of course, some of the buyers were actor friends of Ruby's, who were under strict instructions not to let on that she'd primed them over which paintings to buy. But not all of them were.

'Wonders will never cease,' Joss said, nodding at a rapturous-looking Henry. 'He's actually sold one.'

'Three actually,' Sam said, straight-faced. 'Credit where credit's due.'

Joss patted the beer pump in front of him. 'I'd better test the strength of this stuff tomorrow.'

Owen arrived at the bar, Luke at his side. 'Another pint of the Bishop, please, Joss,' he said, handing over his glass. 'And an orange juice for Luke.'

'Dad,' Luke protested loudly. 'I wanted a Coke.'

Owen glanced down, eyeing his son's flushed cheeks and bright eyes. 'I think you've had more than enough for now. You don't want to crash out before the fireworks on the green, do you?'

'No,' Luke sighed, then brightened. 'Although Nessie said I can sleep here if I do. I wonder if Elijah will be on the prowl.'

Owen grimaced, then turned to Sam. 'I think the entire village might be here. Nice job.'

'Thanks,' Sam said, smiling. 'It was a real team effort, though. Team Star and Sixpence.'

Joss placed a foaming pint on the bar in front of Owen. 'Just Franny to go and the boycott will be well and truly busted.'

Owen nodded at the doorway. 'Speak of the devil.'

Sam's gaze flew to the door. Sure enough, Franny was stood there, gazing around as though there was a bad smell under her nose. Squaring her shoulders, Sam plastered a welcoming smile on her face and began to weave through the crowd.

'Franny, how lovely to see you,' she said once she reached the door, injecting as much warmth as she could into her voice. 'Are you in the market for some new art? Or can I tempt you with the house cocktail, a Silver Sixpence? It's gin and elderflower with a drop of moonlight to give a gorgeous silvery shimmer.'

Franny glanced around, wrinkling her nose at the bright lights. 'I don't really hold with all that fancy rubbish.'

Sam caught Nessie watching from across the room and knew she'd be holding her breath. 'We've got plenty of the more traditional drinks too. Joss has done a great job with the cellars – the beers are getting rave reviews from the real-ale drinkers.'

'Is that so?' Franny sniffed, firing a hard look Joss's way. 'It's nice to see him working at something other than his love-life.'

Sam bit back a grimace. 'I wondered if you might like to give a talk one evening in the new year,' she said, changing the subject. 'About the history of the village and the pub's place at its heart. You are the resident expert, after all.'

There was a short silence, and Sam could tell that Franny was struggling not to feel flattered. Then the older woman gave a terse nod. 'I suppose I could do that.'

'Fantastic,' Sam enthused, as though Franny had just agreed to address the United Nations. 'Let's compare diaries soon and sort out a date. Now, what can I get you to drink?'

Franny's eyes met hers and Sam thought she detected a flicker of something – maybe *humour*? – in their frozen depths. 'I think I'll try a Silver Sixpence, if you don't mind. They sound like just my kind of thing.'

An hour later, there was dancing. Kathryn and the band had whipped everyone into a frenzy with some fast-paced covers that included everything from Bellowhead to Beyoncé. Sam was impressed. Booking the band without having heard them had been risky in the extreme but it looked like Nessie's instincts had paid off – the villagers were loving Sonic Folk, mostly because the band members seemed to be just as much fun as the dancers. Kathryn was beaming from ear to ear as she played. On the makeshift dancefloor, Ruby had kicked off her stilettos to strut her stuff barefoot to 'Single Ladies' with Martha and most of the other women, while Luke and the other children were having a dance-off of their own. Over in one corner, some of the men had challenged Owen to an arm-wrestling. As far as Sam could tell, he hadn't lost a round yet. Even Franny was swaying to the infectious tunes, although Sam thought the number of Silver Sixpences she'd put away might have something to do with it too.

Henry was holding court in one corner, his regimental tie loose and his face flushed, and Sam suddenly felt guilty that she'd been so dismissive of him when she'd first arrived, although not guilty enough to accept his stilted request for the pleasure of a dance as she passed by collecting glasses. 'Some other time, Henry,' she replied, hurrying for the safety of the bar. 'It's all work, work, work tonight.'

At eleven-thirty, Sonic Folk wound up their set and Sam teed up her playlist full of guaranteed floor-fillers. Nessie rang the bell and announced that the bar was temporarily closing. 'There'll be complimentary champagne to see in the New Year but if you want anything else, come and get it now.'

There was a minor stampede, mostly the men ordering pints but Sam noticed Franny ordered another cocktail and Ruby lined up a double whiskey. Once everyone was served, Sam began to lay out champagne flutes. Nessie started to fill them but Sam touched her arm. 'Joss and I can do this,' she said, smiling at her sister's red cheeks. 'Why don't you take a break?'

Nessie opened her mouth to argue but Sam cut her off. 'Owen's glass is empty,' she said meaningfully. 'Why don't you see if he wants another pint?'

She and Joss worked side by side without speaking for a moment. Then they both reached for the last champagne bottle and her hand brushed his. She felt goosebumps crackle on her skin. 'Sorry,' she said automatically.

'Don't be,' Joss said. 'We both know you're desperate to get your hands on me.'

Sam sighed, determined not to let him get to her. 'It was an accident, Joss. When are you going to stop kidding yourself?'

Joss glanced across at her. 'I'm not the one who's living a lie.'

Sam froze. He couldn't know the reason she'd fled London. No one knew, apart from Sam and Nessie. She forced herself to take a deep breath and lowered her voice. 'What's that supposed to mean?'

'You, refusing to admit you're interested.'

'There's nothing to admit,' Sam countered, hoping her face didn't give her away. On the other side of the bar, the revellers continued to party, oblivious. 'We've been over this, Joss. I'm not interested in you that way.'

He raised an eyebrow. 'So you won't be tempted to kiss me when the clocks strike midnight, is that what you're saying? You're not secretly wondering what it would be like?'

'It doesn't matter one way or another,' Sam ground out. 'It's not going to happen.'

'Then it's your loss,' Joss said with rueful shake of his head. 'But sooner or later, you'll have to face the truth, Sam. The question is whether I'll still be interested.'

Picking up an empty box, he headed for the stairs. 'I'll get some more champagne.'

Sam stared after him for a moment, infuriated and amused in equal amounts. He really was the most insufferably arrogant man she'd ever met and yet – she saw a lot of herself in him. He wasn't as ambitious as her but striving too hard was one of the reasons she'd ended up in Little Monkham. He was very good at his job, though, and for all his laid-back attitude she knew he was driven. And he was certainly tenacious.

Sam thought back to this time last year. She'd been at a rooftop bar overlooking the Thames, watching the fireworks explode over the river with – well, not with friends, because she worked too hard to have those, but with people she knew and liked. A lot of champagne had been drunk and she'd gone home with someone whose name she'd probably known at the time but hadn't remembered the next day. At the time it had felt liberating but now, looking back, it seemed empty and meaningless. And suddenly, she realised why the occasional night she'd spent with Nick had been so memorable – apart from his amazing body and blissful technique, it had been good to wake up next to someone familiar. Maybe Nessie was right – maybe there was something to be said for giving her feelings a chance to grow. And there were feelings there for Joss – mostly lust but behind that there was something else, a shoot of something that she could either nurture or uproot . . .

Glancing over her shoulder to check no one was watching, Sam hurried to the cellar door. Joss was standing at the bottom of the stairs, filling the box with champagne.

'What if you were right?' she said, the breath catching in the back of her throat. 'What if I was thinking about kissing you?'

Joss lowered the bottle he held and turned to stare at her. 'Then I'd be a very happy man.'

'You wouldn't gloat and tell me you told me so?' Sam said, her pulse starting to race as she walked down the stairs.

'No,' Joss said solemnly. 'I wouldn't do that.'

She took the final few steps and reached up to touch the soft hair of his beard. 'You wouldn't be unbearably smug?'

'I wouldn't.'

'And you won't do anything stupid like falling in love with me, will you?' she murmured, pulling his face towards hers. 'We're just two adults having a bit of fun, right?'

His answer was lost in the kiss, which went on and on until Sam lost all track of who and where she was. When they finally broke apart, it was with a gasp. Sam took a step back, her lips still tingling, and cleared her throat. 'I want you to know I'm still your employer. We have to be professional about this.'

He smiled gently. 'Yes, boss.'

Sam glanced over her shoulder. 'I don't want to be the talk of the village.'

'Whatever you say.'

Sam bit her lip. Already she wanted to kiss him again, to see if it was even better second time around. 'We should get back upstairs, it's almost midnight.' Reluctantly, she stepped back. 'And I didn't hear you answer my last question.'

Joss pulled her close and lowered his mouth again. 'Oh, we're definitely going to have fun,' he whispered and kissed her again.

Chapter Thirteen

It was five minutes to midnight. Unable to see either Sam or Joss, Nessie invited everyone to take a glass of champagne and gather on the green to start the countdown. In the distance, she could make out the shadowy shapes of Martha's husband, Rob, and a couple of other men as they made sure the fireworks were ready. Someone else was handing out sparklers and Father Goodluck was lighting them. Nessie watched as Owen instructed Luke on how to hold the shimmering stick and she smiled as he twirled it against the dark.

'Want one?' Owen asked.

Nessie shook her head. 'No, let the kids have them.'

He gazed at her for a moment, then disappeared into the crowd. When he returned, he was holding two twinkling sparklers. 'You're never too old for these. Look, I can write my name.'

She laughed. 'And I can draw a star, to go with all the others up there.'

Once the sparklers died, they put them into the bucket of sand. It was a clear night, cold without being bitterly so, and the air was filled with chatter and laughter. Above their heads, the blue-black sky glittered with an infinite number of diamonds. Nessie shivered, not because she was cold but more because of the sense of anticipation that was running through her. At midnight it would be a brand new year, full of possibility and hope, and she was looking forward to it more than she could say. Owen saw her shiver and wordlessly draped his scarf over her shoulders. She smiled her thanks and held his gaze for longer than she should, ignoring the flutter it caused in her stomach. Midnight was magical any time, she thought, regardless of whether it was the turn of the year.

'Thirty seconds!' someone shouted nearby.

It occurred to Nessie that she still hadn't seen Sam. Twisting around, she peered into the crowd but couldn't find her in the semi-darkness. Where was she? Nessie wondered. Had something gone wrong in the cellar? She was about to make her excuses to Owen and go to look but another shout rang out. 'Fifteen seconds!'

As the countdown from ten began, a movement caught her eye and she saw Sam hurry into view. Joss was right behind her, laughing at something she'd said. Nessie let out a silent sigh of relief and relaxed.

'Five, four, three ...'

She felt a fumbling at her side and realised someone was trying to take her hand. A moment later, her fingers were entwined with Owen's.

'Two, one . . . Happy New Year!'

The first fireworks boomed overhead in a riot of red and green sparks. Now that she came to think about it, perhaps it hadn't been the best idea to stand so close to Owen – all around her, people were hugging and kissing each other – but it was too late now. She felt her cheeks flame as she turned to Owen. 'Happy New Year!'

He smiled. 'Happy New Year to you too, Nessie. I hope it brings you your heart's desire.'

His dark eyes glittered by the light of the fireworks as he gazed at her and Nessie felt a thudding in her chest. If she moved just a tiny bit closer now, his mouth would be almost within kissing distance. He'd noticed too, she was sure. All she had to do was edge forwards and close her eyes. All she had to do was—

'Happy New Year, Dad!' Luke shouted, bursting onto Owen with an enthusiastic cuddle. 'Happy New Year, Nessie!'

Another round of screeches and bangs exploded overhead and the moment vanished. Owen held her gaze for a fraction of a second then lifted his son into his arms. 'The same to you, you little scallywag.'

Nessie stepped back, laughing. 'Happy New Year, Luke.'

The crowd broke into 'Auld Lang Syne'. Grinning, Luke raced off, bellowing good wishes at everyone he bumped into. Owen smiled wryly and opened his mouth to speak but Nessie felt a hand touch her shoulder.

'Happy New Year, Ness,' Sam said, pulling her into a hug. 'Let's hope it's going to be a good one.'

Nessie hugged her back, then turned to gaze at the Star and Sixpence, crowned by the radiance of the fireworks. It lit up the darkness in a way that was only partly due to the glow from its windows and it seemed to Nessie as though the pub's blood was pumping for the first time since they'd come. Nessie felt a spark of contentment warm her inside. It felt like more than just a place she and Sam had run to when they'd needed somewhere to go. It felt like home.

'Are you kidding?' she said, glancing at her sister with a grin of anticipation. 'It's going to be an *amazing* year!'

Valentine's Day at the Star and Sixpence

Valentine's Day
at the Star and Sixpence

Little Monkham

Shropshire

Sam Chapman and Nessie Blake
are proud to invite you to a one-night-only
pop-up dining experience

7.00pm

Sunday 14th February

Featuring an exclusive menu from Superchef winner

Alyssa di Campo

and drinks designed by London Cocktail
Connoisseur

Tom Collins

Tickets cost £40 and include
a three-course meal plus welcome drink

BOOKING ESSENTIAL

Chapter Fourteen

Sam Chapman was cleaning the coffee machine when she felt Joss's arms encircle her waist.

'Happy anniversary,' he said, kissing her neck.

For a fleeting second Sam tensed, before forcing herself to relax. The pub had yet to open, there was no one to see them and even if there had been, it wouldn't have mattered; what she did with the cellarman was no one else's business. The only person with a legitimate reason to object was Sam's sister, Nessie, and she'd already made it clear she didn't have a problem with Joss and Sam's relationship.

She twisted round to kiss him, enjoying the soft scratch of his beard against her skin. 'Anniversary?'

Joss smiled. 'Yep. It's exactly six weeks since you jumped me on New Year's Eve.'

'Charmingly put,' Sam said, trying not to smile. 'I don't remember it happening *quite* like that.'

Had it really only been six weeks ago? It felt longer. In fact, she was starting to wonder if her old life as a PR golden girl in London was a half-remembered dream, instead of a career she hoped to go back to one day. Life in the country was certainly keeping her busy.

She reached up to kiss Joss again, before turning back to the coffee machine. 'I think we can both agree on that last bit. Happy anniversary!'

He stepped back, watching her work. 'How are the big Valentine's Day plans coming along?'

Sam hesitated for a brief second, then began stacking the cups on top of the machine. He meant her plan to turn the Star and Sixpence into a restaurant for the night – or at least she hoped he did. Between sweet-talking the up-and-coming chef she had in mind to provide the meals, arranging enough waiting staff to serve the punters and persuading Nessie that this was a perfect PR opportunity, she didn't have time to worry about grand romantic gestures for Joss – six-week anniversary or not. It didn't help that she'd never had to think about Valentine's Day before – she'd always been single. Plenty of cards had arrived at work, of course, but Sam had binned them all. In fact, six weeks was the longest any of her relationships had lasted and she had a sneaking suspicion the same was true for Joss.

'I think it's all coming along,' she said. 'Franny has demanded a table, although I can't imagine her bringing a date.'

Joss grimaced and Sam knew he was wondering what kind of man would have the courage to woo Little Monkham's fearsome postmistress. 'Me neither.' He paused. 'Just to be clear, *we're* not doing anything for Valentine's Day, are we? As in, you and me?'

'We've been over this, Joss,' Sam said, trying not to sigh. 'No, we are not celebrating. No flowers, no cards, no grand romantic gestures. I'm allergic to romance, remember?'

He held up his hands in mock surrender. 'Okay, I get it. It's just that I've been caught out before by girls who've said that and then accused me of not making an effort. I don't want any misunderstandings.'

Sam was well aware that Joss had history with several of Little Monkham's female residents. It had never really troubled her – until now. Just how many hearts had he broken in the village? But when she glanced up at him she saw a shadow in his blue eyes, making him look younger than twenty-nine. He wasn't playing a game with her now – this was something he meant. 'No tricks,' she said, softening her voice. 'And definitely no cards.'

He nodded. 'Got it.'

Sam turned round to survey the bar. 'The chef is coming to inspect the place this morning, to see if it's up to standard,' she said. 'I want her to like what she sees.'

Joss glanced towards the stairs that led to the rooms Sam and Nessie lived in over the pub. 'So that's why Nessie is scrubbing the kitchen walls. I did wonder.'

Sam bit her lip. She knew Nessie was worried and with good reason – Sam had been so sure she could persuade Alyssa di Campo to travel from London for the pop-up event that she'd started selling tickets before the *Superchef* winner had totally committed. If she didn't like what she saw, she might easily pull out, leaving them with no cook and a lot of explaining to do.

'Speaking of which, I'd better go and meet Alyssa's train,' she said, dropping her cloth into the bucket of hot, soapy water. 'Can you make sure this place is gleaming by the time we get back?'

Joss picked up the bucket. 'Yes, boss.'

'This is the kitchen?'

Alyssa di Campo stared around the tiny room, taking in the single sink, the cluttered worktops and the slender fridge-freezer. 'You expect me to produce fifty Michelin-star-worthy meals in a room that is smaller than my shed?'

Nessie cringed inside. 'At least the oven is new,' she said, waving at the shiny chrome and black cooker they'd bought to replace the ancient model their father had left. 'It's got a plate-warmer function.'

The look Alyssa gave her said it all.

'Come on, Al,' Sam said, linking her arm through the chef's. 'You know you love a challenge. It'll be like the old days, before you had gadgets and sous chefs to dance on your every whim.'

Alyssa threw her a withering glare. 'A challenge is one thing, but this? Even Gordon Ramsey would throw the towel in.'

Nessie pictured the kitchen at Snowdrop Cottage next door, with its cherry-red range and American-style fridge and fairy lights. 'What if there was somewhere else, some-where with more space and a killer oven?'

'You're not thinking of the forge?' Sam said, her eyebrows shooting upwards. 'Because that has *great* PR possibilities.'

'The forge?' Alyssa repeated. 'I'm confused.'

'Nessie has a thing going on with the village blacksmith, who just happens to have his forge right next door to us,' Sam said. 'I'm sure she could persuade him to let you use it to cook on.'

Nessie shook her head. 'Firstly, I do not have a thing with Owen. And secondly, I don't think you could cook anything on the forge. It would burn to a crisp in minutes.'

'You are right, it would be too hot,' Alyssa said, looking regretful. 'Where did you actually mean, Nessie?'

Nessie described the kitchen at Snowdrop Cottage. 'I'd have to ask first,' she warned, as Alyssa's eyes lit up. 'And we'd have to find a way to keep the dishes hot when we carry them across the yard. But if you think it sounds like an option—'

'Show me,' Alyssa demanded.

Nessie felt bad for disturbing Owen at work but Kathryn's Land Rover wasn't in the yard, and Alyssa didn't seem like the type to be kept waiting. So Nessie had left Sam and the chef waiting in the yard while she slipped inside the forge, hoping it might make the intrusion less – well – intrusive.

The fire blazed yellowy-orange under its steel hood, almost too bright to look at, and she could feel the heat even from across the room. Dressed in a slate-grey t-shirt that clung to his biceps, Owen was fiddling with a dial on the wall, the one she vaguely remembered did something to the air flow across the burning coke. His dark curls gleamed with the faintest hint of copper as he turned and saw her.

'Nessie,' he said, his deep Welsh lilt wrapping her name in warmth. 'What a lovely surprise.'

She tried hard not to stare. 'Sorry to bother you, but I need to ask a favour.'

'Sure,' he said, dusting his hands on the leather apron he wore. 'What can I do for you?'

'It's not so much me, more us,' Nessie said, opening the forge door to a blast of welcome cool air. 'We've got a bit of a logistics problem and I think you might be able to help . . .'

'It's not perfect, but it will have to do,' Alyssa announced, once she'd finished her inspection of Owen's kitchen.

'Kathryn will be delighted to hear it,' Owen said wryly. 'This is her domain, although I like to think I can find my way round it when I need to.'

Sam raised her eyebrows suggestively and Nessie knew exactly what her sister was getting at – *he cooks, too!*

'Good,' Alyssa said, glancing at Owen with renewed curiosity. 'Because I'm going to need some help. Unless you have plans for Valentine's Day?'

Nessie held her breath, suddenly feeling nervous. News travelled fast in a village the size of Little Monkham and widower Owen was a prize catch; she would have heard if he was seeing anyone. Wouldn't she?

He hesitated for a fraction of a second. 'No,' he said, his eyes flickering towards Nessie. 'No plans.'

'Then it's settled,' Alyssa said. 'You can be my sous chef for the night.'

Relieved, Nessie lingered at the cottage doorway as Sam took Alyssa back to the pub.

'You don't really have to help with the cooking,' she told Owen. 'It's enough that you're giving up your kitchen.'

He smiled. 'I don't mind. Besides, I might pick up some tips. It's not every day you get the chance to watch a superstar chef at work.'

She smiled back. 'You haven't been over to the pub for a few days. Busy?'

Owen grimaced. 'That, and Kathryn has been out a lot in the evenings. Did she tell you the band has a new drummer? He's taking a bit of breaking in apparently.'

'She did mention it,' Nessie said wryly, remembering Kathryn's grumpy rant earlier that week. 'Are you going to their gig in Gloucester on Saturday?'

'I can't – no babysitter.'

'I could look after Luke.' The words were out of Nessie's mouth before she could stop them. 'Um . . . you know, if you wanted to go.'

He frowned. 'Won't you be needed in the bar? It might be busy.'

Nessie shook her head. 'We've taken on a new barmaid – Martha's daughter, Tilly. Sam is spending the night in London but Joss will be around; they can manage without me for a few hours.' She hesitated as another possibility occurred to her. 'Unless you'd rather I didn't.'

'No, it's nothing like that,' Owen said. 'I'd be more than happy and I know Luke would be over the moon. But it's a lot to ask and you've got enough to do.'

'Honestly, it's fine,' Nessie said. 'You're lending us your kitchen, it's the least I can do.'

He studied her for a moment, then nodded. 'Okay then. Around seven o'clock, would that be all right? He goes to bed at eight-thirty and I'll be home before midnight.'

The warmth in his voice filled Nessie with happiness. 'Looking forward to it already,' she said.

Sam's Kensington flat looked the same as always from the outside. The elegant cream-walled and wrought-iron exterior was picture-postcard perfect and the intricately tiled communal hallway was as pristine as ever. Weary from the long drive and the battle with Saturday traffic, Sam climbed the stairs to the top floor and thrust her key into the lock.

It wasn't untidy. The caretaker had a key and had been popping in to leave her post: it was neatly stacked on the hall table. The flat was cold, though, and there was a faint mustiness in the air. Sam walked from room to room, flicking on the lights and opening the windows to let the sharp evening air blast away the staleness. Finally, she sat on the sofa and looked around. This had been her home for several years, her first and only big purchase, and she'd always been happy here. Or at least she thought she had. Had it always felt so drab and impersonal? She'd never been one for clutter but when she compared it to the warmth and vibrancy of the Star and Sixpence, she found her old home lacking somehow. Perhaps it was the silence – there was always noise in the pub even when it was empty: the hum of the glass machine or the rumble of the boiler. She shook her head wryly – who knew a country pub would be noisier than a London cul-de-sac?

Sighing, she went to the bedroom and shook out fresh sheets. She didn't plan to be there for long – a quick shower to freshen up, then out to meet Nick Borrowdale for dinner. In the morning, she'd collect Alyssa and her cooking equipment before driving back up to the Star and Sixpence. After a few glasses of champagne with Nick the atmosphere in the flat wouldn't bother her so much.

An hour later, she was on her way out again. She paused in the hallway to flick through the mail: nothing that needed her attention, the bills were all paid automatically and everything else was junk. Franny had suggested she set up a redirect but from the looks of things she didn't need to. And the truth was, she had good reason to be hard to reach. It had been four months since the mistake that had sent her scurrying away from the bright lights of London and into the anonymity of the countryside – time enough for the fear of discovery and public shaming to start to fade. But it never went away entirely.

Shivering a little, Sam dropped the post back onto the table and headed for the door.

★　★　★

The Soho restaurant Nick had booked was full of people Sam either knew in person or recognised from the big and small screen, although she was relieved not to spot any ex-clients. Even so, she felt all eyes were on them as the *maître d'* led them to their discreet table tucked away at the back of the room. Well, she was with the star of *Smugglers' Inn*, the hottest show on TV. What else had she expected?

'That's quite an impact you have,' she said to Nick once they were seated. 'Does it bother you, being so super famous?'

'What makes you think they were looking at me?' he said, grinning. 'At least half of them were eyeing you up. You look amazing.'

Sam batted away the compliment. 'At least half the men in here are gay so they were imagining you topless, just like most of the women. And every single one of them hates me simply for sitting here.'

'Let's just agree that we're both sex on legs and leave it at that,' Nick said, as a waiter appeared at their table, holding the wine list. 'Champagne?'

Sam tipped her head. 'You read my mind.'

'So,' Nick said, once the waiter had gone. 'How's life at my favourite country pub?'

Sam filled him in on the past few weeks, making him laugh with her descriptions of Franny's extreme nosiness and the village gossip network. Once they'd ordered and the starters had arrived, she asked him how filming was going and they talked and laughed and argued their way through three delicious courses and two bottles of champagne. Sam sat back, feeling more than a little tipsy. She shouldn't have drunk so much but it was hard when the waiter was constantly topping up her glass and she was enjoying herself so much. She'd forgotten how much she loved Nick's dry sense of humour and razor-sharp observations. But underneath the fizz of the alcohol and her enjoyment of Nick's company, there was a nagging sense of disquiet, a feeling that she didn't quite fit into this life any more. Chinatown had been packed, still decked in red and gold from the New Year celebrations, but the glitz and crowds hadn't blinded her to the creeping commercialisation around her. Soho was changing. Several quirky shops were gone and some of her favourite places to eat had closed, replaced by chain restaurants. She couldn't help feeling it lacked the charm of Little Monkham, where every shop was family-run and had been for decades. The Star and Sixpence was at the heart of the village, a sixteenth-century coaching inn that had rarely closed, until the death of Sam and Nessie's father. Then they'd taken over and coaxed the rundown building back to health. Sam had lived in London for her entire adult life but it felt distant and unfamiliar now, like she'd run into an old friend and found they had nothing in common. She realised, with a start, that the Star and Sixpence had become home.

'You know, I've got another bottle of this on ice back at my place.' Nick tapped the champagne bucket, his gaze meeting hers. 'We could drink it together and have some fun, for old times' sake.'

Sam looked into his gorgeous deep brown eyes. Two months ago she wouldn't have hesitated – it wouldn't be the first time they'd indulged in a no-strings night of passion and satisfaction was definitely guaranteed. But she was surprised to discover she wasn't remotely tempted. He wasn't Joss. 'I can't,' she said. 'Sorry.'

Nick didn't appear in the least upset. 'You do realise you're probably the only woman in the country who would turn that offer down, right?'

Sam laughed. 'Exactly why I don't feel bad about leaving you to it. All you have to do is smile and you'll have someone to take my place.'

Nick shook his head. 'The trouble is, they don't want to leave the next day. Whereas you and I have an understanding.' He grinned. 'Fabulous sex, excellent company and zero chance you'll sell your story to the newspapers.'

Sam felt heat flood her cheeks.

Nick groaned. 'Shit, Sam, that didn't come out the way I meant it,' he said, looking stricken. 'I'm an insensitive moron, sorry.'

Forcing herself to stay calm, Sam dabbed at her lips with her napkin. 'It's fine. Honestly, don't worry about it.'

He took her hand. 'Are you sure? God, I'm an idiot.'

She summoned up a smile, knowing he'd meant nothing by the comment. And realistically, the chances of her seeing her own face splashed across the newspapers with damning headlines grew less and less with each week that passed. She'd made a mistake, trusted the wrong person, and been forced to hide away at the Star and Sixpence. Even Nessie didn't know everything and that was the way Sam planned to keep it. But although her lapse of judgement had cost Sam a lot, it had also opened the door to change. It had given her Joss too and she was gradually starting to realise what a gift he had been. A vision of his summer-blue eyes flashed in her mind and she suddenly wished it was him sitting across from her. She'd been unfair, pushing him away when all he'd tried to do was show her how much he cared, and in denial about how much he was starting to mean to her.

Shaking her head, she reached across and touched Nick's hand. 'Really, don't worry. But we should probably call it a night. Tomorrow's going to be a big day.'

He raised an eyebrow. 'Of course. Wall-to-wall romance, right? I bet you can't wait.'

By the time the bill arrived, Sam had the start of a headache. They had the usual tussle over who would pay but she was tired so didn't argue as much as she might have done and let him treat her. The sooner she slept, the sooner she could go home.

Nick kept a solicitous hand on the small of her back as they wove through the tables. It felt as though everyone was firing covert glances their way. Nick was clearly used to it but being so obviously on display was a sensation Sam had forgotten about. It was a relief to slip into her coat and reach the door.

She wasn't prepared for the explosion of lights when she pushed back the door. Confused for a second, Sam blinked hard, and then the barrage of voices began.

'New girlfriend, Nick?'

'Over this way, darlin', so we get your face.'

'Smile, sweetheart! What's your name?'

Nick's hand pressed against her back once more. 'Head down, keep walking,' he murmured into her ear. 'Pretend they're not there.'

The shouts continued as they hurried forwards. Seconds later they were through and Nick was hailing a cab.

'Night, lads,' Nick called as they climbed into the back, his tone friendly. 'Have a good one.'

Settling into the leather seat, Sam closed her eyes and waited for the sickening flashes behind her eyelids to fade.

'Sorry about that,' Nick said. 'I had no idea they'd be hanging around.'

Wearily, Sam nodded. She'd seen clients get ambushed by the paparazzi before but it was the first time she'd been caught up in the spotlight herself. Nick's advice had been spot on – in fact, she'd probably taught *him* how to deal with the cameras back when his career had just been taking off. 'It's a shame you weren't with anyone newsworthy,' she said, opening her eyes.

Nick grinned and took her hand. 'That's what I love about you, Sam. You're always thinking of the angle.'

Nessie liked the living room of Snowdrop Cottage. The sofa was deep and comfortable, the kind that supported and cradled you at the same time. Soft lamps chased the darkness into the corners and a fire burned cosily inside the wood-burner. Snuggled up at one end of the sofa, surrounded by cushions and with a book in her hands, Nessie felt a sense of deep contentment and her shoulders relaxed for the first time in months.

Owen's son, Luke, had been a delight. She'd been worried he would try to play up, refuse to go to bed or trick her into doing something he wouldn't normally be allowed, but he'd been an angel. She'd listened as he told her all about his Lego character collection and helped him with his English homework, although she was sure he knew more about writing the perfect haiku than she did. Then at bedtime, she'd read a chapter from the book he was reading with Owen and Kathryn, and watched as his eyes grew heavier and heavier until she'd said goodnight and left him to sleep. She doubted whether every evening was as smooth but for her first effort at babysitting, it seemed to have gone pretty well.

There was a photograph in a frame on the coffee table beside the sofa. It was a family shot, sunshine framing two laughing parents and a much younger Luke. Nessie picked it up and felt her heart ache. She'd glimpsed it before, of course, but had never had the time or the opportunity to study it so closely.

The Owen in the photo seemed much lighter than the one she knew, although he was as black-haired as ever. Perhaps it was the fairness of Luke's mother, balancing out his dark-ness, or perhaps he was simply untouched by the sorrow to come. There was no mistaking who the woman was: she was so like Luke, asleep upstairs, that Nessie thought she would have known Eliza Rhys even without the giveaway of Luke and Owen in the picture with her. She was beautiful, caught in such a moment of pure happiness that Nessie's eyes welled up with tears. It wasn't fair that she'd died so young. It wasn't fair that Luke had lost such a mother, or that Owen had been robbed of a wife he clearly adored. And another realisation dawned, something that made the hope Nessie had been cherishing since New Year's Eve crumble away. There was no way she could compete with the memory of Eliza. Not timid, mousy Nessie. Not when half the village women thought they were competing too.

Taking great care, she placed the frame back onto the table and picked up her book. She must have eventually dozed off because the next thing she knew, the front door was opening and Owen was smiling in front of her. 'Sorry to wake you.'

Kathryn appeared behind him. Nessie lifted her head, blinking hard. 'Hello. How was the gig?'

'Amazing,' Kathryn said, bubbling over with enthusiasm. 'We've got another booking next month.'

'I'm not surprised,' Nessie said warmly, remembering how good the band had been when they played at the Star and Sixpence on New Year's Eve. She glanced at Owen. 'Did you have fun?'

'Apart from being the oldest person there by about a hundred years, yes,' he said, his tone dry. 'Everything okay here?'

'Fine,' she said, and recounted everything she and Luke had done.

'You got the Lego lecture,' Kathryn said, picking up a tiny black-suited toy from the table. 'I'm impressed. He only does that with people he really likes.'

'Thank you,' Owen said. 'You didn't have to do this and I'm – *we're* – very grateful.'

Nessie checked her watch. 'Honestly, it was my pleasure. But I should probably get back now and see what Joss has been getting up to.'

'Let me walk you across,' Owen said.

It didn't matter how many times Nessie told him not to trouble himself, Owen was determined. Nessie was torn between enjoying a few moments more of his company and the worry that he'd be able to hear her heart thudding beneath her chunky knitted cardigan. An awkward silence stretched between then as they crossed the yard to the Star and Sixpence.

'So you want to come in for a drink?' Nessie said as they reached the pub.

Owen cleared his throat. 'Not tonight,' he said, but he made no move to go. Instead, he gazed down at her as though weighing something up. 'Look, Nessie, I'm not really—'

The door of the pub opened and Tilly the barmaid walked out. 'Ooh, sorry!' she squeaked. 'Didn't see you there.'

Nessie felt her cheeks flush as though she was sixteen again and she stepped hurriedly away from Owen. 'Hi, Tilly. How was it tonight?'

The teenager smiled. 'Busy, but nothing we couldn't handle.' She glanced over her shoulder and lowered her voice.

'Ruby's had one too many. Joss is trying to persuade her to go home now.'

Nessie sighed. It was the second time that week that Ruby had drunk too much. 'Right. I should probably give him a hand.' She flashed an apologetic glance at Owen. 'Thanks for walking me over.'

'No problem,' he said. 'Thanks for looking after Luke.'

He glanced at Tilly, and Nessie wondered whether he was deciding whether to finish his sentence. But then he raised a hand in farewell and disappeared into the darkness. Waving away Tilly's offer to hang around, Nessie turned and went inside the pub.

It wasn't until Nessie was lying in bed much later, having guided an unsteady Ruby home, that she had time to wonder what Owen had been about to say before Tilly interrupted. From his body language it had been something important. He wasn't really *what*? Over his wife? Oh God, that must be it, Nessie decided, feeling her cheeks flame in the darkness – he'd seen the way she'd been looking at him and was trying to let her down gently. *Ugh.* Just the thought of it made her die a little inside. Turning her face against the cool cotton pillow, Nessie closed her eyes. Thank goodness Tilly had appeared before he'd actually managed to say it, she thought with a shudder. At least this way she could salvage a little pride.

Sam arrived home with Alyssa and a car packed with equipment around midday. The journey had been pleasant, although

Sam had spent a restless night tossing and turning in her now unfamiliar bed so she let her companion do the talking. She pulled into the car park and stretched, before glancing quickly at her phone. Three missed calls from Nessie. What did that mean?

Replacing her frown with a smile, Sam turned to Alyssa. 'Let's get you settled in.'

Nessie met her at the door of the pub. 'We need to talk.'

Sam's uneasiness grew. Nessie was prone to unnecessary worrying but there was something about her expression that made Sam pause. 'What's the problem? Is it about tonight?'

Nessie held up a copy of a tabloid newspaper. 'You're a cover star.'

A sudden icy chill made Sam shiver as she gazed at the photo beneath the red banner. It was unmistakably her, Nick looming at her shoulder. *NICK'S MYSTERY WENCH!* screamed the headline. She let out an exasperated groan – it must have been a slow news night for that to make the front page.

Alyssa leaned forwards for a closer look. 'I didn't know you and Nick Borrowdale were a couple.'

'We're not,' Sam said tersely. She glanced towards the bar. 'I suppose Joss has seen it?'

Nessie nodded. 'And that's not all. Some flowers came for you and I'm guessing from Joss's reaction that they're not from him. He's not in the best mood . . .'

Flowers? Sam blinked. Who on earth would send her flowers on Valentine's Day? Hardly anyone knew where she lived.

Rubbing her eyes, she threw an apologetic glance Alyssa's way. 'Sorry, it's not normally so dramatic around here. Why don't I take you upstairs? It looks like I've got some damage limitation to do.'

The flowers were on the living room table. Sam left Alyssa to unpack her overnight bag and went to investigate. She was surprised to discover there were not one but two bouquets.

'One for each of us,' Nessie explained, her cheeks turning rosy.

Sam's eyes widened. 'From Owen?'

'From Patrick,' Nessie said. 'Can you believe it?'

It *was* hard to believe, Sam thought, especially when Nessie's husband had conspicuously failed to bother with any kind of romantic gesture in the fifteen years before Nessie had left him. But that was men, she supposed, always wanting what they couldn't have.

'How do you feel about it?' she asked her sister warily. It would be just like Nessie to feel guilty.

'It was a nice thing to do,' Nessie replied, stroking a red rose petal. 'The message on the card was quite sweet too. He hopes we'll always be close.'

Sam sniffed. 'I bet he does. You're not thinking about calling him, are you?'

'No!' Nessie exclaimed. 'Of course not. It's just . . .' She let out a wistful sigh. 'It's just nice to know someone is thinking of you, even if it isn't the person you hoped.'

She meant Owen of course, Sam realised. 'Maybe he'll give you something in person,' she said. 'Tonight.'

Nessie shook her head. 'I don't think so. Aren't you going to open yours?' She fired a hard look Sam's way. 'I know Joss thinks they're from Nick but I hope you're not that stupid.'

'I'm not,' Sam said, thinking back to Nick's offer the night before. 'I know it looks bad but there's nothing like that going on.'

'So who sent the flowers?' Nessie asked. 'They must have cost a fortune; they look much more expensive than mine.'

A faint alarm bell started to ring at the back of Sam's mind. She took a closer look at the huge bouquet – velvety red roses nestled next to gorgeous purple orchids and pale lilac blooms she didn't recognise. Who knew where she lived and expected such an ostentatious gesture to impress her? Her gaze settled on the small white envelope peeping out from beneath a leaf. There was only one way to find out …

I'm sorry.

There was no name, not even an initial. Silently, she held it out to Nessie.

'Are you sure they're not from Nick?' Nessie ventured, after turning the card over. 'Maybe he means the newspaper thing.'

Sam shook her head. 'Nick doesn't have anything to be sorry for.'

She stared at the blooms for a moment. There was one person who owed her an apology but she'd forbidden him ever from contacting her. Surely he wouldn't be so idiotic?

'What are you going to do with yours?' she asked, nodding at the comparatively modest bouquet next to her own.

Nessie blinked. 'Find a vase for them, I guess. I don't hate Patrick even if I don't love him either.' She paused. 'Shall I find one for yours, too?'

'No need,' Sam said decisively, sweeping the flowers off the table and into the wastepaper basket. 'Out of sight, out of mind. Now, I'd better go and explain a few things to Joss.'

Nessie waited until Sam had gone downstairs to rescue the bouquet from the bin. Pulling on her coat, she slipped out of the side door and walked across to St Mary's, hoping Father Goodluck might be able to use the flowers on the altar.

'Sadly it is Lent and the church remains bare to reflect the sacrifice of the good Lord,' he said, gazing at the flowers sadly. 'But thank you for the thought. I hope you find someone who will appreciate their beauty.'

Nessie said goodbye and took the bouquet outside. Now what? Put them on a grave? It seemed like a terrible waste to leave them to rot on the damp grass but she supposed it was better than having them rot in the bin.

The worst of the February frost had melted and the air in the graveyard was crisp but not too cold. There was only one person buried there that Nessie knew – her father – and since he'd abandoned both her and Sam when they were very young, she wasn't in the habit of laying flowers on his grave. Keeping to the path, she made her way around the back of the church to the willow tree that overhung the newer burial plots. As she got nearer, she saw that someone was already standing by Andrew Chapman's grave, someone wrapped in a cobalt-blue swing coat, with red hair glinting in the sunshine: Ruby Cabernet, looking every inch the faded actress.

Nessie hesitated, not wanting to intrude, but it was too late; Ruby had heard her approaching. She turned around and waved, leaving Nessie no choice but to move closer.

'Darling, I wanted to thank you for seeing me home last night,' the older woman called, adjusting her enormous black sunglasses. 'I must learn not to drink on an empty stomach; it never does me any good.'

Nessie smiled. Ruby was warm and funny and popular among Little Monkham residents but there was no denying she drank too much, whether on an empty stomach or otherwise. In fact, Nessie had begun to suspect Ruby preferred a liquid lunch and perhaps a liquid breakfast too. It wasn't any of her business, of course, except that it caused the occasional problem in the pub at closing time. 'Don't mention it,' she said. 'We all get a little tipsy from time to time.'

Ruby tapped her nose. 'Do you know, that's exactly what Richard Burton used to say? "Ruby, darling," he told me, "there isn't a man-jack among us who hasn't been as pissed as a lord at one time or another."'

Nessie couldn't help laughing. Ruby had a fascinating supply of stories from her acting days and both sisters could see how she would have captivated their father. Less clear was what she'd seen in him, a chronic alcoholic who'd chosen drink over his family, but Nessie had no doubt that Ruby had loved Andrew. Why else would she have brought a single red rose to him on Valentine's Day?

A flash of yellow caught Nessie's eye. Burials in the churchyard were few and far between and so Eliza Rhys was buried only a few plots away. The vibrant yellow was a fresh bouquet, laid neatly at the base of her gravestone. Leaning against the stone itself was what looked like a hand-made child's card.

Nessie's eyes prickled with unexpected tears. It had only been a few years since Eliza's death; of course Owen and Luke would still be struggling with their loss. A worm of guilt wriggled through her, too, because for a fleeting second that morning, she'd hoped – dreamed – that the bouquet in the florist's arms had been from Owen. And she'd promised herself she wasn't going to feel that way – it could only lead to heartbreak. Then the flowers had turned out to be from Patrick and she'd felt a stirring of something else, of comfort and feeling flattered. Someone wanted her, even if Owen didn't.

Ruby cleared her throat. 'Those are lovely. Have you got an admirer?'

'No,' Nessie said, dragging herself back from her thoughts. 'They're not even mine.'

'Oh. I thought for a moment that Owen had pulled his finger out.' She shook her head. 'He's a lovely man but by God does he need a rocket up his arse.'

'Ruby!' Nessie exclaimed, half scandalised and half amused. 'His wife's grave is just over there.'

The older woman peered over her sunglasses, her gaze sharp. 'I know. And I also know that the dead don't keep you

144

warm on a cold winter's night. They don't laugh at your stories and they don't cheer you up when you're down. Only the living do that. So if Owen is still holding a torch for Eliza then he's a bloody fool.' She looked away, her gaze coming to rest on the rose at her feet. 'Don't let him be a fool, Nessie. Make him see you.'

Nessie swallowed hard. 'I – I'm not sure he wants to.'

'He wants to,' Ruby said firmly. 'I've seen how he looks at you, and how you look at him. What the two of you need is less looking and more action.'

Could she be right? Nessie wondered. Did Owen think about her the way she thought about him? It didn't seem possible, not after his words last night but then he'd never finished the sentence. Maybe he hadn't been about to let her down gently after all.

'I'll think about it,' she told Ruby and held out Sam's unwanted bouquet. 'Would you like these? They're only going to waste otherwise.'

Ruby took the display and inhaled deeply. 'Vanda orchids and Grand Prix roses, my favourites. Thank you.'

Nessie took a deep breath and smiled back at her. 'No, Ruby. Thank you.'

Joss met Sam with a humourless smile when she approached him behind the bar.

'Good night last night?' he asked, his tone carefully neutral. 'It certainly sounds like it. "The couple consumed two bottles of champagne and shared a Lobster Thermidor before

145

catching a cab together," the newspaper said. "An eyewitness said Nick Borrowdale seemed completely smitten." '

'It's not what you think,' Sam said, sighing. 'You know what the papers are like, they never let the facts get in the way of a good story.'

'So you didn't drink two bottles of champagne, then?' Joss demanded. 'You didn't leave together?'

His tone wasn't so even now. Sam glanced around, checking who was within earshot but the pub was quiet. 'Those parts are true but he dropped me off at my flat and went home alone. He most certainly was not completely smitten,' she said. 'I promise you, there's nothing going on between Nick and me.'

He looked away, his shoulders hunched. 'So why is he sending you flowers? I bet you didn't tell him you're allergic to romance.'

Sam hesitated. 'The flowers aren't from Nick.'

His eyes searched hers, obviously trying to decide whether to believe her. She met his gaze, held it, and after a moment the accusation on his face faded. 'Then who are they from?' he asked quietly. 'How many of us are there, Sam?'

'Just you,' Sam said, stepping nearer and laying a hand on his arm. 'The flowers were from someone I used to know, nobody important. You're the only one for me.' She took a deep breath and held out the envelope she'd kept behind her back. 'And here's the proof. Happy Valentine's Day.'

Joss stared at the envelope for a moment, then took it from her. 'I thought we weren't doing cards,' he said, tearing it open.

She shrugged. 'I had a bit of a change of heart. It's okay, I know you haven't got me one. I just wanted you to know that you're my Valentine, that's all.'

He read the card and pulled her into a hug. 'Thank you,' he murmured into her hair, before stepping away and reaching into his back pocket. 'Happy Valentine's Day to you, too.'

Sam grinned as she opened the envelope. He'd written her a poem, one that compared her favourably to his precious best bitter. 'Joss Felstead, you're a hopeless romantic.'

'Guilty as charged,' he said, dipping his head to kiss her. 'Give me time and I'll turn you into one too.'

The lights were dimmed. The candles were lit. A roaring fire crackled in the huge fireplace and the tables were set with floating red roses in tall slender vases. Upstairs, the fridge groaned with chilled smoked salmon starters and an enormous pan of delicately flavoured tomato and mascarpone soup steamed on the hob. Over in Snowdrop Cottage, Alyssa, Owen and Kathryn waited for the first orders to arrive. Nessie watched Sam give the tables one last check.

'Ready?' she asked.

Sam pursed her lips. 'There's something missing.'

'Music?' Joss called from behind the bar. 'I hope you put some Barry White on that playlist, he always gets me in the mood.'

Sam laughed. 'Remind me how old you are again?'

Joss grinned as he polished the beer pumps. 'He's timelessly sexy. A bit like me.'

Sam rolled her eyes but Nessie could see it was all an act. In fact, Sam had something of a glow about her tonight, a softness that Nessie had never seen before and she was sure it was all down to Joss. *Wonders will never cease*, Nessie thought with a smile. *My play-the-field sister might just be settling down.*

'It's time,' Sam said, flicking the sound system on. Ed Sheeran's voice filled the air.

Nessie raised her eyebrows. 'This is romantic. I'm impressed.'

'All thanks to DJ Joss over there,' Sam replied. 'If I didn't know better I'd think he was secretly Cupid.'

'He's certainly made you happy,' Nessie observed, lowering her voice so that only Sam could hear.

'He has,' Sam said. 'I don't think I've ever been happier. All we need to do now is get you and Owen fixed up and we'll both be sorted.'

Nessie sighed. 'That's not likely tonight, is it? He's at the cottage and I'm over here.'

'Never underestimate St Valentine,' Sam said, with a surreptitious wink. 'I hear he works in mysterious ways.'

It seemed as though half the village had come to the Star and Sixpence for their annual slice of romance, and plenty of strangers too. Nessie didn't know whether it was the pull of Sam's celebrity chef or the novelty of eating somewhere they normally couldn't, but every table was taken and there was a stream of hopeful walk-in diners. She did her best to accommodate as many as possible but there were some disappointed faces at the door when she turned them away.

She made a point of squeezing Ruby in, though; a table for one in a quiet corner, sheltered from the wall-to-wall romance. It felt right that she was there, even if her lover was only a memory.

Joss and Tilly were running the bar, keeping up with drinks orders. The specialist cocktails designed by connoisseur Tom Collins were going down especially well and Joss seemed to be enjoying his temporary role as Mixologist so much that Nessie thought they might keep the Red Roses cocktail on the menu permanently. Once all the tables were full, she left Sam to supervise the service and hurried upstairs to fulfil the orders. The starters were considered less fiddly and Alyssa had reluctantly agreed to leave them up to Nessie, although Nessie wouldn't have been surprised to discover a hidden camera somewhere, to allow Alyssa to supervise. She couldn't blame her – a chef's reputation was only as good as the food served, after all.

Charlotte, one of the temporary waitresses, appeared in the kitchen doorway. 'Okay, I need eight soups, six salmon, and two mushroom terrines. Then one liver in Chianti, ten spatchcock chicken and five Beef Wellingtons.'

Nessie nodded towards the phone. 'Great. Ring the main courses through to the cottage, will you?'

She bent to check the bread rolls warming in the oven, deciding they needed a few minutes more, before ladling soup into pre-warmed bowls.

Another waitress, who Nessie remembered was called Sarah, craned her head around the door. 'I need nine salmon and five soups.' She checked the notepad in her hand. 'And Table Nine wants to know if the beef is ethically sourced.'

'Tell them to ask Table Four,' Nessie said, adding more bowls to the plate warmer. 'He's the butcher we bought it from.'

'Nessie?' a third voice called from the landing. 'Can I have six mushroom terrines, ten soups and a smoked salmon with no watercress dressing?'

Sarah clicked her fingers. 'Oh, one of my tables wanted to know if the goat's cheese is organic. And another asked for gluten-free bread. Is that possible?'

'I think so,' Nessie said, glancing around. 'Alyssa said she'd ordered some. The cheese is definitely organic.'

She rummaged among the paper bags containing the rolls, mentally adding up the orders. *Twenty-three soups, sixteen salmon (one with no dressing) and eight terrines.*

'What do I need to do with the rest of my orders?' the third girl said.

Nessie waved her towards the phone. Charlotte passed the handset across and sniffed the air. 'Is something burning?'

Nessie dropped the bag of rolls and yanked a pan of onions for the terrine off the heat. They weren't so much caramelised as cremated. 'Okay, this system isn't working,' she said, dumping the pan into the sink. 'I can't do the food and keep track of the orders at the same time.'

Owen loomed in the doorway. 'Can I help?'

Nessie resisted the urge to physically drag him into the already-crowded kitchen. 'Shouldn't you be over at the cottage?'

'I've been ordered over here as reinforcement,' he said. 'But I can help Joss behind the bar if you don't need me.'

'No!' Nessie half yelped and this time she did pull him into the room. 'If I serve up the food, can you assemble it on the trays? Girls, you'll need to help each other serve and for God's sake, be careful going up and down the stairs.'

With Owen to help, Nessie felt her stress levels start to drop. With military precision, he co-ordinated the orders so that she could concentrate on ensuring each dish that left the kitchen met Alyssa's exacting standards. There was a constant stream of feet on the stairs outside but Nessie did her best to ignore it. She also tried to ignore how close Owen was, through necessity rather than choice, and how warm his presence was making her feel. Thank goodness she could blame her rosy cheeks on the oven.

At last all the starters were served. Nessie leaned back against the sink and briefly closed her eyes. 'Wow. It's safe to say, any ambitions I had to cook for the masses are well and truly incinerated.'

Owen smiled. 'That's a shame. Your food looked delicious.'

'No thanks to me,' Nessie said, turning around and filling the sink with hot water. 'It's all Alyssa's hard work. Thanks for coming over, by the way. You saved me from disaster.'

Owen picked up a tea towel and took the freshly washed chopping board from Nessie. 'I can't take the credit for that, either,' he said ruefully. 'Alyssa said I got in her way.'

Nessie felt a spark of indignation. Bloody cheek – he hadn't got in her way and this kitchen was much smaller than the one over in the cottage. 'Well, I'm glad you did. I'd probably have drowned myself in the soup if you hadn't turned up.'

He regarded her steadily. 'We make a good team.'

The breath caught in Nessie's throat. *Don't read too much into it*, she told herself sternly, *he means here, tonight*. She managed a careful nod. 'We do.'

His dark-eyed gaze held hers. 'I was wondering, maybe once this evening is out of the way and things have settled down again, whether you'd consider—'

He was interrupted by a clatter of feet on the stairs. Nessie could have screamed. *Not again* . . .

'Sorry, Owen,' Sarah said from the doorway. 'Alyssa says she can't spare you any longer. She needs you back at the cottage.'

She waited, clearly under orders not to return alone. Owen shook his head. 'I thought I got in her way. Sorry, Nessie, I hate to leave you with all the clearing up to do.'

Nessie bit back a sigh. 'Honestly, don't worry. It's my kitchen, my mess. You'd better hurry. I don't think Alyssa likes to be kept waiting.'

With an apologetic look, Owen ducked under the door-frame and left. Nessie stared after him for a few seconds then plunged her hands into the soapy water. Whatever he wanted her to consider was going to have to wait.

'We're running out of raspberries,' Joss told Sam in a low voice as she slipped behind the bar. 'I've got enough for maybe three more cocktails and then we're done.'

Sam surveyed the room thoughtfully. Most of the guests had finished their main course and were onto dessert, and after that they'd probably want coffee, not more alcohol. Except for Ruby, of course, tucked away at a table for one in the corner. She'd insisted on coming, had told Sam that the Star and Sixpence was where she felt closest to Andrew, and neither sister had wanted to refuse her. Still, Sam thought, it must be hard to sit alone among so many couples. Maybe that was why Ruby was on her fifth cocktail, while her food lay barely touched.

She turned back to Joss. 'Once they're gone, they're gone. First rule of pretty much everything: always leave them wanting more.'

He raised an eyebrow. 'You're the boss.'

Grabbing a bottle of Rioja, Sam plastered on a warm smile and headed for table twelve. Franny was dining with old Henry Fitzsimmons, a match that had instantly set tongues wagging. At first, Sam had thought the pair were simply keeping each other company but now she saw Henry reach across to pat Franny's hand. *Whoever saw that coming?* Sam wondered, taking care to keep her face perfectly straight.

She cleared her throat as she neared the table. Henry snatched his hand away and Franny blushed a pretty girlish pink. 'Compliments of the house,' Sam said, holding out the wine. 'As a thank you for your continued custom.'

Henry thanked her gruffly. Franny offered a gracious smile, like a queen accepting a gift from a loyal subject. Gritting her teeth slightly, Sam opened the wine for Henry to sample.

'Not bad,' he grunted. 'Leave it to breathe a bit and it'll be better.'

Sam set the bottle on the table. 'How was your food?'

Franny's eyes gleamed. 'Delicious. You might not know much about running a business but you certainly have some talented friends, Samantha.'

'Oh yes, compliments to the chef,' Henry said. 'Marvellous grub, although you could mention that the beef could have done with a bit longer in the oven. It wasn't quite cooked.'

Sam summoned up her best PR face. 'Thank you. I'll be sure to pass on your comments to Alyssa.'

Flashing a final smile, Sam made her way around the other diners, checking from a distance that everything was as it should be. Martha from the bakery and her husband were feeding each other lychee cheesecake as though they were the only people in the room and love seemed to be blossoming on many of the other tables too. Sam took a few more drinks orders as she went and hurried to the bar.

'I see Cupid's been busy,' Joss said, nodding at Franny and Henry.

'Hasn't he?' Sam replied, as the smooth sound of Nat King Cole drifted out of the speakers. 'Who knows, maybe a bit of romance will mellow them both.'

Joss shook his head. 'Get serious. There's not enough love in the world to mellow Franny Forster.'

Sam laughed. 'People used to say the same about me.'

'Ah, but you have something Franny doesn't,' Joss replied confidently, balancing a raspberry on top of a finished cocktail with infinite care.

'Oh?' Sam said. 'What's that?'

Joss pushed the drink towards her and winked. 'Me.'

'I think we can call that a success, don't you?'

Sam was leaning against the bar, sipping a cherry cosmopolitan. Nessie thought she looked tired – they all did. As soon as the last of the diners had left, Sam had popped over to Snowdrop Cottage and invited everyone over for a celebratory drink. Owen had opted to stay with a sleeping Luke but Kathryn and Alyssa had come. Joss had provided everyone with a cocktail and Sam had declared a toast to the Star and Sixpence and their visiting superchef.

'You certainly impressed Franny and she's notoriously hard to please,' Nessie observed. 'Never mind the Michelin Star, you've won the Forster seal of approval.'

'I'm honoured,' Alyssa said. 'The evening was a great success. Hard work, but running a kitchen always is.'

Nessie thought back to the chaos earlier and shivered. 'I don't think we'll make it a permanent feature. Once a year is quite enough.'

'But you could open up those rooms you have, and offer bed and breakfast,' Alyssa said thoughtfully. 'They're really quite charming and I'm sure people would pay to stay somewhere as lovely as this.'

Sam's eyes glittered. 'That's a great idea. We could go

boutique, make them unique and add all kinds of great touches. What do you think, Nessie?'

'Ask me again tomorrow,' Nessie said, laughing. 'When the terror of tonight has faded.'

'It's a shame Owen couldn't be here,' Alyssa said. 'He was surprisingly helpful, actually.'

Nessie frowned. 'I thought he got in your way.'

She saw Sam and Alyssa exchange a conspiratorial look. 'He did, at first,' the chef said. 'But then he got better. I think he'd make someone a great husband.'

Nessie felt a hot rush of embarrassment. So that's what this was about – Sam must have recruited Alyssa into her match-making scheme. But did they have to do it in front of Owen's sister? She risked a quick glance at Kathryn, who grinned. Another surge of embarrassment washed over Nessie.

'Speaking of Owen, I think he deserves a drink too,' she said, more loudly than she needed to. 'Joss, can you do me a pint of Thirsty Bishop, please? I'll take it over to the cottage.'

'Great idea,' Joss said, completely straight-faced.

He placed the foaming beer onto the bar and Nessie snatched it up, desperate to escape their knowing looks. Did everyone in the village have an interest in her love-life or was that just how it felt?

'Take your time,' Sam called as she made her way to the door. 'I won't wait up.'

The cold air was a relief to Nessie's mortified cheeks. Sam meant well but she wasn't exactly subtle. What if Kathryn told

Owen what Alyssa had said? He'd think Nessie was dreaming of wedding dresses instead of nervously wondering whether he was even interested.

She almost bottled it at the front door of the cottage. But the thought of going back to the pub was more excruciating than a few minutes of Owen's company so she lifted the brass door knocker and tapped as gently as she could, aware that Luke's room was directly above.

'Nessie,' Owen said, looking surprised but pleased. 'I thought you'd be busy clearing up.'

She held out the pint. 'We thought you might need this. A little thank you for everything you did.'

He smiled and held the door open. 'Come on in.'

The living room was just as warm and inviting as Nessie remembered. The woodburner glowed red and a battered paperback lay spine up across the arm of the sofa. She glanced curiously at the cover but her eye was caught by the photo of Eliza and she looked away again fast.

'Can I get you a drink?' Owen asked. 'There's a bottle of red open if you fancy it?'

Nessie hesitated, then thought of the welcoming committee back at the pub. 'Maybe just a small one.'

He disappeared into the kitchen. Moments later he was back, a brimming glass in his hand. 'Cheers,' he said, once he'd given it to Nessie. 'Here's to another roaring success at the Star and Sixpence.'

'Cheers,' Nessie said. She took a gulp of wine, feeling its warmth curl in her stomach. 'Thanks again for your help.'

Owen sat on the sofa. 'My pleasure. It's great to see the old place full of life again. Your father would be proud.'

Nessie glanced at the space on the sofa and instantly dismissed it: too close. Instead, she perched on the edge of the armchair opposite. 'I expect he would,' she said, doing her best to keep her tone neutral.

It was no secret that she and Sam had been estranged from their father for years before his death, but Nessie had come to learn that the village view of Andrew Chapman had been very different from that of his daughters. In Little Monkham he'd been liked and respected and she saw no reason to alter that view.

She swallowed another mouthful of wine. It was really good, probably a Malbec, she decided, although Alyssa had made a Chianti sauce to go with one of the main courses so perhaps it was that. It was certainly taking the edge off her nerves, she thought, relaxing a little more into the chair.

'You remind me of a little bird,' Owen said, cutting into her thoughts. 'Always about to take flight.'

Nessie looked over at him, expecting to see a smile in his eyes but she saw only concern. 'You wouldn't be the first to say something like that. Sam thinks I'm too timid for my own good.'

'I don't think you're timid,' he said. 'I think you're one of the strongest women I've ever met. Think about it – you moved to a strange village, took on an ailing business and turned it around in the face of some pretty fierce animosity. That doesn't sound timid to me.'

Nessie smiled. When he put it like that, she felt braver. It had been a difficult undertaking to get the Star and Sixpence back on its feet, especially when Franny and Henry were set against them, but she and Sam had managed it. 'Thank you.'

They gazed at each other for a moment and Nessie was aware of another kind of warmth creeping through her, one that had nothing to do with the wine. She thought back to Ruby's suggestion in the graveyard earlier. *Less looking, more action.* If Ruby and Sam were right and Owen really was interested in her, then really there was nothing to stop her making the first move.

Emboldened by his praise, Nessie swallowed some more wine and cleared her throat. 'Do you want to go for a drink sometime? Not over at the pub, somewhere else. Somewhere different.'

The words came out faster than she'd intended and she finished on an anxious squeak. So much for being brave, she thought with an inward groan. But Owen didn't seem to have noticed. His eyes never left hers. 'I'd like that,' he said quietly. 'I'd like that a lot.'

She let out her breath in a rush. 'Me too.'

He shook his head wryly. 'I've been trying to ask you for days, only something always seemed to get in the way. I was beginning to think it was a sign.'

Nessie smiled, as a mixture of relief and happiness flooded through her. 'We got there in the end.'

Owen stood up and held out his glass. 'To future drinks.'

'To future drinks,' Nessie echoed and tapped her glass against his.

Summer at the Star and Sixpence

Jo Jo and Jamie

are delighted to invite you

to celebrate their wedding

at St Mary's Church,

Little Monkham, Shropshire

and afterwards at the Village Green outside the

Star and Sixpence, Sixpence Lane,

Little Monkham

on Saturday 4 June at 1.30 p.m.

Chapter Fifteen

The renovations were not going exactly to plan, Nessie Blake decided, as muffled swearing floated down the stairs from the attic rooms. With a sigh, she got up from the tiny kitchen table and closed the door that led to the landing. Why had she let her sister talk her into opening the rooms above the Star and Sixpence to guests? The project had already overrun, although it was probably better that they'd discovered the missing roof tiles sooner rather than later, and was costing more than they had originally budgeted. Didn't they have enough to do making sure that the pub ran smoothly, without the added stress of dust, clumping boots and roaring testosterone? Sam insisted it would all be worth it eventually but Nessie wasn't so sure.

Her natural instinct was to take things slowly but, as usual, Sam had bulldozed ahead and booked in an overnight wedding party for the start of June, less than a month away. It was too soon, Nessie thought, cradling her coffee as the curses got louder. They'd only moved into the pub six months ago, and heaping on extra responsibility now felt like running before they could walk.

Nessie glanced at the clock; she'd have to go downstairs soon. Joss usually let himself into the bar, but Nessie liked to be around to say good morning; although more and more frequently she found herself bumping into him on the landing as he came out of Sam's room after staying the night. He never showed the least sign of embarrassment but Nessie felt her own cheeks flame every time. It wasn't that she disapproved of the relationship – in fact, she'd never seen Sam so happy – but running into an employee dressed in only your sister's dressing gown wasn't something they'd covered on the pub management course she'd done.

There was a crash from upstairs, followed by a thud and a furious shout. Nessie gulped down her last mouthful of coffee and took refuge in the bar, where it seemed less likely the ceiling would fall on her head. There wasn't much to be done – Tilly and Joss made an efficient team and had done most of the work after closing time the night before. Nessie busied herself clearing out the wide hearth, sweeping out the ashes and setting the fire again ready for the evening. She stood, glancing out of the diamond-leaded windows as she moved to take the ashes outside. Bright sunshine played over the village green, dazzling her eyes with emerald and gold. After the threat of snow in March, it had been a mild April and a warm May so far – some customers had ventured into the beer garden around the back of the pub to enjoy the blue skies and sun, although the evenings were still chilly once night fell. Last night, Owen had stopped by with Luke, and Nessie had spent so long watching them that her sister had wryly joked she was worse than a teenager mooning over her boyfriend.

'He's not my boyfriend,' Nessie had said, cringing inside. Did thirty-four-year-old women have boyfriends?

'Whatever you want to call him then,' Sam replied with a grin. 'You can't keep your eyes off him.'

Embarrassed, Nessie had found some work to get on with and when she'd glanced out again, Owen and Luke were gone. The truth was, she didn't really know where she stood with Owen. They'd been on one date since Valentine's Day and Nessie thought it had gone well, but between the renovations at the pub, the demands of the forge and a nasty bout of a winter sickness bug from Luke, they'd somehow failed to get together again. Now they were in a sort of friendly no-man's-land and Nessie didn't know how to get out. You couldn't call a few drinks at a nearby pub dating . . .

'You wouldn't believe the traffic.' Sam burst through the front door, her arms full of catering supplies. 'Mick McCluskey's tractor shed its load up by the bridge. The queue goes back at least half a mile.'

Nessie smiled. 'It could be worse. It could be the M25.'

Sam shuddered. 'Point taken.' She glanced around the bar. 'No Joss?'

'Not yet, which is a shame because I wanted him to speak to the builders, see how things are going up there. There's been a lot of shouting this morning.'

Her sister dropped the packages onto the bar. 'Why don't you ask them? It's 2016, not 1816.'

'I tried,' Nessie said, pulling a face. 'They did their best to skirt around the question and then practically patted me on the head and told me to run along.'

Sam stared at her. 'Bloody cheek – who do they think is paying for all this work? Give me a hand to unload the car and I'll go and sort them out.'

Nessie tried not to mind the implied criticism. Why had she let the builders patronise her? Why hadn't she stood up to them and demanded to know what was going on, the way Sam was about to? She was the older sister after all, although maybe that was part of the problem; Sam was twenty-nine and turned heads. Nessie was four years older and although she had the same green eyes as her sister, the similarities ended there. They had different personalities too: Sam was confident and together, whereas Nessie was naturally cautious and reserved. All in all, Nessie knew she wasn't in the same league. Even her husband, Patrick, had stopped fancying her by the end of their relationship. No wonder the builders barely noticed when she spoke to them: she might as well be invisible.

'I've got a better idea,' Nessie said, squaring her shoulders. 'Why don't we unload the car and then go and speak to them together? At the very least I can hold your coat.'

'Deal,' Sam said. 'And if they don't play ball, we'll deploy the F-bomb.'

For a moment, Nessie frowned; Sam wasn't scared of

swearing but she didn't usually plan it in advance. Then the penny dropped. 'Oh, you mean Franny.'

'Yep. There isn't a builder between here and Birmingham that isn't terrified of her. If the threat of Franny Forster doesn't get them working, nothing will.'

Nessie smiled wryly. 'Rather them than me,' she said.

'Although I think she might have mellowed a bit since Valentine's Day,' Sam said. 'Whatever old Henry Fitzsimmons is doing, he needs to keep doing it.'

And that was another thing, Nessie thought: how could Cupid's arrow have struck fearsome Franny and cantankerous Henry but have entirely missed her and Owen? It didn't seem fair.

The faint tinkle of broken glass drifted down from above. Sam pushed up her sleeves and made for the stairs. 'On second thoughts, the unloading can wait. There are some builders' arses up there that need a good kicking.'

The title of champion at the monthly Monday Night Quiz was always hotly contested. The Little Monkham regulars viewed teams made up of visitors from other villages in much the same way Nessie supposed Boudicca must have regarded the Romans; invaders to be stopped and quite possibly crushed at all costs. They hadn't quite come to blows yet but some stiffly worded remarks had been traded. Nessie tried to ensure that Father Goodluck from St Mary's Church was there whenever possible, to exert a peaceful and calming presence. Unsurprisingly, Franny's team was the most competitive of the lot.

The questions were set by a TV quiz researcher Sam knew and she did her best to secure a celebrity quiz master each month too. Since the sisters had launched the quiz in March, they'd had the sneering ex-host of late-night TV show *News Tonight* and a return visit from swoon-worthy actor Nick Borrowdale. Nessie was sure the female quizzers hadn't played with full concentration that night; even Franny had seemed distracted, a little less cut-throat. Nessie smiled at the memory. Perhaps they should ask Nick to pose the questions every month.

Their host tonight was razor-sharp comedian, Shania Khan, and Nessie was looking forward to her banter enormously. As always, they'd had to squeeze some extra tables in to accommodate all the teams and Sam had refused entry to a couple of late-arriving teams, although she'd said they were more than welcome to watch from the bar and answer the questions unofficially. An expectant hush settled over the pub as Shania raised the microphone.

'Okay, teams, welcome to the Star and Sixpence Monday Night Quiz,' she said, raising her eyebrows. 'Answer sheets ready, biros steady? Then let's do it.'

She worked her way through the first round. Whispered conversations broke out after each question and some fierce hissing could be heard over on Franny's table. She was sitting with her usual team-mates: Henry Fitzsimmons, Martha White from the bakery, and Owen. Nessie didn't envy them – ever since the team had won the very first quiz, Franny had been cracking the whip and chasing further glory. In April, they'd been beaten into second place by a team from Purdon and Owen had laughingly admitted to Nessie that Franny had scheduled cramming classes to ensure they retook the title this month.

'Round two – geography,' Shania called. 'Question one: There is actually only one lake in the Lake District. What is it called?'

Heads beetled together and murmurs filled the room. Nessie took the opportunity to glance over at Owen. He was whispering to his team-mates, his dark eyebrows furrowed in concentration. Martha didn't appear to be listening; she was staring at Owen with a dreamy expression on her face. Nessie couldn't say she blamed her – with his gentle Welsh lilt, almost everything Owen said sounded like poetry.

Shania lifted the microphone again. 'Question two: There are two landlocked countries in South America. Can you name their capital cities?'

The questions went on. The music round was always entertaining – this time, their quiz setter had sourced ten advert jingles and the teams had to identify both the product and the decade the advert had first aired. Sam and Nessie patrolled the pub for this round; no one had been caught cheating yet but Franny demanded they were extra vigilant against mobile phone use. By the time they'd reached the final round, Franny's team was neck and neck with Purdon.

'Our last round is history,' Shania announced, glancing over at the scores. 'It's looking very tight at the top. I'm told that in the event of a tie, the quiz will be settled by a duel to the death. So, for the sake of Sam and Nessie, let's try to make sure that doesn't happen. Blood is tough to clean off a wood-beamed ceiling.'

The questions were the hardest yet, Nessie thought. Even Henry looked stumped a few times and he was the village history buff. Relieved conversations ensued once the last answer sheets were collected and teams began to talk to each other, sharing their answers. Franny sat straight-backed and rigid, waiting in dignified silence. Nessie shared a conspiratorial smile with Owen. She was meant to be neutral but she couldn't help hoping all the extra revision had paid off.

The sheets were marked and checked by scorers of unimpeachable good character; this time Father Goodluck and a fellow vicar from a neighbouring church had been enlisted. A tense silence fell over the crowd as Shania held up the microphone. 'I'm pleased to say that we have a clear winner, so no blood will be spilled tonight. In third place, we have – and I'm not sure I can read the team name without groaning – Agatha Quiztie.' Cheering broke out from one of the tables, everyone else clapped politely. 'In second place we have ... Purdon Warriors. And in first place, it's The Inquizitors!'

The Purdon Warriors put their heads in their hands while Franny's table celebrated. Martha and Owen high-fived and Nessie was amused to see Franny tentatively copy the action with Henry, although it was possibly the most awkward celebration she'd ever witnessed. She made her way over to congratulate them.

'Well done,' she said warmly, holding up the trophy. 'Who's having it this time?'

Franny reached out and took it. 'It will be on display in the Post Office, the same as before.'

Nessie bit the inside of her cheek and avoided Owen's gaze; woe betide anyone who came between Franny and her prize.

Bill, the captain of the Purdon Warriors, came across and held out his hand to each winning team member. 'Congratulations,' he said in a grudging tone. 'You know, our local pub has a quiz night too. Maybe you'd like to come to our home ground, see how well you do there?'

Franny's eyes gleamed. 'Is that a challenge?'

'Yeah, I reckon it is,' Bill said, raising his chin. 'Last Thursday of the month, if you're not too chicken.'

'We'll be there,' snapped Franny. She waited until he had gone back to his own table before rounding on the rest of her team. 'This means war. Cramming sessions every Wednesday and you'll be set homework, too. There's no way I'm losing to that jumped-up little general.'

Nessie leaned closer to Owen. 'Sorry,' she whispered, trying not to laugh. 'I think we've created a monster.'

'It wasn't you,' he murmured back. 'Wait until the Britain's Best Village competition gets going in August. She takes competitiveness to a whole new level then.'

Nessie watched Franny drawing up a battle plan on a spare answer sheet and grimaced. 'I can hardly wait.'

Chapter Sixteen

Sam's mobile rang as she sat on the living-room sofa after lunch on Friday, poring over a copy of *Woman and Home* in search of inspiration for the guest rooms. She glanced without interest at the screen – gone were the days when she was ruled by her phone – and saw with a frown that it was the same City number that had called several times over the last few days. PPI calls, she assumed, or a salesperson; certainly no one she knew. She'd changed the number when she left her PR job in London and only a handful of people had the new one. Whoever was calling, it wasn't a friend. She blocked the number and went back to her magazine. Could they get away with a roll-top bath in one of the rooms, she wondered, admiring a scroll-footed tub in one of the glossy photos. Or was it asking for a flooded ceiling?

Her phone buzzed and rang again. Sam glared at it, noting the similar but not quite the same number on its screen. 'Go away,' she muttered, hitting the mute button.

Almost immediately, it vibrated and rang once more. She stared at it, uneasiness creeping over her. An automatic redialler? she thought. A lot of cold-call companies used them; it must be something like that. She tapped the number into Google – surely she wasn't the only person being harassed by them. But the search returned no definitive hits. Either the caller was targeting her specifically or they were minnows at whatever business they were in. Sighing in irritation, Sam closed the browser window and blocked the second number.

When it rang again, something snapped in Sam. She snatched up the handset. 'Whatever you're selling, I'm not interested.'

There was a pause. 'Sam? Is that you?'

Sam felt as though someone had tipped a bucket of icy water down her back. It was a man's voice, well spoken and perfectly pitched. The last time she'd heard it, it had been telling her it couldn't live without her. And then she'd discovered what a liar and a cheat it belonged to and she'd never wanted to hear it again. In fact, she'd banned its owner from ever contacting her again. Right after she'd been *encouraged* to leave her job and warned to stay away from the press.

'Listen, Sam, we need to talk—'

She didn't wait to hear any more. With a savage stab, she ended the call and switched the phone off. A second later, she buried it beneath a cushion and went back to her interior design plans. But she could sense it there, glowing like a radioactive particle, poisoning her with its presence. Abruptly, she stood up and went downstairs.

She left the phone where it was.

*　　*　　*

'The wedding caterer called,' Nessie announced later that afternoon in the bar. 'They want champagne and Pimm's for welcome drinks, more fizz for the speeches, plus Chablis for the starters and Shiraz for the main course.'

Sam wrinkled her forehead. The bride, JoJo, had grown up in Little Monkham, although she was now a journalist in London, and both Sam and Nessie had got to know her during her frequent visits to plan the wedding. The day was going to be a whole village celebration, with the ceremony at St Mary's Church and a huge marquee on the green outside the Star and Sixpence afterwards. Her parents were stalwarts of the Preservation Society and Franny had let it be known that anything less than a perfect day would not be tolerated. The rumour was that she'd even considered getting the grass on the village green dyed, to make the wedding photographs look even more stunning. The PR girl in Sam thought it was a great idea.

'So let's say a hundred bottles of champagne, thirty Pimm's and fifty each of the Chablis and Shiraz. Joss is setting up beer and cider kegs on the green but I'll get him to double stock everything else in the cellar too, just to be safe.' Sam raised an eyebrow. 'We don't want the wedding of the year to run dry.'

Her sister looked anxious. 'I'm not sure our credit limit will stretch to all this.'

'Just explain that we're catering for a big wedding and need a temporary increase,' Sam said patiently. 'They'll understand. Oh, and we'll need a few bottles of vintage champagne – some for the bridal party before the wedding and one to leave in the bride and groom's room.'

'And that's another thing,' Nessie said. 'Are you sure the rooms are going to be ready in time? I don't want JoJo and Jamie to spend their wedding night in a building site.'

Sam took a deep breath. It was just like Nessie to fret when there really was no need. 'This time next week the builders will be finished. Then we can get the new carpets laid and the furniture in. Don't worry, it's going to be fine.' She smiled. 'In fact, it's going to be perfect. What better way to launch a B&B than by hosting the travel editor for the *Observer* on her wedding night?'

Nessie hesitated, then smiled too. 'Okay, I'll stop worrying and phone the wholesaler.'

'Great. Don't forget Joss and I won't be around tonight.'

'Doing anything nice?'

'Not exactly,' Sam replied wryly. 'The Friday Night Film Club is showing *Star Wars* in the church hall. Hey, Owen and Luke are going, why don't you come too? We'll be the only sane people there.'

'Oh, I don't think that's a good—' Nessie said, shaking her head.

'Of course it is,' Sam cut her sister off before she could think of a plausible excuse. 'Tilly can cope here, especially since most of the village will be over at the hall. And we'll only be a few minutes' walk away.'

'Even so—'

Sam swallowed a groan of frustration. Nessie was her sister and she loved her dearly but sometimes she wished she could shake the caution out of her. 'Nothing's going to happen between you and Owen unless you spend more time together,' she said, as gently as she could. 'And tonight is a perfect, no-pressure way to do that. So come and watch the film.'

Conflicting emotions chased each other across Nessie's face before she finally nodded. 'Okay.'

'Good,' Sam said in satisfaction and fired a wicked look her sister's way. 'And who knows, if you're really lucky he might show you his Millennium Falcon.'

Joss had dressed up. He wore a beige wraparound tunic, baggy cream trousers and his coppery blond beard had been groomed to perfection. From the look on his face, he also expected Sam to know which character he was.

'The lightsaber is a clue, isn't it?' she said as they walked to the church hall.

Joss stretched out a solemn hand towards her. 'The force is strong with this one.'

Sam tried a guess. 'I don't know. Are you Harrison Ford?'

His fingers dropped to his side. 'I can't believe you've never seen *Star Wars*.'

'It's a bit before my time. I'm more of a *Toy Story* girl,' she said. 'If the film club ever show that, believe me I am *there*. You should see my Bo Peep.'

'But it's a classic!' Joss insisted. 'Everyone's seen it. Nessie!' he called, as they reached the hall. 'You've seen *Star Wars*, right?'

'Oh yes,' Nessie said. 'Approximately three million times, I think.'

'See?' Joss said. 'How can your sister have seen it that many times when you've never even watched it once?'

Sam spread out her hands. 'Because Nessie married Patrick and Patrick was a nerd. I have never dated a nerd so I've never been forced to watch dodgy sci-fi films.' She grimaced. 'Until now.'

He stared at her, outraged. 'Take that back. *Star Wars* is the best film of all time. It's got everything – adventure, thrills, laser swords that sound like a swarm of bees on speed.'

Nessie laughed. 'You'll get no argument from me, I love it too.'

Owen appeared behind her, with eight-year-old Luke at his side. 'And obviously we're fans.' He ruffled his son's white blond hair. 'It's where this one got his name, although if his grandmother ever asks, he's named after the saint.'

Luke was dressed like a smaller version of Joss and carried the same blue lightsaber. Sam's gaze flickered back to Joss. 'Luke . . . Stormtrooper?'

Joss shook his head. 'Come on,' he said, leading her towards the door of the hall. 'It's time to begin your education.'

Inside, Sam groaned when she saw Kathryn had saved them front row seats – no sneaking out unseen halfway through. Kathryn had also dressed up, as the princess with the ridiculous hair. Sam waited until the opening text began to roll across the screen before leaning towards Nessie. 'I've changed my mind about Owen – the Rhys family are clearly a bunch of nutters. Get out while you still can.'

Nessie grinned. 'Give in to the dark side, Sam. We've got popcorn.'

'So, are you a convert?' Joss asked as they strolled with the rest of the filmgoers beneath a sliver of moon on their way back to the pub. 'Can I tempt you with *The Empire Strikes Back* on DVD?'

'It wasn't as bad as I was expecting,' Sam admitted in a grudging voice. 'I still don't know who you're dressed as, though.'

Joss laughed. 'To be fair, he doesn't look anything like this in the film we just watched. But it doesn't matter.'

Up ahead, Luke stopped pretending to carve the air with his lightsaber. 'He's Obi-Wan Kenobi, but the young version, from the prequels,' he called. 'Watch out for him, he can do mind tricks.'

'I can,' Joss said. He lowered his voice. 'I bet I could even persuade you to sleep with me tonight if I wanted to.'

Sam raised her eyebrows. 'If you wanted to? I don't think there's ever been any doubt about that, Joss Felstead.'

'Not the night before the match,' Owen said over one shoulder. 'We're playing Lower Seddon in the Shropshire Village Cricket League tomorrow and Joss is our star bowler. We need him to be as fresh as he can be.'

Joss grinned and winked at Sam. 'Trust me, Owen, I'm a Jedi.'

The Little Monkham cricket team was a haphazard mix of a few good players and a lot of others who thought they could play or had been good once upon a time. They played their home matches on the village green and as the Star and Sixpence was the unofficial clubhouse, Sam and Nessie soon realised they were expected to provide lunchtime refreshments for the players. Although now that Sam had seen Joss thundering down the wicket to bowl a few times, she didn't mind quite so much and often sneaked out to watch: who knew cricket could be sexy? She didn't suppose Nessie minded either, not when it gave her the perfect opportunity to watch Owen flex his delicious blacksmith muscles with a cricket bat.

She watched the two of them now, walking ahead of her, their fingers tantalisingly close to touching. Anyone could see they fancied each other; if only one of them would take the other's hand, make the first move, she was sure the laws of attraction would take care of the rest. If Sam had been Nessie she'd have gone for it with Owen months ago. But she wasn't Nessie and she just had to accept that her sister had a different way of doing things: a less direct, more circuitous, infuriatingly hesitant way. The trouble was that Owen also seemed happy to take the long way round – if they weren't careful, they'd be so busy taking things slowly that they'd end up in the dreaded friend zone, each feeling it was too awkward to make a move.

Something was needed to force the two of them together, Sam decided. Something or some*one* . . .

Chapter Seventeen

The Saturday morning sky held the promise of the perfect summer's day. By ten-thirty there was already a shimmering haze over the middle of the green and the breeze that had set the pub sign swaying was gone. Nessie stood in the doorway of the Star and Sixpence, watching a pair of blue tits swoop over a cluster of deck chairs nestled outside the freshly laid boundary rope. In half an hour the chairs would be occupied and the air would be filled with the resounding smack of bat on ball and a smattering of polite applause. It was quite possibly the most English scene Nessie could imagine.

A flicker of movement caught her eye: Kathryn and Luke at the door of Snowdrop Cottage, framed by freshly bloomed wisteria. Kathryn waved when she saw Nessie and the two of them walked across the yard outside the forge to meet her.

'It's going to be a hot one,' Kathryn observed. 'Too hot for running about chasing a ball.'

Nessie smiled. 'You'll get no argument from me. I've got some cold lemonade inside if you'd like some?'

Luke nodded enthusiastically. 'Yes, please.'

'I wouldn't say no,' Kathryn said, then shielded her eyes and looked towards the war memorial on the far side of the green. 'It looks like there's a crowd on their way. We'd better grab a spot.'

They headed for the chairs. Nessie went inside to pour the lemonade and was just adding a straw to Luke's when an elegant voice floated across the bar. 'Who does a lady have to sleep with to get a G and T around here?'

Nessie turned. 'Good morning, Ruby. Come to watch the cricket?'

Ruby was dressed in typically glamorous fashion: a wide-brimmed hat covered her glorious red hair and enormous dark glasses shaded her eyes. She looked every inch the faded actress – far too dazzling to belong in Little Monkham.

'Of course, darling,' she said, reaching up to lower her sunglasses with a crimson-tipped finger. 'It takes me back to the garden parties Larry Olivier used to hold – one of the boys would always dig out a bat and before we knew it the greenhouse was smashed to smithereens.'

Nessie smiled. One of her favourite things about Ruby was the stories she told about her days as a star of the British acting scene. Sometimes, Nessie tried to picture Ruby and her father as a couple but she could never make the scene work: her memories of Andrew Chapman were of an incoherent alcoholic who'd never quite loved his wife and family enough, and left when he was forced to choose between them and the drink. Ruby, on the other hand, was charming and vivacious and even though Nessie knew her father had tried hard to change in his later years, she still couldn't grasp what someone as full of life as Ruby had seen in him.

'I hope there'll be no broken windows today,' she said, pouring Ruby's gin and adding a minimalist splash of tonic, the way she knew she liked it. 'Martha says she'll have Owen's guts for garters if the bakery window gets hit again.'

Ruby reached for her drink and took a long sip. 'Perfect,' she said, smacking her lips together. 'Olivier would simply have adored you.'

Nessie led the way outside, where the deckchairs were filling up and blankets were being spread across the grass. She made sure Ruby had a seat and passed the lemonade to Kathryn and Luke before hurrying back inside. The heat would make everyone thirsty and trade would be brisk.

Sam and Nessie took it in turns to tend the bar. At lunchtime, Nessie brought trays of sandwiches down to the bar and laid them out for the players, along with cold meats and cheese. Between the teams and the spectators, the pub was pleasingly busy. Nessie felt her stomach flip more than once when she caught sight of Owen in his cricket whites.

'If only I was twenty years younger,' Ruby sighed, following Nessie's gaze. 'There's something sexy about a man in sports kit, isn't there? Not that Owen needs any help in that department, but even old Henry Fitzsimmons looks better.' Her eyes twinkled mischievously. 'I can almost see why Franny is so taken with him.'

'Mmm,' Nessie agreed, keeping her face poker-straight. She didn't like to think what would happen if Ruby turned her charms on Henry. Armageddon, probably.

Kathryn was at the bar, deep in conversation with Sam. They broke off as Nessie approached. 'What are you two cooking up?' she asked, dumping a handful of empty glasses on the bar.

'Nothing,' Sam said innocently. 'Kathryn was just telling me how gorgeous the bluebells in the woods are at this time of year.'

'They're like an ocean,' Kathryn said, her Welsh lilt dancing. 'Ask Owen if you don't believe me.'

Nessie glanced across at him at exactly the moment Kathryn called out. 'Owen! Come and tell Nessie about the bluebells.'

His dark eyes met hers. Smiling, he excused himself from the other cricketers and came towards her. 'Thanks for the delicious lunch, Nessie; you've done us proud again. Now, what do you want to know about the woods?'

Sam got in first. 'Nessie was just saying how desperate she is to see the bluebells,' she said, lightning-fast.

'And I was telling her how you know all the best places in the woods to find them,' Kathryn went on. Her eyes widened, as though something had just occurred to her. 'Hey, I know, why don't you take Nessie to see them? The weather is meant to be glorious tomorrow.'

Nessie felt her insides squirm with embarrassment. It wasn't the first time Sam and Kathryn had tried their hands at match-making and she suspected it wouldn't be the last, but did they have to be quite so obvious?

'Luke has football in the morning,' Owen said and hesitated. 'And you know what tomorrow is.'

'Of course I know.' Kathryn fixed a determined gaze on her brother. 'It's just a walk in the woods, Owen. You're always telling me that they look their best in the morning light.'

When he still didn't seem convinced, she touched his hand. 'Go. I'll take Luke to football.'

'And I can manage here,' Sam said, evidently anticipating Nessie's own objection to the idea. 'You could take your time, maybe even have a picnic. No need to rush back.'

Owen shook his head and fired a rueful smile at Nessie. 'Do you ever get the feeling you've been set up?'

Nessie turned hot and cold. Oh God, he thought she was in on this, didn't he? Poor Nessie, so desperate for a date that she got her sister and her friend to trick him into taking her out. She wanted the ground to swallow her up. 'Don't feel you have to,' she mumbled, fighting for composure. 'I'm sure I can find them on my own.'

His gaze was steady. 'I have no doubt you can. But the thing I've noticed about nature's beauty is that it's often better when you have someone to share it with.' His eyes crinkled at the edges. 'Would you share it with me, Nessie?'

She stared up at him and the resolve she had to make an excuse – any excuse – melted away. 'What time do you want to leave?'

★   ★   ★

When Nessie entered the kitchen at eight-thirty the next morning, she found a wicker basket packed with fresh fruit and croissants and tiny pots of jam, and an enormous tartan blanket pinned with a note. *What could be more romantic than a picnic in the woods? Just saying.*

Half smiling and half frowning, she stepped into the hallway and gazed at Sam's door. It was firmly closed, with no sounds indicating movement on the other side. Shaking her head, Nessie went back to the kitchen. It was a smart move, she thought; her sister must have known that Nessie wouldn't be rude enough to leave it behind. Nothing to drink, she noted, as she weighed the basket in one hand. Sam was probably being practical, trying to keep the weight down. Or maybe Owen had found a bottle of something on his kitchen table – that sounded more like her sister's style. Grabbing some water from the fridge, she went to see if her suspicions were correct.

Owen was waiting at the edge of the green. 'Let me take that,' he said the moment she was near enough and took the picnic basket from her.

'Why don't we swap?' she said, taking a cool bag with what looked like a champagne bottle peeking out of the top. 'Let me guess – a present from Kathryn.'

Owen nodded. 'I found it in the kitchen, with a note saying: "Drink me". There's some freshly squeezed orange juice too.'

'We can make Buck's Fizz,' Nessie said. Drinking champagne on an empty stomach wasn't a risk she was willing to take.

'Good idea,' Owen said and gestured across the green. 'Shall we?'

The sun was every bit as strong as it had been the day before. If the weather held for the wedding it would be fabulous, Nessie thought, although she knew JoJo had left nothing to chance; come rain or shine, guests would be able to shelter inside a vast luxury marquee, where they'd dine and dance until midnight. The wedding breakfast was restricted to family and friends but the whole village would join the evening celebration, with a free bar courtesy of the bride's parents. It really did promise to be the wedding of the year.

Owen and Nessie walked through the village, past the church and over the bridge that crossed the small river until they reached a wooden kissing gate. The air was filled with birdsong and the distant babble of the river. Beyond the gate, the trees were in full leaf, green and glossy, shading the path from the sun. Nessie took a long deep breath and felt some of the stress of the last few weeks slip away.

'Lovely, isn't it?' Owen said as they walked. 'It's always peaceful here but I think the morning light makes it especially soothing if you're feeling the strain.'

They'd been walking for around half an hour when Owen stopped suddenly and gripped her arm. 'Look,' he whispered, pointing surreptitiously at the top of a tree. 'We're being watched.'

Nessie peered along the branch and then let out a stifled gasp as she saw a reddish-brown face staring down at them. 'Oh! He looks just like Squirrel Nutkin.'

'They're endangered, so you hardly ever see them. Grey squirrels are more aggressive and carry a disease that kills the reds too.'

Scarcely daring to breathe, Nessie watched the little creature scurry along the branch. 'Poor things. It doesn't seem fair.'

Owen smiled. 'That one seems happy enough. Come on, let's leave him in peace.'

The trees grew thicker as they went deeper into the woods. Owen kept up a comfortable pace, although Nessie suspected he was walking more slowly than he might if he was alone. She noticed the occasional bluebell here and there but nothing like the sea Kathryn had described. And then she saw a larger splash of blue among the green. Moments later, they rounded a corner and she was greeted by a carpet of delicate flowers. It looked exactly like a wave, washing over the woodland floor.

'Oh,' she said, 'how beautiful.'

'This is just a taster,' Owen said, glancing at her warmly. 'Wait until you see the next bit.'

And sure enough, around the next twist in the path, there was something even better: a small, crystal-clear waterfall tumbling over grey rocks, surrounded on either side by a forest of bluebells. Nessie stopped dead: it was one of the loveliest sights she'd ever seen. 'Wow.'

Owen stood for a moment, surveying the scene with a faraway look in his eyes. Then he seemed to give himself a mental shake. 'We can eat on that rock over there,' he said, pointing to a wide flat area off to one side, about halfway up the waterfall. 'If you're up for a bit of climbing?'

Nessie bit her lip. The climb didn't look too precarious but the last thing she wanted was to tumble headlong into the water. Then again, she didn't want to come across as unadventurous. She nodded. 'Okay.'

Owen led the way. Nessie felt her feet wobble a few times but he was there each time to steady her. The last time he took her hand he didn't let go.

They spread the blanket out and started to unpack. Underneath the croissants and jams, Nessie discovered some Scotch eggs from the village butcher, crumbly slices of cheese and juicy cherry tomatoes. She laid everything out onto the plates which had been strapped against the lid of the basket as Owen pulled out two champagne flutes.

'They really have thought of everything,' Nessie said, surveying the feast.

He laughed. 'I don't know about Sam, but my sister is pretty determined once she gets an idea into her head.' He passed her a glass brimming with champagne. 'Cheers.'

Too late for Buck's Fizz now, Nessie thought. She tapped her glass against his. 'Cheers,' she echoed. 'Thank you for showing me the bluebells, even though you were pretty much forced into it.'

'I wasn't forced into anything,' he protested. 'Like I said, beauty is better when it's shared and I'm glad of the chance to share with you.'

His eyes met hers and warmth flooded through Nessie.

One of his dark curls had escaped from the others and was resting on his forehead; she had a sudden overwhelming urge to brush it away, back to where it belonged. It wouldn't take much, she mused, she was close enough to reach. And while she was at it, she could run her fingers down the side of his face, pull him near enough to kiss ...

She glanced away, focusing instead on the bluebells, and took a gulp of champagne. The bubbles hit her stomach sharply, exploding into heat that did nothing to cool her frazzled thoughts. Drinking on an empty stomach *was* a bad idea, except that it sometimes made her feel a tiny bit braver. Maybe even brave enough to do what was on her mind, to make the first move. There was no law that said she had to let Owen take the lead, after all. She'd certainly never have a more romantic setting.

She took another sip of champagne and looked back at Owen, only to find him still watching her. Without stopping to think, she leaned towards him and pressed her lips against his. For a heartbeat, neither of them moved, then Owen's hand tangled in Nessie's hair and his lips parted. A jolt of electricity surged through her as the kiss deepened; the sound of the waterfall faded away and all she could think was how right it felt.

And then it ended. Owen pulled away, a stormy look in his deep brown eyes. 'Nessie, I ...'

He trailed off and a wave of embarrassment and shame flooded over her. She'd done the wrong thing, misread his intentions and now he was trying to find a way to let her down gently. 'I'm sorry,' she said, taking a deep breath. 'I shouldn't have done that.'

Owen sat back, puffing out a long, frustrated-sounding huff. 'No, you should. And I don't want you to think it wasn't good because it was. It's just—' His gaze skittered away, over the top of the bluebells and back again. 'Today isn't the best day, that's all.'

Nessie stared at him in confusion. 'Why?'

'It's my wedding anniversary,' he said. 'Eliza and I would have been married ten years today.'

Nessie groaned. 'I'm so sorry. I had no idea.'

He shook his head and smiled bleakly. 'Why would you? It's my fault, I should have said no when Kathryn suggested a walk. But I wanted to show you the bluebells and I thought maybe it was time to ... time to make some fresh memories.'

The world lurched as Nessie's skin began to crawl. 'You used to come here with Eliza.'

Owen sighed and hung his head. 'She loved the bluebells too.'

He looked so sad that Nessie wanted to hug him, to reassure him that it was okay. She didn't dare touch him again, though. Instead, she busied herself with rearranging the plates, giving him time to recover himself. 'You know, we should probably eat some of this,' she said, after a while. 'Sam and Kathryn will be cross if we don't.'

He sat for a moment, staring at the ground. Then he lifted his head and gave her a wry smile. 'Hell hath no fury like a sister scorned. And they meant well. Their timing was off, that's all.'

Twin spots of heat pricked Nessie's cheeks and she hid behind filling her plate with food she didn't want. Her timing had been off, too, catastrophically so. Because the ghost of Eliza felt like a physical presence between them now, in a way that she never had before. And Nessie wasn't at all sure how to lay her to rest.

Chapter Eighteen

Sam stared at her phone on the bedside table.

It hadn't rung since yesterday morning, not since she'd answered Will Pargeter's call and cut him off before he could utter more than a few words. They were etched into her memory, though, and as much as she tried to forget them, she was worried. *Listen, Sam, we need to talk . . .*

What could he possibly have to say that she might want to hear, she wondered. He was the reason she'd lost her job – lost everything, in fact, while he got to carry on as normal. If only she could turn back the clock to the night they'd met; go to a different bar, ignore his flirtatious smiles, tell him where to shove his bottle of Bollinger. But then she might not be here, at the Star and Sixpence. And she wouldn't have Joss.

It had been reckless of her to accept the first drink. But she'd recognised his face, although she couldn't say where from, and he'd been very charming. Her defences had been deployed elsewhere, at the other man trying to chat her up in the noisy bar and who wouldn't take no for an answer. Will had intervened, told the man to stop hitting on his girlfriend, and Sam had been vulnerable for a few minutes. That had been all Will Pargeter needed.

'I don't normally do that kind of thing,' he'd said, once the other man had got the message. 'Especially not when the damsel in distress looks like she's more than capable of handling herself. To be honest, I was more concerned for him than you.'

Sam laughed. 'Thank you. I'll take that as a compliment.'

She looked at him properly then. He was tall, around 6′ 4′′, in his early thirties with wavy brown hair and pale blue eyes. Good looking too, especially in that expensive suit and crisp white shirt, and she had the oddest feeling she already knew him. He wasn't a client; she was sure she'd remember but she couldn't place where she'd seen him before. Maybe television – he was very well spoken and had the air of someone who was used to being watched.

'I can't blame him for trying,' he said. 'You're by far the most eye-catching woman in here.' He held out a hand. 'I'm Will Pargeter.'

She considered the name: definitely no one she knew. 'Sam Chapman. Pleased to meet you.'

She took his hand and he instantly raised it to his lips. 'Trust me, the pleasure is all mine.'

From anyone else, it would have been cheesy. But whether it was the twinkle in his eye when he said it or the consummate confidence behind the delivery, it worked. Sam felt a shiver of attraction when she met his gaze.

'Can I buy you a drink?' he asked.

She shook her head. 'I should buy you one, to thank you for saving me.'

Will grinned. 'Ah, but you didn't actually need saving. So we're all square.'

'A vodka martini, then,' Sam said and surreptitiously glanced down at his left hand. No wedding ring and no tell-tale signs that he normally wore one, either.

Nodding, he turned to go.

'Actually,' Sam said impulsively, laying a hand on his arm. 'Make it dirty.'

Will's eyes met hers. 'Whatever you want,' he said and in that second Sam knew they were going to have sex. How long it took them to get there depended on how well he played the game.

He came back with her drink and they began a court-ship dance. Sam established early on that he was thirty-three and single, ran his own consultancy business in the City, although she couldn't quite get to the bottom of what his business actually was. He'd just sealed the biggest deal of his career, he said, and was in the mood to celebrate. The next time he went to the bar he returned with a bottle of Bollinger and things got hazy after that. They'd gone back to his hotel, The Landmark in Marylebone – by that time she already knew money wasn't something Will Pargeter struggled with – and hadn't wasted much time on sleep. Just before seven, Sam had scrawled her number on the hotel notepaper and left Will sprawled across the king-size bed.

He called later that day to thank her for a wonderful night and sent an extravagant bouquet of lilies and roses to the office. The next time she'd seen him had been on the BBC news the following morning. He looked, if anything, even better than he had in person. Sam had sat up in her bed and turned the sound up.

'Thank you for joining us, Lord Pargeter,' the anchor-woman said, with a smile that seemed a little more coy than usual. 'So tell me – what is a "Morality Tsar" and why does the government need one?'

Sam blinked hard. *Lord* Pargeter? Her gaze slid to the caption at the bottom of the screen: *Lord William Pargeter – New Morality Advisor to Prime Minister.*

Will looked serious. 'I wouldn't call myself a tsar, exactly, but I have been brought in to ensure certain moral standards are observed in politics. Anyone who reads the papers will know there have been too many lapses in judgement recently among members of both the House of Commons and the Lords. These men and women are meant to be role models and it's my job to ensure they behave accordingly.'

The newsreader raised her eyebrows. 'And how do you propose to do that?'

He leaned forward earnestly. 'There are a number of things I plan to put in place. A transparent, clearly accountable system of expenses for MPs and Lords, so that everyone can see where public money is being spent. Strict moral guidelines to ensure that my colleagues in public service fully understand their positions as beacons of integrity and decency.'

He waved a hand. 'And of course, I'll be encouraging them to remember their family responsibilities too.'

Sam went cold as the studio lights caught on his left hand: it was unmistakably a wedding ring. Her eyes slammed shut. To make things even worse, she now remembered where she'd seen him before; in the foyer of Brightman and Burgess where she worked. Her boss, Myles Brightman, had mentioned doing some media training with a newly appointed advisor to Number Ten and Sam had seen them fleetingly as she'd gone out to meet a client. She hadn't made the connection. Until now . . .

Scrambling out of bed, she hurried through to the living room for her laptop, tapping impatiently with her nails as she waited for her browser to load. All of her worst fears were confirmed. Will Pargeter wasn't just married; he was married with two children; a three-year-old and a six-month-old baby. His wife was the daughter of a viscount and they lived in a sprawling country pile somewhere in Sussex. His title was hereditary but he'd been working his way up through the corridors of power for the last few years – rumour had it he was tipped to be London Mayor – and now he'd 'sealed the biggest deal' of his career. Sam felt sick. Apart from the fact that she'd been taken in by his lies, there were strict rules of conduct at the PR agency about sleeping with clients – it was a definite no-no, whether they were married or not. If anyone found out she'd slept with the so-called morality tsar, she'd be in major trouble. Thankfully, it seemed that he had much more to lose than her and wouldn't be telling anyone about that night either. His poor wife, Sam thought. How many other women had he charmed into bed while she was looking after a toddler and a new baby?

Sam picked up her phone and stabbed out a furious text. *Never contact me again.*

There'd been calls, of course, and more flowers. She'd ignored them all. And then the worst had happened – she'd run into Will somewhere she couldn't escape: the office.

She'd known there was a possibility she'd see him at some point but had banked on the fact that he had too much at stake to try anything. So she was unprepared when she walked into the conference room and saw him on the other side of the table, between two other colleagues who looked less pleased to see her.

'Ah, Sam, thanks for joining us,' her boss, Myles, said briskly. 'I'm sure you already know who this is but I'd like to formally introduce you to Will Pargeter. We're handling some of his PR while he's working with Downing Street and he's asked if you could come aboard.'

So that was it, Sam thought. The flowers and phone calls had failed so he was trying to get her attention another way. She plastered on the blandest of smiles to hide her anger and reached one hand across the table. 'Lord Pargeter.'

Will's eyes danced as he gripped her fingers. 'Call me Will, please. Myles has told me so much about you that I feel like we know each other already.'

She flashed him a stiff look. 'As you wish.'

Sam felt his eyes on her often as the meeting progressed. She kept her own gaze averted, looking anywhere but at him unless he addressed her directly, which he did more and more until Sam was sure everyone in the room must have guessed what was going on. But Myles seemed oblivious, even when Will held her hand far too long at the end. 'I look forward to working more closely with you, Sam.'

Once he'd gone, she'd asked Myles to be excused from the project.

'But he asked for you specifically, Sam. By name.' Myles frowned as he studied her. 'I thought you'd be pleased.'

Sam's mind raced as she searched for a plausible excuse. 'I don't usually work with the political clients,' she said, and gritted her teeth slightly. 'I'm not sure I can handle it.'

Myles threw her a disbelieving look. 'What's this really about?'

She should come clean, admit her mistake, Sam knew, but she couldn't bear to see the disappointment on Myles' face. 'I . . . I don't trust him, that's all.'

Her boss laughed. 'Since when has that been important? I don't trust a lot of our clients but I still work with them. No, you stick with Will Pargeter. I've got a feeling he'll be good for you.'

Sam had remembered those words a month later, when Myles had summoned her to his office and stared at her in thunderous silence from behind his desk.

When he did speak, his voice was like a whip. 'Explain.'

She took a moment to compose herself before answering.

'I know what you're thinking, but he kissed me, not the other way around.'

Myles thumped the desk. 'It doesn't matter! What matters is that you were kissing at all. In the conference room, of all fucking places, where anyone could have walked in.'

Sam closed her eyes briefly, remembering the flash of panic she'd felt at the end of the meeting when she'd realised everyone else had left the room apart from Will. He'd moved fast, trapping her against the table and before she could react he was pressing his lips upon hers. 'I wanted to do this for so long,' he'd murmured in anguish, before kissing her again. 'I can't live without you, Sam, please stop punishing me. I'll do anything.'

She'd twisted away immediately, outraged and furious, only to see Myles watching from the doorway ...

'I can assure you, it wasn't my idea,' she snapped. 'I did try to warn you he couldn't be trusted.'

Myles narrowed his eyes. 'How long has this been going on?'

'Nothing is going on,' Sam protested. 'Today was a one-off and, believe me, it won't happen again.'

'I'm not an idiot, Sam. Tell me the truth.'

She'd spilled out the whole story then, determined to defend herself.

'I didn't know he was a client until a few days later,' she finished. 'And I definitely didn't know he was married. He lied about that.'

Myles rubbed his face wearily. 'It doesn't matter, Sam.

Tongues are wagging already. If – *when* – this gets out, people are going to assume what I did – that you're having an affair. No one is going to believe you didn't know he was married. I'm not sure I believe it.'

'Honestly, I—'

'You should have told me as soon as you realised who he was,' he interrupted. 'I might have been able to do something then, protected you or moved you to another office. Now I don't have any choice.'

Sam tensed, knowing what was coming next. 'Myles—'

'I'm sorry it's come to this,' he went on, looking as regretful as he sounded. 'You're one of the best PRs I have. But we both know you've got to go. You're a ticking bomb, Sam, and I won't let you drag Brightman and Burgess into a scandal.'

She watched him in silence, digging her nails into her palm to stop the tears that pressed the backs of her eyes. She should fight, threaten unfair dismissal or a sexual harassment case, except that all the details would have to come out and she'd be ruined. Unemployable. Not only that, but the lives of Will's wife and children would be ruined too and she couldn't have that on her conscience.

Myles shook his head. 'It's easier if you resign. I can offer you six months' salary in lieu of notice, if you pack your things and leave immediately. A solid reference, if you want one.'

A solid reference, she noted, the kind that gave dates of employment and not much else. The kind that spoke volumes by saying nothing at all. Who was she trying to kid? Sam wondered, feeling sick. She was practically unemployable now. 'I suppose you'll keep him as a client?' she said, unable to prevent bitterness from sharpening her words.

'I have to,' Myles said, shrugging. 'He's powerful, his star is on the rise. And since it seems he can't keep it in his trousers, I imagine he's going to need us for more than just media training eventually.'

Without another word, she got up to go. She reached the door before Myles spoke again. 'One last piece of advice, Sam. I know you're angry and you have a right to be, but don't even think about going to the press with this. It won't end well if you do.'

She raised her chin. 'Threats, Myles? You know me better than that.'

'*Advice*, from one PR to another. When you've calmed down you'll know I'm right.' He shook his head sadly. 'Look after yourself, okay?'

And just like that her career was over.

Listen, Sam, we need to talk. What could Will Pargeter possibly have to say that she wanted to hear? Her mind skittered back to her last conversation with Myles. *Tongues are wagging*, he'd said. She'd always known there was a strong possibility that her secret would be found out. Could someone else have put two and two together? Could it be Will's wife?

She picked up the phone and brought up the number again. Maybe she should speak to Will, find out whether her fears were true. If they were, and the shit was about to hit the fan, she needed to know sooner rather than later.

The bedroom door bumped open and Joss appeared in the doorway, wearing boxer shorts and carrying a tray bearing tea and toast. He stopped when he saw Sam's face. 'What?'

For a moment, Sam thought about telling him everything. And then the moment passed and she dredged up a smile. 'Nothing,' she said. 'Work stuff, that's all.'

He started forwards again and slid the tray onto the bedside table. 'Anything I can do to help?'

'Yes,' she said, pulling him towards her. 'Distract me.'

Chapter Nineteen

'Got time for a cuppa?'

Nessie looked up from the delivery paperwork she was checking off. Kathryn was hovering on the other side of the bar, a box from the village bakery in her hands.

It was one-thirty on Wednesday afternoon and the pub was quiet, or as quiet as it could be with the builders still working on the attic renovations. A few village stalwarts were dotted here and there but they were reading the papers or chatting amongst themselves. They wouldn't care if she took a quick break.

'If you've got some of Martha's macarons in that box, then it's love,' Nessie said.

Kathryn grimaced. 'I went for doughnuts. Sorry.'

Nessie laughed as she walked to the coffee machine. 'Don't be. Macarons taste gorgeous but they're gone too fast. Give me a doughnut to sink my teeth into any day.'

She made a pot of tea and joined Kathryn at one of the tables in front of the fireplace. The weather was too warm for a fire now, with forecasters predicting a heatwave that would last until early June at least. Long enough for the wedding, Nessie thought to herself. After that, she didn't really mind if it snowed.

'So?' Kathryn said, peering with unashamed interest over the top of her tea. 'How were the bluebells?'

Nessie hesitated. She might have known it would be the first thing Kathryn asked. In fact, she was amazed it had taken so long; Sam had been on her almost as soon as she'd walked through the door, although she'd been dismayed by what Nessie had told her.

'The bluebells were beautiful,' she answered carefully. 'Every bit as gorgeous as you said they'd be.'

'Good,' Kathryn said, leaning forward. 'And?'

'And I wish I'd known what day it was before we went,' Nessie said, sighing. 'Before I made a great big fool of myself.'

The sparkle faded from Kathryn's eyes. 'Ah, the wedding anniversary. What happened?'

Feeling like she'd rather crawl under the table than relive the embarrassment, Nessie gave her friend a brief rundown of events. 'So I think I'm wasting my time,' she finished. 'Owen obviously still carries a torch for Eliza and I can't compete with her. More than that, I don't want to.'

Kathryn opened up the cake box and bit glumly into a doughnut. 'I do love my brother but there are times when I could cheerfully thump him.'

'Kathryn!' Nessie exclaimed, half shocked, half amused. 'It's hardly his fault. If anything it's mine, for rushing things.'

The other woman chewed for a moment. 'How many times have you and Owen gone out now?'

'Twice,' Nessie said. 'Not counting the film last Friday.'

'You've been on two dates,' Kathryn repeated. 'In six months. And how many times have you kissed?'

'Once,' Nessie admitted, feeling her cheeks turn pink. Kathryn was her friend but she was also Owen's sister. It felt weird discussing this with her.

'Once,' Kathryn said solemnly, 'initiated by you. That's not rushing things. People have got married faster.'

Nessie shuddered. 'And that's the other thing. Technically, I'm still married to Patrick. I'm not sure I should be kissing anyone.'

'Don't give me that, Vanessa Blake,' Kathryn said, shaking a finger at her. 'Sam says Patrick is ancient history, whether you've got a piece of paper that says so or not. Just like Eliza is history. Owen might not want to face up to that fact but it's time he did.'

Nessie fiddled with her teaspoon. 'You can't make him move on if he's not ready.'

Kathryn sighed. 'I know. But I also know I've never seen him happier than he has been these last six months. So you'll forgive me if I seem to be pushing the two of you together. I don't mean to meddle, I just think he deserves a bit of happiness, that's all. And from what Sam says, you do too.'

Nessie thought back to Sunday, when Owen had mentioned how much Eliza had loved the bluebells. He'd looked so sad and alone. 'You're right,' she said, swallowing hard. 'But maybe I'm not the one to give it to him.'

'Rubbish,' Kathryn snorted. 'I've seen how you two are with each other. Do you think I'd be going to all this trouble if I didn't think you were the one?' She leaned forward, her expression suddenly serious. 'Listen, I'm going to tell you something I've never told another soul. I know it seems like Owen and Eliza had the perfect marriage but things were pretty rocky between them just before she got sick. I don't think they'd have gone the distance if – well – if circumstances had been different.'

'But they weren't different,' Nessie said gently. 'And Eliza is always going to be there. If Owen's not ready to let go then I'm better off knowing now, before I make an even bigger fool of myself.'

Kathryn's shoulders sagged. 'Don't give up hope, that's all. He'll realise that for himself, if he's got any sense.'

Nessie managed a strained smile and reached for the cake box. 'Best not to hold my breath, though, right?'

'Maybe,' Kathryn admitted.

Nessie breathed a heartfelt sigh of relief when the builders packed up the last of their things later on Friday afternoon. She and Sam spent the weekend clearing the worst of the dust from the attic rooms ready for the decorator to start early on Monday morning. And although she wouldn't admit it to anyone except herself, Nessie was glad of the excuse to stay upstairs, out of sight. She hadn't seen Owen since the weekend, although she'd heard from Franny that he'd contributed a vital answer to their narrow victory over Purdon Warriors at the Farmers Arms the night before. She wasn't sure what she'd say to him anyway. The walk back from the woods had been pleasant enough and he'd kissed her on the cheek when they'd parted, but she'd seen a guarded look in his eyes that hadn't been there before. After Kathryn's revelation about Eliza, Nessie didn't know what to think. But it was easier to keep her distance than to face the certainty that their relationship might be over before it had really even begun.

Sam seemed just as preoccupied. Nessie had found her staring out of the narrow attic windows several times, a distant expression on her face. It was so out of character that Nessie had asked if she was having problems with Joss.

'It's nothing like that,' Sam had replied. 'I'm just worried about the wedding.'

And Nessie had let it go. She knew from experience that Sam only shared what she wanted to share. But she found it was adding to her own sense of disquiet. She tried to shake it off but it stuck, so much so that Ruby commented when she called into the Star and Sixpence on Monday afternoon.

'Is everything all right, Nessie?' the older woman asked a few minutes into their conversation.

'Fine,' Nessie said, knowing her voice was too bright. 'I think Sam and I will be glad once JoJo's wedding is out of the way.' Ruby raised an immaculate eyebrow, causing Nessie to replay the last sentence in her head. 'Not out of the way. Underway.'

Ruby nodded. 'You do mean out of the way and who can blame you? It's not every day you have a friend's wedding to cater for, and an important friend at that.' She let out a contented sigh. 'I do love a summer wedding, though, especially when the whole village joins in. I can't remember the last time we had one. Of course, Andrew and I planned a big celebration for ours but it wasn't to be, sadly.'

Nessie blinked. Ruby and her father had been *engaged*? That was news to her. Once again she was reminded that the Andrew Chapman who ran the Star and Sixpence was not the same man she knew. 'He proposed?' she said, trying to keep the surprise from her voice.

'Not in so many words,' Ruby said, waving a dismissive hand. 'But we had an understanding, darling. I suppose you might call it a pact. One day we'd stand before God and forsake all others to make a fresh start. In your father's case it meant giving up the booze, which is probably why we never quite made it down the aisle.'

It was hard for Nessie to imagine her father sober. She couldn't picture him without a glass in his hand, could only recall him drunk and the arguments it had caused. She remembered her mother weeping late at night too, when she thought her daughters were fast asleep. Her memories of those years were ingrained with the scent of whiskey and tobacco and the salty taste of tears.

'I think you would have liked him better in your adult years,' Ruby went on. 'Or maybe *liked* is the wrong word – you might have *understood* him better, been able to see past the booze to what lay underneath. He was a good man who tried his best to do the right thing.'

Tell that to the wife he abandoned, Nessie thought, but she didn't say it. 'Maybe I would.'

Ruby gave a small smile. 'He dreamed of seeing you and Sam again, of making up for all those lost years. He'd cut down a lot on the drinking but he didn't want to get in touch with you until he was completely sober. He didn't want to let you down again.'

'Do you think he'd have managed it?' Nessie asked, swallowing to dislodge the sudden lump Ruby's last sentence had caused. 'Stopped drinking, I mean.'

Ruby gave an elegant shrug. 'I like to think he would. I had a dress all picked out, ready for the day he made an honest woman of me. Then he went and died on me and now we'll never know.'

Nessie wanted to hug her. Whatever she thought about her father, it was clear Ruby had adored him. 'It's just a piece of paper. I'm sure he loved you just as much without it.'

'And yet we set so much store by it,' Ruby said. 'JoJo and Jamie are spending a small fortune on this wedding. Then there's you and Owen, both hiding behind your old marriage certificates instead of taking a chance and embracing love.'

Nessie felt her mouth drop open. That hardly seemed fair – Owen did right to honour his wife's memory, and Nessie's separation from Patrick was less than a year old. Neither of them were exactly hiding. And yet . . .

'You think I should get a divorce,' she said baldly.

'It would be a start,' Ruby replied. 'Not because you need to — you're a free woman, after all — but because of what it represents. You'd have a clean slate, a fresh start. It might make Owen feel better about giving up the memory of Eliza too.'

'What if he's not ready?' Nessie asked.

'Then do it for you,' Ruby urged. 'Look at your own future. Reclaim who you are.'

In a strange way it made sense, Nessie was surprised to discover. She *was* in a sort of limbo at the moment, neither married nor single. It would be liberating to cut her ties with Patrick, not because she wanted to forget him but because Ruby had a point; a fresh start was exactly what she needed. Hadn't that been what coming to the Star and Sixpence had been all about?

Impulsively, she reached out and wrapped her arms around the older woman. 'You're so right,' she said, breathing in the scent of Chanel No. 5 mingled with gin. 'Thanks, Ruby, I could kiss you.'

Ruby laughed. 'That's what Richard Burton used to say, every time I told him to get his arse back to Elizabeth.'

Chapter Twenty

Sam waited until she was out of Little Monkham, on a trip to stock up on luxury towels and bed linen for the guest rooms, to call Will. The car park at John Lewis seemed as good a place as any.

'It's me,' she said when he answered.

'Sam,' he said, sounding far too pleased to hear her voice. 'How are you?'

She exhaled sharply. 'Never mind how I am. What do you want?'

There was a pause. 'I need to see you.'

A wave of disbelief washed over Sam. Was that what this was about after all this time – his refusal to accept that she didn't want him? 'Why?'

'Marina knows about you. About us.'

Sam closed her eyes. 'How?'

'Does it matter?'

'Of course it matters,' she snapped.

'Someone told her,' he sighed. 'A friend of a friend, some-one who used to work at Brightman and Burgess.'

Myles' voice echoed in Sam's head: *tongues are wagging* . . . She leaned her head against the steering wheel. 'What is she going to do?'

'I don't know,' Will said. 'We should meet up, work out a strategy.'

She snorted. 'That's the last thing we should do. She's probably having you watched.'

'Myles is talking about breaking the story first, before Marina can.'

Sam's eyes widened. 'Myles?'

'Of course,' Will said. 'He's the one who tipped me off.'

He hadn't warned her, Sam thought bitterly, but it was hardly a surprise. Myles made it perfectly clear where his loyalties lay when he'd told her to leave. 'And gave you this number, I suppose.'

'No, I had to call in a few favours to get this, and to find out where you'd disappeared to. How on earth did you end up running a pub?'

Her mouth dropped open. 'All those silent calls . . . they were you?'

'At first I just wanted to hear your voice. I – I still think about that night, Sam. I don't want you to think you're one of many.' He took a deep, shaky-sounding breath. 'Marina was so wrapped up in the baby, I was lonely. And there you were, fascinating and funny and irresistible. I'm a good man, Sam, I didn't mean for any of this to happen.'

'Oh please,' she snarled. 'You weren't wearing your wedding ring, Will. Who does that unless they're out on the pull? And

don't even get me started about what happened in the conference room that day.'

'My ring was at the jeweller's,' he said patiently. 'It wasn't
fitting properly and I kept fiddling with it. Myles said it would
look bad in my television interviews so I sent it to be fixed. I
got it back the day after we spent the night together.' He hesitated. 'I'm sorry about that day too. I just wanted you so
much, it was driving me crazy.'

He had an answer for everything, Sam thought, not believing
a single word. It was a good thing he was moving in political
circles now; he had the right personality for it. 'You know what?
None of it matters,' she said wearily. 'I don't have to believe you
– I'm not the one who has to spin a way out of this for you.'

'But you do need to limit the damage, just the same as I do.
Myles says if we handle things the right way, we might still
manage to find a way out of this.'

He might find a way out, Sam realised, not *we*, which was
why he was so keen to take control and break the story before
his wife could. The trouble was that in order to paint Will as
a good man who'd made a mistake he bitterly regretted, Sam
would have to be cast as a predatory bitch who'd knowingly
had an affair with a married man. The media would want
blood to spice up the story and if it wasn't Will's, it had to be
hers. But she wasn't about to throw herself on her sword: she
might not have a high-flying career to protect any more but
she still had plenty to lose.

'I'm not meeting you,' she insisted. 'It will look bad if it
gets out, like we're cooking up a story to cover our tracks.

And I really don't want to be in the same room as you, not after what happened last time. Tell Myles I'll speak to him instead.'

'He won't talk to you. He says he can't represent both of us – conflict of interest.'

Sam felt her temper flare. 'I'm not asking him to represent me. But if he wants me on board with this then he'll have to communicate somehow.'

'Okay, I'll pass that along. We'll get through this, don't worry.'

The implication that the whole sorry situation was something they shared equal responsibility for was almost more than Sam could take. She gritted her teeth. 'Goodbye, Will.'

'Bye, Sam,' he said, and his voice was suddenly filled with warmth. 'It's great to hear your voice.'

Sam hung up. With her hands folded in her lap, she sat perfectly still and waited for her anger to die down. As it began to fade, the practical PR side of her brain began to kick in. She needed to know how vindictive Will's wife was likely to be, who she blamed for the whole mess and whether she was the type to go straight to the press. Sam rummaged in her bag for her little black address book. It was time to call in a few favours.

'Earth to Sam, come in, Sam.'

Joss waved a hand in front of her face as they stood behind the bar on Friday morning, his face amused.

Sam started. 'What?' she snapped.

His smile drained away. 'You were miles away. I thought you might like to know that the marquee's going up. Look.'

He pointed past the few customers to the open door, through which Sam could see a gigantic white tent had begun to take shape in the distance.

'Oh,' she said, rousing herself. 'Good.'

Joss frowned. 'What's going on? You've been snapping like a crocodile with toothache all week and your phone hasn't stopped ringing.' He held up a hand. 'And don't tell me it's work stuff again because I'm not an idiot. Something is wrong, Sam, and I want to know what it is.'

She should tell him, Sam knew, before he found out through lurid headlines and wildly exaggerated claims. It had happened before they'd met, so technically it didn't concern him, but he'd still be caught in the crossfire and so would Nessie. Sam was hoping it wouldn't come to that; her sources suggested Marina Pargeter wasn't the kind to air her dirty laundry in public. The danger now was Myles and his determination to own the story. In fact, Sam wouldn't be surprised if he leaked the news himself. The sensible thing would be for her to tell Nessie and Joss now, minimise the damage; if she was advising a client that was exactly what she'd tell them to do. But she was scared of how the two people she cared about most would react. Nessie knew some of it already, the bare bones but not the detail. Joss was oblivious to it all. Only Nick Borrowdale knew everything; he'd been the one she'd run to after packing up her office, a friend in her time of need, and she'd sworn him to total secrecy.

'It's nothing,' Sam told Joss. 'I've been stressed about the rooms being finished in time, that's all.'

'But they are,' Joss objected. 'And they look amazing, top of the range stuff. The cellar is bursting with stock for the wedding and everything is in hand. So why are you walking around looking like the sky is going to crash down upon our heads at any minute?'

'I—' Sam hesitated. She was going to have to tell him; she wanted to. But not here, where there were customers to over-hear her toe-curling, shameful confession. Not now. 'I suppose I am being a bit pessimistic. Sorry.'

His blue eyes bored into hers. 'And you're sure that's all it is? You're not angry with me over something I have or haven't done, or something I've said or not said?'

Her eyes widened. 'No! Honestly, it's nothing like that.'

Joss stared at her for a long moment. 'Okay,' he said at last and his expression relaxed. 'Just think, this time tomorrow, JoJo will be upstairs getting ready and Jamie will be some-where, terrified beyond belief.'

Sam smiled in spite of herself. 'How do you know? He might be looking forward to the best day of his life.'

'That too,' Joss agreed. 'But he'll still be terrified. All men are.'

'In which case I'm amazed anyone ever makes it down the aisle,' she said drily.

Joss laughed. 'But that's the best part – we feel the fear and do it anyway. Because when you meet the one, you know, and you don't let anything stop you from spending the rest of your life with her.'

Now it was Sam's turn to stare. 'You really are a romantic, aren't you?'

He stepped closer. 'Yes. And just so we're clear, I already know you're the one. So give it a few years and it'll be you getting ready and me feeling the fear.'

He bent his head to brush her lips with his.

'Get a room, you two,' Bryan from the butchers joked, across the other side of the bar.

'Sorry,' Joss called, stepping back with a wry smile. 'What can I get you?'

As he walked away, Sam felt a shiver of anxiety work its way down her spine. She'd spent all of her adult life running away from commitment and it had found her anyway, in someone she'd never have expected. And the weird thing was, she wasn't scared any more, not of settling down at least. Things felt right with Joss, as though she was where she was meant to be, and it made her heart sing to know he felt the same way.

She watched him laughing with Bryan and made up her mind: she had to find time to tell him what was going on and soon. She couldn't – wouldn't – risk losing him.

Not now she knew she loved him.

Chapter Twenty-One

Nessie stood in the middle of JoJo and Jamie's bridal suite on Saturday morning and gazed around. The room was dominated by a superking-size four-poster bed with exquisitely carved dark oak posts, complete with billowing cream curtains, fine Egyptian cotton sheets and plump inviting pillows. Later this evening the bed would be strewn with rose petals, and the antique claw-footed champagne bucket would be brimming with ice beside the bed. She crossed the room and entered the bathroom: a double-ended slipper bath gleamed under the dimmable spotlights in the sloping beamed ceiling. Fluffy white towels hung from the heated towel rail and a basket of Molton Brown goodies sat beside the twin sinks; Nessie had tested a few before buying them for the rooms and had fallen in love with the Gingerlily body wash.

Cleverly tucked away behind the tiled wall was a walk-through rainfall shower. The guest room next door had a similar layout with a teal blue colour scheme, no bath and a sleigh bed instead of a four-poster. Sam had insisted they spared no expense and Nessie had to agree the overall effect was worth it. The question was, would JoJo agree? Apart from the fact that it was her bridal suite, a good write-up from her would be worth its weight in gold.

Nessie had been up since five-thirty, unable to sleep, fretting about the day ahead. A couple's wedding day was arguably the most important of their entire lives: what if she or Sam had forgotten something? A tiny detail that made everything else unravel?

That fear had mingled with her worries about Owen, another thing to haunt her dreams. She'd taken a cup of tea outside, cradling it as she watched the sunrise over the eastern side of the village. Maybe it was time to take a step away from Owen. She knew Sam and Kathryn wouldn't agree, nor Ruby for that matter – she was all about seizing the day and making every moment count. The thought made Nessie feel a little bereft, as though she'd uprooted a rose before it had ever truly begun to bloom, but it felt good to be making a decision instead of clinging on to a withering hope. She'd reclaimed a bit of herself, just like Ruby had told her to. And as the sun's rays turned the amber walls of the Star and Sixpence to gold, Nessie came to another decision. She'd get a divorce from Patrick. Ruby was right; until she did she'd be in limbo.

So on the day when she'd be helping one couple to start out their married life, Nessie had downloaded a divorce petition, filled it in and printed it off, ready to be sent to the nearest court. Patrick would have to agree, of course, but she couldn't see why he wouldn't – their separation had been amicable, the result of drifting apart. And even though he'd sent her flowers on Valentine's Day, she didn't imagine he saw any kind of reconciliation in their future.

She'd spent a quiet half hour contemplating the end of her marriage and then she'd put on some make-up and prepared herself for what lay ahead. Now it was ten-thirty and there was no time left for anything; JoJo and her bridesmaids were due any minute.

'Nessie?' Joss's voice floated up the stairs from the floor below. 'They're here.'

With a final glance around to reassure herself everything was where it should be, Nessie went down to welcome the bride.

'How lovely to see you, JoJo,' Nessie said, enveloping the petite blonde-haired woman in a warm hug. 'You look radiant.'

JoJo laughed and patted her cheeks. 'That's what a chemical peel and Botox does for you. Having friends who are beauty editors really pays off sometimes.'

Nessie grinned – she'd never seen JoJo looking anything other than perfect. But today she had an extra glow, the kind only brides seemed to have. If someone could bottle that, they'd be an instant billionaire, Nessie thought.

JoJo looped her arm through her sister's. 'You already know Kate, of course, and these are my best friends, Brid and Amanda.'

'Hi,' Nessie said, smiling at the others. 'Welcome to the Star and Sixpence.'

'I'm so excited about staying here,' JoJo went on. 'When my parents told us you were opening the rooms upstairs to guests, I knew exactly where Jamie and I would spend our wedding night.'

Nessie spread out her hands. 'In that case, let me give you the tour. I can't wait to hear what you think.'

Upstairs in the bridal suite, JoJo stood open-mouthed in admiration. 'Wow,' she said, gazing around in delight. 'This is amazing. Really gorgeous, Nessie, well done!'

'I've had more than one sleepless night worrying whether we'd get it all finished,' Nessie admitted, feeling shaky but relieved at the journalist's praise. 'At one point I thought Sam might actually punch the plumber.'

Everyone laughed. 'I doubt even Franny could have fixed it if she had,' JoJo said. She crossed the room to stroke the curtains on the four-poster bed. 'Just look at this – Jamie's going to have a hard job getting me out of it in the morning.'

'I don't suppose he'll try too hard,' Kate said with a wink. She glanced around. 'No sign of the ghost, then?'

She meant Elijah Blackheart, Nessie realised, the ghost of an ill-fated highwayman who was said to roam the corridors of the sixteenth-century inn at night. Beside her, Amanda's eyes widened.

'Not so far,' Nessie said. 'Although I'm not supposed to tell people that. Sam says ghosts are great for the B&B business.'

Brid shook her head. 'The only spirits I like are the kind you drink.'

Nessie smiled. 'Let me show you the room next door. The champagne is already on ice.'

'Wow,' Sam said when she stepped outside just after lunch-time and saw the plumed white horses and the flower-decked carriage in front of the Star and Sixpence. 'This isn't just the wedding of the year, it's the wedding of the decade.'

The driver, dressed in a grey morning suit with an azure blue cravat, tipped his hat. 'Good morning. Lovely day for it.'

Nessie smiled. 'JoJo and her party will be down soon. Can I get you a drink while you wait?'

The driver shook his head. 'I daren't spill anything down this suit. More than my job's worth.'

Sam grimaced in sympathy – the temperature was about to hit thirty degrees, too hot to go without liquids for long. She hoped he had a water bottle stashed somewhere to swig from once he'd delivered the bride to St Mary's. JoJo and Jamie planned to walk back through the village after the ceremony, greeting friends and neighbours who hadn't been in the church as they went, followed by their families and guests. It was a lovely tradition, Sam thought. She only hoped the ladies had thought to wear sensible shoes.

JoJo's parents had arrived just before midday. While Mrs Smith had hurried upstairs to help her daughter dress, JoJo's father had promptly ordered a large whiskey and had been joined by a crowd of friends and well-wishers. Joss had been kept busy serving them until Tilly had arrived to take over, then he'd slipped over to the green to set up the beer and cider kegs outside the marquee. Sam had watched him go, conscious that she still hadn't found the time to talk to him about Will. It would have to keep now, everything would. She wasn't about to let anything jeopardise the smooth running of the wedding.

When JoJo appeared, both Sam and Nessie let out gasps of admiration. Her dress was brilliant white, fitted until it bloomed into a fishtail. A breathtakingly intricate lace bodice danced and shimmered with sequins and tiny seed pearls, flowing up to cover her shoulders and arms. Her long blonde hair was swept up into an elegant arrangement of loosely pinned curls. She looked perfect, as though she had stepped straight from the pages of a magazine.

Behind her, the bridesmaids wore the same azure blue as the carriage driver's cravat. Mrs Smith came last, looking radiant in rose taffeta, carrying a hand-tied bouquet of peonies and roses.

'You look beautiful, JoJo,' Mr Smith said, hurrying over to clasp his daughter's hands. 'You make an old man proud.'

'Dad,' JoJo said, smiling. 'You're not even sixty yet.'

Mr Smith took her hand and tucked it underneath the crook of his elbow. 'I feel old today. It seems like only yesterday I was changing your nappy.'

JoJo laughed but Sam saw her exchange a misty-eyed look with her father. 'The carriage is ready when you are,' she said.

It took two trips – Mrs Smith and the bridesmaids in one, and JoJo and her father in the second. 'You should get going,

Ness,' Sam said, as they waved the carriage off with the bride and Mr Smith inside it.

Her sister nodded. 'You're sure you can manage?'

'Of course,' Sam said, giving her a little push. 'Go and ogle Owen in a suit.'

Nessie's smile faltered a little but she didn't argue. 'Okay. I'll get back as soon as I can.'

Sam watched her make her way across the green: taking the direct route that would be quicker than the roads the carriage had to travel and she'd easily make it before the bride. Just as Sam was about to go in search of Joss, she felt her phone vibrate in her pocket. She pulled it out and smiled when she saw the name on the screen. 'Nick Borrowdale, how are you?'

'I've just taken a call from a tabloid journalist about you, Sam.' Nick's voice was urgent and grim. 'He wanted to know how I felt about being two-timed with the government's married Morality Tsar.'

Sam's smile vanished like the sun behind a rain cloud. 'What? When?'

'Around twenty minutes ago,' Nick said. 'What the fuck is going on, Sam? How do they know about you and Will?'

It was a good question, Sam thought numbly. Someone had obviously talked. But who – Marina Pargeter or Will himself?

'Tell me everything,' she demanded.

An hour later Sam greeted her sister at the door of the pub, feeling like she might throw up at any moment. 'Nessie, I'm sorry to dump this on you but I've got to go.'

Nessie's mouth fell open. 'What? Go where?'

'To London. Nick called – my secret is out. *The Sunday Planet* is running it on the front page tomorrow.'

She watched the blood drain from her sister's face. 'How?'

Sam tightened her lips: she had a pretty good idea what had happened but she wasn't ready to share it with Nessie yet, not without the facts. 'His wife has known for a while. I expect this is something to do with her.'

'Sam!' Nessie gasped. 'Why didn't you tell me?'

'I don't have time to explain,' Sam said, feeling a stab of guilt at the hurt and bewilderment on her sister's face. 'You'll be fine without me. I've asked Tilly to take care of setting up the bridal suite later and the caterers will look after the drinks during the meal. All you need to do is keep an eye on the bar staff and remember to smile.'

Nessie stared at her. 'For God's sake, Sam, how am I supposed to do that?'

Sam felt her eyes prickle with tears and blinked them away; she didn't have time to feel sorry for herself now. She needed to get to London to confront Will and see if there was a way to stop the story from going to print. And if there wasn't, she'd need the services of a bloody good PR.

'Just do your best,' she told Nessie, squeezing her arms. 'It'll be fine.'

Her sister gave a reluctant nod. 'Drive carefully.'

'I will,' Sam said, hurrying out of the door.

The village green was beginning to get crowded. Sam craned her head, searching for Joss, but there were too many people in the way. She couldn't see him. Once again, she regretted not having told him what was going on. He'd have to wait until she got back, she decided, heading towards her car. And she'd just have to hope he understood.

Chapter Twenty-Two

Nessie knew she needed to keep her mind on the job but it was hard, knowing that her sister was racing towards London, probably in no fit state to drive. How could this happen, today of all days? She'd known Sam's secret lover was someone explosive – it had to be for her to have lost her job – and her sister had always said it was someone the newspapers would tear apart. But since they'd taken over the Star and Sixpence, Sam had started to relax a little. Maybe she'd even convinced herself that her ill-judged one-night stand wasn't coming back to bite her. Nessie had certainly almost forgotten about it. Now it had raised its head again and its mouth appeared to be full of sharp fangs. She hoped this last-minute journey to London was worth it.

Most of the guests for the wedding reception and meal had arrived from the church now and were mingling on the village green. The catering staff wove through the crowd, offering perfectly chilled glasses of Pimm's and tall flutes of crisp champagne. Nessie spotted Joss doing a roaring trade with his kegs of Thirsty Bishop and Sycamore cider, not far from the Punch and Judy stand. Elsewhere, there was a coconut shy and a giant game of Jenga and plenty of other village fête-type games to keep the guests happy while the newly wed Mr and Mrs Brady had their photographs taken. There wasn't much for Nessie to do but she found herself standing in the middle of the green feeling suddenly overwhelmed.

'Are you all right, Nessie?' Kathryn asked, as she passed by with Luke. 'You look a bit lost.'

Nessie gave herself a mental shake. 'It's nothing really, just a slight hiccup.'

She explained Sam's absence, although she kept the reason for her sister's abrupt departure to herself.

'What can I do to help?' Kathryn said, as Luke scampered away to play with friends. Spotting her brother, she raised her voice. 'Owen, come over here. Sam's had to leave and Nessie is a bit short-handed.'

'I'm fine, honestly,' Nessie said, striving to hide her embarrassment as Owen approached. 'It's mostly keeping an eye on the bar, making sure any drinks are being run through correctly so that we can generate a bill at the end of the night, letting the bar staff take a break when they need to. But really, I can manage.'

Owen glanced towards the almost empty pub. 'I don't think there's too much to worry about at the moment. Everyone is too busy enjoying the sunshine and fun on the green.'

Nessie allowed herself to be momentarily distracted by how good he looked in his tailored black suit. More used to seeing him in work clothes, she wouldn't have believed he owned such a well-cut suit if she hadn't seen him in it. She'd been at the back of the church – far enough away to be able to stare at him out of the corner of her eye without being noticed. 'There's nothing to worry about at all,' she said to Kathryn and Owen. 'Everything is going to be fine.'

The mood on the green was joyous. The sun beamed down and there wasn't a cloud in the sky – JoJo had thoughtfully arranged for tubes of sun cream to be left in the luxury toilet trailers, as well as flip-flops for aching feet. An ice-cream van served mini cornets and delicious fresh fruit ice lollies to anyone who wanted one and the queue was long. The air rang with the sound of chatter and laughter and the sound of people enjoying themselves. After an hour or so, the guests began to drift into the marquee and Nessie assumed they were being seated for dinner. After checking all was well behind the bar, she followed them in.

The marquee was a vision of loveliness. The grass had been covered with a hard floor and fully carpeted. Nessie counted more than thirty tables, each with beautiful cascades of peonies in the centre and seats decked with azure blue ribbon that matched the bridesmaids' dresses. Gradually, the guests made their way to the numbered tables. And at the head of the room, in pride of place, was the top table.

Mr and Mrs Smith were sitting down already, with the groom's parents, Mr and Mrs Brady. Best Man Jed was there too, shuffling through his notes and looking nervous. Thank goodness he didn't seem to have taken too much Dutch courage, the way Patrick's Best Man had; he'd passed out just before the speeches and hadn't woken up again until just after their first dance.

Nessie hovered unobtrusively at the back of the tent and tried not to stare too much at Owen. Once it was clear everyone had found their table, Jed lifted a microphone to his lips. 'Pray be upstanding for the brand new Mr and Mrs Brady!'

The room erupted into thunderous applause as JoJo and Jamie entered the marquee. Nessie spotted Franny dabbing at her eyes with a handkerchief and smiling at Henry Fitzsimmons in a way he seemed oblivious to. Maybe that would be the next wedding of the year, Nessie thought, struggling to keep her face straight.

She slipped out midway through the speeches to check for messages from Sam. She wasn't expecting anything yet – it was a good few hours' drive to London and her sister wouldn't get in touch until she had news. But she checked all the same. After that, she headed back to the Star and Sixpence, looking resplendent at the top of the green in the glorious late-afternoon sun. Apart from the fact that Sam should have been there, basking in the glory of a job well done, Nessie realised she wasn't really missing her sister in a professional capacity. The hard work had been done in the days and weeks preceding the wedding, and she'd have been lost without her then. Unless this was the calm before the storm, Nessie thought, biting her lip. She hoped not: she wasn't sure she could handle any more surprises today.

*   *   *

Sam met Nick in Golden Square. It had always been one of her favourite London gems, tucked away almost unnoticed behind the bustling Soho streets, like an emerald nestled behind a flashy, attention-grabbing diamond. Nick wore a baseball cap and dark glasses to disguise himself and Sam was grateful for his thoughtfulness – the last thing she needed was a throng of adoring *Smugglers' Inn* fans following them on their way to the office of his PR advisor.

'Lizzy knows the basics but I've left the details for you to fill in,' Nick said as they arrived at the deserted offices. 'Between the three of us we should be able to manage the situation.'

Sam placed her hand on his arm. 'Thanks, Nick. I really appreciate this.'

He took off his sunglasses and smiled at her. 'No problem. Anything for you.'

The door buzzed and they took the lift up to the fifth-floor offices of Goldman PR. Lizzy greeted them both with warmth in spite of the fact that Sam knew she'd been pulled away from her family to deal with this. Then again, when your client was Nick Borrowdale, you went the extra mile.

'Tell me everything,' Lizzy said, once they were seated in her office with a steaming pot of coffee between them. 'I'm sure I don't need to tell you that honesty is the best policy here – whatever you tell me will remain strictly between us.'

It felt strange to Sam to be on the other side of the desk. She knew Lizzy by reputation and had always been impressed by the way she'd managed Nick's public persona. Not that he needed much handling – once his star had gone well and truly supernova he'd become a PR dream. Which made it all the more important that his role in this mess be managed the right way.

After Sam had spilled out the whole sorry tale, Lizzy sat back, looking thoughtfully between Sam and Nick. 'Forgive me for asking this, but what is your actual relationship? Are you seeing each other?'

'No,' Nick said. 'We spent the night together on occasion if it suited us, but not since Sam left London.'

Was it Sam's imagination or was there a hint of regret behind his words? She shook the thought away. 'I'm in a relationship with someone else. The thing with Will happened before I met him but he doesn't know about it.' She paused. 'Yet.'

Lizzy sighed. 'You worked in PR for years, Sam, so you know how this is likely to go. From the sounds of things, the story is going to run. We need to think about damage limitation and how we do that depends on who's running the story.'

'The journalist I spoke to was from *The Sunday Planet*,' Nick said.

'She means the source,' Sam explained. 'Not the outlet.'

Lizzy nodded. 'If Marina Pargeter is behind the story then we could try to cloud the waters, suggest that Sam isn't the only other woman or maybe even issue a flat-out denial. But if it's Will himself, then we're in trouble.' She paused. 'I have to say that if Will was my client, I'd be tempted to break the story first to get his side of events into the public consciousness.'

'That's what I'd do too,' Sam said.

'Have you had any contact with him since the start of the week?' the other woman asked.

'No. I've called in a few favours with journalists to see if any of them could find out whether any deals were being done and spoke to a few friends at Brightman and Burgess. Nobody had anything concrete – even the ones who work closely with Myles hadn't heard much.' Sam shook her head. 'I thought about arranging a meeting today and confronting him but decided not to on the drive down.'

'Good,' Lizzy said as she picked up the phone. 'Let's go straight to the horse's mouth. I'm going to call Myles.'

Sam fixed her gaze out of the window as the conversation wore on and tried to resist the urge to tear the phone out of Lizzy's hand. Myles was clearly being slippery but Lizzy was a pro.

'My client is concerned about how the revelations will affect her relationships and reputation,' she said, fixing her eyes on Sam. 'And since it was your client who failed to mention his wife and young children before spending the night with her, I don't think there's any doubt who is in the wrong.'

Her gaze hardened as she listened. 'If you do that my client will sue.'

Sam's heart sank. It was abundantly clear who the source of the story was now. He was going to hang her out to dry to save himself. She waited for Lizzy to finish the conversation before venting her fury.

'Those bastards! They're putting all of this on me, aren't they?'

Lizzy let out a humourless laugh. 'Pretty much. Reading between the lines, Myles has set up some kind of heartfelt confessional interview between Will and *The Sunday Planet*. Myles suggested that Marina's post-natal depression left Will vulnerable and you made a play for him, knowing exactly who he was.'

'Bull,' Sam snapped. 'Will came onto me, not the other way round. I had no idea who he was until afterwards. Myles knows that.'

'That's why Will's version of events sounds so plausible,' Lizzy said. 'Myles is holding all the cards. So, how do you want to handle it?'

Sam passed a weary hand across her eyes. 'I don't think there's any way we can suppress the story. So you're right, we need to limit the damage. I suppose I could tell my side of things but no one will be interested in me until I make the headlines.'

'We could make you more interesting,' Nick said.

'How?' Lizzy asked dubiously. 'No offence, Sam. You know what we mean.'

'What if we staged a romance between Sam and me?' Nick said. 'The papers already think there's something going on. What if we build on that and get snapped out together, very clearly in love?'

'No,' Sam said immediately. 'Thanks, Nick, but I don't think that's going to help my relationship.'

'But it might save your reputation, and weaken Will's lies,' Lizzy mused. 'Think about it: Will is involved with politics and people naturally distrust politicians, whereas Nick is practically a national treasure, his likeability is sky-high. Coming out as being in a committed relationship with you won't hurt that, in fact, women will probably love him more for standing by you at a difficult time.'

Sam pictured the look on Joss's face when she tried to explain. 'No,' she repeated. 'Thank you, Nick, I love you for offering but there must be another way.'

'Then you could ride it out,' Lizzy suggested. 'Keep a dignified silence, refuse all interview requests. The trouble with that is it makes you look guilty and Will gets away with it.'

Nick shook his head. 'You might get dragged into the divorce, too. Marina Pargeter could name you as the other woman.'

'That's if they get divorced,' Sam argued. 'There's more mileage in an emotional reunion and glossy magazine feature showing them as stronger than ever.'

'You're thinking like a PR,' Nick said gently. 'Marina is a woman scorned, remember? Would you take someone back after they'd cheated on you and broadcast it to the nation, dragging your mental health through the mud in the process?'

'No,' Sam admitted, feeling another rush of indignant fury on Marina's behalf. 'I'd string him up by his balls.'

Lizzy narrowed her eyes. 'The post-natal depression angle might backfire on Will. What he's actually doing is subtly laying some of the blame on Marina – if she'd been looking after him properly at home, he'd never have strayed.'

It was a good point, Sam realised. 'Maybe we can use that. Can we prime a few friendly female journalists? Get a media-friendly health professional lined up to denounce him for blaming his wife?'

'I think we should target his role as advisor to Number Ten, too,' Lizzy said. 'How can he preach to anyone about morality when he can't respect his wedding vows? Let's play up the young family angle as well – he abandoned his respon-sibilities there. Didn't the government publish a report on the impact of divorce on children's achievement not so long ago?'

Nick looked back and forth between them, his expression half-admiring, half-amused. 'You two are ruthless. I almost feel sorry for this guy.'

'Will Pargeter is a class A manipulator,' Lizzy said. 'I have no issues with taking him down.'

Sam sat back, trying to be objective. The next few days were going to be tough. If they went with the angle she and Lizzy had just worked out, Will would win the opening round but there was every chance Sam would win the war. And she knew only too well that today's news was tomorrow's tumble-weed. She'd always be known as Will Pargeter's other woman, though, a situation that would be made even worse if Marina cited her in any divorce petition. Sam glanced sideways at Nick. If it wasn't for Joss, she'd have accepted his offer in a heartbeat. Pretending to be loved up with him would be no hardship whatsoever.

'Okay,' she said with a decisive nod. 'Let's do it that way. Lizzy, you see if you can dig up a journo or two to run opinion pieces.'

She pulled her phone from her bag and began to dial.

'Who are you calling?' Nick asked sympathetically. 'Joss?'

'An old friend,' Sam said, with a grim smile. 'When the Archbishop of Canterbury condemns a man for cheating on his wife, people pay attention.'

Nick whistled. 'Wow, go Sam. Will Pargeter is about to find out he messed with the wrong PR.'

Chapter Twenty-Three

The wedding meal went without a hitch. Once again, it was clear that no expense had been spared; the service was perfect and the food looked mouth-watering. Nessie didn't see every course but the crab and fennel tart starters smelled divine, as did the chocolate orange crème brûlée dessert. But it was the aroma of the freshly percolated coffee that gave her the most envy and, realising she hadn't eaten or drunk since before the wedding ceremony itself, she headed back to the pub for a break.

The rest of the villagers began to arrive at the green around six-thirty. JoJo and Jamie had issued an open invitation to join them for dancing and drinks into the night and it looked as though Little Monkham's residents had taken them at their word. The bar of the Star and Sixpence began to get busy and Nessie was glad they'd taken on some extra staff for the night; the free bar was definitely whetting people's whistles.

She hadn't heard from Sam and it was worrying her. Of course, she knew that Sam had more important things to think about, but even so, by seven o'clock, Nessie was picturing her sister arrested for assault, or worse. She did her best to put it out of her mind and took the opportunity of a lull in trade to wander over to the marquee to catch JoJo and Jamie's first dance.

The tables hadn't been moved after the meal; most of the guests were still seated at them, although they'd moved around a lot. Nessie frowned as she wove her way between the tables – where exactly was the first dance going to take place? Wasn't there supposed to be a band later too? She felt a stab of anxiety even though it wasn't part of her remit. Had something gone wrong?

At the top table, Jed tapped the microphone and raised it to his lips. 'Ladies and gentlemen, your attention please. Put your hands together for Mr and Mrs Brady's first dance!'

The curtain at the end of the marquee fell away, revealing another, black-roofed tent complete with twinkling starlight overhead and a glitter ball. A band was poised on a small stage near the back and the sides of the tent had been opened up to allow guests to gather around the edges. With a murmur of delight, people got to their feet and made their way over to watch.

A collective *aaah* filled the air as Jamie led JoJo to the middle of the dance floor and the band began to play the opening bars of *Can't Take My Eyes Off You*. Cameras started to flash almost instantly. Nessie found herself standing next to Martha from the village bakery and her husband, Rob.

'Doesn't she look beautiful?' Martha sniffed, dabbing at

her eyes with a napkin. 'I remember her being born. Now look at her.'

Nessie smiled. Everyone she'd spoken to had a story about JoJo, a memory to share. It was one of the things that made it such a lovely wedding, a day Nessie knew she'd remember for a long time.

Around halfway through the song, Kate and Jed joined the bride and groom on the dance floor. They beckoned the other guests to dance too. Nessie smiled as Martha dragged Rob to join in. Reminded once more of her own wedding, Nessie turned to slip away and found Owen there.

'They make a lovely couple, don't they?' he said, nodding at JoJo and Jamie, who were gazing into each other's eyes as though they were the only two people there.

'They do,' Nessie agreed. 'But doesn't every bride and groom? They'll never be more in love than they are at this moment.'

Owen tipped his head. 'True.'

They watched in silence for a few seconds. Nessie was aware of Owen shifting restlessly beside her, as though he was trying to decide something. Finally, he spoke. 'Want to dance?'

Nessie hesitated. 'Owen—'

'I'm tired of always trying to work out how I should act and what I should feel,' he said, his expression unreadable. 'So I'm going with my gut and right here, right now, it's telling me to dance with you.'

She gazed at him in an agony of indecision. There was less than half the song left and they were in a crowd of people.

What harm could it do to dance with him? Without another word, she took his hand and led him onto the dance floor.

Neither spoke as they moved. One of Owen's hands clasped hers, the other rested lightly on Nessie's waist. It burned through the cotton of her shirt. Slowly, she slid her fingers up his arm, feeling the curve of his muscles under the fabric of his suit. His eyes seemed darker than ever, stormy and intense as their bodies swayed. Nessie's gaze slid down to his mouth, reminding her of the last time she'd been this close, near enough to kiss him. Was he remembering too? Or was he thinking of Eliza and the way she'd danced at their wedding. Nessie closed her eyes briefly, her heart aching. This had been a mistake. How could she have thought it wouldn't affect her?

The song ended. All around them, people broke into applause. Nessie broke the hold and stepped back, forcing her mouth into an easy smile. 'I should be getting back to the pub. Thanks for the dance.'

He watched her for a moment then returned her smile. 'No problem. Let me know if you need any help over there.'

Nessie nodded and made her way out of the marquee. Her skin still tingled from where he'd held her.

The next time Nessie left the Star and Sixpence, the skies had begun to darken. The trees outside had been festooned with fairy lights, giving the approaching twilight a magical, other-worldly feel, so that Nessie half felt as though she had stumbled into *A Midsummer Night's Dream*. The music floating across the air from the marquee was quite different, though;

Jamie's family were from Edinburgh and they had organised a traditional Scottish Country dance, complete with ceilidh band and a caller to instruct their guests on the steps. Any other time, Nessie would have loved to join in but after the way half a dance with Owen had made her feel, she wasn't sure she wanted to risk meeting him on the dance floor again.

She made her way around the green, collecting the empty glasses that were dotted here and there and loading them into the glass tray she'd brought. The catering company had stopped serving drinks at the end of the meal, passing on the party baton to the Star and Sixpence. Most people were inside the marquee, enjoying the dancing, although the night air was still warm. Later it would be chilly but for now Nessie could see scattered groups and couples seated on hay bales or standing around chatting.

Luke flew past, his face aglow with happiness as he chased another child across the grass. She looked around, wondering where Owen was. And then she saw him, standing underneath a twinkling tree. She wasn't sure whether he was watching her or Luke, but she raised a hand to wave anyway. He waved back. Then he started towards her.

'It looks pretty full on in there,' he said, nodding at the crowded pub at the top of the green, with light spilling from its windows and laughter drifting through its door. 'How's it going?'

'Not bad,' she said. 'Joss and Tilly are great and the extra staff we hired are a huge help.'

He nodded. 'Good. Have you heard from Sam?'

'About ten minutes ago. She's on her way home.'

'Emergency sorted?'

Nessie shifted uneasily. 'I have no idea. All she said was that she was heading home. I'll have to wait until she gets here to find out more.'

Owen tipped his head. 'Again, if there's anything I can do to help, just shout.'

'Thank you,' Nessie said with a smile. 'I'll keep that in mind.'

She spotted an empty glass upside down under the next tree and lowered the glass tray to the ground while she collected it. When she straightened up, Owen had picked up the tray. 'It's no bother,' he said, when she protested. 'It won't take long if we work together.'

Nessie didn't argue. They strolled across the green in silence for a moment then Owen spoke. 'Has it been hard for you today?'

Nessie stared at him, wondering what he meant. Having Sam disappear in a fog of uncertainty hadn't been a picnic but she'd coped. Dancing with him had been harder.

Owen saw her confusion. 'The wedding,' he explained. 'I wondered whether it made you think about Patrick at all.'

Nessie pictured the divorce papers lying on her bed, neatly addressed and ready to be posted. 'A bit,' she answered warily. 'There were some good times, and our wedding day was one of them.'

'Of course,' he said, and Nessie thought he sounded embarrassed. 'I didn't mean to imply you and Patrick weren't happy.'

They had been neither happy nor unhappy towards the

end, Nessie wanted to say, they'd just *been*. But she swallowed the thought. 'How about you?' she said instead. 'I expect it was harder for you.'

'In some ways,' Owen said, with a sigh that made Nessie ache for him. 'Being in the church was tough, although I've been in there countless times since Eliza's funeral. But it wasn't as hard as I thought it would be. Maybe Kathryn is right. It's time I got over her.'

Nessie's heart started to beat a little faster as she stooped to collect another glass. Did that mean what she thought it meant? 'I've always thought that was an odd thing to say, when someone you love dies,' she said slowly. 'Because you never really get *over* losing a loved one, do you? You come to terms with it, eventually, and you might get used to their absence but you're never the same person you were before. It'll always affect you, one way or another.'

He glanced sideways at her. 'You're right. Losing Eliza did change me. It made me more afraid, for one thing, scared of something happening to Luke. Frightened to take risks.'

'I can understand that,' Nessie said quietly. 'It's a perfectly natural reaction.'

'But it's no way to live your life,' Owen replied. 'And what I've realised since — well, since last week, is that I don't want fear to rule me any more. I'm going to take more chances and see where they take me. Do you know what I mean?'

Nessie thought again of the envelope on her bed. In a way, she was doing exactly the same thing. What had Ruby called it? Reinventing herself. 'Yes,' she said. 'I think I do.'

They reached the entrance of the pub. Owen stopped in a puddle of light from the door and turned to Nessie. 'So I guess what I'm trying to say is, maybe we could take a few chances together?'

Nessie smiled. It wasn't a heady declaration of love but it was a start. 'I think that sounds like a plan, Owen.'

'What time did Sam say she'd be back?'

Joss looked tired and stressed, Nessie thought. Sam had been in too much of a hurry to tell him she was going, leaving it to her sister to break the news, and Nessie knew it had bothered him. Then she'd made matters worse by failing to contact him all day. Nessie hadn't known how much to say, so she'd kept to the same story she'd given Kathryn and Owen, that Sam had some urgent business in London to deal with. The trouble was, Joss was much harder to fob off than everyone else. Sam's behaviour had been out of character for weeks and her sudden departure had set alarm bells ringing.

'It's not Nick Borrowdale, is it?' he'd asked as evening fell, and Nessie had struggled to answer because Nick was involved and she didn't want to lie. In the end, she'd settled for a half-truth.

'Sam did mention his name but it was only in passing. It's not him she's gone to see.'

Now she gave him a sympathetic smile. 'She'll be back around ten-thirty, depending on traffic. Look, why don't you call it a night? Go and have a drink, enjoy what's left of the party. I can manage here.'

He shook his head. 'I want to see Sam when she arrives. I want to know what's going on.'

Ah, Nessie thought unhappily as he went to serve a customer, but is Sam going to want to see you?

Chapter Twenty-Four

The fireworks went off just after ten-thirty. Sam could see them exploding into the darkened sky as she drove into the village. In some ways it worked in her favour because it meant hardly anyone was in the Star and Sixpence when she walked in, they were all outside watching the sky, including most of the bar staff. And in other ways it wasn't so good, because there was nothing to stop Joss from demanding to know where she'd been, before she'd even sat down.

'Let me get you a drink,' Nessie said, firing a warning glance his way. 'You must be shattered.'

'God, yes,' Sam said. 'Make it a double.'

She kicked off her shoes and stretched into one of the leather armchairs in front of the unlit fire, resting her head against the back of the chair and closing her eyes. She was bone weary, too exhausted to have to explain herself to Joss, who she could sense was pacing the bar like a caged tiger. She didn't open her eyes again until Nessie returned with a large vodka and tonic, and then she lifted the glass to her lips and drained it. 'Thanks,' she said, handing the glass back to her sister. 'I think I'm going to need another.'

Sighing, she wiggled her toes and risked a glance at Joss. 'How has it been here? Okay?'

He stopped walking to scowl at her, tight-lipped and furious. 'Fine. But maybe next time you decide to take off without so much as goodbye, don't do it on the busiest day of the year.'

'Joss!' Nessie exclaimed, crossing the pub with a second vodka and tonic. 'That's enough.'

Sam ran a tired hand over her face. 'No, he's got a right to be angry. You both do. I let you down and I'm sorry.' She looked at Joss and took a deep breath. 'But I promise there was a good reason for it, although you're not going to like what it is.'

Joss's face darkened. She pointed at the seats beside her. 'You should both probably sit down.'

For a moment, she thought he would refuse, but then he seemed to realise how unreasonable he was being and sat down. Nessie looked grave as she perched on the edge of another chair. 'Is it as bad as you expected?'

Sam sighed. 'Worse. But before I get into that, I owe Joss an explanation.' She cleared her throat, suddenly nervous all over again. She'd rehearsed this moment many times in the car on her drive back from London but now she came to deliver the speech she'd decided on, she was certain it would only make him more furious. 'There's something I've never told you, the reason I came to the Star and Sixpence with Nessie last December.'

Joss went still, his gaze wary. 'Go on.'

'It happened before I met you, a stupid one-night stand that blew up in my face and cost me my job and my career. I thought it was done with, all in the past, until a few weeks ago when I got a phone call from the man I'd spent the night with.'

'Nick Borrowdale,' Joss said, his tone grim.

'No,' Sam said, trying not to sound impatient. 'Of course it wasn't Nick. It was ... someone else, a man with important friends. Someone with a lot to lose if the night we'd spent together ever got out. I thought that meant he'd work as hard as me to make sure that didn't happen. I found out today I was wrong.'

Slowly, she explained. Nessie's mouth fell open when she heard Will's name and Sam's explanation of who he was. Joss's face grew more and more closed. By the time she'd finished, he looked angrier than Sam had ever seen him.

'Did you manage to stop the story going to press?' Nessie asked.

Sam shook her head. 'We couldn't. It'll be headline news tomorrow. Everyone is going to know the sordid details.'

'I knew there was something going on,' Joss exploded. 'Why didn't you tell me the truth when I asked? Why did you lie and say you were stressed about the wedding preparations?'

Sam hung her head. She didn't know how to answer because he was right – she should have told him. 'I suppose I was hoping I wouldn't have to explain anything. Things have been better here than I ever dreamed possible and I guess I just stuck my head in the sand and hoped Will Pargeter would go away.'

'But who leaked the story?' Nessie asked. 'Was it his wife?'

'That's the worst part,' Sam said, fighting to keep her voice steady. 'Will and Myles leaked it in exchange for the chance to paint Will as a repenting husband, someone who made a mistake and is willing to apologise for it. Nick suggested we try—'

She stopped talking, suddenly aware of what she'd been about to say. It was too late, though; Joss had heard Nick's name.

'*He* was there?' he said incredulously. 'You couldn't tell me or your sister what was going on but Nick bloody Borrowdale knew everything?'

Sam shook her head. 'It wasn't like that. Nick's one of my closest friends; he's known about Will from the beginning. I went to meet with his PR advisor today, to get her take on things. In fact, he was the one who tipped me off that the story was going to break.'

'And how did he know?' Joss demanded.

Sam felt her temper start to slip. It had been a long hellish day and the last thing she needed were accusations and an interrogation to round it off. 'A journalist called to ask him how he felt about it, if you must know.'

'Of course they did,' Joss snarled, getting to his feet. 'Because everyone knows you and him have a thing going on. Christ, Sam, has one man ever been enough for you? Or are there more dirty little secrets waiting to fall out of the closet?'

Sam was on her feet within milliseconds, her hand ringing against his cheek so hard it left a white imprint. 'How dare you?'

'How dare I? You need to take a long hard look at yourself, Sam,' Joss said, his eyes blazing. 'Because from where I'm standing, you look pretty cheap.'

'Get out.' Sam's voice was flat.

'Don't worry, I'm going.' In one fluid movement, he pulled a bunch of keys from his pocket and hurled them to the floor. 'And don't expect me back in the morning.'

He turned and stormed from the pub, just as the fireworks outside reached a crescendo of noise. Sam and Nessie stared after him, silent and shocked. Then Sam sank to the floor, her head buried in her hands, and all the tears she'd suppressed over the last few weeks came flooding out of her.

Nessie wrapped her arms around her and let her cry. 'We'll get through this, Sam, don't worry.'

Sam shook her head. 'I don't know, Ness. We've got a plan in place but it'll take time to start working. And Joss is—' Her throat closed up on the word *gone*. She sighed. 'It feels like Will's already won.'

A shape loomed in the doorway. Sam looked up through her tears and saw it was Owen, his face a mask of concern. 'Everyone's heading this way,' he warned. 'I'll buy you some time.'

Nessie flashed him a grateful look. 'Thanks.' Gently, she pulled Sam to her feet. 'Come on, let's get you to bed. Things will look better in the morning.'

'They won't,' Sam said with a shudder. 'They're going to look much, much worse.'

'Then they'll look better the morning after that,' Nessie insisted. 'Nobody even reads the papers these days, anyway.'

Sam knew she was trying to make her feel better. 'You'd better hope Franny doesn't,' she said, as Nessie helped her up the stairs and into her bedroom. 'She'll probably have us run out of Little Monkham for bringing the village into disrepute.'

'Leave Franny to me,' Nessie said firmly. 'In fact, leave everything to me. We've made more friends than you think since we've moved in, I'm sure they'll all rally round when we need them.'

Sam sat forlornly on her bed. 'I'm sorry, Ness. I've made a real mess of things.'

'You haven't,' Nessie said, wrapping her in a hug. 'None of this is your fault. And like I said, we'll get through this. Together, just like we always have.'

When Nessie got downstairs, she found Owen behind the bar, serving up pints like he'd worked there all his life. He flashed her a quizzical look. 'Is Sam all right? I saw Joss go flying out with a face like thunder and guessed they must have argued.'

'It's a bit more complicated than that,' Nessie said in a low voice. 'I'll explain everything later but let's just say the next few days are going to be a challenge.'

'Ah,' Owen said soberly. 'Well, I like a challenge. And I quite fancy myself as a bartender, so if you're in the market for a temp until he calms down, let me know.'

Nessie smiled and felt some of the stress fall away from her. 'Be careful what you wish for, Owen. I might just take you up on that.'

Chapter Twenty-Five

Nessie let Sam sleep the next morning. The party had gone on until midnight, although JoJo and Jamie had gone up to their room not long after the firework display. Nessie was grateful to Tilly, who'd remembered to put the vintage champagne on ice in their room and chocolates on the pillows. She'd already planned to pay the barmaid for a few extra hours, by way of a thank-you, but with Joss at least temporarily out of the picture she'd be relying on Tilly even more and it wouldn't hurt to make her feel appreciated.

At nine o'clock, Nessie carried breakfast up to JoJo and Jamie. It took her two trips: the first tray was laden with tea, coffee and orange juice, the second had two sizzling full English breakfasts complete with local bacon and sausages, eggs from Martha's hens and bread Nessie had got up at six-thirty to make. She slid the trays onto the stands outside the room and tapped on the door.

'Room service,' she called, listening for signs of move-ment. Once she was sure she could hear someone heading for the door, she slipped unobtrusively down the stairs. What was the point in breakfast in bed if you had to get dressed to collect it?

In the bar, Nessie took stock of the damage. The wine supplies needed topping up but since most of the village would be nursing headaches today, she didn't imagine they'd be drinking much. At some point she'd need to venture into the cellar to confront the pipes and barrels that had always been Joss's domain; if it took more than a few days for him to calm down, she'd need to ring round a few agencies first thing on Monday to find a temporary cellarman. And if he didn't come round at all – well, as she'd told Sam once before, no matter how good Joss was in the cellar, employees were easier to replace than sisters.

By the time JoJo and Jamie came downstairs at ten-thirty, Nessie had dealt with any remaining glasses, vacuumed, and polished the bar until it gleamed. The Star and Sixpence might be in freefall behind the scenes but she was satisfied that no one would know it from the outside.

'I really can't thank you enough, Nessie,' JoJo said, beaming. 'Everything was perfect, just perfect. Thank you so much.'

Nessie smiled. 'I'm glad. I hope you slept well. Was the bed comfortable?'

'It was divine,' JoJo said, then grinned. 'Although I can't say we got much sleep. We'll have to come and stay again to test out its rest-giving qualities.'

'Please do,' Nessie said, laughing. 'You're welcome any time.'

'And I'll give you a glowing write-up in the paper,' JoJo went on. 'Just as soon as we're back from our honeymoon.'

'Great,' Nessie replied, trying not to think of the headlines people up and down the country would be reading right that very moment. 'We need all the help we can get.'

JoJo nodded. 'The rooms are both gorgeous and staying here is such a treat. I'm sure you're going to be turning guests away really soon.'

Nessie waved the couple goodbye, with promises to pass on their thanks to Sam. Heaving a sigh of relief, she grabbed herself a coffee and leaned against the fridge, wondering how long to let her sister sleep.

A shadow fell across her, and Nessie looked up to see Franny stood on the other side of the bar, unsmiling and forbidding. She slapped a folded copy of *The Sunday Planet* onto the bar. 'What is the meaning of this?'

Nessie glanced down. The lurid headline made her wince: THE LORD AND THE BARMAID. Unfolding the paper, she skimmed the article; it was pretty much what Sam had anticipated. She steeled herself to meet Franny's gaze. 'You shouldn't believe everything you read.'

The postmistress stared over her wire-rimmed glasses. 'This isn't the first time I've had to speak to you about negative publicity, Vanessa. I've told you before, behaviour like this simply won't be tolerated. I demand an explanation. Now.'

The last word was like a gunshot. Nessie felt her own temper start to rise. Who did Franny think she was? She opened her mouth to say exactly that and then thought better of it. What if there was a better way to handle the situation? A way that might get Franny on side . . . What would Sam do if she was her own client?

Nessie took a deep breath. 'There's some truth to it,' she said candidly. 'The part where Sam spent the night with Lord Pargeter. But that's all. She had no idea who he was, didn't know he was married. He lied then and he's lying now, only this time it's to save himself. Come on, Franny, haven't you ever been lied to, been fooled by a smooth talker?'

To her surprise, Franny's gimlet gaze faltered. She glanced at the paper and Nessie saw a hint of uncertainty flicker across her face. 'I . . .'

Nessie took her chance. 'You know Sam,' she said, softening her tone. 'She came here to get away from this, from him, after he cost her her job. What does she have to gain from a single night with a married man?'

Franny's eyes remained on the paper for a moment and then her expression hardened. 'So you're saying she's the victim, is that it?'

'Sam is no angel, but she doesn't deserve this,' Nessie said, waving a hand at the headline. 'Come on, Franny, you're an intelligent woman. You know how the newspapers work.'

'I don't know what to think, quite frankly,' the other woman snapped. 'But mark my words, the Village Preservation Society will have something to say about it.'

She spun on her heel and marched out, leaving the paper on the bar.

Nessie was flicking through the paper, scowling at the lies Will and Myles had spun, when Owen poked his head around the door. 'Everything okay? I saw Franny thunder in. Do you need an ambulance or is it only a flesh wound?'

Nessie smiled and lifted her arms. 'No wounds at all. See?'

Owen raised his eyebrows. 'Amazing. She looked like she was going to take someone's head off. Did you draw first blood?'

Nessie's smile melted away as she offered him the paper. 'Not exactly. She brought this.'

He took it and glanced down at the front page. Frowning, he read on. Once he'd finished, he lowered it to the bar and whistled. 'That's what all this is about. No wonder Joss was upset.'

'It's not all true,' Nessie objected. 'And the bits that are happened long before Sam even met Joss.'

Owen nodded. 'I believe you. So, what's the battle plan?'

'Plan?' Nessie repeated and shrugged. 'Wait out the storm, I guess. Hope we don't get drummed out of the village in the meantime.'

'We're not all like Franny,' he said. 'Some of us understand.'

Nessie sighed. 'Not the Village Preservation Society. I think they've forgotten what it's like to be young.'

He touched her arm, sending a fizzle of energy to the pit of her stomach. 'Let me know if there's anything I can do.'

She was about to thank him when JoJo stormed into the bar. 'I've just run into Franny.'

259

Nessie's heart fell into her boots. Franny certainly hadn't wasted any time with her campaign to turn everyone against them but she was disappointed to see JoJo was her first recruit. 'It's not what it looks like.'

The other woman raised an outraged eyebrow. 'Isn't it? It looks pretty obvious to me – Sam's been hung out to dry to save Will Pargeter's bacon.'

Nessie gaped at her. 'That's right – that's exactly what's happened. But I thought—'

'I've seen this kind of thing so many times before,' JoJo said, looking furious. 'But Sam is a friend and I want to help. Do you want me to call a few colleagues, see what they can dig up about this Pargeter guy?'

'You'll need to speak to Sam about that,' Nessie said, blinking. 'She's working with a PR advisor in London. But you shouldn't be worrying about this now. You're supposed to be jetting off on honeymoon.'

'Not until tomorrow,' JoJo replied. 'Plenty of time to launch Operation Love Rat.'

Nessie felt the leaden weight on her shoulders shift a little bit. 'Thank you. I know Sam will really appreciate it.'

JoJo nodded. 'Franny is on her way around the village, knocking on doors and rallying the troops. We thought a village barbecue on the green this afternoon might help to take Sam's mind off things?'

'But—' Nessie began, then trailed off in bewilderment. What was going on?

Owen smiled at her. 'Maybe Franny remembers what it's like to be young after all.'

For the second time that weekend, the Little Monkham green was thronging with villagers. The marquees were gone, dismantled earlier in the day and replaced by a mixture of tables and chairs from the Star and Sixpence and every house in the village. Three barbecues were on the go, sizzling with sausages, burgers and steaks supplied by the butchers, and music pumped from a sound system hooked up to an extension lead through the pub window. Everywhere Sam looked, she saw friendly, sympathetic faces, although Joss was conspicuously absent. The wave of support was almost enough to tip her into tears but she'd sworn she wouldn't cry again. Not over a lowlife like Will Pargeter.

She couldn't decide whether Henry or Franny had surprised her the most. At first Sam had thought she was dreaming when Nessie had brought her breakfast in bed along with the news that Little Monkham was behind her all the way. Then she'd come downstairs and seen for herself: Henry had placed himself in charge of operations and was directing Owen and the other village men in setting up the green. Franny was organising the food – Martha had opened up the bakery especially to supply rolls for the barbecue and her husband had been despatched to the nearest supermarket with a shopping list. Ruby was in charge of music and had amazed everyone by announcing she had a Spotify playlist that would suit the occasion perfectly. Sam didn't know what reaction she'd expected when her secret hit the headlines but it definitely wasn't this.

'Is there anything I can do, Henry?' Sam had asked, as the ex-military man consulted his clipboard. 'Carry some of the tables or chairs outside, maybe?'

'All under control,' he said. 'But I think JoJo was looking for you. Something about getting an interview with your chap's wife?'

Sam frowned. 'He's not "my chap". Quite the opposite.'

'No,' Henry said, and his expression became uncharacteristically soft. 'Franny explained. The man's an utter bounder, but don't worry, he'll get what's coming to him.'

He looked so fierce that Sam was almost worried for Will. But Henry meant well and she was touched by the sentiment. 'Thank you.'

She'd caught up with JoJo under the shade of one of the trees. 'There you are, Sam,' JoJo said. 'I've got some great news. The friend of a friend went to school with Marina Pargeter and they've managed to secure an exclusive interview with her.'

Sam's mind raced. Whose story would the interview support? It was no good if Marina was about to divorce her husband and blame Sam. 'Any idea how she's feeling about being splashed all over the front page of the Sunday papers?'

JoJo's eyes gleamed. 'Furious, by all accounts,' she said triumphantly. 'And get this – it's not the first time Will has cheated on her. So his claims that you're the one who instigated his downfall look pretty shaky.'

Sam grinned in delight. 'JoJo, I could kiss you.'

'Careful,' JoJo said, returning the smile with a wink. 'I'm a married woman now, you know. People will talk.'

Sam had sought out Franny last, partly because she was still a tiny bit scared that the postmistress secretly disapproved of her apparent bed-hopping ways. But Franny had smiled when she'd seen Sam approach and had even clasped her hand in support.

'I must admit, I thought you'd be angry,' Sam said, once Franny had told her what she thought of the headlines.

'I was, at first,' Franny said, peering over her glasses. 'But something Nessie said made me think. She asked me if I'd ever been fooled by a smooth talker and – well – as a matter of fact, I had.'

Sam blinked. 'Oh?'

Franny sighed. 'There was a man I knew, when I was young.' She paused, as though remembering. 'He said I was the love of his life. Except it turned out I wasn't the only one. And when his wife found out, he told her I'd thrown myself at him. Told everyone, in fact. I had quite a reputation after that.'

Sam swallowed a gasp of astonishment. Had she heard correctly? Had the buttoned-up pillar of the Little Monkham community been through something similar to her? It didn't seem possible, and yet ... Franny couldn't possibly have always been the way she was now. Maybe something had made her that way.

The other woman looked up. 'Of course, it was years and

years ago. But I never forgot it. He put me off love for a very long time.'

Sam squeezed Franny's bony fingers, feeling her pain. 'I'm sorry to hear that. Really, I am.'

Franny gave a little shrug. 'So, when Nessie explained what had happened with you, I knew the village had to do something to help, even if there wasn't much we could actually do.'

'You've helped,' Sam said in a rush of gratitude. 'Believe me, you have.'

'And try not to worry about Joss,' Franny said. 'He'll come round eventually.'

Sam pictured the anger and hurt on Joss's face the night before. Deep down, she wasn't sure Joss was ever going to forgive her, but she did her best to smile at Franny. 'I'm sure you're right.'

The other woman nodded. 'And if he doesn't, I'll send my Henry round to have a little word.'

Halfway through the afternoon, Franny plugged a microphone into the sound system and asked for the music to be turned down. With Henry's help, she climbed onto a chair and an unexpected hush fell over the crowd. Sam held her breath, wondering what Franny was up to now: surely she wasn't about to rally the villagers to march on London?

'Friends,' she began. 'You know why we're here today. A scurrilous lie has been spread about a Little Monkham resident. And when one of our own is attacked, we close ranks to protect them.' She fixed an imperious gaze on Sam. 'The days to come will be difficult, Sam, but I can assure you that every single one of us is with you. You are not alone.'

Her eyes met Sam's and a flash of understanding passed between them. Then a burst of applause rang out, swelling into cheers, and Sam found herself pulled into one supportive hug after another. Finally, she ended up face to face with her sister.

'Who'd have thought Franny would come out fighting for us?' Nessie said, wrapping her arms around Sam.

Laughing, Sam returned the hug. 'I know! Remember how against us she was when we first arrived?'

'I never thought I'd be grateful to Dad for anything but I'm glad he left us the Star and Sixpence,' Nessie said. 'I'm glad we came here.'

Sam closed her eyes against the sudden rush of tears threatening to spill down her cheeks. She swallowed to dislodge the lump in her throat and managed a watery smile. 'Me too,' she replied. 'Best decision we ever made.'

Autumn at the Star and Sixpence

You are invited to a
Halloween Masked Ball
at the Star and Sixpence,
Little Monkham, Shropshire.

Join us for an evening of music, mystery and magic

8.00 p.m.
Saturday 29th October

Cocktails, canapés and curdled blood until
the witching hour

Chapter Twenty-Six

'Nessie?'

Nessie Blake looked up from the sheet she was smoothing over the mattress of the four-poster bed in one of the guest rooms to see Connor, the new cellarman, standing in the doorway. She'd have to stop thinking of him as 'new', she reminded herself as she straightened up – he'd worked at the Star and Sixpence since June, a temporary replacement who'd become permanent after Joss Felstead made it clear he wasn't coming back. It was now early October, and Connor was as much a part of the team as she and her sister, Sam, were.

'Is everything okay?' she asked, frowning. It wasn't like him to venture up to the guest rooms – the bar and cellar were his usual territory. In fact, if she didn't know better she'd say he looked unsettled, or as unsettled as a strapping forty-year-old ex-fireman ever did.

'There's a man in the bar asking for you,' he said.

'Me?' Nessie said, frowning. It couldn't be one of the regulars – Connor wouldn't be looking so wary if it was someone he knew. A journalist maybe, snooping around for gossip about Sam? Most of them had given up by now although they'd been pretty relentless in the days immediately after the headlines had hit, constantly trying to trap Nessie into commenting about her sister's infamous fling with Lord Pargeter. But the press could be persistent, even when the story had gone stone cold.

'He asked for you by name,' Connor said. 'Mrs Nessie Blake. No company name or card. Said just to tell you that you'd know him when you saw him.'

Before the Pargeter debacle turned their lives upside down, Nessie might have sent Sam to see who it was. But her sister kept out of the bar as much as she could these days, even now. And in any case she wasn't on the premises: she was getting her hair cut. Nessie was on her own.

She was being over cautious, Nessie decided; it was probably a sales rep, or someone else who'd seen her name above the pub door. 'Okay,' she said, squaring her shoulders. 'Give me a minute to finish up here and I'll be there.'

By the time she walked down the stairs to the pub, Nessie had convinced herself it must be someone from the brewery, although it was practically unheard of for them to call in on a Saturday. So she was totally unprepared for the jolt of recognition that went through her when she looked across the bar and met the gaze of her husband.

'Hello, Nessie,' Patrick said, his blue eyes crinkling into a smile she'd once found irresistible. 'It's so good to see you.'

'I can't get over how good you look,' Patrick marvelled, his gaze travelling over her face and hair in undisguised admiration. 'Were you always this gorgeous?'

Nessie smiled uncomfortably. They were tucked away in one of the pub's little nooks, away from the curious stares of the lunchtime regulars but even so, she knew word would be spreading all over the village that her husband had come looking for her. It didn't mean a thing, of course. Why shouldn't Patrick come to see her? They'd separated amicably enough the year before; their fifteen-year relationship had drifted slowly from love into friendship and from there into housemates who shared a history but not much else any more. It was strange seeing him here, she thought, his face so familiar and yet so out of place but she couldn't deny the tiny lurch her heart had given at the sight of him again. That, along with his uncharacteristic flattery, was what was making her feel so uncomfortable.

'What do you want, Patrick?'

It came out flatter than she'd intended. His smile faded. 'Who says I want something? Maybe I'm just here to talk.'

She stared at him. 'Our Decree Nisi comes through in a few weeks. I haven't seen you since I left last year, and I can't think of anything we need to say to each other that couldn't be said on the phone or by email.'

His eyes met hers. 'I've missed you.'

Nessie felt her stomach somersault. It was the last thing she'd expected him to say; for the last few years of their marriage he'd barely noticed she was there. Surely he couldn't mean it. 'Patrick—'

'Just listen,' he interrupted, leaning forward. 'I know we had our problems but this divorce thing has been a wake-up call for me. What's that old saying – you don't know what you've got until it's gone?' He reached across and took her hand. 'Tell me it's not too late.'

A dull roaring filled Nessie's ears. This couldn't be happening. Patrick had signed the paperwork from the court without a murmur. She'd held off from applying for the divorce for over a month in the summer because she'd wanted to speak to him first and he'd taken his time returning her call. Even then, he'd seemed in agreement that it was the best course of action for both of them. So what had changed his mind?

'Is this about the house?' she asked. 'Because I've told you there's no rush to buy me out.'

He flashed her a frustrated look. 'No, of course it isn't. You're not listening to me. I'm telling you I still love you, Ness. I want you to give me – *us* – another chance.'

Nessie pulled her hand away. 'I don't think that's—'

'Don't answer now,' Patrick urged. 'Take some time to think about it. You've got rooms here, haven't you? I'll stay in one of those.'

'They're booked,' Nessie said faintly. 'And even if they weren't—'

'Then I'll sleep on the sofa,' he said. 'Whatever it takes. I'm serious about this, Ness. I want you back and I don't care how long it takes to convince you.'

She ought to tell him about Owen, Nessie thought, trying to control the panicky fluttering of her heart. Patrick sounded uncharacteristically determined; he didn't seem to have considered the fact that there might be someone else. *Typical Patrick*, a little voice whispered inside Nessie's head. But he looked so desperate and vulnerable that she couldn't bring herself to say the words. She would have to tell him, of course, even though she and Owen were still taking baby steps with their relationship. Just not here. And not now.

'I'm not sure Sam is going to be pleased to see you,' she said eventually, struggling to think of anything else to say.

Patrick took a sip of his pint and smiled. 'She'll come round. After all, she only wants what's best for you, right?'

That was exactly what Nessie was afraid of: Sam did want what was best for her sister and Nessie knew only too well that Patrick didn't fit into that description. He'd be lucky if Sam let him stay the night.

'Just give me a chance,' he said, giving her the puppy-eyed look that used to work so well when they were younger. 'After fifteen years you owe me that at least.'

She didn't want to say yes. But the way things were looking she didn't have a choice. 'Okay,' she said, managing to swallow the sigh that followed. 'It doesn't mean anything, though, and I don't know what Sam is going to say.'

Patrick smiled confidently. 'You leave Sam to me.'

'Have you lost your mind?'

Sam cast an incredulous look at Patrick, sitting on the living-room sofa, before rounding on her sister again. 'Seriously, are you mad?'

'Keep your voice down,' Nessie said, as she pulled Sam further along the landing, out of Patrick's earshot. 'He'll hear you.'

'So what if he does?' Sam demanded. 'You're getting divorced, Nessie. How Patrick feels shouldn't be top of your agenda right now.'

'It isn't,' Nessie insisted, feeling her cheeks grow warm. 'But that doesn't mean I'm going to be rude to him. He's driven all the way from Surrey to see me; the least I can do is hear him out.'

Sam folded her arms. 'Right. And what does he have to say for himself? Is he trying to wriggle out of paying you for your share of the house? Because if he is—'

Nessie took a deep breath. This was the bit she'd been dreading. 'No, he says it's not about the money.' She glanced over her shoulder at her soon-to-be ex-husband. 'He says he's not sure he wants a divorce.'

'What?' Sam exploded.

'He says it's all happened so quickly; he wants us to talk things through before it's too late.'

'But it is too late,' Sam said, with some satisfaction. 'You've got Owen now.'

'I know,' Nessie said, biting her lip. She didn't dare mention what else Patrick had said: that he still loved her.

'So all you have to do is tell Patrick that and we're done, right?'

Except it wasn't that simple, Nessie thought wretchedly. In theory, Sam was right – surely Patrick would accept the inevitability of the divorce if he knew she'd met someone else? So why didn't it feel like the right thing to do?

'Right, Nessie?' Sam repeated, her eyes narrowing slightly.

'Right,' Nessie replied in a subdued voice. 'But not now. He wants to take me out for dinner tonight. I'll tell him then.'

'Dinner?' Sam echoed in disbelief. 'When was the last time Patrick took you out anywhere?'

Nessie thought for a moment; she genuinely couldn't remember the last time she and Patrick had done anything together. He'd been wrapped up in building his business and she – well, she couldn't bear the awkward silences as they sat opposite each other, or the feeling that she was evidently a lot less interesting than his phone.

'My thirtieth birthday,' she said, shaking off the memories. 'We went to the Dirty Duck – you know that place run by the experimental chef – and Patrick wouldn't try anything on the menu. Made-up muck, he called it.'

'Marvellous,' Sam muttered. She let out a long, loud

sigh. 'I suppose he can stay tonight, since he's here. You have to promise me you'll nip this in the bud, though.'

Nessie summoned up a mental picture of Owen, working in his forge next door, striking sparks from a glowing piece of metal as he bent over the anvil. He was tall and muscular, with wild black curls and flashing dark eyes – everything Patrick wasn't. When Owen looked at her sometimes, she felt a shiver of something indescribably delicious run through her. The trouble was, she wasn't sure he was over his first wife, childhood sweetheart Eliza, who'd died several years earlier, leaving Owen to bring up their son, Luke, alone. That was why he and Nessie had been taking things slowly, cementing a friendship first that could blossom into more once they were both sure it was the right thing to do. But Nessie would be lying if she didn't occasionally find it hard constantly second-guessing how Owen felt about her. Sometimes she wished she was more like Sam, who decided what she wanted and took it. Except look where that had got her with Will Pargeter . . .

And then there was Patrick – steady, dependable Patrick, whose main crime had been to stop noticing Nessie was there. He hadn't always been that way; once, he'd wooed her and said all the right things. They'd been happy enough at first, until time and familiarity and an unhealthy dose of indifference had worn both Nessie and their marriage down. Nessie wasn't sure the relationship could be rekindled, even if she wanted it to be. Sam was right;

Patrick belonged in her past and it wasn't fair to let him believe otherwise.

'Okay,' she said, managing a fragile smile. 'I'll tell him tonight that there's no hope.'

Chapter Twenty-Seven

It wasn't that she disliked her brother-in-law, Sam thought as she opened her laptop on the kitchen table and tried not to resent the fact that he was sitting in *her* spot on the sofa next door. She just didn't like the way Nessie had gradually lost her confidence over the years she'd been with Patrick, a side-effect of his disinterest. And she'd bitten her tongue more than once over his expectation that Nessie would do all the cooking and the cleaning while holding down a full-time job of her own, plus helping Patrick with the admin for his IT support business. But Sam didn't dislike him as a person. She just thought Nessie was much better suited to Owen Rhys. Together with his sister, Kathryn, Sam had been gently pushing Nessie towards him. So the sudden arrival of Patrick in Little Monkham, with his divorce-related cold feet, did not please Sam at all. The sooner Nessie told him things were definitely over, the better.

Feeling another needle of irritation, Sam checked her email. There was a message from Nick Borrowdale, confirming he'd be at the Halloween Masked Ball she had planned for the end of October. Sam felt a thrill of anticipation that was only half to do with the party. Smiling, Sam fired off a quick reply to Nick and switched to the Star and Sixpence account. There were several emails about Oktoberfest, the beer and cider festival weekend she and Nessie had planned for a week's time. And there was one from the Real Ale Drinkers' Association. Sam clicked open, expecting it to be about Oktoberfest. The message made her shout instead.

'Sam?' Patrick said, poking his head around the kitchen door. 'Is everything okay?'

'Better than okay,' Sam said, getting to her feet with an elated grin. 'The Star and Sixpence has been voted Regional Pub of the Year by the Real Ale Drinkers' Association!'

Hugging her laptop to her chest, she squeezed past him and went downstairs to find Nessie.

'Really?' her sister gasped when she heard the news. 'But I didn't even know we'd been judged.'

'Neither did I,' Sam said, shrugging. 'I emailed them when we first reopened, to let them know the pub was back in business, but they sent what seemed like a standard reply and I haven't heard from them since.'

'I wonder who came,' Nessie said. 'And when?'

'They visited sometime over the summer,' Sam replied. 'But whenever it was, they liked what they saw. I'm going to slap that "award-winning pub" logo straight on our website. And we should give Connor a pay rise – the quality of the beer will have played a big part.'

Nessie beamed at her. 'We should. Wow, I can't believe it. Is there a trophy or something?'

Sam scanned the email again. 'It says we'll be presented with a framed certificate and invited to the national finals in December.'

'So you could be voted the best pub in the entire country?' Patrick said from behind her.

Some of Sam's elation ebbed away at the sound of his voice. She'd almost forgotten he was there. 'In theory,' she said. 'But I expect the competition is pretty fierce and we've only been in business for nine months. I don't expect we'll win.'

'It's not bad going for nine months, though,' Patrick said, sounding impressed. 'This place must be a right little goldmine.'

Nessie shifted uncomfortably. 'It's been a lot of hard work.'

'But it's paying off big time,' Patrick persisted. He threw an admiring glance her way. 'You're amazing, Ness.'

'It's not just me,' Nessie said, looking flustered.

'It's your name above the door,' he said, shrugging. 'So I reckon you can bask in the glory. I'd forgotten how smart you are. How smart you *both* are.'

Sam frowned. Patrick had never been one for wild flattery before – he really was pulling out all the stops.

And although she'd be the first to agree that her sister was resourceful and clever, she hoped Nessie was wise enough to see through Patrick's charm offensive. 'We've had a lot of local support,' she said in a meaningful tone. 'From our friends in the village.'

She gazed pointedly at Nessie as she added the last few words, hoping her sister would get the hint. Patrick was starting to attract interest from a few of the regulars dotted around the pub – once they worked out who he was, his presence would be the talk of Little Monkham. Two pink spots appeared on Nessie's cheeks: she understood exactly what Sam was getting at.

'It's really only meant to be pub employees behind the bar, Patrick,' she said, sounding awkward. 'Health and Safety, you know how it is.'

Patrick smiled. 'No problem,' he said, walking around to the customers' side. 'What drink does the landlady recommend?'

Sam bit back a sarcastic response and let Nessie pour him a pint of Thirsty Bishop. But she didn't return upstairs; she balanced her laptop on the end of the bar and kept a watchful eye on her brother-in-law. If Nessie didn't make it clear Patrick wasn't welcome at the Star and Sixpence later, she would.

It was unusually quiet for a Saturday night. Rain had set in during the afternoon, along with blustering winds that whistled around the Star and Sixpence and across the village green, the tail end of a hurricane from the States that everyone had hoped would blow itself out across the Atlantic. Patrick and Nessie had headed to nearby Purdon for their meal.

'Rather you than me,' Sam had called with a shiver as they'd vanished into the gloomy twilight, and she'd meant more than just the weather. She couldn't think of much she'd like to do less than sit opposite Patrick making small talk.

She'd built a roaring fire in the huge fireplace at the heart of the pub and lit as many candles as she could find to create a cosy atmosphere, although she doubted many villagers would brave the wind and the rain to join her and Tilly the barmaid. On nights like this, when the wind sighed around the old coaching inn and the beams creaked as they settled, Sam could almost feel the shadows of the people who'd lived there before. The pub was said to be haunted by the ghost of a highwayman, a story Sam played on with some of their more credulous overnight guests. It had also given her the idea for the Halloween Masked Ball; Sam was nothing if not practical and although she didn't believe in ghosts herself, she wasn't above exploiting the idea of them. Even so, on a night like this she could easily believe that the creaks and moans were not all caused by the old building settling down for the night . . .

There was one regular Sam could always rely on to stop by: Ruby Cabernet.

'Awful night,' Ruby said as she pushed the pub door

shut and shook the raindrops from her fur-trimmed hood. 'There's a tempest worthy of Prospero himself blowing out there.'

She unhooked her heavy-looking cape and draped it across one of the chairs facing the fire to dry. Typical Ruby, Sam thought, eyeing the older woman's forest green wiggle dress and kitten heels; anyone else would be in boots and a waterproof coat but Ruby maintained she had *standards* and never looked anything other than extraordinary. Her red hair was always perfectly set, her make-up immaculate. She was Little Monkham's style icon and the PR girl in Sam was itching to find out more about her. *One day*, she told herself.

Ruby glanced around the bar with wide eyes. 'Don't tell me I'm the only one brave enough to battle the elements?'

Sam managed a rueful smile. 'It looks that way. I could have George Clooney here tonight and we'd still be on our own.'

'Then I'd better have a double G&T, if I'm your only patron,' Ruby said, arching a delicately drawn eyebrow. 'And perhaps one for George, too.'

Tilly set to work pouring Ruby's drink while Sam joined her at a table by the fire. The older woman took a long sip of gin then smacked her lips together in appreciation. 'The first one always hits the spot.'

Sam dredged up a smile, doubting very much that this was Ruby's first drink of the day. 'We aim to please.'

Ruby leaned back into her seat. 'No Nessie tonight?'

Sam hesitated. Had word got around about Patrick already? But she only saw friendly interest in Ruby's eyes; if she was on a fact-finding mission she was hiding it well. 'She's out for dinner with an old friend.'

'Old friends,' Ruby sighed. 'The best kind. Of course, when you get to my age most of your old friends have gone to that great green room in the sky.'

'Ruby!' Sam exclaimed. 'You're not old.'

The other woman shook her head, her eyes twinkling. 'To quote darling Harrison Ford, it's not the years, honey, it's the mileage.'

Sam laughed. 'I'm sure every mile has been worth it.'

The door swung open again. This time it was Owen. He stood for a moment, rain glistening in his black curls. Ruby's scarlet lips curved into a smile as she winked at Sam. 'Who needs George Clooney when you've got Owen Rhys?'

'Pint of Thirsty Bishop, Owen?' Tilly called, reaching for a glass.

He nodded as he shrugged off his coat. 'It'd be rude not to, especially since I hear it's award-winning.' He glanced around. 'Quiet in here.'

'The important people are present,' Ruby said briskly. 'The stalwarts.'

'The hard core,' Owen replied as he crossed to the bar. He fired a swift smile at Sam.

'Although if you're looking for Nessie, you're going to be disappointed,' Ruby said. 'Sam says she's out on the town.'

'Oh?' Owen said easily. 'I'm sorry to have missed her.'

Sam didn't think Nessie would mind – the last thing she'd want was to run into Owen before she'd given Patrick his marching orders. Maybe Sam wouldn't mention Owen had stopped by. Unless of course Nessie hadn't told Patrick the news ... then Sam might use it to remind her sister where her future lay. And that Patrick wasn't part of it.

Owen carried his pint over to where Ruby and Sam sat beside the fire. The conversation touched on Sam's plans for Oktoberfest and the range of beers Connor planned to offer. Briefly, Sam wondered how different things might have been if Joss was still around but she didn't let her thoughts dwell on him; thanks to Connor, they were doing very well without Joss's help. Ruby had launched into a scandalous tale from eighties Soho when the door opened again and Nessie walked in. She stopped dead when she saw Owen.

'Nessie,' he said, getting to his feet with a smile. 'I thought you were out for the evening.'

Nessie's panic-filled gaze flew to Sam. 'There's a fallen tree blocking the Purdon road so we turned back.'

Ruby patted an empty chair next to her. 'Then Purdon's loss is our gain.'

Sam saw Nessie half-glance over her shoulder and knew Patrick must be on his way into the bar. Her brain flew into damage limitation mode. 'Did the two of you manage to hammer out the details?'

'What?' Nessie said, still distracted. 'Oh ... no, not really.'

Ruby pounced like a tiger. 'Details? Are you and your friend planning a school reunion?'

Sam took a deep breath. 'Not exactly. I know I said Nessie was out with an old friend. In actual fact she was out with her ex-husband.'

Patrick appeared in the doorway. 'Not quite, Sam.' He strode forwards, holding out a hand to Owen. 'Hi, I'm Patrick. Nessie's *husband*.'

Owen blinked at the emphasis on the final word. He took Patrick's outstretched hand almost automatically and his eyes strayed to Nessie's. 'Owen Rhys. I'm—' He paused for a heartbeat and an unspoken communication seemed to pass between them. 'I'm her next-door neighbour.'

Chapter Twenty-Eight

Nessie woke up with her alarm at six o'clock and lay for a moment staring at the cracked ceiling above her bed. This time yesterday, everything had been fine. Not perfect, but moving in the right direction. Then Patrick had arrived and shaken everything up like leaves in a gale, and she wasn't at all sure life would settle back down exactly the way it had been before.

Her thoughts flew back to last night and she covered her gritty eyes with a groan. She'd thought her heart would stop when she'd walked into the bar and found Owen sitting there. Sam had done her best to rescue the situation, but Nessie had known the moment Patrick introduced himself that the damage had been done: Owen had drained his pint and made his excuses not long after. Nessie had watched him go, her heart heavy with anxiety, and longed to follow him to explain, but she couldn't. Not with Patrick watching. So she'd spent a restless night worrying, listening to the howling wind with Sam's whispered goodnight warning bouncing around her brain: *Tell Patrick tomorrow or I will.*

With a broken sigh, Nessie pushed back the covers and pulled on her dressing gown. Patrick was asleep in the living room; she could hear his snores through the door. With a bit of luck the amount of Thirsty Bishop he'd drunk would mean he'd sleep through her breakfast preparations for the guests upstairs. But he wouldn't sleep forever; she'd have to face him sometime and set things straight between them. She needed to speak to Owen too, and explain that it wasn't what it looked like, that Patrick wasn't back in her life the way he'd insinuated he was.

But before any of that, she thought as she padded along the landing to the kitchen, she needed to bake some bread.

She knocked on the door of Snowdrop Cottage just after eight-thirty. The wind and rain had died down, leaving the air smelling clean and fresh but Nessie thought she detected a smoky hint of autumn as she crossed the yard in front of the forge. It took a moment for the door to open and when it did, it wasn't Owen peering out at her but Kathryn. Her dark curls, so like Owen's, were uncharacteristically messy, suggesting she'd just got up.

'Morning, Nessie,' she said, her Welsh lilt lifting into a half-covered yawn. 'You're up and about early for a Sunday. Do you need to borrow something?'

Nessie shook her head. 'I came to see Owen. Is he around?'

'No, he's taken Luke to football,' Kathryn said, with a sympathetic grimace. 'Won't be back for about an hour.'

Nessie felt her shoulders sag. She should have known Owen would have taken Luke to football – he did it every Sunday morning. But her mind had been so full of jumbled thoughts that she'd forgotten. She gnawed at her lip; she didn't want to go back to the pub, not when there was every chance Patrick would be awake. She wanted to see Owen first, to give her the strength to tell Patrick it was over. But it didn't seem as though luck was on her side.

'Why don't you come in and wait,' Kathryn said, as though reading her mind. 'We can have a cuppa and a gossip.'

Nessie frowned. 'But you've just got up.'

'It's no bother,' Kathryn replied. She pulled the door back further. 'I've got some of Martha's triple chocolate chip cookies.'

Nessie smiled. 'You know me too well.'

It wasn't until she was sitting in Kathryn's cosy kitchen, sipping a cup of steaming hot tea, that it occurred to Nessie to wonder whether Owen had told his sister about last night. She didn't think so – Kathryn was famous for her bluntness. She would have brought the subject up the moment Nessie was through the front door if she'd known.

'How are things with you?' she asked.

Kathryn cupped her hands around her tea and sighed.

'Okay, I suppose. Band rehearsals are the usual mess of egos and artistic disagreements, but what can you expect with a bunch of musicians?' She pulled her mouth into a wry smile. 'I sometimes think I'm the only sane one among them.'

Nessie smiled too; she'd seen Sonic Folk play a number of times and they'd never failed to impress her, but she knew from Kathryn that there was a lot of tension beneath the energetic, polished performances. 'Oh?'

'Bookings are up, which is great,' Kathryn said. 'Or it would be if they weren't scattered all over the country. Some of us have responsibilities. We can't just set off to Edinburgh at a moment's notice.'

Nessie shifted uneasily. There was a faint whisper of resentment behind Kathryn's words, something she'd never heard before. She knew Kathryn had sacrificed a lot to help her brother care for Luke after Eliza's death. Could it be that she was starting to feel tied down by Owen and Luke? She was only in her early thirties, after all; could she perhaps be wondering when she might get to lead her own life?

'Have you spoken to Owen about this?' she asked.

Kathryn shrugged. 'You know my brother. He'd tell me to go and then forget to pick Luke up from school at the end of the day.'

Nessie laughed. 'I think he's got more sense than that.'

'You're probably right,' Kathryn admitted. 'But he'd still struggle if I wasn't around to help. I'm not sure they'd eat, for a start.'

'They'd be fine,' she said to Kathryn. 'Honestly, take a bit of time for yourself. You've earned it.'

Kathryn looked unconvinced. 'I dunno . . .'

'At least talk to him about it,' Nessie urged. She smiled. 'You never know, he might be as keen to fly solo as you are.'

'But what if I decided to make it . . . a more permanent arrangement?'

Nessie stared at her. 'You mean move out?'

Kathryn's gaze slid away. 'Perhaps. I don't know.' She sighed. 'Maybe I just need a bit of space. Or maybe I'm just in an odd mood — autumn does that to me sometimes. The change of the season, all the trees losing their leaves, it makes me a bit restless.'

Nessie nodded. The change from summer to autumn was probably the most dramatic of the seasonal shifts — as well as the visual signs, the air seemed different too, rich and smouldering with the scent of delicately spiced wood smoke even when there was no fire for miles. Unlike Kathryn, it didn't make Nessie feel restless. It made her want to reach for warm woollen jumpers and snuggle beside the fire with a good book and a never-ending mug of hot chocolate. 'Talk to Owen,' she said again gently. 'He'll understand.'

The other woman nodded, then pushed the plate of cookies towards Nessie. 'We'd better eat these before Luke gets back. You know he can detect chocolate from two villages away.'

The conversation moved on to the latest village gossip: Franny Forster was rumoured to be thinking about moving in with Henry Fitzsimmons, something Nessie would never have predicted when she'd first met her.

'Good on her, I say,' Kathryn said. 'It just goes to show that it's never too late.'

There was a rumble outside as Owen's battered old Land Rover swept into the yard. Nessie heard Luke chattering at the back door, then he tumbled inside, his freckled face rosy beneath his mop of untidy blond hair. 'I scored three goals,' he announced proudly. 'It would have been four except Robbie Henderson fouled me just as I was about to shoot. Dad said he's a filthy little—'

'Never mind what I said,' Owen cut in, laughing. His dark eyes came to rest on Nessie. 'Good morning.'

All of Nessie's mortification about the night before came rushing back. She did her best to smile but it was a weak effort. 'Good morning. Kathryn and I were just having a gossip.'

Luke's eyes lit up when he saw the crumb-covered plate. 'You've had triple chocolate chip cookies! Did you save one for me?'

Kathryn mock-frowned. 'Maybe.' She eyed his mud-caked knees and grubby football kit. 'But you're not getting anything until you've had a shower.'

She chivvied him towards the kitchen door. 'Thanks for the advice, Nessie,' she called over one shoulder as Luke thundered up the stairs. 'Much appreciated.'

Luke's chatter faded away to a dull murmur, leaving a heavy silence behind. Nessie cleared her throat nervously. 'I think I owe you an explanation.'

Owen shook his head. 'You don't owe me anything.'

'I do,' Nessie insisted. 'And it really isn't what you think. Patrick is ... he isn't ... oh God, I don't know. It's complicated.'

There was a loud thud overhead, followed by a squawk from Luke and a cross-sounding mutter from Kathryn. Owen frowned. 'Shall we go for a walk?'

The village green was sparkling with dew, its grass an even deeper emerald than usual. Nessie felt dampness seep through her canvas shoes but the discomfort was nothing compared to the knot of anxiety twisting through her stomach. She cleared her throat again and fixed her gaze on the distant war memorial.

'I had no idea Patrick was coming,' she said. 'He turned up yesterday out of the blue, saying he wanted to talk. And since I couldn't really refuse, it seemed better if we did it away from the pub and the prying eyes of the village.'

A smiled flickered across Owen's features. 'Sounds sensible to me.'

'There's nothing going on between us,' Nessie said in a rush, feeling her cheeks start to burn. 'Between me and Patrick, I mean. We're still getting divorced.'

Owen was quiet for a moment. 'You might think so but it's not the impression I got from Patrick last night. He went out of his way to let me know you were still his wife.'

Nessie felt another wave of embarrassment wash over her. 'I have no idea what's got into him. Honestly, during the last few years we were together I don't think he noticed I was even there, as long as his dinner was on the table. And now he's acting like we're Richard Burton and Elizabeth Taylor.'

'So he's contesting the divorce?'

'It's too late for that,' Nessie said. 'He signed all the paperwork ages ago. No, I think he just wants to be sure it's the right thing for both of us.'

Owen glanced sideways at her. 'And how do you feel about that?'

Nessie kicked at a clump of grass, sending a tiny shower of dew across her already soaking foot. 'Irritated, mostly. If he'd shown this much interest before I left maybe we'd still be together. Sam wants me to send him packing. That's what I was meant to do last night.'

Owen said nothing and Nessie felt a small stab of frustration. Impassioned declarations weren't his style but he could show some emotion, give her a sign that he was bothered by the sudden reappearance of her husband. An irrational desire to make him jealous surfaced in her mind. She pushed it away but the idea persisted. Maybe what Owen needed was a bit of competition, it whispered. She shook her head – it was the kind of thing Sam might do.

'But what if he means it?' Owen said. 'What if he does still love you? Would you ever consider going back to him?'

Nessie stopped walking to stare at him. He was being so bloody impartial, she thought in exasperation, so reasonable; like a good friend who had no interest either way. Which was all very well but friendship wasn't necessarily what she needed right now – not from him. A little bit of passion wouldn't go amiss, the little voice murmured; something to show he felt more for her than friendly concern. Nessie cast a sideways look at Owen. Maybe it *was* time to force his hand.

She took a deep breath. 'He says he wants me back. And he'll do anything to make that happen.'

The last sentence hung between them. *Come on*, Nessie willed him, *tell me not to listen to Patrick. Say you want me too.* But Owen's gaze darkened and he stepped back. 'I won't stand in your way. If you want to save your marriage then you should.'

His jaw tightened, as though he wanted to say more, but he checked himself and turned to walk away.

Nessie felt her stomach clench. 'Owen, wait—' she began but he didn't stop.

Her shoulders slumped. Great – instead of invoking an impassioned response, she'd effectively told Owen she wanted to get back together with Patrick and he'd taken her at her word. Could she have handled the situation any worse? She should run after him, explain that it wasn't Patrick she wanted. But then she'd have to explain why she'd just suggested that she did. No, the best way to deal with the whole situation was to set Patrick straight and send him back to Surrey. Then she could repair the damage with Owen and everything would be as it had been.

Groaning with frustration, she headed back to the Star and Sixpence. As she got nearer, she saw someone standing at the living-room window watching her. It was Patrick. Had he seen her talking to Owen? she wondered, as he lifted his hand to wave. Then she decided it wasn't such a bad thing if he had. It would give her more ammunition to convince him their marriage was over.

Chapter Twenty-Nine

The gate of Weir Cottage creaked as Sam pushed it open. She looked up at the windows and hesitated; the curtains were still drawn, which wasn't entirely surprising given the amount of gin Ruby had put away the night before. But a quick glance at her phone told Sam it was almost eleven-thirty – surely Ruby must be up by now? And if she wasn't, she soon would be.

Ruby answered on Sam's second ring of the doorbell. She opened the door, dressed in a daisy-print tunic and lime-coloured Capri pants that Sam instantly coveted. Her sunglasses were perched on top of her head and she held a muddy trowel in one gloved hand. She looked the picture of health and nothing like the slurring, unsteady drunk Sam had guided home the previous night.

'Sam, darling!' she exclaimed in delight. 'How wonderful to see you! Come in, come in.'

Sam followed her down the hallway. Now that she was inside she could see that the cottage was actually a bungalow and bigger than it looked from the outside. But the thing that amazed her the most was how well Ruby looked. She'd lost count of how many double gins the other woman had put away but she knew it had been a lot. Enough to ensure a hangover of epic proportions in most people.

'What's your secret, Ruby?' she said once she'd reached the tiny cottage kitchen. 'How can you possibly look so fresh this morning?'

Ruby leaned against the counter and patted her cheeks. 'A bespoke beauty cream made by the kind of genius no one talks about for fear everyone will discover her.'

Sam raised her eyebrows. 'A beauty cream that fends off hangovers? Wow, no wonder you don't want anyone else to know – she'd be inundated.'

Ruby smiled. 'I also had some help from a recipe that old reprobate Ollie Reed gave me years ago. It's called a Prairie Oyster – have you heard of it?'

Sam shook her head.

'I used to make it for your father, to take the edge off after a heavy night. You need an egg yolk, Tabasco, Worcestershire sauce and a dash of vinegar.' She winked. 'Oh, and most importantly, a shot of brandy.'

Sam felt her cheeks blanch. 'I think I'll stick with water,' she said. 'I came to make sure you were okay but I can see you're in better health than me.'

'Will you stay for a coffee?' Ruby asked, patting a chrome espresso machine. 'We could sit in the garden.'

There was something behind the words, a faint whisper of neediness that Sam might have missed another time. Maybe Ruby wasn't quite as self-assured as she made out. 'Of course. I'd love to.'

The sun had burned off the autumnal dew and the morning was warm. Sam sat at the chic little patio table and let the heat soak into her skin.

'I do hope you're wearing SPF, Sam,' Ruby called as she finished planting some bulbs in a glistening blue ceramic pot.

'Don't worry,' Sam said. 'My skin cream is packed with SPF and a whole lot more. It's got more vitamins than my five a day.'

'Good. Helen Mirren told me to never to be without it when we were with the Royal Shakespeare Company in the seventies. "Darling Ruby," she said, "the sun is your most vicious critic. Fend it off at all costs." I've never forgotten.'

Sam grinned. Ruby's fondness for spirits certainly hadn't dulled her memory. But it had taken its toll in other ways – there had been an unmistakable tremor to her hand as she'd held the small cups to the espresso machine. Sam's smile faded as she remembered the way her father's hands had trembled the morning after a heavy night. He'd been a fan of the hair-of-the-dog hangover cure too, which had inevitably fed a dependency that had ruined his marriage and driven him from his daughters. Had Ruby been a drinker before she'd met Andrew Chapman or had he turned her into one? Sam didn't know but it looked very much as though Ruby was on the same slippery slope as her father.

She gave her head a slight shake. 'I can't believe it's October already. Are you coming to the masked ball?'

'Wouldn't miss it for the world. I think I've still got my mask from *The Merchant of Venice* in '82. How clever of you to give us the chance to dress up for Halloween.'

'And then it will be Christmas,' Sam observed. 'What are your plans? Have you got family to visit?'

Ruby didn't look up. 'No plans, other than propping up your rather lovely bar and seeing who I can catch under the mistletoe.'

Was it Sam's imagination or was the older woman's carefree tone slightly forced? Did she have family somewhere? Or was it simply that she missed Andrew? Christmas wasn't always a time of good cheer, not for everyone.

'But it's ages away yet – who knows what might happen?' Ruby went on, getting to her feet and dusting the soil from her gloves. 'I might get an invitation from that delightful Hiddleston boy I've seen so much of on the television. Or, even less likely, my son might call.'

She sat on one of the chairs and reached for her coffee while Sam gaped at her. 'Your son? I didn't know you had one.'

Ruby sighed. 'I don't really, not any more. He was something of an *unexpected* delivery, you see, and I was at the height of my career. You couldn't have a baby and a successful career in those days, the two simply didn't mix, so I let his father do most of the upbringing. By the time work slowed down enough for me to draw breath it was too late to be his mother.'

'But he must have understood once he was older,' Sam said, feeling a sting of indignation on Ruby's behalf. 'You needed to work.'

Ruby tipped her head. 'He tried,' she said lightly. 'But he wasn't a fan of my drinking, either. I'm afraid I – I rather disgusted him.'

For the second time in as many minutes, Sam found herself gaping. 'But he – you—'

The other woman patted her hand. 'Really, Sam, it's not so hard to understand. You've felt that way too. It's why you lost contact with your father all those years ago.'

Sam felt heat start to rise up her neck and onto her cheeks. Ruby was right; she *had* felt revulsion when she saw her father drunk and stumbling. But she'd been a child then and Andrew Chapman had never written once he'd left, never given his daughters a way to stay in contact. As she'd grown up she'd understood his addiction, although the deep aversion whenever she'd thought of him had stayed with her, meaning she tried not to think of him at all. And perhaps on a subconscious level she'd chosen to focus on the parent who did want her, not the one who hadn't. Maybe she had more in common with Ruby's son than she liked to admit.

'You're right,' she said quietly, 'that's exactly how I felt. But you're not like my father. I know you loved him but even you must have known what a monster he was when he drank.'

Ruby gazed at her for a long moment. 'I know he hurt you,' she said, reaching for Sam's hand again. 'I know he gave you plenty of reasons to hate him. But I also know he loved you and he tried so many times to stop drinking. The trouble is, once alcohol sinks its claws into you, it doesn't like to let go. Not without a fight.'

'And how about you?' Sam asked, squeezing the other woman's fingers. 'Has it got its claws into you?'

Ruby withdrew her hand and tilted her head to the sun. 'Oh no, darling, I could give it up any time I like. Now, don't let me keep you. I'm sure a busy girl like you has somewhere else to be.'

Nessie left Sam and Connor to handle the Sunday lunchtime rush and took Patrick on a tour of the village. The leaves were just starting to change colour on the trees along the riverbank, turning from glossy green to amber and gold and brown, and the graveyard of St Mary's church was littered with early casualties from the gale the night before. She pointed out her father's grave, passed by the stone belonging to Eliza Rhys, and led Patrick back towards the green, hurrying past the Post Office in case Franny was on the prowl.

'You really love this place, don't you?' Patrick asked, after she had cooed over the cakes in the window of Martha's bakery and run through the familiar family names on the war memorial.

'Yes,' Nessie said simply. She took a deep breath. 'Which is why I'm going to stay here.'

Patrick went still. 'Right,' he said. 'You mean alone. Without me.'

She nodded and glanced towards the Star and Sixpence. 'Sam and I have worked hard to build the pub back up to what it is. I don't want to give all that up to move back to Surrey with you. I'm sorry.'

He took her hand and squeezed it. 'But you wouldn't have to. I'd move up here.'

She stared at him in shock. 'But what about your work? The business?'

'I'd come and work with you,' he said, beaming at her. 'You could do with a new computerised till system, the one you've got looks like it runs on steam. And I could link it into your stock-keeping systems, make it easier to re-order. Your website is a bit cheap-looking too, if you don't mind me saying so.'

He'd better not let Sam hear him say that, Nessie thought faintly as Patrick went on and on listing the things he saw were wrong at the Star and Sixpence; she'd spent a small fortune on getting the site professionally developed and managed all the content herself.

'So you wouldn't have to leave Little Monkham,' Patrick finished, raising her hand to his lips to kiss it. 'I'll give up everything for you instead.'

Nessie felt the world whirling around her. 'Patrick, I don't think that's a very good idea.'

His face fell. 'Obviously I don't mean straight away. We'll take things slowly, get to know each other again and then I'll move in.' He gazed into her eyes. 'Deep down, I know you still love me, Ness.'

'But—'

He placed a finger on her lips. 'Don't answer now.'

She removed his finger and took a step back. 'No. I think we should be really honest with each other—'

'You're right,' he interrupted, 'we should. I didn't want to tell you this, didn't want to put any pressure on you but since we're being honest . . . the business isn't going so well. In fact, it's on the verge of going under.'

Nessie gasped. 'But it was doing so well! What happened?'

'You left,' Patrick said, spreading his hands. 'It all went wrong once you'd gone. I tried to keep on top of the appointments and the invoices but I'd get it all wrong, put the wrong amounts or turn up on the wrong day. Clients started to back out of their contracts and I couldn't persuade them to change their minds.'

Nessie stared, unable to take it in. 'Why didn't you get someone in to help? A PA or an assistant?'

His face flushed as he shrugged. 'I didn't want to face how much you'd done, couldn't admit I needed help. By the time I'd got over that, it was too late and I couldn't afford to employ anyone.'

'So that's why you're really here,' Nessie said, feeling a sick realisation creep over her. 'You want me to come and sort things out.'

'No!' Patrick exclaimed, looking aghast. 'No, that's just a side-effect, one less thing holding me in Surrey. I'm here for you, Ness. I'm nothing without you.'

He gazed at her helplessly and she was horrified to see there were tears in his eyes.

'I love you,' he whispered. 'I've always loved you and I always will. Don't shut the door on us.'

Nessie felt a shiver of fear run through her as she heard the desperation in his voice. How could she tell him about Owen now? What would he do? 'You can't stay here,' she said, her voice sounding rough and strange in her ears. She clutched at the first straw that came to her. 'Sam would kill us both. But I'll take a look at your accounts and see if there's anything I can do.'

He started to interrupt her again, and she held up a hand. 'Don't push it, Patrick.'

Patrick grabbed her fingers again, squeezing so hard her knuckles hurt. 'Thank you. I knew you'd sort me out. You always did.'

Nessie managed an unhappy smile. It looked as though Patrick's problems were hers again, at least until she could find a way to make him let her go.

The Little Monkham Book Club met at the Star and Sixpence on the first Tuesday of the month. Officially, they were there to discuss whatever book Franny had selected for them but Nessie suspected more than one of the members treated it as a wine tasting evening while pretending to have read more than the first few pages.

Nessie tried not to look up hopefully each time the door opened but she couldn't help it. Owen sometimes joined in, if the chosen book appealed to him, and she thought this month's title – a twisty-turny psychological suspense – might have been one he'd enjoy. Franny was there of course, keeping order. Also clustered around the tables in front of the fire was Martha from the bakery, Henry Fitzsimmons, Barbara Smith, whose daughter, JoJo, had held her wedding reception at the Star and Sixpence in June, and Ruby. Nessie wondered whether Henry felt intimidated by the women around him but he appeared to be enjoying himself under Franny's watchful gaze. And then, just as she was calling the meeting to order, Owen arrived.

Nessie did her best to smile as he came up to the bar. 'The usual?'

Owen nodded. 'Please. I wasn't sure I was going to make it; Kathryn thought she might have plans for this evening but they fell through at the last minute.'

'Oh?' Nessie said, wondering whether Kathryn had taken her advice and spoken to her brother about taking some time away from him and Luke.

'Still, her loss is my gain.' He glanced over his shoulder and lowered his voice. 'Martha told me earlier that she

Googled a few reviews of the book and read the last few pages. A tenner says Franny rumbles her by the end of the evening.'

Nessie laughed. 'I don't think you'll find anyone in Little Monkham crazy enough to take that bet. Franny makes Sherlock look slow on the uptake sometimes.'

She placed his drink on the bar. He took a sip then glanced around as though looking for someone. 'Are you on your own tonight?'

Was he asking where Patrick was, Nessie wondered, or Sam? 'Yes. It's Connor's night off and Sam is upstairs working on a press release. Did you hear we'd won the Real Ale Drinkers' Regional Pub of the Year award?'

'No,' Owen replied, looking delighted. 'But I'm not surprised. Does Franny know?'

'Not yet. I think Sam wants to keep it for protection in case we do something to annoy her within the next few weeks.'

Owen laughed. 'Good plan. Distraction is often the best way with Franny.'

He looked around again and seemed to be about to ask her something else when Franny's imperious voice rang out. 'Owen, are you here to talk books or to romance the landlady?'

Mouth twisting with amusement, Owen gave Nessie an apologetic shrug and made his way over to the table, where Henry clapped him on the shoulder. 'I didn't know the second one was an option,' he said.

'Not for you, it isn't,' Franny said, peering over her wire glasses sternly. She held up a copy of the book, neatly divided by different coloured Post-it notes. 'Now, let's get down to business. Who thought the hero was a spoiled, whining moron?'

The discussion began to flow and things were just getting heated between Franny and Ruby when there was a loud click and the room was plunged into darkness.

Nessie hissed in irritation. The electrics had been temperamental when they'd first moved into the Star and Sixpence and they'd spent a small fortune having the building rewired. But this was the second time the switch had tripped this month. 'Don't panic, everyone,' she called, fumbling under the bar. 'I've got a torch here somewhere.'

The fridges had stayed on, as had the beer pumps, so Nessie knew it wasn't a power cut. In the light from the fire, she saw Owen get up and make his way towards her. 'Need any help?'

'Not unless you've got a torch on you,' Nessie replied. 'There's no way I'm going down those cellar steps in the dark — a-ha!'

She pulled out a thin black cylinder and switched it on. A beam of light cut through the gloom. 'Come on then,' she told Owen. 'You can teach me the ways of the fuse box, oh wise one.'

It was strange being in the cellar with Owen. Nessie was careful to keep her distance but she couldn't stay too far away or he'd be left in total darkness. They edged their way down the stairs, navigated around the barrels and past the stacked boxes of wine for Oktoberfest to reach the furthest corner. Once there, Owen flicked up the plastic casing and ran his fingers across the switches until he found the problem. Suddenly the cellar was full of light and both Owen and Nessie found themselves blinking.

'It's usually this middle one,' Owen said, pointing to a small plastic lever that looked like all the others. 'That's the one that controls the lights.'

Nessie sighed. 'I thought the electricians had fixed this when they put the new lights in.'

'They probably did,' Owen said, shrugging. 'But sometimes the switches just trip for no apparent reason.'

'And sometimes they have a very good reason,' Nessie added. 'We'll keep an eye on things, thanks.'

She started to turn away but Owen touched her arm. 'Before you go, there's something I've been meaning to ask you.'

Nessie felt her heartbeat quicken. Was he going to ask her about Patrick? Or – her heart stuttered – was he going to ask her out? 'Go on,' she said warily.

Owen gazed down at her. 'I don't know if you're aware but there's a very good meteor shower due about halfway through October. They're called the Orionids, and Kathryn, Luke and I usually head out around midnight to watch them from one of the fields away from the light pollution of the village.'

Nessie frowned. She'd heard of the other meteor shower, the one that usually happened in August, but she hadn't thought to go outside to watch them.

'And since Kathryn can't make it this year, Luke wondered – well, both of us really – we wondered whether you might like to come stargazing with us.'

Nessie hesitated. It sounded wonderful but a night beneath the stars seemed like a romantic thing to do and she wasn't sure she could handle any more confusion right now. Then again, Luke would be there and after Owen's reaction the last time they'd spoken, Nessie was almost certain romance was the last thing on his mind.

'You could bring Patrick if you wanted to,' he said, flattening any remaining worries Nessie had about his intentions.

'Can I think about it?' she asked. Then she replayed the words in her head and cringed. 'I don't mean I want to think about bringing Patrick – I can't, he's gone back to Surrey. I meant I want to think about going with you. We've got Oktoberfest this weekend and then Sam will be busy organising the Halloween ball so I'll probably be busier than normal.'

'I understand,' Owen said. He paused and Nessie wondered if he was going to dig further about Patrick. But he smiled instead. 'It would be lovely if you could join us but even if you don't come, can I ask you to cross your fingers for clear skies? It's no fun watching the stars in a storm.'

Amen to that, Nessie thought as she climbed the stairs back to the bar. The last thing they needed was more choppy weather, either inside or outside their relationship.

Chapter Thirty

'Ooh, I bet he's going to introduce you to the big dipper!' Sam exclaimed the next morning when Nessie told her the news over breakfast.

Nessie gave her a level look. 'Really, Sam, is there any sexual innuendo you won't stoop to?'

'Nope,' Sam said with an unrepentant grin. 'You keep setting them up and I'll keep knocking them out of the park. But sitting out under the stars is very romantic, that's all I'm saying.'

'Luke will be there,' Nessie pointed out.

'That's where snuggling under blankets comes into its own,' Sam said. 'They cover a multitude of sins.'

'It's not a date,' Nessie insisted. 'Owen made that very clear. He even invited Patrick.'

Sam sighed. What was it with her sister and Owen? They seemed to go out of their way to invent reasons not to be together. It was maddening. 'He was being polite. You did kind of suggest you might get back together with Patrick.'

'But I didn't mean it!' Nessie protested, going red. 'I just wanted to make him jealous, that's all.'

Sam regarded her sister with a mixture of amusement and affection. 'You're my sister and I love you, Nessie, but you're terrible at this kind of thing. Honesty is the best policy here – just tell Owen the truth.'

Nessie put her head in her hands. 'I don't know what to say. It was easier when I thought all Patrick wanted was me but now I know about all his other problems it's harder to walk away.'

Sam frowned. She was beginning to wonder whether she'd severely underestimated her brother-in-law. He was turning out to be more manipulative than she'd thought. 'Do you still love Patrick?'

'No,' Nessie said without hesitation. 'I mean, I still care about him, obviously. But I'm not in love with him.'

'Then don't you think you should let him find someone who is?' Sam asked, her voice gently reproachful. 'The longer he keeps hoping you'll rescue him, the longer it will be before he sorts himself out and moves on.'

Nessie stared at her wordlessly for a moment, then nodded. 'You're right.'

'And that frees you up to follow your own heart, with Owen,' Sam went on. 'You deserve to be happy too.'

Her sister's eyes filled with tears. 'I know.'

Sam squeezed her arm. 'Tell Owen everything,' she said.

315

'And do it soon, before he convinces himself you've slipped away. Then you can let the stars work their magic and we can all breathe a sigh of relief.'

Friday lunchtime arrived faster than Sam would have liked, and with it the final preparations for Oktoberfest. She finished draping the red, yellow and black material across the pub ceiling and stepped down from the stepladder.

'What do you think?' she asked Connor, who'd been steadying the ladder while she worked. 'Does this say "Bavarian Beer Tent" to you?'

The cellarman gazed around thoughtfully, taking in the colourful drapes, the red and white checked tablecloths on the long trestle tables and the distinctly Germanic decorations adorning the walls. He grunted. 'I hope you're not expecting me to wear Lederhosen.'

'No more than I'll be dressed as a beer wench,' Sam said, pulling a face. 'I have got us all hats, though. How are the kegs looking?'

One end of the pub had been taken over by a row of steel barrels, manhandled into place by Connor and each filled with authentic German ales. Customers bought tokens at the bar, which Connor would then exchange for a foaming stein of beer. A gazebo had been set up in the garden where visitors could try a variety of different bratwurst and sauerkraut. It was shaping up to be a great weekend but Sam knew Connor was worried about the temperamental

Bavarian barrels. A beer festival was only as good as its beer, after all.

'They're okay,' Connor said. 'Tasting good, which is the important thing.'

Sam made her way behind the bar and fired up the playlist of traditional oompah band music she'd compiled especially for the Oktoberfest weekend. Connor looked pained.

'Do we have to listen to this all weekend?'

Sam nodded. 'Of course. When in Bavaria, Connor . . .'

The cellarman muttered about ear plugs and wandered over to the beer barrels. Wait until he heard the oompah cover versions she'd slipped in here and there, Sam thought with a grin. Britney's *Toxic* had never sounded so good.

Trade built up steadily from lunchtime to a decent-sized crowd by around five-thirty. As the evening went on, Sam was pleased to see many of the village regulars among the throng – Owen, Franny and Henry, Martha's husband, Rob, and a couple of the lads from the butcher's next door, as well as some less familiar faces – sampling the Oktoberfest delights. Even Father Goodluck put in an appearance and Sam was glad to see him. He'd been supportive of Sam and her sister and often did the scoring for the monthly quiz night. Knowing he had a soft spot for Guinness, Sam encouraged him to try one of the darker German ales and was delighted by the grin that split his face.

'Excellent, Sam,' he said, taking another long swig. 'Truly delicious.'

She was so busy that she didn't see Joss come in. It wasn't until Nessie nudged her and nodded towards the bar that Sam noticed he was there, with a pretty brunette on his arm. The sight of him there, with what was obviously a new girlfriend, was like a sledgehammer into Sam's stomach. You're over him, she reminded herself, trying not to stare at his freshly shaven face. Joss had always had a beard, well-kept but not too groomed, and it was one of the things that had attracted Sam to him. She found it very odd to see him without it now, like he'd somehow forgotten to get fully dressed that morning. He looked younger, more boyish, as though he'd lost five years off his age. Sam wasn't sure she liked it.

'Who's that he's with?' Nessie whispered during a brief lull in trade.

Sam risked another glance, pretty sure she'd never seen the girl before. She couldn't live in Little Monkham, she decided, unless she'd been hiding under a rock for the last ten months or so. Whoever she was, it meant Joss was happy and moving on, which Sam knew should have made her glad – things hadn't worked out between them but she didn't bear him any ill-will. The trouble was she *didn't* feel glad. The trouble was her immediate reaction had been quite a different emotion, one she recognised immediately: jealousy.

She gave herself a mental shake. 'I don't know but she looks nice.'

Nessie slipped an arm around her shoulders. 'Courage, Sam. I know it's hard.'

Sam blinked hard against the sudden rush of heat behind her eyes. 'He looks happy, don't you think?'

'He looks *different*,' her sister said, raising her eyebrows. 'What on earth possessed him to shave off his beard?'

'Maybe his new girlfriend doesn't like it,' Sam suggested, remembering how soft and silky the blond hair had felt beneath her fingers. 'Some women hate them.'

'He looks about twelve,' Nessie replied, with a dismissive shake of her head. 'It's a good job he doesn't work behind the bar any more – no one would believe he was old enough.'

Worried he would catch them staring, Sam changed the subject and did her best to push Joss out of her mind, something that was helped by an unexpected arrival just before nine o'clock.

'Nick!' Sam exclaimed as he appeared before her at the bar. 'What are you doing here?'

He grinned at her, causing audible sighs from several nearby women, and shrugged. 'What can I say? I missed you and you made it very clear you couldn't leave the pub this weekend so . . . here I am.'

Sam felt her spirits lift. He'd been filming in Cornwall again and must have driven for hours to reach her. 'It's good to see you,' she admitted with a smile. 'Can I get you a drink?'

He lifted his bag. 'Actually, I think I'd like you to show me to my room.'

She shook her head. 'You mean my room?'

'Nope,' Nick said, his grin widening. 'I mean my room. If you check your bookings, I think you'll find the four-poster room is reserved for a Mr Turner, who said he'd be checking in late – around nine o'clock?'

Nessie gasped. 'It is – I was just wondering where he was.'

Nick fixed his eyes on Sam. 'I wanted to surprise you.'

Sam had never seen so many women swoon at once. She gazed into his dark eyes and felt something inside her shift. It was very good to see him. 'You've certainly achieved that,' she said, smiling. 'Come on, I'll show you the way.'

Nessie winked as she walked past. 'Don't rush back.'

The lights were low in the four-poster guest room. Nessie must have sneaked up at some point in the last hour, Sam realised, because there was a bottle of Prosecco on ice in the antique champagne bucket by the bed and fresh cookies on the table beneath the window.

Nick dropped his bag by the door and ran a hand over his stubbly chin. 'You don't mind, do you?' he said in an uncertain voice. 'Me just turning up out of the blue like this, I mean?'

Sam stared at him. She'd never seen him unsure before; Nick Borrowdale was usually supremely confident in everything he did. 'Why would I mind? I love having you here and God knows, you're good for business.'

'Yes, but I've never turned up uninvited before,' he said.

'I've booked the room for tomorrow as well but I don't have to stay, not if you'd rather I went.'

She let out an astonished laugh. 'Of course you can stay. Bloody hell, Nick, what's got into you? You're acting like a lovesick teenager.'

He smiled and a touch of his trademark smoothness returned. 'Sorry. It's been a long week.'

Sam crossed the room and reached up to plant a kiss on his cheek. 'Tell me about it. But seeing you makes everything better.'

He gazed at her for a moment. 'Good. Now, I suppose we'd better get back downstairs before Franny decides we're up to something naughty.'

His eyes lingered on hers for a fraction too long, just enough to remind Sam of the nights they'd spent together in the past, and she realised with a jolt that something naughty was exactly what she felt like getting up to. She shook the thought away and summoned up a smile. 'Don't. I'm pretty sure some of the village women are sticking pins into an effigy of me already over you.'

He nodded at the bottle in the champagne bucket. 'Are you going to help me to drink that?'

Sam hesitated. Prosecco and Nick were a dangerous combination. 'Ask me again later.'

Nick's mouth quirked into a smile, his confidence obviously restored. 'Don't worry, I will.'

★　★　★

Sam knew Joss would be watching her when she came back downstairs with Nick. They hadn't been gone long enough to be accused of anything – not that it was any of Joss's business anyway – but she still felt his gaze burning into her. He'd always suspected there was more to her relationship with Nick than she admitted, had never accepted the two of them were just friends no matter how many times Sam had tried to reassure him. She supposed he must be taking a grim satisfaction in seeing the newspaper photos of her and Nick together now, congratulating himself on being right. Let him, she decided. He'd made his choice when he'd walked out.

Nick, on the other hand, didn't seem to have noticed Joss was there; he was too busy charming the rest of the villagers. Sam saw Joss and his new girlfriend leave not long after – sour grapes, she wondered, or fear that he might lose another girlfriend to the actor.

It took longer than usual to get everyone to leave at closing time but eventually the bar was empty. Nick nodded at Connor.

'I'm amazed Sam hasn't got you in costume,' he said, smirking. 'A big lad like you in leather would certainly bring in the ladies.'

Connor grinned. 'I'm not sure the wife would approve.'

Sam shook her head. 'We're saving the costumes for the masked ball and letting the beer do the talking this weekend.' She fixed Nick with a look. 'Speaking of costumes, do you know what you're planning to wear?'

Nick tapped his nose. 'It's a surprise.'

'Only, a few of the village ladies have asked whether you'd be prepared to recreate the topless scene from *Smugglers' Inn* and I said I'd ask,' Sam said innocently.

Nick sighed. 'It's a good thing I don't mind being objectified, isn't it?'

Sam sent him a level look. 'You love it, Nick Borrowdale. Don't pretend otherwise.'

'Don't worry, I have my costume sorted,' he said, winking. 'You won't be disappointed.'

Shortly after that, Connor and Tilly said goodnight and headed off. Nessie made her excuses and left Sam and Nick sitting beside the fire, talking over old times until Sam yawned and stretched.

Nick took her hand. 'You don't have to, you know.'

Sam felt her cheeks flush as she looked away. This was ridiculous, she thought, she'd spent the night with Nick plenty of times before and they'd always had a good time. Why was she suddenly coming over all coy and embarrassed?

'I know.'

Nick studied her. 'I've put you on the spot by coming here.'

'No, it's not that. It's . . .' Sam trailed off, not sure what was troubling her. And then it dawned on her: the problem was Joss. This was his territory; if she slept with Nick here it would seem disrespectful somehow. Although Joss hadn't respected her very much, a little voice whispered, when he'd brought his new girlfriend to the pub. So did it matter very much if she slept with Nick again? Joss had moved on; it was time she did too. And who better to move on with than gorgeous, sexy Nick?

'It's nothing,' she said firmly. Slowly and deliberately, she leaned forwards until her face was close to his. 'Shall we have some fun?'

One hand cupped her face, drawing her closer still. 'Only if you're sure?'

Her lips brushed his and she felt a slow burn start in her belly. 'I'm sure.'

Nick pulled her close and kissed her. It was new and familiar both at the same time. After a few moments, they broke apart. Sam's breath felt ragged in her throat; she'd forgotten just how good he was. 'So do you – uh – think that Prosecco will be chilled enough by now?' she asked, gazing into his eyes.

Nick smiled. 'I think it's going to be perfect.'

'Good,' Sam said, pulling him to his feet. 'Let's go and find out.'

Chapter Thirty-One

It took Sam a few bleary-eyed blinks to remember she was in the guest room upstairs, and a couple more to remember the sequence of events that had led her there. She twisted sideways to find Nick sprawled beside her, his dark hair tousled against the white Egyptian cotton bedsheets. There had been Prosecco, she recalled, and many long kisses. Then she and Nick had undressed each other, taking more time to explore than they ever had during their previous encounters. He hadn't changed much – more toned and muscular than she remembered but essentially the same Nick. What was different was Sam's sense that this meant more to him than it had before. Previously their nights together had been based on a shared sense of fun and mutual convenience but this time, Nick had sought her out, made a deliberate and long journey to be with her. This time the stakes felt higher and that troubled her.

She checked the time: seven-thirty. Nessie would be in the kitchen preparing breakfast; there was no way Sam could sneak back to her room without being caught – not with the creaky floorboards that littered the route. Then again, she was pretty sure Nessie would have put two and two together already, a suspicion that was confirmed when breakfast for two was left outside the door just after eight.

Sam woke Nick, avoiding the arm that tried to snake around her waist. 'Breakfast. There's a full English here with your name on it if you want it.'

She lifted the silver cloche cover from the plate and the aroma of bacon rose into the air. Nick smiled. 'Oh, I want it. But if my personal trainer ever asks, I had a protein shake and peanut butter on wholemeal toast, okay?'

Nessie made no comment when Sam brought the empty trays down an hour later, her hair damp from the shower. She watched over the top of the newspaper as Sam loaded the dishwasher and poured herself a mug of tea.

'How's the weather looking?' Sam asked as she settled at the kitchen table.

'Not bad,' Nessie said. 'A bit crisp but that should burn off once the sun comes out. How's our Mr Turner?'

Sam couldn't help smiling. 'Fine, as far as I can tell. He says the bed is very comfortable and he's happy to stay a second night.'

Nessie fired a curious look her way. 'And?'

'And what?' Sam replied. 'I'm fine too.'

'Not that,' Nessie said dismissively. 'The bed. What did you think of it?'

'Oh,' Sam said. 'Very nice. The posts came in very handy when we—'

Nessie held up a hand. 'Spare me the details,' she said with a delicate shudder. 'As long as you didn't break anything then I don't need to know.'

The only thing Sam was worried about breaking was her friendship with Nick. But this wasn't the first time they'd spent the night together; surely that wasn't going to be a problem? 'We didn't,' she assured her sister. 'Now, what's the plan for today?'

They discussed the day's schedule: Connor was introducing a couple of new ales to encourage return visits among the beer aficionados, and come rain or shine, sausages and pretzels would be on sale in the garden, beneath the gazebo. In the evening, Sam had booked a live oompah band to perform and she was hoping they'd play some of the cheeky covers she'd added to the pub's playlist: there was only so much traditional Bavarian music she could take in one day after all.

'How about you?' Sam asked her sister. 'Will Owen be sampling some more of the ales tonight?'

'No,' Nessie said. 'Kathryn has an overnight gig so Owen needs to stay in with Luke. He said he'd try to pop in tomorrow lunchtime.'

'Good,' Sam said in satisfaction. 'You can tell him you accept his kind invitation to snog under the stars.'

Nessie laughed. 'It's hardly that. But yes, I'll tell him I'd love to come.'

Sam grinned mischievously. 'Everything comes to she who grasps it, Nessie. Trust me on this.'

'You've got such a filthy mind,' Nessie said, batting her arm with the folded-up newspaper. Then her expression softened a bit. 'But it's good to see you happy with someone again, especially after what happened over Will.'

'It feels good,' Sam said, pushing away the momentary pang when she thought of everything that particular mistake had cost her. 'And it's your turn next.'

Nessie opened her mouth and Sam knew she was about to demur, to make some kind of self-deprecating comment. Then she smiled. 'I hope so. I really do. There's just the small matter of my divorce to settle before then.'

Patrick, Sam thought, a prickle of irritation piercing her own contentment. The sooner Nessie got her Decree Nisi through, the better.

Sam was on her way back from the butcher's with a fresh load of bratwurst when she saw Joss heading down Star Lane towards her. She hesitated, thought about doubling back, and then squared her shoulders. It was time she and Joss acted like grown-ups and cleared the air instead of avoiding each other all the time. The Star and Sixpence was the only pub in the village, part of the community, and she didn't want him to feel as though he wasn't welcome. But Joss clearly had other ideas – the moment he saw her he turned around and hurried in the opposite direction.

Sam sighed and continued on her way back to the pub. Clearing the air was going to have to wait.

Chapter Thirty-Two

Patrick's accounts were driving Nessie to distraction. He hadn't exaggerated when he'd said the business was in danger of going under – his income had dwindled away alarmingly and from the looks of things he had serious cash-flow issues. No wonder he seemed so keen on moving to Little Monkham, Nessie thought, passing a weary hand over her face; it must seem like the answer to all his problems. And it could easily be enough to convince him he still loved her – desperation did strange things to people, after all, and she and Patrick hadn't ever really fallen out. They'd just drifted apart.

She stretched and wandered over to gaze out of the living-room window. The trees on the green were fully dressed for autumn now, their leaves a glorious mix of tawny and russet and red. A few leaves were swirling lazily across the grass but most had accumulated in piles around the base of the trunks, filling Nessie with the sudden urge to gather great armfuls to throw into the air. Soon it would be winter and a year since she and Sam had arrived at the Star and Sixpence. So much had changed . . .

She still hadn't explained the situation with Patrick to Owen. He'd popped into the bar a few days after Oktoberfest to let her know he and Luke planned to watch the meteors on Friday 21st and she'd almost told him then. But the middle of the pub felt too public for such a personal conversation, no matter how quiet it was, and she'd simply said she'd see what she could do. Sam had accused her of chickening out and Nessie hadn't been able to deny it. And now it was the 18th. If she wanted to join Owen and Luke beneath the stars, she needed to come clean with Owen soon.

'A penny for your thoughts,' Sam said, walking into the living room.

Nessie turned around and her gaze came to rest on the haphazard pile of paperwork next to the laptop on the coffee table. 'I'm going to need much more than a penny,' she said with a sigh.

Sam pulled a face. 'Let me guess. Patrick.'

Nessie nodded. 'It's a mess. I can't believe he didn't get anyone in to help him.'

'Like he said, he didn't want to admit he needed it,' Sam said. 'Typical man.'

'It has made me wonder whether he really wants what he thinks he wants,' Nessie said hesitantly. 'For him and me, I mean.'

331

'I must admit I've wondered that too,' Sam said. 'Obviously, I think he was crazy to let you slip away in the first place, but there's something off in the way he's acting, don't you think? If he's so keen to rekindle your relationship, why didn't he say something earlier – when you first applied for the divorce, for example?'

'He says he suddenly realised he didn't want to lose me.'

Sam sniffed. 'That didn't seem to worry him when you moved out. Look, Ness, I don't mean to suggest he's got an ulterior motive in all this, but I think you need to be careful not to get sucked in. By all means do what you can with the accounts. But don't try to bail him out.' She shook her head wryly. 'He got himself into this mess, he can get himself out.'

Sam was right, Nessie decided. She'd work out an action plan to turn the business around but she wouldn't do the work for him.

'Have you told Owen about any of this yet?' Sam said.

Nessie tried not to flinch. How did Sam seem to know what she was thinking? 'No.'

Sam glanced at her phone. 'Go and find him now. It's almost lunchtime, he'll probably be ready for a break.' She fixed Nessie with a determined stare. 'Get it over with.'

'He'll be in the forge,' Nessie objected. 'I don't want to interrupt him.'

Sam let out a growl of frustration. 'Dear God, Nessie, you can dither for England. Just go and do it. Now.'

Taking a deep breath, Nessie did as she was told. She

knew from years of experience that Sam didn't let go once she had the bit between her teeth. And in any case, her sister was right. This was a conversation Nessie and Owen needed to have.

The forge was warm when she slipped inside, although the fire beneath the wide steel hood on the far side of the room was banked low and burned a sullen red instead of its usual incandescent orange. As always, the air was faintly tinged with smoke and the scent of sulphur. Owen stood beside the workbench in one corner, polishing a beautifully twisted toasting fork in a vice. His grey t-shirt was smudged with dust and his expression was intent as he turned the blackened steel into burnished silver. Nessie watched in fascination for a few seconds; she loved seeing Owen at work, loved his total absorption in the task at hand. And she couldn't deny that she'd found watching him swing the hammer hard enough to send sparks flying from a glowing piece of metal incredibly sexy in the past. It was probably a good thing he was engaged in a less-active task today. She didn't need any distractions.

She cleared her throat. Owen looked up. 'Hello, Nessie,' he said, lifting the protective glasses from his eyes and smiling. 'What brings you here?'

Nessie felt her mouth go dry. Now that she was here she didn't want to talk about Patrick. She could make an excuse, invent a reason for her visit that had nothing to do with her husband . . . but then she'd have to face Sam. She swallowed hard and forced herself to speak. 'There's something I need to tell you. Have you got a minute?'

He stepped away from the workbench, his eyes concerned. 'Of course. Let me just clean up and we can go somewhere a bit more comfortable.'

They opted for a walk down to the bridge. Nessie didn't waste any time – she knew that if she didn't start talking immediately she'd lose her nerve. When she'd finished, Owen leaned against the stone parapet and studied her carefully. 'You're sure you don't want to give things another go? With Patrick, I mean.'

Nessie took a deep breath and met his questioning gaze. 'I'm sure. And in time, he'll see that it's all for the best too. Sam says it's time we all moved on.'

Owen tilted his head. 'She's a wise woman, your sister.'

They stood in silence for a moment, gazing at the branches swaying in the breeze, listening to the music of the river as it gushed under the bridge. 'It doesn't seem like five minutes since these were all green,' Owen said after a while, as a flurry of crisp brown leaves cascaded by. 'Nothing stays the same for long, does it?'

Nessie hesitated. Did he mean the trees or life in general? 'When I was young I used to feel sad when I saw the leaves all curled up and dead,' she said, watching the leaves twirl. 'Then one day, my mother explained that it's all part of a bigger pattern. That the old leaves have to make way for new ones in the spring, so the tree can grow.'

Owen's eyes crinkled at the edges. 'We can learn a lot from nature, don't you think?'

This time Nessie was sure he wasn't just talking about the trees. She held his gaze and smiled. 'Yes, I think we probably can.'

Sam stared at the packed rucksack on the kitchen table in disbelief.

'Bloody hell, Nessie, you're going for a few hours, not a week!'

Nessie folded her arms defensively. 'Owen said to wrap up warm, so I'm taking our picnic blanket and the tartan rug. I've also packed a flask of hot chocolate, in case Luke wants a drink; three hot water bottles and a few snacks.'

'Hardly anything at all, then,' Sam said, shaking her head in amusement. 'You've probably got room for the sink if you want it.'

'Go ahead,' Nessie said. 'Laugh if you want. But if I'm going to be spending the next two hours sitting in a pitch black field staring at the sky, I want to be properly prepared.'

'Fair enough,' Sam conceded. 'Hadn't you better get going, though? It's eleven o'clock already.'

Nessie pulled on her warmest coat and hoisted the rucksack onto her shoulders. 'Okay,' she said, wondering whether the hot water bottles had been a mistake. 'I'm ready.'

Her sister smiled. 'May the force be with you, or

whatever that ridiculous saying is. And if the opportunity for a fumble under the blanket presents itself, then go for it.'

'Sam!' Nessie couldn't help laughing. 'All right, maybe I will.'

'Good girl,' Sam said. 'There's hope for you yet.'

Owen and Luke were waiting at the door of Snowdrop Cottage.

'Ready?' Owen asked as Nessie reached them.

'Can't wait,' she replied warmly.

Luke showed no signs of tiredness as they walked, even though Nessie knew it was several hours past his bedtime. His gaze was fixed hopefully on the sky. 'We might see a few meteors now, if we keep our eyes open.'

At the edge of the village, away from the glow of the street lamps, Owen handed out head torches. 'The moonlight is helpful but we don't want any accidents.'

Luke grinned, his face pale beneath the brightness of his torch. 'One year, Dad trod in a cowpat.'

'Yuck,' Nessie said, thinking of Sam's insistence that she was off for an evening of romance: there was nothing romantic about cow poo. But she was glad she'd worn her wellies. She wasn't looking forward to lying down in a field full of dung – picnic blanket or no picnic blanket – but she'd cross that bridge when she came to it.

As they got further into the field, however, she saw that she needn't have brought any blankets at all. Owen had clearly been here earlier: laid out in the middle of the bumpy grass were three deck chairs, complete with pillows and thick fleecy throws. A wicker picnic basket rested beside them.

Nessie turned to Owen. 'You've done this before.'

He smiled. 'Once or twice. I'm not going to lie, watching the Perseid meteors in August is usually more pleasant but at least it's not raining.'

Luke threw his father a scornful look. 'Obviously. We wouldn't be able to see the sky if it was raining.'

Nessie was just about to reply when a silver streak seared across the sky. 'Oh!' she gasped. 'What was that?'

Owen lifted the blanket from the nearest deck chair and ushered her into it. 'It looks like the show's about to start. Let's get comfortable.'

He draped the throw across her legs, taking the time to ensure she was snugly wrapped up, before settling into the chair beside her. Luke wriggled into position in the final seat and they sat for a moment, staring upwards.

'Oh,' Nessie said, rummaging in her rucksack. 'I almost forgot. We should drink this before it gets cold.'

She pulled out her flask. Owen grinned and reached into the wicker basket. 'Snap,' he said, holding up a flask of his own. 'I think we're sorted for hot chocolate.'

Nessie grinned. 'But did you also bring these?' she asked, pulling out a bag of mini-marshmallows.

'All right!' Luke exclaimed, his eyes lighting up. 'You can come with us again, Nessie!'

Once the hot chocolate was poured, they switched off

their head torches and settled down to watch the sky. Nessie laid her head against the pillow and gazed upwards, glad of the warm fleece to ward off the chilly night air. The stars seemed much brighter here, away from the village, and they twinkled in a way she hadn't really noticed before, as though they were trying extra hard.

'Meteor showers are named after the constellation they originate from,' Owen said softly. 'In this case, that's Orion. They're made when debris from passing comets hits our atmosphere and burns up.'

'How many will we see?' Nessie asked, scanning the sky for tell-tale flares of light.

'It's hard to say – sometimes, it's only one or two. But on a clear night like this, we could see between ten and twenty an hour.'

'There!' Luke shouted suddenly and Nessie caught a bright burst out of the corner of one eye.

'I see it!' she called excitedly. 'Oh, and there's another!'

It seemed as though they spotted one every few minutes after that. Some were brighter than others and Nessie found it was easier to relax than actively seek the flashes out.

'Wow, that one was huge,' Luke exclaimed, sounding every bit as thrilled as Nessie felt. 'Don't forget to make a wish!'

I wish I knew how Owen felt, Nessie thought, turning her face towards him even though all she could see was a faint pale outline. And then she felt a gentle tug at her blanket as

Owen's fingers crept underneath and wrapped themselves around her own. Nessie smiled in the darkness as a sudden burst of warmth flooded through her. *Wow*, she thought, turning her gaze towards the sky once more. The universe worked *fast*.

Chapter Thirty-Three

'So?' Sam demanded when she ran into Nessie on the landing the next morning.

'It was lovely,' Nessie replied, smiling. 'I think the final count was over twenty, which Luke says is better than last year.'

'I don't mean the meteors,' Sam said in exasperation. 'I mean you and Owen. Did anything happen?'

Nessie thought back to the night before when Owen had taken her hand beneath the blanket. Sam clearly expected more but for Nessie, it had been enough. 'Maybe.'

Sam groaned. 'This is like watching one of those terrible period dramas, where everyone is too uptight to even flirt. Why can't the two of you just get a room and have done with it? Then we can all get on with our lives.'

Her sister blushed. 'There's no rush, Sam. Owen and I are happy to take our time.'

'There's taking your time and then there's taking forever,' Sam said with a sigh. 'Glaciers have defrosted faster than you two move.'

Nessie pushed past her and went into the bathroom. 'If you must know, he held my hand.'

'And?'

'And nothing,' Nessie said. 'Like I said, we're taking our time.'

She closed the door, leaving Sam staring at it in disbelief. She supposed it was a step in the right direction but at this rate, she'd be fifty before the two of them got together. It was time for another strategy meeting with Kathryn.

Sam was on her way over to Snowdrop Cottage on Saturday afternoon when she saw Joss coming towards her. Her first instinct was to keep walking but he had a determined air about him and she knew there was no escape.

'Joss,' she said in a brisk tone. 'How are you?'

His blue eyes rested on hers. 'Not bad. How are things with you?'

'Fine. Busy, as always.'

He nodded. 'Oktoberfest seemed to go well. You had a good selection of beer available.'

Sam shrugged. 'I can't take the credit for that; it's all down to Connor. He's great.'

Not as good as you, she wanted to say but she knew there was nothing to be gained from praising him. He'd made his choice in the summer.

Joss shifted his weight from one foot to the other. 'Well. Like I said, it seemed to go down well.'

Sam said nothing. Up close he looked even younger without his beard, although the lines around his eyes gave his true age away. She had seen those eyes crinkle with laughter so many times while they'd been a couple. They'd laughed a lot.

'I saw you with Nick.'

It was a statement of fact, with no accusation behind the words, but Sam knew Joss well. He was needling her, trying to get a reaction. 'And I saw you with your new girlfriend. What's your point?'

He stared at her. 'Nothing. I ... I just wish you'd been honest with me from the beginning, Sam. If I'd known about you and Nick I would never have started seeing you, and we might all have been saved a lot of heartache.'

His mask of indifference slipped a little, giving her a glimpse of the hurt he clearly still nursed underneath. 'There was nothing to tell,' Sam said.

'I read the papers. I know that's not true.'

Sam growled in frustration. 'It was all an act – Nick and I were friends. And if you hadn't thrown your toys out of the pram, that's all we'd still be now.'

She knew it was the wrong thing to say but she couldn't help herself; his accusations hurt just as much now as they had months ago.

His expression closed and his lips set in a tight, thin line. 'You act like I'm just a kid, Sam, when I'm only a little bit younger than you. And whether you like it or not, you're just as much to blame for what happened with us as I am.' His hands clenched by his side. 'You kept things back, didn't tell me about Will or that you were sneaking off to meet Nick in London. You weren't honest with me – what was I supposed to think?'

'You're right,' Sam said quietly. 'I am equally to blame. And for what it's worth, I'm sorry.'

He paused. 'Do you mean that?'

She laid her hand on his arm. 'Of course I do, Joss. We were good together. I – miss you.'

Joss gazed at her for a moment, then shook her hand away. 'I don't get it. All I ever wanted was for you to let me in, to let your guard down. But you never really trusted me and that made it impossible for me to trust you.'

Sam stared at him in consternation. 'I *did* trust you!'

'Not enough,' Joss ground out. He glanced across at the Star and Sixpence. 'And you trusted Nick Borrowdale more.'

He turned on his heel.

'At least he was there for me,' she called. 'At least he showed he cared!'

Joss stopped and spun round to glare at her. 'I cared, Sam. That's the whole bloody problem.'

He strode away, leaving Sam staring after him in shock. *I cared too*, she felt like shouting, except that she knew he wouldn't believe her. He'd made up his mind about her the moment he'd found out about Will, and nothing was going to convince him otherwise.

'You look like you've seen a ghost,' Kathryn said when she opened the door to Sam. 'Don't tell me Elijah Blackheart has been up to his old tricks again?'

Sam slumped onto the living-room sofa and put her head in her hands.

'Why does everything in my life have to be so complicated?' she asked. 'Why can't things just go smoothly for a change?'

Kathryn sat down opposite her. 'What are we talking about here? Work? Relationships? A tricky new cocktail recipe?'

Sam shook her head. 'Men. I just ran into Joss and – well – let's just say I don't think we'll ever be friends.'

Kathryn raised her eyebrows. 'He's stubborn. And proud – it can't be easy for him seeing you splashed all over the papers with Nick.' She held up her hands as Sam started to speak. 'I know why you did it. I'm just saying it fanned the flames of Joss's anger, that's all.'

'His unfounded anger,' Sam pointed out defensively. 'The thing with Will happened before I'd even met Joss, remember?'

'I remember,' Kathryn replied. 'But he was always a bit jealous of Nick, a bit insecure over you. Knowing you and Nick are together now might be hard for him to take, especially if he's realised he had no one to blame but himself.'

Sam frowned. 'Do you think he has realised that?'

'What – that he acted like an idiot?' Kathryn snorted. 'Plenty of people told him he had, so I imagine the seed has been planted. Don't worry, he'll calm down. Eventually.'

Sam took a deep breath and pushed Joss from her mind. 'It doesn't really matter if he doesn't. How are things with you?'

Kathryn sat back. 'They're okay. I spoke to Owen, told him I wanted to do more gigs.'

'And?'

'And he took it well,' Kathryn said. 'So now we just need to find a way to get him out of the house and Nessie over here to babysit. Any ideas?'

Mentally, Sam flicked through the coming month. 'We've got the Halloween Ball soon but obviously they'd both be attending that, along with Luke. Can't you invite Owen to a gig, the way you did before?'

Kathryn tipped her head to one side. 'I could. I don't think he really enjoyed it but I could apply a bit of pressure, make him feel guilty for not being more supportive.'

Sam flashed her an admiring look. 'I like your thinking. When's your next gig?'

They compared diaries and picked a date when Sam thought Nessie would be free. Kathryn promised to get to work on Owen as soon as she could and Sam agreed to soften Nessie up, although she knew her sister doted on Luke and loved looking after him. The more Owen and Nessie were pushed together, the more likely it was they would give in to their obvious attraction and the happier everyone would be.

After plotting with Kathryn, Sam headed over to Weir Cottage to visit Ruby. She hadn't been in the pub the night before and while that wasn't unheard of, it was unusual. There'd been a nasty bout of flu working its way around some of the village residents and Sam wanted to be sure Ruby hadn't fallen victim to it.

There was no answer at the front door. Frowning, Sam glanced at the windows, which were still curtained even though it was now mid-afternoon. Then she let herself through the side-gate; maybe Ruby was in the garden and hadn't heard her knock.

There was no sign of her in the garden and the back door was shut too. Sam gave it an experimental rattle. It was locked. Shading her eyes, she peered through the window. What she saw made her blood run cold. Ruby was lying on the kitchen floor, motionless. A shattered bottle lay by her side.

Sam rapped sharply on the window. 'Ruby!' she shouted. 'Can you hear me?'

There was no sign that she'd heard. Pulling out her phone, Sam called Nessie.

'Does anyone have a key to Ruby's cottage?' she asked, the moment Nessie answered.

'I – I don't know,' Nessie stammered. 'I think Franny might have one, or maybe Joss – he used to take her home a lot when he still worked here. Why, what's happened?'

Joss, Sam thought, why did it have to be Joss? But there was no time to worry about that now.

'Phone them both and see if either of them can get over to Weir Cottage right now,' Sam barked. 'Ruby's had some kind of accident but I can't get in to help her. She's not moving.'

She hung up on Nessie and immediately dialled 999. She could only hope it wasn't too late.

Chapter Thirty-Four

Joss was out of breath when he met Sam by the cottage gate.

'What's wrong?' he puffed. 'Nessie said Ruby was hurt?'

'I think she's had a fall,' Sam said, leading him to the back of the cottage. 'The ambulance is on its way but I'm worried. She's not moving.'

Joss's expression was grim as he peered through the window. 'Stand back,' he told Sam, waving to one side as he lined himself up with the back door.

'What are you doing?' Sam asked in alarm. 'Don't you have a key?'

He shook his head. 'I gave it back when I left the pub. Now keep out of the way. I don't want you to get hurt too.'

Sam did as she was told, glancing down the side-path for Franny or the ambulance. There was no sign of either and every minute that passed could mean the difference between life and death for Ruby. She watched as Joss bunched his muscles and put his shoulder to the door.

The woodwork creaked but held under the first barge. Joss clenched his jaw and hit the door again, and again. On the third hit, the wood gave way and the door flew back. Joss tumbled inside.

'Are you okay?' Sam called, hurrying inside the cottage after him.

Joss rubbed and flexed his shoulder. 'I'm fine,' he said shortly. 'Check Ruby.'

Sam knelt down carefully among the shattered glass and peered at Ruby. She was pale but breathing, her eyes fluttering beneath her strangely naked eyelids. 'She's still with us,' Sam said. 'Should we try to move her? Put her into the recovery position?'

There was a clatter from outside and Franny appeared, leading the paramedics. 'Thank God,' Sam said, exchanging a relieved look with Joss.

Sam went with Ruby in the ambulance. She'd wanted to speak to Joss, to thank him for his help but he'd been deep in conversation with Franny and there'd been no time, anyway; understandably, the paramedics were keen to get Ruby to hospital as soon as possible. They thought she'd fallen in the kitchen, hitting her head on the tiled floor and knocking herself unconscious. What was really worrying them was a suspected fractured hip but they couldn't confirm without an X-ray.

So Sam had contented herself with sending a grateful smile Joss's way as the ambulance doors closed, pleased when he'd nodded in reply. Maybe, just maybe, it was the start of a ceasefire between them.

Nessie stayed behind to clear up the mess. Franny offered to help but Nessie saw a gleam in the other woman's eye that suggested she was itching to nose around and she didn't think Ruby would appreciate that so she declined.

She packaged up the broken glass – from a bottle of decent Chablis – and mopped up the spilled wine. There was an empty gin bottle on the side, which she took out to the recycling bin and what she saw there made her pause. The black basket had five empty wine bottles and another large gin bottle nestling at the bottom. The recycling van called round on Thursday mornings, suggesting that this was two days' worth of drinking for Ruby. Nessie bit her lip. She hadn't realised it was so bad. No wonder Ruby had fallen.

Back inside the cottage, she opened up the cupboards, searching for cleaning products. There wasn't much in the way of Flash but she found plenty of alcohol. It was everywhere she looked: stashed under the sink, in the cupboards next to the tins of soup, in the freezer. She even found a half-empty bottle of gin beside Ruby's bed, a glass with a shrivelled-up slice of lemon at the bottom next to it.

Nessie collected everything she found and put it on the draining board. There were twenty-eight bottles of wine, port, vodka and gin. Some were open, others were still sealed. She stared at the collection in mute horror. Ruby didn't just like a drink; she was an alcoholic, just like Nessie's father had been.

Feeling sick, she poured the contents of the open bottles down the sink. Then she found some bags and packed up what was left. At some point Ruby would be coming home and Nessie didn't want there to be a single drop of alcohol left in the house.

She did another sweep before she left, making sure she hadn't missed anything. There was one room that was locked, a bedroom at the front of the cottage. Nessie rummaged around on Ruby's dressing table, taking care not to disturb any of her precious make-up, until she found the key. She turned the handle slowly, dreading what she was about to find.

It was a shrine to Ruby's acting days. There was no bed. The walls were lined with framed photographs – some black and white, some colour – of a much younger-looking Ruby with a plethora of famous faces. Nessie recognised all the greats – Laurence Olivier, Cary Grant, a young Judi Dench and many more besides. There were other pictures too, of Ruby with a little boy, both of them smiling into the camera, and with a man Nessie didn't recognise but assumed must be her husband. And then there were photographs Nessie hadn't expected to find – ones of her and Sam when they were children. These must have belonged to her father, she guessed; Ruby must have rescued them from the pub after he'd died.

'Oh Ruby,' Nessie murmured, gazing at the pictures sadly.

Her gaze strayed to the desk beneath the pictures of her and her sister, to a neatly bundled parcel of handwritten envelopes. They were addressed to Sam and Nessie Chapman, at their mother's address. All were marked 'Return to Sender' in defiant red ink.

Nessie didn't know how long she stood there staring at the envelopes. Her mother had always claimed their father had vanished without trace and had never tried to contact his daughters again. The sight of those letters was proof that she'd lied. Nessie reached out a hand and traced her name on the uppermost envelope; for a moment, she was tempted to open them but even though they were meant for her and Sam, it felt somehow wrong to read them behind Ruby's back. Once the other woman was back to full health Nessie would ask about them. Until then, the letters would remain where they were, unread and waiting.

The hospital confirmed Ruby had broken her hip. The operation to pin the fracture had to wait until her bloodstream was clear of alcohol, during which time Ruby was alternately charming or difficult. Sam and Nessie took it in turns to go to the hospital during the days that followed but she had no shortage of visitors; when it came to looking after their own, Little Monkham rallied round.

By the time the evening of the Halloween Ball rolled around, decorating the Star and Sixpence was the last thing Sam and Nessie felt like doing. But the guests would be arriving soon, incognito and expecting a bloodthirsty evening – there was no way they could cancel.

Nick arrived just as Sam was dangling glittery spiders from the ceiling. He pulled on a black tricorn hat low over his eyes and glowered up at her. 'Elijah Blackheart, at your service, ma'am,' he rasped. 'If you'd just hand over all your jewels and valuables I'd be much obliged.'

Sam climbed down the ladder and stared at him suspiciously. 'That's a very convincing hat. Is it the one you wear in *Smugglers' Inn*?'

Nick grinned. 'Might be. Don't tell the props department.'

Sam laughed. 'You'd better hang on to it, then. You know what your fans are like, they'll do anything to own their very own bit of *Smugglers'* swag.'

'Who are you dressing up as?' Nick asked, kissing her cheek. He'd shaved his trademark stubble for the role too. 'Please tell me it's something fabulous.'

Sam smiled, thinking of the skin-tight Catwoman costume in her wardrobe upstairs. 'I'll see your highwayman and raise you a superhero.'

'Wait until you see it,' Nessie called from the other side of the bar. 'I'm pretty sure she's going to give Franny a coronary.'

'Or Henry,' Sam said, with a wicked smile. 'How are

you, anyway? The guest rooms are fully booked, I'm afraid – JoJo and her sister are staying up there – so you'll have to bunk in with me. Is that all right?'

'I'm sure I'll cope,' Nick replied, his eyes twinkling. He waved a hand around the bar. 'Is there anything I can do to help?'

Sam grinned and handed him a fistful of drawing pins. 'I'm glad you asked that. How are you with bats?'

By nine-thirty, Sam was regretting her costume choice. It was too hot, too tight and had definite drawbacks in the comfort break department. But it had certainly turned heads; Nick's eyes had lit up when she'd appeared in the bedroom door and he'd kissed her in a way that left no doubt of his appreciation. There'd been a gratifying moment of silence when she'd entered the crowded bar, broken by a long, low wolf whistle that had almost made her blush. Even so, Sam was beginning to wish she'd gone for a classical Venetian vampire costume like Nessie – anything that meant a visit to the toilet didn't take half an hour.

Owen and Luke had come as Batman and Robin, which was cute. Connor was cutting an elegant figure as Zorro, complete with a wicked-looking rapier. Franny appeared to be dressed as Elizabeth I and Henry looked very much like Henry VIII, which Sam found an oddly incestuous pairing. Nick was getting an unbelievable amount of attention as Elijah Blackheart – as Sam had predicted, die-hard *Smugglers' Inn* fans had recognised the authentic hat almost instantly and she'd heard more than one over-excited guest plotting to steal it by the end of the night. Inevitably, some guests had turned up in similar outfits but most just laughed it off. There were one or two whose costumes were so good that Sam couldn't identify exactly who was underneath. She hadn't spotted Joss and assumed he'd decided not to come.

By ten-thirty, the party was in full swing. Connor's Dark and Stormy cocktails were going down well – cider and rum topped with ginger ale was proving a potent mix and more than one guest was looking the worse for wear. The band Sam had booked to play had everyone up dancing with a mixture of covers from every decade. Nick had dragged Sam to join in with the Time Warp, although she had to go outside for some fresh air afterwards. And then, just before eleven o'clock, the lights went out.

'Don't panic, everyone,' she called, with a silent groan. 'The switch has just tripped. Let me find a torch and I'll have the lights back on in a heartbeat.'

Down in the cellar, it only took her a moment to flick the switch. A cheer from upstairs told her the lights had come back on, although the cellar remained stubbornly dark. Frowning, she stared at the switch, checking to see if any of the other buttons looked wrong but everything seemed to be in order. Maybe the bulb had gone, she thought, swinging her torch upwards to look at the fitting. It would have to wait until the morning, if it had.

Carefully, she picked her way back to the stairs. A shadow appeared in the doorway and she peered up to see the outline of a tricorn hat. 'Bloody hell, Nick, you scared me!'

She reached the top of the stairs but stopped when Nick didn't move. He stared at her in silence for a moment, his face shrouded in shadow, then suddenly one arm swooped behind her back to pull her close and he leaned in to kiss her hard.

A burst of heat exploded through Sam. One hand clasped the banister to ensure she didn't fall, the other wound itself around Nick's neck. The kiss went on, growing deeper and more passionate with each passing second, until Sam thought he might sweep her into his arms and carry her up the stairs to take things further. It was unlike any kiss Nick had given her before; strange and yearning but familiar all at the same time.

Then he broke off, as suddenly as he'd started. With a swirl of his cape, he turned and went, leaving Sam staring after him in confusion. He'd never got into a role that much before, she thought, touching her bruised lips, not even when she'd visited him on location. Maybe it was something to do with the mask. Or maybe it was her Catwoman outfit. She'd certainly received enough compliments about the way it fitted her.

At midnight Nessie called time and the guests reluctantly began to leave. Nick was still surrounded by a crowd of adoring fans – smiling, Sam edged her way to his side. 'That was some kiss earlier, Mr Highwayman,' she murmured into his ear. 'Anyone would think you were an actor.'

Nick blinked at her. 'What? When?'

'At the cellar door,' Sam said, gazing quizzically at him. 'Just after the lights went out.'

He frowned. 'Sam, I don't know who it was you kissed but it definitely wasn't me. Martha hasn't let me move from this spot all night.'

Sam stepped back in alarm. She'd been so sure it was Nick – he'd had the same tricorn hat, the same cloth mask, everything. But it wasn't beyond the realms of possibility that someone else had been at the ball in the same costume . . . in fact, why hadn't she thought of that earlier? The kiss hadn't been Nick's usual style; it had been harder, more desperate. An opportunistic, stolen kiss by someone who knew exactly where she'd be . . .

Sam's head whipped around as she scanned the remaining guests. At first she couldn't see another highwayman, then she spotted him on his way out of the door. His hat was different – cheap-looking and plastic. He reached up to take it off and now she could see his hair was fair, not dark like Nick's. He glanced over his shoulder as he went and locked eyes with hers: blue eyes, the colour of the summer sky. And suddenly she knew who the mystery kisser had been, and why it had seemed different but familiar all at the same time: Joss had come as Elijah Blackheart too.

Chapter Thirty-Five

Luke was yawning, struggling to keep his eyes open as Owen and Nessie said goodnight in the doorway of the Star and Sixpence.

'And you're sure you don't mind?' Owen said for the third time, gazing anxiously at Nessie.

She laughed. 'I've told you, I'm happy to help. Go and see Kathryn's gig. Luke and I will have a great time while you're gone, won't we?'

Luke nodded and yawned again.

Nessie lowered her voice. 'Any time you need help, just give me a shout. I know Kathryn loves looking after Luke but she deserves a bit of me time too.'

Owen smiled. 'Thank you, I will.'

He gazed down at her, his eyes alive with warmth behind their mask. Nessie held her breath, wondering if he was about to kiss her, and then Luke let out a third noisy yawn and the spell broke.

'So I'll see you on Thursday,' Owen said, with a rueful glance at Luke. 'About half past seven?'

'But hopefully I'll see you before then,' Nessie said, feeling suddenly emboldened by her costume. If you couldn't be forward when you were dressed as a Venetian vampire, when could you be?

Something flared in Owen's gaze. 'I hope so too. Goodnight, Nessie.'

She watched him vanish across the yard and into the doorway of Snowdrop Cottage. Tiny steps, she reminded herself with a secret smile. She should wish on meteors more often.

Back inside the bar, there was a noticeable strain in the air. Sam and Nick were clearly mid-argument, although they stopped as Nessie came nearer.

'Everything okay?' she asked cautiously, looking back and forth between them.

'Fine,' Sam snapped.

'If you consider the news that Sam's been snogging other men *fine*,' Nick said dryly.

'I've told you, it was a case of mistaken identity. It was dark, he kissed me and I assumed it was you so I kissed him back. It wasn't until later that I realised it was Joss.'

'Joss?' Nessie gasped. 'What the hell does he think he's playing at?'

'I've got no idea,' Sam said, shaking her head. 'Maybe he thought I was someone else.'

'Of course he did,' Nick said, raising an eyebrow. 'He confused you with the other Catwoman who was here.'

359

Nessie stared at her sister with a mixture of consternation and pity. What was it about Sam that attracted drama? It seemed as though every relationship she had was tarred with the same brush.

'Look, Nick, I don't think you can blame Sam for this,' Nessie said.

Nick stared first at her, then at Sam. He sighed. 'I suppose not. You do look bloody amazing in that costume – I'm not surprised he was tempted.'

Sam shook her head. 'I really did think it was you.' She glanced over at Nessie. 'I saw you and Owen getting pretty cosy out there just now.'

'I'm babysitting for him Thursday so he can go to Kathryn's gig,' Nessie explained. 'We were just sorting everything out.'

'And speaking of sorting things out, you need to call Patrick,' Sam said in a stern tone of voice. 'You've written him a new business plan, now you need to hand it over, along with a firm goodbye.'

Nessie sighed. 'I know. It's just—'

'It's just nothing,' Sam cut in. 'He'll try to talk you round, Nessie. Don't let him.'

'Okay,' Nessie said, raising her hands in mock-surrender. 'I'll call him tomorrow.'

Sam nodded once and glanced over at Nick. 'Right, are we good, Mr Highwayman, or do you want to sleep on the sofa?'

Nick hung his head. 'We're good, Catwoman. I'm sorry.'

'Excellent,' Sam said. 'Are you all right to lock up, Ness?'

'Of course,' Nessie said. 'You two go on up.'

Sam headed for the stairs behind the bar. 'Oh, and Nick?' she called over one shoulder. 'Bring the hat, okay?'

Nessie waited until the guests from the upstairs rooms had checked out before she called Patrick. There was no sign of life from her sister's room but that wasn't exactly a surprise, given the look in Sam's eyes when she'd led Nick up to bed. Carrying the phone downstairs to the empty bar, Nessie dialled Patrick's number with shaking fingers.

'It's me,' she said, when he answered. 'Nessie.'

'Ness!' His voice was instantly warm and happy. 'How are you, darling?'

Nessie winced. This was going to be harder than she'd expected. She took a deep breath and steeled herself. 'I'm okay. Listen, I've been looking at your accounts and I think I can see a way out of this.'

She explained the business plan she'd put together with Sam, detailing in simple terms how Patrick could repair the damage to both his finances and his reputation. There was a long silence on the other end of the phone when she'd finished.

'Patrick?' Nessie said, after a little while. 'What do you think?'

Another pause. 'So I guess this means I'm not moving to Little Monkham.'

Nessie closed her eyes. 'No.'

'And I guess it means we're not getting back together either.'

There was no mistaking the bitterness in his voice now. She took a deep breath and fixed her gaze on a sparkling spider that was twirling lazily from the ceiling. 'No, Patrick. I'm sorry. I should have told you this before but I've actually met someone else.'

A bark of laughter ricocheted through the phone. 'Fucking hell, Nessie, you didn't waste any time. It's that blacksmith, isn't it? I saw he was sniffing round you.'

'It doesn't matter who it is,' Nessie said, fighting to keep her voice steady. 'What matters is that you can move on now, find someone new for yourself.'

'Don't pretend you're doing this for me.' His snort of derision rattled through the handset. 'I don't know why I'm surprised, actually. You always did put yourself first.'

'That's not true—'

'It is,' Patrick snapped. 'If you cared about anyone other than yourself you wouldn't have left in the first place.'

Nessie dug her nails into her palm. 'Goodbye, Patrick.'

'Yeah, yeah, hang up on me. Pretend I don't exist,' he said and now his tone was whiny and petulant. 'Good luck getting the money for the house, by the way. It'll be a long time before I can afford to buy you out, not when I've got a business to bail out too.'

There was a loud clatter as he slammed the phone down. Nessie disconnected the call and sat quietly for a moment, staring into space. Had she been selfish to leave him, to want more than a half-interested friendship, to expect love from her husband? She didn't think so. Patrick was hurt and worried about his business now, but in time he'd come to see that she'd made the right choice for both of them. But that didn't mean his words didn't sting, she realised, as tears prickled the backs of her eyes. She let them fall, unchecked, for a minute, then dried her face with her sleeve and started to take down the Halloween decorations.

'You're sure you got it all?' Sam asked Nessie in an undertone, as they waited on the doorstep of Weir Cottage on Tuesday morning, with what appeared to be half the village. 'You didn't miss any?'

'If I did, it's pretty well hidden,' Nessie replied. 'I guess we'll soon find out.'

Owen pulled the car up to the kerb and got out to help Ruby onto her crutches. The crowd burst into applause as she started to make her way up the path and Nessie was pleased to see Ruby had a full face of make-up on. She had gathered up what she thought Ruby would need and taken it to the hospital shortly after her fall, along with nightclothes and clean underwear, but she had no idea whether she'd chosen the right products. Either she'd done well or Ruby had made the best of what she had; Nessie suspected Ruby would rather die than face an audience without her make-up.

'Oh stop it,' Ruby called, trying and failing to look displeased. 'You're embarrassing me.'

'Welcome home, Ruby,' Sam called, joining in with the applause. 'We missed you.'

'You mean you missed my bar bill,' Ruby replied. 'I bet your takings have halved.'

There was a smattering of dutiful laughter but Nessie and Sam exchanged worried looks. How would Ruby react when she discovered every drop of drink had been removed from the cottage? How would she feel when she walked into the Star and Sixpence and found no one would serve her alcohol? And what would she say when she realised that every shop in the village had agreed not to sell her wine or spirits? Would she see it as a well-meaning attempt to save her life or an intolerable interference?

Ruby's consultant at the hospital had taken Nessie and Sam to one side after the operation.

'Are you Miss Cabernet's immediate family?'

'We're the closest thing she has to family,' Sam said firmly.

'Then I'm sure you're aware that she has a drink problem. The results from her blood tests show some elevated enzyme levels that are indicative of quite severe liver damage and her bones are quite thin.' He consulted his notes. 'We can't tell more without a biopsy but I would suggest that Ruby stops drinking at once, or at least cuts down drastically. Her body can't take much more.'

The sisters had worked out a plan on the way back from the hospital and had agreed that Franny had to be in on it. As much as Ruby would hate the thought of Franny knowing her secret, saving her life mattered more and they needed the weight of the village behind them if it was going to work.

Ruby reached the front door and turned to face the crowd. 'I owe you thanks, my friends, for taking the time to welcome me home.' She smiled. 'I can't tell you how happy I am to be here. The NHS is wonderful and they've looked after me well, but as the incomparable Judy Garland once said, there's no place like home.'

She managed to get her keys into the lock on the third attempt and manoeuvred her crutches inside. Nessie and Sam followed her and closed the door while Ruby looked around.

'Someone's been busy,' she remarked. 'It wasn't this tidy before.'

'I did a bit of cleaning,' Nessie said cautiously. 'But it didn't need much.'

'Fibber,' Ruby said, giving her a knowing look. 'Housework has never been my strong suit – there was always something more interesting to do.'

'Can we get you a cup of tea, Ruby?' Sam asked, heading towards the kitchen.

'God, no,' Ruby said, settling into a hard chair with a pained expression. 'I've been living on the stuff for over a week now. Get me a proper drink, there's a good girl. G&T, on the rocks, just how I like it.'

Sam stopped and turned slowly around. 'I can't do that, Ruby. I'm sorry.'

'Of course you can,' Ruby said in a brisk voice. 'There's some gin in the cereal cupboard and the tonic is in the fridge. I assume I don't need to tell you where to find the ice.'

'There's no gin in the cereal cupboard,' Nessie said. 'It's all gone.'

Ruby let out an incredulous laugh. 'Did you throw a party while I was gone?'

Nessie knelt at the older woman's side. 'The doctor spoke to us about your drinking. You need to stop, Ruby.'

'No, what I need is a gin and tonic,' Ruby said and her voice had an edge Nessie had never heard before. 'Without the lecture chaser, thank you.'

'You won't find any alcohol here,' Sam said. 'You won't be served at the Star and Sixpence or at any of the shops in Little Monkham. We mean it. You have to stop.'

Ruby's scarlet lips pressed together so hard they became white. 'What gives you the right to decide this?' she snapped. 'You and some doctor who's probably fresh out of medical school think you know what's good for me? It's my life, girls, I can live it however I want and if that means I drink myself into an early grave, then so be it.'

Nessie looked at Sam helplessly. Ruby was right; if she wanted to drink then she'd find a way. They needed something more, something stronger than the need for alcohol. 'Won't you even try?' she asked. 'Maybe your son would come to see you if – if you cut down a bit. We could help you find him if you like?'

The older woman struggled to her feet, her eyes flashing. 'My son is none of your business. My drinking is none of your business. And unless one of you interfering kill-joys has got a hipflask, I'd like you to leave. Now.'

Nessie stood up. She couldn't see that they had any choice. They had to do what Ruby asked.

'We only want what's best for you,' Sam said over her shoulder, as Nessie opened the door.

Ruby didn't reply.

Sam pulled the door shut behind her and spread her hands. 'Now what?'

'Now we wait,' Nessie said, with a long sigh. 'It will go one of two ways – either she'll come to her senses and realise we're telling the truth, or she'll find a way to drink again and all we've done is delay the inevitable.'

She did her best to sound optimistic but one look at Sam's doubting expression told her they both had the sinking feeling Ruby had already made her choice.

Chapter Thirty-Six

When her phone rang early the next morning, Nessie somehow knew it was Ruby before she'd even glanced at the screen.

'Nessie,' the other woman croaked when she answered. 'Can you come?'

She dressed as quickly as she could and shook Sam awake. 'Ruby called; she needs help. You'll have to take over the guests' breakfasts.'

The streets were still dark as Nessie hurried to Weir Cottage. A light shone over the front door, which was ajar, and she slipped inside, taking care to close it behind her.

'Ruby?'

'In here.'

Nessie followed the sound of her voice into the bedroom with all the photographs and found Ruby clasping the picture of herself and her son. She was still wearing the same clothes she'd had on to come home from hospital and Nessie couldn't help wondering whether she'd been up all night. 'What's the matter, Ruby? Are you in pain?'

'Of a kind,' she said, holding it out for Nessie to see and admire. 'He was such a darling boy. So affectionate and loving.'

Nessie took the frame, discreetly trying to work out if Nessie had been drinking. There was no tell-tale smell of juniper berries to suggest gin, no sharp tang of white wine and no fruity aroma from red. There was no smell at all and her words were clear and crisp. Nessie felt a tiny spring of hope grow inside her. Maybe there was a chance after all.

'You must miss him terribly,' she said.

Ruby sighed. 'You know, I'd be lying if I said I did. Does that make me a terrible mother? I was so busy that I hardly had time to miss anyone but that doesn't mean I stopped loving him.'

She took the photo back from Nessie and stared at it for a long moment. 'But that isn't why I called you here. I wanted to apologise to you, to Sam too, but I know she likes her beauty sleep so I'll catch up with her later.'

'No apology needed,' Nessie said gently. 'You were surprised and angry.'

'And addicted,' Ruby admitted. 'This isn't the first time someone has tried to help me. Last time, it was your father, ironically. We tried everything, from cold turkey to Alcoholics Anonymous but each time one or the other of us would slip off the wagon and we'd be right back where we started. Of course, living in a pub was disastrous for your father. He could never get away from it.'

'I know it's hard to stop,' Nessie said in a low voice. 'And it must be even harder when there's alcohol everywhere you look. That's why we poured it all away, so you wouldn't be tempted.'

Ruby smiled and opened up a small drawer underneath the table. She pulled out a small bottle of vodka and handed it to Nessie. 'You missed this one,' she said. 'Take it now before I change my mind.'

Nessie hurried to the kitchen and poured the alcohol down the sink. She hadn't even noticed the drawer under the table; surely there must be more she'd overlooked, tucked away in secret pockets, ready to lead Ruby astray. She'd have to keep her eyes open, or perhaps Ruby would give up more of her stash in time.

When she walked back into the room, Ruby had the parcel of envelopes addressed to Sam and Nessie in her hands. 'I'd forgotten I even had these,' she said, passing the bundle to Nessie. 'They're all the letters Andrew wrote over the years that your mother sent back. Read them when you have a chance. I think they'll show you he wasn't entirely a monster.'

Nessie held on to the envelopes tightly. 'Thank you,' she said, her throat suddenly tight and aching at the thought of all the missed opportunities the letters represented. 'Ruby, would you like us to help you find your son?'

The other woman hesitated. 'Perhaps, in time. But let's

concentrate on getting through today first, shall we? There will be times when I fail, Nessie, but I hope I can count on you and Sam to help me get back onto the path.'

Nessie reached out to squeeze Ruby's shoulder. 'Of course you can. We're family now, aren't we?'

Ruby reached up to take her hand. 'Your father would have been so pleased to hear you say that. Thank you.'

Nessie smiled. 'No problem.' She waved at one of the photographs on the wall. 'Now, when were you planning to tell us about you and Cary Grant?'

'Well?' Sam demanded when Nessie came home over an hour later. 'How bad is it?'

Nessie shook her head in cautious wonder. 'Not at all what I was expecting. I think she's going to try and stop drinking.'

'No,' Sam breathed, looking amazed. 'Really?'

'Yes. She even gave me a bottle of vodka to pour away, said I'd missed it when I tidied up.' Nessie held up the bundle of envelopes. 'She gave me these too – they're letters to us from Dad.'

Sam stared at her in shock. 'Letters? But Mum always said he never wrote.'

Nessie sighed. 'She lied. I thought we could set aside an evening, go through them together.'

Her sister looked apprehensive. 'Not tonight – we're both working. And not tomorrow – you're babysitting Luke.'

'Friday then?'

Sam shook her head. 'I thought I might pop down to London. Nick's filming in New Zealand soon and I'd like to see him before he goes.'

Nessie studied her sister for a moment. Sam was right – they were busy – but Nessie couldn't help wondering if there was more to her reluctance to read the letters than that. Then again, if Nick was going away it made sense that she spent some time with him. 'Sure,' Nessie said, then hesitated. 'Have you seen Joss since the ball?'

'No,' Sam replied and blew out a long puff of air. 'If he wasn't avoiding me before, he is now.'

Something in her sister's expression made Nessie frown. 'Sam? Is there something you're not telling me?'

'No,' Sam snapped, scowling. Her shoulders sagged. 'Yes. Maybe.'

Nessie raised her eyebrows. 'Meaning?'

'Meaning maybe I enjoyed kissing Joss more than I let on,' Sam said, sounding guilty. 'That doesn't make me a bad person, does it? It's not like I was the one doing the kissing, after all.'

'No, it doesn't make you a bad person,' Nessie said slowly. 'And of course you enjoyed it – you thought he was Nick.'

Sam threw her a hunted look. 'But that's the thing: when I think back, I've got a feeling I did know. Not consciously, but deep down, I knew it was Joss. And I didn't stop him.'

Nessie felt a wave of sympathy for her sister; it was hard to juggle feelings for two men at the same time. 'Of course you're confused, Sam. But try not to read too much into it. Joss meant a lot to you and things ended badly – this kiss has probably stirred up a lot of feelings you didn't get to deal with when you broke up.' She paused and smiled gently. 'But none of that is Nick's fault. Don't let this tarnish what you have with him.'

Sam stared at her for a few seconds, then nodded. 'You're right. God, you're so right, Ness. What would I do without you?'

Nessie reached over and gave Sam a hug. 'That's what sisters are for.'

Chapter Thirty-Seven

Snowdrop Cottage was one of Nessie's favourite places to be. Whether it was the warm amber glow of the lamps playing over the beamed ceiling, or the all-enveloping warmth from the wood burner she couldn't say, but she found a special sense of contentment when she settled into the comfortable sofa. She'd spent the evening playing with Luke – losing several times at an impossibly hard racing game on his PlayStation. Then it had been bedtime and she'd discovered that Owen had been reading *The Prisoner of Azkaban* with him, a chapter a night. So she'd thrown herself into the story, attempting to do all the voices, watching the magic unfold before Luke's eyes. Just before he'd fallen asleep, he'd clutched at her hand and thanked her in a way that made the breath catch in Nessie's throat. She'd caught a glimpse then of what motherhood was like.

Downstairs, she'd tidied up the kitchen and poured herself a glass of wine. She'd brought a book of her own to read but decided to carry on with Harry Potter, practising the voices for another evening. And eventually, she'd sat in silence, listening to the crackle of the fire and enjoying the peace of the cottage.

She glanced sideways at the photograph of Eliza Rhys, laughing with Owen and a much younger Luke, and felt her usual stab of sadness that Owen and Luke had lost her so young. Often, she'd felt guilty when she looked at that picture, as though she was somehow being disrespectful when her thoughts towards Owen were frequently impure. But tonight, she felt a spirit of kinship with Eliza, almost as though they were friends.

'Luke's a great boy,' she told the picture, raising her glass. 'You'd be proud of him. And Owen – well, I hope you won't mind me saying that he's pretty great too.'

It was long after eleven when the front door opened and Owen walked back in. Nessie was engrossed in Luke's book and looked up blinking, half expecting him to be wearing wizarding robes.

'How was the gig?' she asked with a smile.

He stood for a moment, gazing at her with an unreadable expression on his face. Then he seemed to give himself a mental shake.

'Good, thanks,' he said finally. 'They're a great band and of course Kathryn is amazing.' He crossed the room in a few strides to sit beside her on the sofa, leaning back into the soft cushions and closing his eyes. 'It's nice to sit down, though. I'm not much of a dancer.'

Nessie thought back to the dance they'd shared in the summer, at JoJo's wedding on the village green; he'd been pretty good then but she didn't like to say so.

'Shall I get you some wine?' she said instead, shifting her weight to stand up.

Owen's eyes flicked open. 'Eh? No, not yet. There's something I want to say first.'

Immediately, Nessie's heart began to thud. 'Oh?'

He fixed her with a dark-eyed, serious gaze. 'I haven't been very honest with you, Nessie.'

Now Nessie's heart plummeted into her feet. 'In what way?'

'When you told me Patrick wanted you to take him back, I pretended not to care one way or another,' he said, his voice low. 'That wasn't how I felt at all.'

Nessie held her breath, not trusting herself to speak. Was it her imagination or was Owen leaning closer?

'The truth is, it made me furious – not with you, but with myself, for not being brave enough to say what I wanted to say.' His eyes were fixed on hers. 'I can't stop thinking about you, Nessie. I think I might even – well, if it's all right with you, I'd really like to kiss you.'

She hesitated for as long as it took her heart to beat once, then leaned forwards to close the distance between them. 'Yes,' she whispered.

From the moment their lips met, Nessie was lost. The last

time she and Owen had kissed, he'd pulled away, leaving her confused and embarrassed. This time was different – the kiss went on and on, deepening until it was clear neither of them wanted to stop. Eventually, they broke apart however, and Nessie could see in Owen's eyes that it had meant as much to him as it had to her.

She let out a long shaky breath. 'So.'

Owen smiled. 'So.'

'What happens now?'

'I think I should take you to dinner,' he said, his gaze solemn. 'And afterwards, I think I'd like to kiss you again.'

Nessie felt her lips tingle as she thought of the way his mouth had felt on hers. 'Perhaps then I could take *you* to dinner,' she said, smiling. 'And I could kiss you.'

Owen reached out a hand to cup her face, drawing her near to brush his lips against hers. 'Now you're getting the idea.'

Nessie had seemed different on Friday morning, soft and contented and, above all, happy. Sam had even heard her humming along to the radio as she'd emptied the dishwasher in the bar. She'd messaged Kathryn, who'd said that Owen seemed in an unusually good mood too but there'd been no time for Sam to interrogate her sister; she'd had to leave for London to see Nick.

They took in a new West End play and then went out to eat, heading back to Nick's apartment in the early hours of the morning.

'I could get used to this,' Nick murmured against her hair as they lay in bed listening to the wind together.

'Me too,' Sam said. 'Except that you're flying to New Zealand and I've got a pub to run, so we'd better not get too comfortable.'

There was a brief silence. 'You could always come back to London for good,' Nick said after a while. 'The only reason you left was to escape Will Pargeter and that's all over and done with now.'

'Is it?' she asked doubtfully. 'I'm still *persona non grata* at Brightman and Burgess and I can't see any other PR firms falling over themselves to give me a job, can you? Not after the kind of headlines I made.'

Nick snorted. 'Hardly anyone remembers that. Don't forget you've been making better headlines since then, with me. I'm sure you'd get snapped up right away.' He paused. 'You could move in here if you wanted to, rent your flat out and make some money.'

Sam pulled away and propped her head up on her hands. 'You're serious, aren't you?'

'Of course,' Nick said. 'I'm not here a lot of the time but you could come and visit me on location and I'd love to have you around when I came home. It's . . . well, it's a lonely business being an actor sometimes.'

Now it was Sam's turn to let out a delicate snort of disbelief. Nick had always had women throwing themselves at him every single day – he couldn't possibly be lonely. Then again, she remembered him telling her before that he never

378

knew who to trust; a kiss and tell story with the star of *Smugglers' Inn* would be worth a lot of money to the papers. And now she came to think of it, there hadn't been anyone else for quite a while – not since before they'd decided to go tabloid–official with their made-up relationship. She also had the growing feeling that something was different about Nick these days. He was attentive and committed – just like a real boyfriend. Sam was beginning to wonder if this had been his real agenda all along. 'Nick—'

He reached up to stroke her cheek. 'Don't decide now. I'll be back from New Zealand just before Christmas. Think about it and let me know, okay?'

He drifted off to sleep not long after that, leaving Sam wide-eyed and restless beside him. When she'd left London, she had never dreamed she'd find life in Little Monkham so satisfying. But working alongside Nessie to restore the pub had proved unexpectedly rewarding and the Star and Sixpence was so much a part of her now that it would be a real wrench to leave. And then there was her sister: they were a team; it wouldn't be fair to abandon her, even for a life of glamour with Nick Borrowdale. Sam had made a lot of friends in the village, too, she'd miss them if she went back to London. But she couldn't say she wasn't tempted. London had been home for most of her adult life and she'd be lying if she didn't admit there were times when she missed the bright lights, the excitement of the city.

She lay back against the cool cotton pillow and stared at the ceiling. And then there was Joss: angry, confused Joss, who couldn't decide if he wanted her or hated her. She hadn't thought about him once while she'd been with Nick, but back in Little Monkham it was a different story. And now that Nick was going to be away for weeks, did that mean she'd find her mind straying back to the way Joss's lips had felt on hers more often?

Maybe Nick was right, she thought, turning into him and snuggling against his shoulder. Maybe spending more time in London was a good idea.

The letters lay on the coffee table in front of Nessie and Sam. It was early evening, the bar was in the capable hands of Connor and Tilly, and two glasses of Merlot sat on either side of the envelopes.

Nessie picked up the bundle and studied the curly handwriting as though it could tell her what was inside. 'Is it weird that I'm quite looking forward to finding out what Dad had to say?'

'I'm not sure I am,' Sam replied honestly. 'But he took the trouble to write the letters. I suppose the least we can do is read them.'

Slowly, Nessie slid the ribbon holding the bundle together over one end. She understood Sam's reticence; their father had been missing from most of their childhood and all of their adult lives. Was there anything to be gained from going back over old ground now? And then she remembered Ruby, gazing misty-eyed at the photograph of the son who'd turned his back on her, and she came to a decision. Whatever Andrew Chapman's letters said, one thing was certain: they'd help Sam and Nessie to understand their father better.

'Ready?' she asked, picking up the first envelope and lifting the flap on the back.

Sam reached for her wine glass and took a long gulp of the ruby liquid. 'Ready.'

Nessie unfolded the letter and held it so that her sister could see it. And together, they began to read.

Star and Sixpence
Sixpence Lane,
Little Monkham,
Shropshire,
SY6 2XY

12th June 1990
Dearest Vanessa and Samantha
How are you, my girls? I hope you haven't grown up too much in the six months since I last saw you?
I am sorry to be so slow to write. It has taken me a long time to find a new home and I didn't want to get in touch before I had, because I wanted to have somewhere you might be able to come and visit. You'll see from the address that I have moved into a pub, which seems like a crazy choice but it actually suits me rather well. Little Monkham is the loveliest village – they play cricket on the green every Saturday and there are plenty of other children for you to

make friends with. The village even has its own Post Office
and the postmistress says she will let you stamp some letters
if you are sensible and good. I think you'll like it here.
I hope that your mother will see that I am making an effort
to sort things out and will allow you to come for a visit.
Until then, I am sending some hugs with this letter. I hope
they don't leak out of the sides before it reaches you.
Missing you both,
Love, Dad x

Christmas at the Star and Sixpence

Season's Greetings!
Please join us for
Carols by Candlelight
3.30 p.m.
Christmas Eve
at St Mary's Church,
Little Monkham, Shropshire
followed by a Festive Fayre on the village green.
Mulled Wine – Roasted Chestnuts –
Warm Mince Pies
All welcome!

Chapter Thirty-Eight

Eight-foot Christmas trees and sixteenth-century coaching inns did not mix, Nessie Blake decided, as she paused halfway across the Star and Sixpence bar to watch her sister put the finishing touches to the pub's festive decorations. Sam was doing a great job but there was no escaping that the top of the tree she'd chosen was almost brushing the oak-beamed ceiling.

'What do you think?' Sam called, draping silver strands along the already-laden branches. 'Christmassy enough?'

Nessie's gaze took in the colour co-ordinated baubles, the thick strings of tinsel and cool white fairy lights; Sam's eye for detail was second to none. 'It looks great. Franny will be unhappy that there's no star on the top, though.'

Christmas was the highlight of Franny's year and she'd made sure everyone knew how important it was that everything was perfect. Both sisters had learned fast that she was not someone to cross.

Sam let out a short sigh. 'But our ceiling is too low. I can't magic a higher one out of thin air.'

'Then why didn't you buy a smaller tree?' Nessie asked, feeling a little exasperated.

'I told you, this was the last one they had,' Sam said. 'The guy said there were more arriving tomorrow but we couldn't wait.'

They certainly couldn't, Nessie thought; the village Christmas lights were due to be switched on in less than three hours' time and the pub was acting as HQ. It simply had to have a tree, with or without a star, just as there had to be a mulled something to drink and mince pies to eat. Nessie drew the line at snow, though – Sam had been all for finding a way to blast the village green with fake whiteness but Nessie had refused. Unfortunately, the weather wasn't helping to set the scene – the odds on a white Christmas were slim.

'Maybe Franny won't notice,' Nessie suggested, knowing how unlikely the idea was: Franny noticed *everything*.

'With a bit of luck, she'll be distracted by our VIP,' Sam said. 'I'm sure I heard her say the Flames were her favourite band when she was a teenager. Although I'm not convinced Franny ever *was* a teenager.'

Nessie grinned. She'd seen pictures of the Flames in the seventies, when they were at the height of their considerable fame – they'd been very good-looking, especially lead singer, Micky Holiday. The band had recently finished a world tour so it was even more amazing that Sam had managed to call in a few old PR favours to entice him to turn on the Little Monkham Christmas lights; it turned out Micky had grown up in a nearby village and was only too happy to do the honours. If the object of Franny's teenage desire couldn't distract her from noticing Sam's less-than-perfect decorations then nothing would, Nessie decided. 'Where is Micky, anyway?'

Sam stepped back to admire the tree. 'Tucking into a bottle of champagne in the guest rooms upstairs, staying out of sight so that he doesn't give the game away.'

The identity of the mystery guest had been a closely guarded secret and not even Franny knew whom Sam had booked. The posters had hinted at a not-to-be-missed celebrity and the Star and Sixpence regulars had done their best to weasel the truth out of Sam and Nessie, without success. The rumours were that curiosity had been piqued in the neighbouring villages as well and a bumper crowd was expected. Nessie had to hand it to her sister – she certainly knew how to get people's attention.

'As long as he doesn't miss it,' she said, picturing the rock star passed out on the four-poster bed.

'No chance,' Sam said firmly. 'Speaking of missing things, hadn't you better get going? You don't want to miss the post.'

She nodded at the envelope in Nessie's hands: the paperwork for the Real Ale Drinkers' Association Pub of the Year award. The Star and Sixpence had already won Regional Pub of the Year – now they were in the running for the biggest prize of all and a glitzy award ceremony in London beckoned. As long as Nessie posted the forms in time.

'I'd better go. If I'm not back in half an hour, start baking the mince pies without me.'

Sam snorted. 'Then Franny really would be furious. Burnt mince pies definitely won't get her seal of approval. I'll start mulling the cider instead.'

There was a queue in the post office.

Nessie shifted from one foot to the other and resisted the temptation to check her watch again. She supposed it was to be expected – there were only twenty-two shopping days until Christmas, the busiest time of the year for the postal service – but that didn't explain why Franny was currently engaged in a seven-minute-and-counting conversation about the varied merits of goose fat with Mrs Glossop. She must know she had a queue of customers, so why wasn't she moving Gossipy Glossop along with a firm but unmistakably final Franny smile?

The bell above the door jingled, suggesting the queue had just become longer. Nessie glanced around and her feeling of irritation melted away when she saw it was Owen Rhys. Nessie still felt a jolt of electricity whenever she saw him, an attraction that had only deepened as the months passed. She almost blushed when she remembered their last date – a romantic meal in a restaurant far away from the village that had ended in the kind of kiss that had steamed up the car windows to practically indecent levels. Yes, she thought now, as Owen's dark eyes crinkled into a smile, it was safe to say things were hotting up between them. She was even starting to hope they might—

'Next!'

Nessie's head whipped around to see Franny frowning over the top of her wire-rimmed glasses. 'Come along, Vanessa, I haven't got all day and nor have you.'

Biting her tongue, Nessie stepped forwards and slid her bulky envelope through the gap at the bottom of the window. 'Special Delivery, please.'

Franny zoomed in on the address. 'Your Pub of the Year award paperwork?'

Nessie nodded. 'It needs to arrive by Monday.'

'You've left it to the last minute.' The postmistress tapped at her keyboard, each click somehow resounding with disapproval. She sniffed. 'But better late than never, especially with the might of the Royal Mail behind you. We'll make sure it gets there on time.'

Nessie hid a smile. Franny's fearsome reputation reached far beyond Little Monkham – she wouldn't be surprised if the entire postal network was terrified of her – but underneath the older woman's brittle exterior there was a surprisingly soft centre. Nessie knew she was proud that the Star and Sixpence was flourishing and felt she'd played no small part in its triumph. Even so, Nessie didn't really want to antagonise her.

She handed over a ten-pound note, tucking the change and the receipt into her purse. 'Thank you.'

The postmistress nodded. 'You're welcome. Is everything ready for later?'

Nessie thought of the starless Christmas tree, the unbaked mince pies in the kitchen and the VIP guest snoozing upstairs. 'Of course,' she said, crossing her fingers underneath the counter. 'We're all set.'

'Good,' Franny replied, her eyes gleaming. 'The Little Monkham Christmas lights switch-on heralds the beginning of the festive season. I hope you and Samantha appreciate its importance.'

Nessie smiled weakly. 'We do, Franny. Now, I must be getting back. See you later.'

She hurried for the door, almost forgetting Owen was waiting in the queue. 'No pressure,' he murmured as she passed.

She threw him an agonised look but didn't dare to stop, not with Franny's gimlet gaze burning a hole in her back. Instead, she hurried out of the door and across the green, shivering at the hint of frost in the air. To quote her sister's favourite TV show, winter was coming and it would arrive a lot sooner if the Christmas lights switch-on didn't go exactly as Franny expected.

'Three . . . two . . . one . . .'

On the steps of the Star and Sixpence, perma-tanned pop veteran Micky Holiday hit the oversized switch in front of him and the village green lit up. The Christmas tree beside the pub burst into multi-coloured glory too and the crowd cheered.

Micky leaned close to the microphone stand and grinned. 'It's officially Christmas! I hope none of you have been naughty? Because if you have I might have to—'

Next to the sound system, Sam dropped the microphone volume and swept up the music. The sound of Kirsty MacColl and The Pogues filled the air. Micky threw her an injured glance. 'I wasn't going to be rude. Anyone would think you didn't trust me, Sam.'

Sam smiled as she handed him a steaming cup of richly spiced cider. 'You forget how well I know you, Micky. Remember the time you mooned the Prince of Wales?'

Micky shrugged. 'That was years ago. I've grown up since then.'

'It was two years ago,' Sam corrected with a laugh. 'And I'm pretty sure rockers like you never grow up.'

Ruby appeared at Micky's elbow. 'I can vouch for that.'

Micky beamed in delight. 'Ruby!' he cried, sweeping her into a hug. 'It's been too bloody long.'

The retired actress smiled as he kissed her cheek. 'Lovely to see you, darling. You haven't changed a bit.'

'Nor have you – still as glamorous as ever,' Micky said, standing back to study her. 'Although the cane is new. Been in the wars?'

Ruby pulled a face as she glanced down at the elegant walking stick in her hand. 'I took a little tumble. Nothing serious, but these chilly December nights don't help.'

Micky nudged her. 'You need something to warm your cockles, my girl.' He held out his mulled cider. 'Wrap your lips around this.'

For a moment, it looked to Sam as though Ruby would take it, but then she shook her head. 'Not for me, Micky.'

He pushed the drink nearer. 'Go on, take it. It's good stuff.'

Sam felt herself tense on the other woman's behalf. Ruby had been teetotal for just over a month now and Sam knew every day was a struggle for her. Sam stepped forwards, intending to intervene but Ruby held up a hand. 'It's okay, Sam.' She fixed Micky with an honest look. '*You* might not have changed, but I have. I'm not much of a drinker these days.'

A flash of comprehension crossed Micky's face. He handed his cup back to Sam. 'Thank God for that. It's exhausting being a wild man of rock – sometimes all I want is a nice cup of tea, but do you think anyone ever offers me one?'

'I'm sure you can get one inside,' Sam said, feeling a rush of warmth towards him. 'Tilly will sort you out at the bar.'

Micky gave Ruby a sideways glance. 'I can bring you one out, if you like? I know going into pubs can be tricky.'

'Goodness no,' Ruby said, slipping her arm through Micky's. 'I might have given up the demon drink but I could never give up the Star and Sixpence.'

Sam smiled. 'And we couldn't do without you, Ruby.'

She watched as the two of them made their way through the entrance, which was festooned with fairy lights. Nessie hurried over. 'Is that a good idea?' she said, tipping her head in the direction Ruby and Micky had taken. 'I thought you said he was a champion boozer?'

'He is,' Sam replied. 'But he's also been around the block a few times and knows a bit about addiction. As soon as he worked out Ruby was an alcoholic, he handed over his drink and asked for a cup of tea.'

Nessie's gaze widened in surprise. 'Really?'

Sam nodded. 'He was actually the perfect gentleman.' Her own eyes narrowed in thought. 'In fact, I wouldn't be surprised if there's a spark of something between them.'

Franny appeared before Nessie could respond. 'Ah, there you are, Vanessa. I just want to make sure that you're aware of your Christmas Eve responsibilities.'

Nessie exchanged glances with Sam. 'What responsibilities?'

'The landlord of the Star and Sixpence always attends our candlelit carol service,' Franny said. 'It's a tradition that has been in place for more than four hundred years.'

Sam frowned. 'But what about last year? Nessie's name was over the door then too but you didn't demand she went.'

'Last year was different,' Franny replied briskly. 'You'd only just arrived and we weren't sure how long you would be staying.'

Sam stared at her with mounting indignation. Nessie placed a calming hand on Sam's arm. 'I'd be happy to attend. I'm – er – not required to sing, am I?'

Franny pursed her lips. 'It's a carol service, not a karaoke evening. Joining in with the rest of the congregation will do.'

Nessie looked visibly relieved. 'Then count me in.'

The postmistress glanced at Sam. 'You'd be very welcome too, of course.'

'I'll be busy here, mulling the wine for all you thirsty carollers and making sure the Festive Fayre is under control,' Sam replied quickly. 'But I'll hum a few Christmassy tunes while I'm doing it.'

Franny gave a stiff nod. 'That will have to do, then.' Her expression softened and became almost girlish as she glanced over Sam's shoulder. 'Now, did either of you see which way Micky went? I want to thank him personally for doing such a wonderful job.'

'Of course.' Sam kept her face perfectly straight as she pointed inside the Star and Sixpence. 'I think he went that way.'

The older woman patted her hair as she hurried away. 'Good. I wouldn't want him to think we didn't appreciate him.'

'I think Franny has a crush,' Nessie said, shaking her head. She glanced over at Henry Fitzsimmons, who had been stepping out with the postmistress for a few months now. 'Poor Henry.'

'Poor Henry?' Sam almost snorted. 'Poor Micky, more like. He's about to meet the most intense old Flamer ever.'

★ ★ ★

'I've got some news.'

Sam paused in the act of stirring her latte. Further along the bar, Nessie stopped loading bottles of wine into the fridges. They both looked at Kathryn, who was standing on the other side of the empty bar with an excited, apprehensive look on her face.

'What kind of news?' Sam asked. 'The kind that needs bubbles or the kind that means we need to be sitting down?'

'Bubbles, I think.' Kathryn hesitated. 'The band is going on tour.'

Sam grinned. A Sonic Folk tour was a sign that they were more in demand than ever. 'Definitely bubbles,' she said. 'Although eleven o'clock in the morning is probably too early for champagne, even on a Saturday.'

'That's great news,' Nessie said, straightening up. 'When do you go?'

Kathryn pulled a face. 'That's the thing – in typical musician fashion, we've left all the actual planning to the last minute so the first gig is this Thursday. In Newcastle. Then it's on to Leeds, Hull and Manchester and after that it's all a bit of a blur.'

'Good for you, it's about time you guys hit the big time,' Sam said. She fired a covert glance at Nessie. 'How has Owen taken the news?'

'He's pleased,' Kathryn said. 'And he won't be solo parenting for long – Luke's grandmother is coming to stay for a few weeks.'

Sam considered her careful choice of words; Kathryn hadn't said 'my mum', meaning that the grandparent in question must be Eliza's mother. Sam sneaked another look at Nessie, who looked a little rattled, suggesting the inference wasn't lost on her either.

'How lovely,' Nessie said. 'It's been a while since Luke saw her, hasn't it?'

Kathryn paused. 'A few years – she took Eliza's death very hard. And Luke is so like Eliza that I imagine it must be difficult to see past the resemblance sometimes, which is probably part of the reason.'

'Part of the reason?' Nessie echoed, wondering how anyone could stay away from a child as lovable as Luke. 'What's the rest?'

'She's . . .' Kathryn hesitated. 'She's not the warmest person I've ever met, that's all. Not what you'd call maternal. But she's very capable and I know she'll take care of my boys.'

Sam raised her eyebrows. 'Owen is old enough to take care of them both, surely?'

Kathryn laughed. 'Of course he is. But he needs to work, too, and school hours don't lend themselves to working parents. Having Gweneth around will be a big help.'

'I think it's a lovely idea,' Nessie said. 'You deserve a break too.'

'Don't forget us when you're famous, will you?' Sam teased. 'You're booked to play at our New Year Party – last night Micky Holiday was talking about coming back to join you.'

Kathryn's mouth fell open. 'Really?'

Sam nodded. 'He's taken a bit of a shine to Ruby, much to Franny's disappointment. I think we might be seeing a bit more of him, actually.'

Kathryn's expression became a little less star-struck. 'Good. Ruby deserves a bit of TLC – she's had a rough couple of months.' She sighed. 'Micky Holiday, though – he's a rock and roll legend. If I was ten years older I definitely would.'

'Don't let him hear you say that,' Sam warned, her eyes twinkling. 'Micky's got a silver tongue – I've heard him charm younger women than you into bed.'

Kathryn grinned. 'Don't worry, I've spent enough time around musicians to be immune. Anyway, I only popped in to tell you my news. I'd better get back before Luke realises I've gone and empties the biscuit jar.'

Sam waited until she was alone with her sister before clearing her throat. 'So, Owen's mother-in-law is coming to stay.'

Nessie bent down and continued to stock the fridge. 'I think it will be good for Luke to see her.'

'But perhaps not so good for Owen.'

'I don't know,' Nessie said. 'We haven't talked about Eliza much, or her family. He's certainly never suggested there's a problem.'

But Kathryn had, Sam wanted to say. Reading between the lines, Gweneth didn't like Owen – surely she'd be more of a feature in her grandson's life otherwise? She hadn't even visited for his birthday in November. 'And how do you feel about meeting her? Do you think she'll mind that Owen has someone new in his life?'

The smile Nessie sent her way was strained. 'Of course she won't. Eliza died three years ago; she must expect Owen to move on at some point.'

'I think she's going to be trouble,' Sam said, with a direct look at Nessie.

Her sister's shoulders sagged. 'I do too,' she replied quietly. 'Let's hope we're wrong.'

Chapter Thirty-Nine

'When are we seeing that gorgeous man of yours again?'

Martha's eyes danced across the bakery counter as she handed Sam a freshly sliced loaf of bread and a box of crumble-topped mince pies. She made no secret of her crush on Nick Borrowdale, and was constantly dreaming up ways to tempt him back to Little Monkham.

Sam laughed. 'Not for a while, sorry. He's still away filming.'

Martha pouted beneath her white hat. 'Not *Smugglers' Inn*? Cornwall is lovely at any time of year but surely they can't be filming in December. He'll catch his death.'

'He's in New Zealand, working on a big blockbuster. I can't say more than that.'

'Oh,' Martha breathed, her face lighting up. 'Any chance of tickets for the premiere? There's a lifetime's supply of doughnuts in it if you get me there.'

Sam laughed again. 'I'll see what I can do.'

She said goodbye to Martha and called into the butcher's next door to place Nessie's Christmas order and check they were still okay to run their sizzling turkey sausage stall at the Festive Fayre. It wasn't just Martha who loved Nick, Sam mused as she made her way back to the pub. The whole village had embraced him as one of their own, which made things difficult for Joss, who still held a grudge against him. It didn't matter that the reasons behind the grudge were unfounded; Joss disliked Nick and it couldn't be easy constantly hearing his name everywhere he went.

Her thoughts flashed back to Nick, and the last night they'd spent together before he left for New Zealand. He'd held her close at the airport when she'd gone to wave him off. 'I'll miss you.'

'I'll miss you too,' she'd said, reaching up to kiss him. 'But it's only six weeks. You'll be back before you know it.'

His brown eyes crinkled into a smile. 'True. And the best thing about being away from you is the reunion. Shall I book the four-poster room at the Star and Sixpence again?'

'You'll be lucky,' Sam said. 'It's booked solid for months. You'll have to slum it downstairs in the staff quarters with me.'

'I don't mind.' He paused for a moment and his expression grew serious. 'Maybe we could grab some time to ourselves in the New Year? Away from Little Monkham and London – just us?'

Sam smiled. 'I'd like that.'

Boarding was announced for his flight and Sam gave him a little push. 'Now go and hang out with all your famous friends. Be amazing.'

Nick pulled her close and swept her into the kind of kiss she was getting used to – the kind that made her almost forget who and where she was. When they broke apart, Nick's eyes seemed darker than ever. 'I'll see you in six weeks.'

Sam touched a finger to her still tingling lips. 'Six weeks,' she echoed as he walked away. Six weeks to make a decision that would change her life again . . .

And now it was only three weeks until Nick was back and Sam was no nearer to deciding what she wanted. She hadn't confided in Nessie, hadn't told anyone that Nick had asked her to move in with him. He hadn't mentioned it during their Skype chats; he seemed to be leaving the ball entirely in her court, so Sam had pushed it to the back of her mind. But she couldn't ignore it forever. By Christmas, she would have to make her choice. The trouble was, whatever way she chose, she was going to break someone's heart: either her sister's or her boyfriend's. And she didn't really want to hurt either.

'What are you wearing for the Pub of the Year awards?'

Nessie looked up from the kitchen table, a hunted look on her face. 'The purple dress I bought for Bev's wedding a few years ago. Why?'

Sam folded her arms. 'No. I am not being seen with you in that; it looks like something Franny would wear. Haven't you got anything else?'

'Come on, Sam, glitzy award ceremonies aren't my thing,' Nessie protested. 'You said it yourself, we're not going to win, so what does it matter what I'm wearing?'

'Trust me, it matters,' Sam said grimly. Her years in PR had taught her to always look her best, no matter what the occasion, and she'd given her clients exactly the same advice. 'Besides, don't you want to look good for Owen?'

Now Nessie looked shamefaced. 'I haven't asked him yet.'

Sam stared at her sister in disbelief. The awards were less than two weeks away, at an expensive hotel in London, and their tickets were plus ones. Connor, the cellarman at the Star and Sixpence, was taking one place and Sam had suggested Nessie invite Owen. 'Why not?'

'Being away from Luke overnight is a big deal – I was waiting for the right moment to test the water with Owen and then Kathryn told us she was going away,' Nessie said. 'So I thought I'd better wait until Gweneth arrived and she doesn't get here until Thursday.'

It kind of made sense, Sam thought, although knowing her sister, there was a healthy dose of over-cautiousness mixed in there too. 'That will only give him a week's notice.'

Nessie bit her lip. 'Look, Sam, I'm not sure it's a good—'

'We've been over this,' Sam interrupted, her tone firm but gentle. 'You and Owen will never get it on in Little

Monkham. You need some time away and the award ceremony is the perfect opportunity.'

'But—'

'But nothing,' Sam said. 'I can't believe I'm practically having to force you to get to grips with those amazing blacksmith's biceps, Nessie.'

Nessie sighed. 'I know. I don't want to rush things, that's all.'

Sam took a deep breath and blew it out slowly. 'Tomorrow is the anniversary of the day we moved here. You and Owen will have known each other for exactly one year and you haven't progressed past the occasional kiss. That is not rushing things, Ness.'

Her sister's cheeks turned pink.

'Or have you?' Sam asked, grinning in surprise.

'No, but . . .' Nessie hesitated, then ploughed on. 'I think I want to.'

'Then ask him to the awards,' Sam said. 'Get a twin room if it helps or book the honeymoon suite. Whatever it takes. Just take the bull by its horn.'

Nessie's blush deepened. 'Sam!'

'I mean it,' Sam went on. 'You haven't slept with anyone since Patrick and I doubt he was up to much. Seriously, get naked with Owen. I bet he knows a trick or two.'

Now Nessie's cheeks were a deep rosy red. 'Okay, if I agree to ask him, do you promise to stop talking?'

Sam held up her hands. 'Only if you promise to do it.'

'I promise.'

'Good,' Sam said in satisfaction. 'You know I'm only making you do this because I love you, right?'

Nessie sighed. 'Yes. And I know how it looks from the outside, but we are getting there, honestly. We're just—'

'Taking your time, I know,' Sam cut in. Her voice softened. 'I only want you to be happy, Ness.'

Her sister stared down at the table for a moment, then looked up shyly. 'I must admit, I am curious about the size of his muscles.'

'Me too,' Sam said, grinning. 'But I can't wait to hear about the size of everything else too.'

Sunday morning was crisp and perfect. The grass of the green was still silvery-white, despite the blue skies and sunshine, as Sam made her way to visit Ruby. She rubbed her hands together as she walked, grateful for the cashmere scarf Nick had given her before he'd left. Winter in Little Monkham seemed much colder than London had ever been but what it lacked in warmth it made up for in beauty; the village looked like a Christmas card, sparkling and fresh. She could only imagine how much prettier it would be in the snow.

Ruby was ready for Sam when she knocked on the front door of Weir Cottage. She hurried her inside, exclaiming over the frosty air, and ushered her into the kitchen, where the air was rich with the scent of croissants and fresh coffee. Breakfast with Ruby had become a Sunday morning habit for Sam and Nessie, one they took it in turns to share. At first, it had been born from a fear that the older woman might fall off the wagon but, as the days and weeks passed and Ruby stayed clean, it had grown into something each of them looked forward to. More than anything, it had given Sam and Nessie a way to get to know Ruby better, and through her, find out more about their estranged father. She'd given them a bundle of letters he'd written that their mother had returned unopened – those had been eye-opening too and had shown Andrew Chapman to be very different from the half-interested waster both sisters had always believed him to be. In spite of this, Sam found it hard to forgive him for putting alcohol before his family, even though she now understood he'd had no choice.

'Happy anniversary,' Ruby said, once they were both seated at the kitchen table with steaming mugs of cappuccino and a plate of warmed pastries before them. 'You've survived a whole year in Little Monkham.'

Sam smiled. 'This time last year, Nessie and I were packing the car and having the mother of all arguments about how long it would take us to get here. Nessie wanted to leave at midday but I'd arranged a farewell lunch with some friends.'

Ruby lifted an eyebrow. 'Who won?'

'I did,' Sam said, sighing. 'And then we got lost in the dark and I wished I'd listened to Nessie.'

'There's been a lot of water under the bridge since then. I'm sure she's forgiven you.'

'Probably.' Sam gave a wry laugh. 'And let's face it, I've done much worse things.'

'But you've also done a lot of good — helped to restore the Star and Sixpence to her former glory, supported your sister through her divorce, tamed the dragon that is Franny Forster.' Ruby's eyes twinkled. 'Those are extraordinary things, darling. Give yourself some credit.'

Sam couldn't help laughing. 'I suppose when you put it like that . . .'

Ruby reached across and patted her hand. 'You are a wonderful young woman, Sam, and I'm very glad you're part of my life.' She reached across the table to pick up a small, beautifully gift-wrapped box. 'Now, I hope you won't mind but I got you a little anniversary gift.'

Sam glanced at her in dismay. 'Oh Ruby, you shouldn't have.'

The older woman waved a dismissive hand. 'Why shouldn't I? You've been good to me and I want to show my gratitude. Go on, open it.'

Shaking her head, Sam tugged at the oyster ribbon and lifted the lid of the cream-coloured box. She gasped. Nestling inside was a perfect silver sixpence hanging from a chain.

'I hope you like it,' Ruby said, watching her carefully. 'Nessie has the star and you can swap with her if you prefer.'

Sam reached out to touch the glistening coin with one finger and shook her head. 'Not a chance. This is perfect — thank you.'

Ruby sat back, looking pleased. 'It's not much, just a little token of my gratitude.'

Sam fastened the chain around her neck. 'It's gorgeous. I love it.'

'Good,' Ruby said. She lifted up the plate of croissants and held it out to Sam. 'Now let's eat, before these pastries get cold. As that charming man who does the baking show says, there's nothing worse than a soggy bottom.'

Sam was so deep in thought as she made her way back to the pub that she didn't see Joss until he was almost right in front of her. She caught the flicker of movement as he approached and looked up, startled. 'Oh!'

He nodded at her, his blue eyes wary beneath his thick beanie hat. 'Hello, Sam. How are you?'

She gazed at him for a moment, marshalling her thoughts. It didn't matter how often she saw him without his golden beard, she just couldn't get over how much younger he looked clean-shaven. But there were shadows under his eyes and she hated the way he was watching her, as though he was waiting for a hammer blow to fall. Then again, he had good reason to be apprehensive, she thought: he'd avoided her ever since the night he'd kissed her.

'I'm fine,' she said. 'How are you?'

'Okay,' he said, his gaze still watchful. 'Getting by.'

Sam nodded. An awkward silence grew; Sam steeled herself not to speak. It was a trick she'd seen her old boss, Myles Brightman, use countless times – people hated awkward silences and would often say the first thing that came into their heads to fill them.

Joss touched his hat nervously. 'Look, about what happened at Halloween . . .'

He trailed off. Again, Sam waited.

'I'm sorry, okay? I shouldn't have done it. But you looked so good in that Catwoman outfit and I'd had a few drinks and it just . . .' His shoulders slumped. 'I missed you, that's all.'

He looked so dejected that Sam's resolve to make him suffer melted away. She took a deep breath. 'I miss you too. But you took an unbelievable liberty – you must have known I couldn't tell it was you.'

'I kind of hoped you could tell,' he said quietly. 'But then you acted like nothing had happened and I realised you had no idea it was me. So I pretended it hadn't happened too.'

'It took me a while to work it out,' she admitted. 'You didn't have to completely avoid me, though. Things didn't work out between us but there's no reason we can't be friends.'

'Friends?' Joss let out a short incredulous laugh. 'We can't be friends, Sam. Not while Nick Borrowdale is around to rub my nose in it.'

Sam stared at him. 'He hardly rubs your nose in it – in fact, he's been away for weeks. And you haven't exactly been a monk yourself – how are things going with that girl you were seeing – Rebecca, wasn't it?'

'We broke up,' he said, looking away with a scowl.

'Oh. I'm sorry to hear that,' Sam said, then hesitated. 'It wasn't – it wasn't because of what happened at Halloween, was it?'

'What difference does it make?' Joss replied with a weary shrug. 'It was never going to work, anyway. We wanted different things.'

Sam didn't dare ask what he meant – she had a horrible suspicion that it would somehow all turn out to be her fault if she opened that particular can of worms. 'For what it's worth, I'm sorry.'

He opened his mouth as though he was about to say something, then seemed to change his mind. 'Me too.'

Another silence grew and this time it was Sam who broke it. 'Did you hear we won regional Pub of the Year?'

Joss nodded. 'I've got a few mates at the Real Ale Drinkers' Association – one of them told me. Congratulations.'

Of course he'd have mates at RAD, Sam thought, he'd been a good cellarman and she knew he was working in a pub over at Purdon now, so he was still in the trade. And the truth was that winning the award must have been in part down to Joss's hard work; if he hadn't looked after the beer so well, Connor would have had a much harder time picking up the reins after he'd left. The Real Ale Drinkers' Association had visited anonymously in the summer and their judge had commented on everything from the friend-liness of the bar staff to the thickness of the toilet paper and they'd had plenty to say about the quality of the beer, all of it good.

'It's the final in a couple of weeks. We're all going to London,' Sam said, knowing as she spoke that he'd probably be aware of that too.

'I hope you win.'

Sam laughed. 'We won't, but thanks anyway. Not unless you know something I don't?'

Joss held up his hands. 'I don't know anything. But you and Nessie have worked hard to make the Star and Sixpence what it is. You deserve some recognition for that.'

He was making a genuine effort, Sam decided. She smiled. 'Thank you. Get us, having an actual conversation like—' She paused, realising she'd been about to say 'grown ups' and knowing Joss hated it when she suggested he was acting like anything other than an adult. 'Like civilised people.'

'I don't know if we can ever be friends, Sam, but I've got no problem with civility,' Joss said, meeting her gaze. 'I genuinely hope you and Nessie win.'

Sam tipped her head. 'Thank you. I'm sure you'll know if we do – you'll probably hear the screams all the way from London.'

Joss studied her. 'I meant what I said earlier. I miss you. I miss working at the Star and Sixpence too.'

She was filled with a sudden sadness at the way things had worked out. 'I know things weren't always great but we did make a good team. I wish you hadn't left.'

He squared his shoulders. 'I couldn't have stayed. But that doesn't mean I don't regret leaving. If you ever get stuck for staff, let me know. I wouldn't mind helping out sometimes, even if it's only serving up the Christmas beer at the Festive Fayre.'

Now it was Sam's turn to study him. 'That's very generous of you – thanks. Maybe there's a chance we can be friends after all.'

Joss smiled. 'Maybe. Catch you later, Sam.'

'Yeah,' Sam said as he began to walk away. 'Catch you later.'

That was part of her problem, Sam thought as she walked inside the pub, thinking of his summer-sky gaze and infectious grin: Joss had already caught her once and she wasn't one hundred per cent sure she'd ever wriggled free.

Chapter Forty

The stars were bright and clear on Sunday evening, and a thin crescent of silvery moon hung in the black satin sky as Nessie headed over to thank Ruby for her thoughtful gift.

She found the older woman in a reminiscent mood.

'Come in, darling. I was just sorting through some old photographs.'

The kitchen table was awash with pictures, newspaper clippings and theatre programmes. The photographs were a mixture of professional shots from Ruby's acting days – Nessie glimpsed a variety of dramatic costumes and poses as her gaze flickered over the colourful pile. The newspaper clippings were yellowed with age and the programmes bore the logos of many famous West End theatres alongside the names of well-known plays. Nessie picked up the nearest programme.

'*Blithe Spirit*,' she read, '*a sparkling romantic comedy by Noel Coward.*'

Ruby nodded. 'I did that one twice – once in '82, when I played the ghost, Elvira, and once in 2004, when I played Madame Arcati, the medium.' She sighed. 'Glorious days.'

Nessie's eye was caught by another photo. 'Is that you and . . . Elizabeth Taylor?'

The older woman smiled. 'Ah, darling Liz. We had many late-night conversations over a bottle or two, putting our love lives to rights.'

'And this one?'

'Me and Micky Holiday,' Ruby admitted, glancing at the picture Nessie had picked up. 'He was quite a looker back in the day.'

'He still is,' Nessie replied with a smile of her own. 'Just ask Franny or Kathryn.'

Ruby winked. 'No need to ask Franny – she made her admiration very clear on Friday. I believe the phrase "silver fox" was used.'

Nessie nodded. 'But he only had eyes for you. I take it you used to be an item?'

'Oh yes,' Ruby said, her eyes twinkling. 'We were quite the power couple, until he broke my heart. Or did I break his? Do you know, I can't remember.'

'He certainly seems to still carry a torch for you,' Nessie said. 'When are you seeing him again?'

Ruby laughed. 'Are you playing matchmaker, Nessie?'

'No!' Nessie said, feeling herself blush. 'Okay, maybe a little bit.'

'He mentioned going out for dinner in the New Year, for old times' sake. I said I'd think about it.' She gazed at the picture for a few seconds. 'It doesn't hurt to play hard to get sometimes, especially with a man like Micky.'

Nessie couldn't help comparing her own situation to Ruby's. 'How do you know all this stuff? I'm terrible at playing games.'

'You are,' Ruby agreed, casting a knowing look at Nessie. 'But Owen is equally bad, which is why the pair of you should just be honest with each other.'

'Easier said than done,' Nessie said ruefully.

There was a smaller pile of photographs at the edge of the table. These ones were clearly family snaps, featuring Ruby and her son, Cal, when he was a child. Nessie let her gaze skitter over those; she knew they held bittersweet memories for Ruby. And next to that pile was an even smaller one: Ruby with Andrew Chapman, Sam and Nessie's father.

It was always a jolt to see him as he was in his later years. Nessie remembered him through the long lens of childhood; in her mind, he was young and handsome, the way he had been just before he'd left them. Drink hadn't affected his looks much then; his face wasn't ruddy and doughy, his nose wasn't pitted and bulbous like it was in the photos with Ruby. He was recognisably her father and a stranger all at the same time.

Nessie gave herself a mental shake. 'I came to thank you

for the lovely present,' she said, touching the silver star dangling around her neck. 'It's very kind of you.'

'The pleasure is entirely mine, darling,' Ruby said. 'You girls are the closest thing to a family I have.'

Her eyes travelled briefly to the photographs of her and her son, causing Nessie to ache for her. 'I know we've talked about this before but do you think it's time we tried to find Cal for you?'

Ruby looked hesitant. 'I don't know ... he wasn't very receptive last time we spoke. In fact, I seem to remember he told me never to contact him again.'

Nessie knew the story: Ruby's career on the stage had meant she was often away from home, and her relationship with both her husband and her son had suffered. By the time Cal was old enough to understand his mother's absence, alcohol had clouded their relationship still further and he'd eventually cut all ties with her.

'How many years ago was that?' Nessie asked.

'Seven,' Ruby replied. 'No, eight. It was just after his twenty-first birthday party. I'm afraid I got rather drunk.'

Nessie gave her an encouraging look. 'A lot can change in eight years. You've changed.'

Ruby let out a short laugh. 'I've stopped drinking, you mean? Yes, I suppose that's something. But I worry that it's too late for Cal and me. I'll always be the mother who wasn't there for him and nothing I can do will change that.'

Her tone was brisk but Nessie wasn't fooled. It didn't

matter how good an actress Ruby was; she couldn't hide her sadness.

'You'll never know unless you try,' Nessie urged. She glanced sideways at the photograph of her father. 'If there's one thing I regret, it's not having the chance to talk to Dad before he died – missing out on the opportunity to hear his side of the story. I know you've given Sam and me the letters he wrote to us when we were children but I would have liked to have had that conversation in person.'

'And I know he would have given anything to see you and Sam again one last time,' Ruby said, sighing. She closed her eyes. 'Okay. I can give you Cal's last known address and his date of birth, if that helps?'

Nessie smiled. 'I'm sure it will. And who knows, maybe we'll find him in time for Christmas.'

She waited while Ruby went to find her address book, flicking through the old theatre programmes and marvelling at the sheer number of roles she had played; everything from Lady Macbeth to Norma Desmond in *Sunset Boulevard*. Nessie had known Ruby's career had been long and rich but she'd never grasped quite how talented and versatile the other woman was. She sifted through some of the newspaper clippings – glowing reviews of Ruby's many performances mingled with write-ups of star-studded celebrity parties. And then she found an article that made her jaw drop.

'Ruby, did you win a BAFTA?' she asked, when the older woman came back into the kitchen.

'Ah, I see you've uncovered my short-lived film career,' Ruby said, her eyes twinkling. 'The BAFTA was for Best Supporting Actress, in a weepy starring me and a terribly ill Laurence Olivier in '83. Of course, he still acted me off the screen, in spite of his failing health.'

Nessie stared at her. 'But they gave you the BAFTA.'

Ruby smiled. 'No, darling, Larry gave me the BAFTA. His talent was so great that I was able to borrow a little and deliver a performance that caught the Academy's eye.'

'I'm sure that's not true,' Nessie said. 'I'm sure you were brilliant in your own right.'

'Well, perhaps just a little bit,' Ruby allowed. 'And who knows what might have followed if I hadn't discovered I was pregnant?'

Understanding dawned on Nessie. 'With Cal.'

Ruby nodded. 'I auditioned for more films but it wasn't like it is nowadays; no one wanted a pregnant leading lady back then, not when there were plenty of other eager young things ready to take her place. So once Cal was born, I took refuge in the theatre.' She paused and managed a wistful smile. 'I think that's when my drinking began.'

Nessie looked at her with mute sympathy. Ruby had always painted her career as a glittering success, one she'd sacrificed everything for; she'd never once hinted that perhaps it hadn't been as fulfilling as she might have hoped.

'But it's all ancient history now, anyway,' Ruby said, giving herself a brisk shake. 'I've had more than my fair share of good fortune over the years.'

'What did you do with the BAFTA?' Nessie asked, curiosity getting the better of her.

'It's gathering dust under the bed. I could never bear to look at it, you see.' She held out a sheet of paper covered in curly copperplate handwriting. 'Cal's details.'

Nessie took it, glancing briefly at the Somerset address.

'And I found this too,' Ruby went on, lifting up an envelope that bore Nessie and Sam's names in spidery handwriting. 'I've kept it back, wondering when to give it to you.'

'Kept it back?' Nessie repeated. 'Why?'

'Because it's the last one,' Ruby said, passing the letter to Nessie. 'He wrote it when he knew he didn't have long left. And I think, given what you've said this evening, that maybe it's time to give it to you.'

Nessie stared down at it for a moment, and then swallowed, *the last one* . . . 'Thank you. I'll read it with Sam later.' She held up the paper with Cal's address. 'And we'll get to work on this right away.'

Ruby sighed. 'I don't hold out much hope.'

Nessie stood up and squeezed her hand. 'Who knows – maybe Cal has changed too.'

Sam held the envelope Nessie had given her for a long time without speaking.

'I'm not sure I'm ready for this,' she said eventually, shifting on the living room sofa so that she was facing Nessie. 'I mean, I've forgiven him a lot since we discovered Mum lied about him not keeping in touch, but this feels . . . very final.'

Nessie nodded – she felt exactly the same way, as though they were somehow saying goodbye to a father they'd come to understand so much better in the last year. 'Ruby didn't say as much but she dropped some pretty broad hints that it's not an easy read.'

Sam sucked in a deep breath and puffed it out fast. 'At the same time, I don't want to put it off. If Ruby thinks we're ready then maybe we are.'

'Okay,' Nessie replied. 'I'll get us a drink.'

It was a little Sunday evening ritual they'd adopted, before they'd run out of letters; sitting on the sofa with a glass of wine, reading their father's words from decades earlier. Nessie felt it was extra poignant tonight.

Sam waited until Nessie was seated beside her, then passed her the letter. 'You open it. You were his favourite, after all.'

Nessie laughed. 'No I wasn't. You should have seen how he doted on you when you were a baby.'

'You're the oldest, then,' Sam insisted. 'So you should open it.'

Nessie slipped her finger under the flap on the envelope, feeling the glue crackle and give. She slid the letter out, noticing instantly how different the handwriting was: old and frail, in spite of the fact that Andrew had only been in his mid-sixties when he'd died. Sam took one side, Nessie held the other and started to read.

Star and Sixpence,
Sixpence Lane,
Little Monkham,
Shropshire,
SY6 2XY

13th July 2015

Dear Vanessa and Samantha

It has been many years since my last letter to you. I don't know if you ever knew that I wrote – I like to think that you didn't but perhaps I am just a foolish old man. Perhaps your mother showed you the envelopes and you chose not to open them. I suppose it doesn't really matter now – what's done is done.

If you are reading this then I assume you have met Ruby. She is very different to your mother but I think you will like her. She has been the light that has kept me going for many years and I thank the blessed star that brought her to me, almost as much as I thank the one that gave me the two of you, my darling daughters. You have always been in my heart, even though you were sadly not in my life.

Ruby is making me write this early in the morning, when I am not at my best but my thoughts are a little sharper, although my head thumps and my hand shakes. So you will have to forgive my terrible handwriting. She tells me I must write it now so that there's a better chance I will remember everything I need to say – unfortunately,

I think it is far too late for that. I do want you to know that losing you both has been the deepest regret of my life. I am sorry that I was not there to see you grow into the accomplished young women I know you must be, and I'm sorry that I will not be there to see everything you will achieve in the future. But most of all, I am sorry for every moment of pain or sadness I caused you – the two of you are the best of me and I have loved you from the second you were born.

You will know by now that I have left you the Star and Sixpence. She is a grand old lady who has looked after me well all these years – I hope she will do the same for you. But perhaps you won't want to live here, in which case I give you my blessing to do whatever you see fit with the building, although you may encounter some opposition from Franny Forster. She's a good woman too, if you look past the prickliness. Anyway, I once wrote that I thought you would like Little Monkham – and whether your time here is long or short, I hope I was right. This place and the people who live here have given me a lot.

I am certain that your memories of me are of a ham-fisted giant who broke your toys and abandoned you. I wish I'd had the opportunity to change that. All I can do is leave you my home and hope it is enough to show you that I loved you, in spite of how it looked.

Be happy, my darling daughters,
Love, Dad xx

Neither sister spoke for a few seconds, then Nessie took a deep, unsteady breath and reached for her wine. Tears spilled down both cheeks as she turned to Sam and raised her glass to chink it against her sister's. 'To Dad. I wish we'd known him better.'

Sam's cheeks were wet too. 'Yeah,' she said, managing a watery smile of her own. 'To Dad.'

'Do you think this sounds okay?'

It was almost eleven o'clock on Tuesday morning and Nessie had been at the kitchen table since before six trying to compose a letter to Ruby's son. A quick check of the electoral roll had told her and Sam that Cal no longer lived at the address Ruby had given them, but they'd managed to track him down to a small town on the outskirts of Oxford. And now it came down to it, Nessie wasn't sure she knew what to say to him.

'*Dear Cal,*' she read, trying to inject some confidence into her voice. '*I'm writing on behalf of your mother, Ruby Cabernet, who is a close family friend. I know that you have not seen each other for many years, and that she regrets this, so I wonder if perhaps you might consider meeting her for a coffee and a chat some time.*'

Sam leaned back against the kitchen counter and pursed her lips. 'It's a bit formal.'

'That's because I don't know him,' Nessie said. 'And actually, I'm sticking my nose right into his business – I think I should be a bit formal, don't you?'

'True,' Sam conceded. 'You probably need to get across

that Ruby has stopped drinking, though. Without actually saying so, obviously.'

Nessie groaned and tossed her pen onto the table. 'Why am I doing this when you're the PR girl? You know how to spin things so that they sound better and appealing.'

Sam shook her head. 'You can do it. Just mention that Ruby has changed and suggest that she deserves a second chance – if he's half as smart as his mother then he'll read between the lines.'

'But what if he doesn't?' Nessie said, anxiety bubbling up inside her. 'What if I mess this up and Ruby never sees him again? Come on, Sam, this is important.'

'Fine,' Sam sighed, taking a seat at the table. 'Pass me the pen.'

Relieved, Nessie sat back and watched as her sister wove her magic on the paper. She'd been thinking about Ruby and Cal a lot more since reading their father's last letter; it had made her determined not to let history repeat itself. Ruby deserved the chance to make things right with her son. Nessie just hoped she and Sam could convince Cal too.

Chapter Forty-One

'Nessie, I'd like you to meet Gweneth.'

Nessie surreptitiously wiped her hand on her jeans and stepped out from behind the bar, hoping she didn't look as nervous as she felt. It was ridiculous to feel intimidated by Owen's mother-in-law, she reminded herself as she summoned up a warm smile; she was thirty-six years old, not sixteen. Meeting her boyfriend's family should be a breeze.

'Hello, Gweneth, it's lovely to meet you at last,' she said, holding out her hand. 'I've heard so much about you.'

The blonde-haired woman did not smile back. Instead, she touched Nessie's outstretched fingers for the briefest of seconds and then let her arm drop. 'Hello.'

Nessie kept her smile in place and tried again. 'Can I get you a drink? A coffee or a glass of wine?'

Gweneth's eyes had been flicking around the pub, taking in every detail. It was Friday lunchtime and the bar was quiet but Nessie still wished she'd made the time to clear the empty glasses that were dotted here and there, especially when Gweneth's cold blue gaze came to rest on her. 'It's a little early for me, thank you.'

Nessie's heart sank; the disapproval in the other woman's voice had been unmistakable. Where was Sam when she needed her? Nessie wondered, resisting the urge to glance wildly around. A bit of charm would work wonders now.

Owen stepped forwards. 'Gweneth arrived yesterday, from Aberystwyth. She's staying with us while Kathryn is away.'

And that was a sign Owen was nervous too, Nessie thought, because he knew she was well aware why Gweneth was staying; they'd talked about it over dinner a few nights ago. 'Oh yes, of course,' Nessie said politely. 'Did you have a good journey?'

'Tolerable, I suppose,' Gweneth replied. 'It's been so long since I've visited Little Monkham that I'd forgotten how far it was.'

There was a faint whisper of accusation behind the words. Nessie cleared her throat hurriedly. 'I'm sure Luke is excited you're here. He's been talking about your visit all week.'

Again, Gweneth's steely gaze swept over Nessie. 'Do you spend a lot of time with my grandson, Nessa?'

Nessie glanced briefly at Owen to see if he was picking up the same vibe she was. She saw his forehead had crinkled into a frown. 'I babysit sometimes.' She felt her cheeks begin to heat up. 'And – well, I suppose you could say we're . . . that we've been—'

'Nessie and I are seeing each other,' Owen cut in easily. 'So of course she spends a lot of time with Luke. He thinks the world of her.'

'The feeling is mutual,' Nessie said, smiling at Owen partly in gratitude and partly in delight. 'He's a very special boy.'

Gweneth looked as though she'd been slapped. 'I see.' Her lips tightened until they were almost white. 'I didn't realise that was the situation, Owen.'

He tipped his head. 'And now you do.'

'Now I do,' Gweneth echoed, aiming a hard stare at Nessie. 'Well, I don't think I need to keep you any longer. It looks like you have plenty of work to do here.'

She produced a smile that went nowhere near her eyes and turned on her heel. Owen flashed Nessie an apologetic look and turned to follow but Nessie grabbed his arm. 'You didn't think to tell her beforehand?'

'Sorry. I didn't think she'd react like that.' He squeezed her fingers. 'I'll pop over later, we can talk more then.'

Nessie watched him go and let out a shaky breath. Sam had been right about Gweneth Morgan; she was going to be trouble.

Nessie kept her distance from Snowdrop Cottage over the next few days, although she was so busy managing Festive

Fayre disasters that it wasn't hard. The merry-go-round Sam had booked had suddenly cancelled and it had taken Nessie a lot of desperate phone calls to find a replacement. A mini-feud, which had broken out between Henry and Martha's husband, Rob, over who was best qualified to be the village Father Christmas, had required all of Father Goodluck's diplomatic skills to resolve it. And if the temperature kept dropping, they were all in danger of freezing, but there was nothing Nessie could do about that.

Owen was true to his word and called into the Star and Sixpence to reassure Nessie that he was sure Gweneth didn't hate her; she was just having trouble adjusting to being in Little Monkham, with its constant reminders of Eliza. Sam had raised her eyebrows and suggested Owen could have handled it better.

'At least Luke is happy she's here,' she said.

Nessie had winced. 'Actually, I'm not sure he is. I watched him leaving for school this morning and you know what he's usually like – he chatters non-stop. But not today. He didn't say a word and he looked so fed up.'

Sam shook her head. 'Huh. When is Kathryn back again?'

'Christmas Eve,' Nessie replied. 'But what if this becomes a regular thing? What if Kathryn decides to move out and Owen needs Gweneth's help more and more?'

'That's not going to happen,' Sam said, but she sounded less than certain.

'It might,' Nessie argued. 'Kathryn has already said she's worried life is passing her by.'

'I meant that Owen wouldn't rely on Gweneth,' Sam said. 'Not if he sees how unhappy Luke is around her.'

Nessie sighed. 'I don't know. I could be wrong – maybe Luke was just in a grump about something.'

'How unhappy you are, then,' Sam said. 'It doesn't sound like Owen has the best relationship with Gweneth himself.'

'I suppose it's hard for her too,' Nessie said. 'She might come round in a day or two, once she's settled in.'

But Gweneth showed no signs of coming round – in fact, she'd crossed the street to avoid Nessie on Saturday morning. Owen had been conspicuously absent from the Star and Sixpence too, something Ruby had been quick to notice.

'No Owen tonight?' she'd asked across the bar as she sipped the peach and elderflower mocktail Connor had rustled up for her.

Nessie had tried her hardest to look casual. 'Not tonight. I expect he's keeping Gweneth company.'

Ruby leaned forwards. 'Not willingly, I bet,' she said in a wicked stage-whisper. 'Have you checked she hasn't chained him to his anvil?'

'Ruby!' Nessie said, trying not to laugh. 'That's not very nice.'

'Nor is Gweneth Morgan,' Ruby replied. 'I know it can't have been easy losing her daughter like that but I seem to remember she could freeze molten lava with a single glance long before Eliza fell ill.'

'Owen and I are going out for a drink on Monday evening,' Nessie said. 'Providing Gweneth doesn't mind babysitting Luke.'

'Ay, there's the rub,' Ruby said, sighing. 'I'm sorry to be a pessimist but I wouldn't count on Gweneth to do anything that allows Owen to spend time with you, Nessie.'

Nessie had tried not to let it bother her, but she almost groaned out loud when she took some flowers to her father's grave on Sunday morning and saw Gweneth standing just a few plots away at Eliza's. She thought about turning around and then squared her shoulders and carried on walking; she wasn't afraid of Gweneth Morgan.

When Gweneth turned around, Nessie nearly changed her mind. The other woman watched her approach in a frosty silence that had little to do with the sub-zero temperature.

'Good morning, Gweneth,' Nessie said, doing her best to sound friendly. 'How are you enjoying your stay in Little Monkham?'

The atmosphere became even colder. 'I'm standing at my daughter's grave. Enjoying is hardly the word I'd choose.'

Nessie felt her face flush. 'Of course – I didn't mean ... I'm very sorry for your loss. From what I've heard, Eliza was a wonderful person.'

Gweneth glanced down at Eliza's gravestone, hiding her face from Nessie. 'Yes, she was. Irreplaceable.'

Unsure what to say next, Nessie started to arrange the flowers she'd brought on her father's grave.

'Of course – you're Andrew Chapman's daughter,'

Gweneth announced suddenly. 'That certainly explains why you were drinking at lunchtime on Friday.'

Nessie felt a thorn sink into her finger as she clenched the stem she was feeding into the sunken vase. 'I wasn't drinking,' she said as evenly as she could manage with her thudding heart. 'I offered you a drink, out of politeness, because you were in a pub and that's what people often do in pubs.'

The other woman sniffed. 'Believe me, I know. You get all kinds of people in those places.'

The words themselves were innocent but the inflection behind them was not. Nessie stood up. 'Do you know, I think I'll come back and do this later.'

Gweneth's eyes narrowed. 'Not so fast. There are a few things you and I need to get straight.'

'I don't think—'

'Owen was married to my daughter and Luke is my grandson,' Gweneth said, as though she hadn't heard Nessie speak. 'They are *my* family.'

Nessie opened her mouth to speak again but Gweneth cut across her. 'And maybe in the fullness of time, Owen might find someone new to settle down with, but I am bloody sure that someone isn't going to be you.'

Nessie stepped back as though she'd been whipped. 'What exactly do you have against me?'

Gweneth glared at her. 'Look at you – you're half the woman Eliza was. You work behind a bar all day and you stink of beer – if you think for one moment I'd let someone like you look after my grandson then you've got another think coming. I'd take him to live with me before that happened.'

The world tipped around Nessie – this was crazy! Had Gweneth really just suggested she might take Luke away from his father? 'What?'

Gweneth shrugged. 'There are signs of neglect everywhere I look. Owen is too busy working in the forge to take proper care of the boy and I don't suppose that sister of his is much better, when she's here. As far as I can tell, Luke spends most of his time playing computer games. He certainly doesn't want to do any of the things I suggest.'

Nessie's mouth fell open. 'Luke isn't neglected.'

'Maybe, maybe not,' Gweneth said, her voice suddenly oily. 'But I can certainly see reasons for suggesting it. I think Social Services would listen to a concerned grandparent, don't you? If I decided it was necessary . . .'

And suddenly, Nessie understood. 'You want me to back off.'

'I wouldn't dream of suggesting such a thing. But if you care about Luke as much as you say you do—'

Nessie felt as though the air had turned to treacle. 'You want me to back off or you'll take Luke away from Owen.'

Gweneth said nothing. She simply stood beside Eliza's grave, watching Nessie with a little half smile. 'I'll leave you to think it over,' she said eventually, sweeping past Nessie. 'I'm sure you'll do what's best for everyone.'

Nessie stared after her, wondering if she'd imagined the

entire conversation. Gweneth couldn't really have suggested she'd report Owen to Social Services if Nessie didn't end their relationship. And yet her final words still rang in Nessie's ears — *I'm sure you'll do what's best for everyone . . .*

Ruby had been more right than she could possibly know, Nessie thought faintly as she bent once more to arrange the flowers on her father's grave. Gweneth might not have Owen chained up with iron but she had him trapped nonetheless.

Nessie's feeling that she was caught in some kind of never-ending nightmare continued throughout Sunday and spilled into Monday. She got the breakfast order wrong for Mr and Mrs Guthrie in the guest rooms and had to offer profuse apologies, then inexplicably managed to wash a red sock in with the white towels, turning them all salmon pink. Sam noticed her preoccupied air and asked her several times what was wrong; Nessie thought about telling her the truth but she knew her sister would be outraged, and that she'd insist on confronting Gweneth, which could have all kinds of unintended consequences. Nessie had no idea whether the woman meant her threat or not but a direct confrontation was the last thing she wanted, especially when Luke's wellbeing was at stake. No, she'd make some discreet enquiries first, Nessie decided; maybe speak to Kathryn about Gweneth Morgan, and then she'd work out what to do next. Unfortunately, that also meant she needed to convince Gweneth that she was going along with her plan without explaining to Owen what was happening. He was going to be confused and disappointed, Nessie thought, closing her eyes. And so was Sam.

'You're quiet this evening,' Owen said, as they sat opposite each other in a restaurant a few miles from Little Monkham.

Nessie did her best to smile but she knew it was a poor effort. 'I've got a bit of a headache, to be honest.'

He threw her a concerned look. 'Why didn't you say something? We could have postponed tonight and gone out when you were feeling better.'

Nessie sighed. 'It seemed a shame to waste a ready-made babysitter.' She paused to gather up some courage and then went on. 'How are you getting on with your new house-mate, anyway?'

Owen took his time chewing a mouthful of steak and Nessie wondered if he was buying himself time to find a diplomatic answer. 'Not bad, I suppose. She's got some old-fashioned ideas about bedtime that I think Luke is struggling with, and she refuses to read him any Harry Potter so he waits until she's gone and reads it under the bed sheets.'

Nessie let out a brief laugh. 'That sounds like Luke.'

'And me, when I was a kid,' Owen said, his eyes crinkling at the edges. 'I was forever staying up late to finish reading a book when I was his age. I still do, to be honest.'

Nessie tried to banish an appealing image of Owen tucked up between white cotton sheets, immersed in a book. 'But Luke is happy around her, isn't he?' she persisted. 'He likes being with her?'

'He seems to, which is probably a good thing seeing as she's suggested he goes and stays with her sometime in the future.'

Nessie almost dropped her fork. 'Has she? What have you told her?'

The words came out sharper than she'd intended, causing Owen to frown. 'I said we'd see how things went. What's with all the questions, Nessie? What's going on?'

'Nothing,' Nessie said wretchedly. 'It's just—'

She stopped as a sudden urge to tell him the truth came over her. It didn't sound as though he was especially enjoying his mother-in-law's visit, nor did she get the feeling Luke was especially happy, either. But Owen was like Sam; if Nessie explained what Gweneth had said, he'd insist on confronting her. And then things could probably only go one way: she would deny everything, making Nessie look neurotic and insecure, and then she'd put her horrible plan into action, causing a lot more heartache for everyone. The suggestion that Luke go and stay with her for a few days could be meant as a reminder to Nessie of what might happen if she didn't do as Gweneth demanded . . .

'I think we should take a break,' Nessie blurted out.

Owen's frown deepened. 'From dinner?'

She took a deep breath. 'No, from us – you and me.'

'Oh,' Owen said, suddenly very still. 'Right.'

Beneath the table, she clenched her hands into fists,

willing herself to say what needed to be said. 'It's just that things seem to be moving so fast these days – my divorce isn't finalised yet and . . . well, I think we should step back a bit, that's all. Work out what we really want.'

Owen lowered his fork and stared at her. 'I already know what I want.'

The look in his eyes made Nessie shiver, in spite of what she was trying to say, and she had to push the feeling aside to concentrate. 'Don't ask me to explain because I can't.'

'Is this about your divorce?' he asked, sounding bewildered. 'Because you know I don't give two hoots whether you've got your Decree Absolute or not.'

Nessie shook her head. 'No, it's nothing to do with that.' She paused, trying to ignore the sickness in the pit of her stomach. 'Look – it's almost Christmas, we're both going to be busy. Why don't we agree to take a break until the New Year?'

Owen studied her in silence for a moment. 'You didn't feel like this last week. What's changed?'

'Nothing,' she said, unable to meet his gaze. 'It's for the best, that's all. You're going to have to trust me.'

The silence grew, until Owen reached across to take Nessie's hand. 'Okay, if that's what you want. I trust you.'

She swallowed as tears blurred her vision. 'It is what I want.'

'Then it's fine with me.' He squeezed her fingers gently. 'You're worth waiting for, Nessie Blake.'

It was all so unfair, Nessie thought, fighting the hot

miserable tears that were threatening to spill down her cheeks. But it was also the only way she could see to protect Luke and Owen from Gweneth. Blinking hard, Nessie took a few seconds to compose herself and then looked up into Owen's dark-eyed gaze.

'Thank you,' she said, managing a wavering smile. 'I hope you're right.'

Chapter Forty-Two

'You've done what?'

Sam stared incredulously at her sister on Tuesday morning, unable to believe what she'd just heard. The last time they'd spoken about Owen, Nessie had been going to invite him to the Pub of the Year awards in London and now, by some twist of logic Sam couldn't even begin to understand, she seemed to have broken up with him instead.

Nessie had the grace to look shamefaced. 'Keep your voice down,' she said, glancing around the quiet bar. 'It's only a temporary break and I do have my reasons.'

'What reasons?' Sam shook her head. 'Honestly, Nessie, I don't understand you sometimes – he's hot and totally into you, you're both single. What possible reason could you have for taking a break?'

'I don't want to go into it, Sam,' Nessie said, raising her

chin. 'I've told you what's going on, now can you please just let it go?'

Sam opened her mouth to argue and then snapped it shut. Her sister was entitled to handle her relationship with Owen however she wanted to, although it made Sam want to scream with frustration. But there was obviously more to this break – temporary or otherwise – than Nessie was letting on.

'Fine.' Sam took a deep breath and let it out slowly. 'As long as you're all right?'

Nessie gave her an unhappy smile. 'I'm all right. So, what's the plan for Thursday?'

Sam switched her mind into work mode. 'The awards don't start until seven in the evening. Tilly has asked her friend, Robin, to help her cover the bar, so I thought we could pick up Connor and drive down to London just after lunch on Thursday, check in at the hotel mid-afternoon and then hit the shops.'

'Hit the shops?' Nessie repeated. 'I thought you already had an outfit.'

Sam pictured the silver cocktail dress hanging on the back of her door upstairs, and the strappy heels in the wardrobe. 'I do,' she said. 'We're going shopping for you.'

Nessie began to argue but Sam cut her off. 'I've already told you that purple dress won't do. You need something knockout, Nessie.' Her voice softened a little. 'Let me treat you, okay? Call it an early Christmas present.'

'Nothing low cut,' Nessie warned. 'Or too tight.'

Sam held her hands up in mock surrender. 'I promise.' She aimed a mischievous glance her sister's way. 'We'll save the trip to Victoria's Secret for another day.'

Sam blinked blearily at the message first thing on Thursday morning before she let out a loud groan of frustration.

'Nessie?' she called, pushing back the duvet and wincing as her feet hit the cold bedroom floor. 'Ness, we've got a problem.'

She pulled on her dressing gown and padded along the landing to the kitchen, where Nessie was putting the finishing touches to the full English breakfast for the latest guests in the rooms above. 'Tilly's got a fever,' Sam said, as Nessie looked up. 'She doesn't think she can come in today.'

Nessie's face fell. 'Oh no. She was complaining about feeling shivery all day yesterday – that's why I sent her home early. I don't suppose her friend Robin will want to come in without her. What are we going to do?'

Sam tapped her phone thoughtfully. 'Call in some favours? Who do we know who's handy behind the pumps?' Her thoughts flew to Joss and his offer to help out if they needed him. Would Nessie be okay with it, if she saw that it didn't trouble Sam?

'Give me a hand to carry these up, will you?' Nessie said, waving a hand at the laden trays. 'And then we can put our heads together properly.'

'What about Owen?' Sam said, once the breakfasts had been safely delivered. 'He's worked the bar before and I'm sure he'd be happy to help, even if you have broken his heart.'

'I haven't broken his heart,' Nessie said, grimacing. 'But all the same I'd rather not ask him. Isn't there anyone else?'

Sam frowned at her sister thoughtfully. What was behind this sudden aversion to Owen? It had come out of nowhere; one minute they'd been discussing his muscles in a moderately inappropriate manner and the next, Nessie practically flinched at the mention of his name. What had changed in the last week, she wondered.

'There is one person we could ask,' she said aloud, still considering Nessie. 'You might not like it, though.'

'Who?' Nessie asked. Her eyebrows shot up. 'Not Franny?'

'God, no!' Sam spluttered. 'We'd have no customers left. No, I meant Joss – I ran into him a few days ago and he said he'd be happy to help out if we ever got stuck.'

'I don't think that's a very good idea,' Nessie said, folding her arms. 'Not with everything that's happened between you.'

'He knows his way around the cellar,' Sam pointed out. 'Whatever else you think of Joss, he's a safe pair of hands.'

Nessie frowned. 'It's not his hands I'm worried about. Have you forgotten what happened at the masked ball?'

Sam shook her head. 'Of course I haven't. But we had a chat and I think we both know where we stand now. Just think about it, Ness.'

Nessie looked unconvinced. 'I don't know.'

Sam knew better than to push it. 'He's probably already working, anyway,' she conceded. 'But maybe I could ring around a few of the other local pubs, see if any of their staff are interested. Someone might fancy a bit of extra cash this close to Christmas.'

'Or they'll be busy working too.' Nessie sighed. 'I suppose one of us will have to stay here.'

Sam reached for her phone, unwilling to accept defeat. 'Let me see what I can do first.'

By mid-morning, she'd run out of options. The landlords she'd spoken to wanted to help, but a lot of the pubs served food and had Christmas parties to cater for – they couldn't spare anyone to help Sam out, no matter how much they wanted to. The agencies were at full stretch too – the run up to Christmas was simply too busy, they told her.

'Why don't I stay here?' Nessie said, when Sam gave her the bad news. 'Obviously you need to go, and Connor has worked so hard that he really deserves to be there. I don't mind missing it.'

Sam gazed at her in dismay; Nessie had worked hard too and it was her name above the door. She ought to be able to enjoy the award ceremony too; it wasn't as though there was much glamour involved in running a pub. 'I know you don't want to ask Owen but is there any chance—'

'No,' Nessie interrupted. 'I don't imagine Gweneth would approve anyway. She told me she's not a big fan of pubs.'

The penny dropped in Sam's head: Gweneth was what

had changed. Her arrival had sparked some kind of problem between Nessie and Owen – something Nessie was unwilling to share with her sister or, from the sound of things, Owen himself. Sam narrowed her eyes reflectively; maybe it was time for Sam to play matchmaker yet again . . .

'Okay, Ness, if the worst comes to the worst then I guess you'll have to stay here,' she said. 'It's a shame, though – I was looking forward to letting our hair down together.'

Nessie gave a little shrug that didn't quite mask her disappointment. 'We'll just have to make sure we get nominated again next year.'

Sam got to her feet and stretched. 'I'm just popping to the shop – do you need anything?'

Nessie glanced at the clock in surprise. 'You're cutting it a bit fine, aren't you? I thought you wanted to leave at lunchtime?'

'That was when I thought we needed to hit Oxford Street,' Sam pointed out, heading for the stairs that led down to the bar. 'I've got plenty of time now. See you in a while.'

Owen was right where Sam expected him to be: in the forge, hammering a piece of white-hot metal on the anvil. She waited until the ringing hammer blows stopped and he plunged the glowing metal into a bucket of water before she called his name.

He looked up. 'Sam. I don't see you in here very often.'

Sam took a few steps forward but kept a safe distance

from the heat of the furnace behind him. He looked every bit a blacksmith; his forehead was smudged with dirt and his curls were wild in the firelight. 'I've got a proposition for you, Owen.'

He listened while she explained what had happened. 'So I wondered whether you'd be able to help out behind the bar for a few hours this evening?'

Owen nodded. 'I'd be happy to. What time do you need me?'

'Around seven would be perfect,' Sam said, smiling. 'Thank you.'

She was almost at the door when she heard Owen call, 'Tell Nessie I said good luck. Enjoy yourselves.'

Sam crossed her fingers as she turned to smile at him. 'Oh, we will. Thanks, Owen.'

The Post Office was quiet, which was exactly what Sam had hoped for as she crunched across the village green. Franny was behind the shop counter, reading the local paper when Sam walked in.

'Hello, Samantha. What can I get you?'

Sam picked up a tube of toothpaste and placed it on the counter. 'Last minute supplies.'

Franny nodded. 'Of course. What time are you setting off?'

'Soon,' Sam said. 'I want to allow a bit of time for traffic once we hit London – we don't want to be late.'

Franny's eyes were sharp over the top of her glasses. 'You

most certainly do not. You and Vanessa are Little Monkham ambassadors – the honour of the entire village is at stake.'

Sam wondered whether she should mention the change in plan as she handed over some money, and decided against it; the postmistress might volunteer to work the bar, or worse, decide she needed to go to London instead. Sam wasn't sure she could cope with twenty-four hours of non-stop Franny. 'Speaking of Little Monkham ambassadors, I heard from Kathryn. The tour seems to be going well.'

'I am delighted to hear it,' Franny said. 'Although strictly speaking, the band is something of a mongrel – only Kathryn is a local girl.'

Sam nodded, mentally shifting her conversational chess pieces into place. 'It's nice that she's having a good time, getting out there a bit more instead of looking after Luke all the time, and it's lovely for Luke to spend some time with his grandmother.' She paused to drop the change Franny had given her into her purse. 'You and Gweneth must be old friends – have you seen her much since she arrived?'

Much to Sam's delight, Franny's nostrils flared. 'We are no such thing. I've barely seen her at all and that's just the way I like it.'

'Oh,' Sam said, widening her eyes. 'Don't you get on?'

Franny pursed her lips. 'It's not that we don't get on,' she said stiffly. 'More that she hasn't got a good word to say about the village. I'm sorry that poor Eliza died here but it wasn't anything we did. The way Gweneth Morgan went on you'd think we were personally responsible for what happened.'

'So she's probably not very happy to be back,' Sam mused. But that still didn't explain her impact on Nessie, she thought. 'How did she feel when Eliza moved here with Owen?'

'I seem to remember she was rather upset,' Franny replied. 'Often tried to make them go back to Wales, especially when Luke was born. But Owen had built his business here by then and so they stayed. Gweneth didn't like that, either.'

Sam picked up her toothpaste. 'She sounds quite controlling.'

Franny snorted. 'You can say that again. I'm amazed she's left Owen and Luke alone as long as she has, to be honest. I thought she'd have been meddling and interfering years ago.'

'There wasn't really room for meddling,' Sam said. 'Not when Kathryn was filling in for Eliza so well.'

The postmistress gave Sam an appraising look. 'You should tell Nessie to watch her back. I don't imagine Gweneth will be pleased that Owen is courting again.'

And there it is, Sam thought, as the last piece of the puzzle fell into place. That's why Nessie was back-pedalling so spectacularly. The question was, what did Gweneth have to threaten her with? And how was Sam going to neutralise her?

'Thanks, Franny,' she said, heading for the door. 'We'll try to uphold the honour of the village tonight.'

Franny sniffed. 'Remember, it's not the taking part that counts – it's the winning. Don't let me down!'

Shaking her head in wry amusement at Franny's ironclad competitiveness, Sam pulled out her phone as she crossed the green.

'Kathryn?' she said, as the call connected. 'It's Sam. Listen, we need to talk . . .'

'You were a long time,' Nessie said, when Sam walked back into the pub.

Sam held up her toothpaste. 'Franny was giving me some last minute instructions for later.'

'About that . . .' Nessie said, unsmiling. 'We've got another problem.'

She waved a hand towards Connor, who was hunched miserably on a bar stool looking like he'd much rather be in bed.

Sam gaped at him in consternation. 'Not him too?'

Nessie nodded grimly. 'It looks like the same thing that Tilly has. I'm sorry to say this, Sam, but I don't think he should be going anywhere.'

Connor looked across and managed a feeble wave, giving Sam the opportunity to take in his flushed face and sweaty forehead. 'You're right,' she told Nessie with a reluctant sigh. 'The only place Connor should be going is bed.'

She crossed the bar and picked up his overnight bag. 'You look like you're about to pass out,' she told him kindly. 'Go home.'

'But the awards—'

'Aren't what's important right now,' Sam finished, as he broke off to cough. 'Christmas is just around the corner, you need to look after yourself, not worry about an award we probably haven't even won.'

The ex-fireman opened his mouth to argue again. This time it was Nessie who interrupted. 'You've got the same symptoms as Tilly and she's tucked up in bed with a hot water bottle and a Lemsip,' she told him. 'Sam can fly the flag for the pub and tell us all about it once she's home.'

Connor looked back and forth between the two of them, his eyes glittering with fever. 'Okay,' he sighed.

'Let me give you a lift,' Sam said, slipping behind the bar to grab the car keys. 'No offence, Connor, but you look like you'd lose a fight with a kitten.'

The cellarman flashed her a grateful look. 'I feel it. Thanks.'

'Don't be long,' Nessie said to Sam, with a meaningful glance at the clock above the bar. 'Time's getting on.'

Connor didn't live far away – a few minutes' journey by car. Sam dropped him at his gate with strict instructions to rest. Then she turned around and headed back to the Star and Sixpence, her mind on the evening ahead. It wasn't the end of the world for her to be attending the awards on her own but she had to admit it would have been nice to have someone to share it with. And then, as she reached the green, she saw a familiar figure: Joss.

Coming to a snap decision, she slowed down and opened her window. 'Are you working tonight?'

Joss blinked at her. 'No, it's my night off.'

Sam nodded. 'Got any other plans?'

'No,' he said, frowning. 'Why?'

She was about to ask him if he'd be able to cover the bar and then another thought occurred to her. Nessie didn't want Joss at the Star and Sixpence but that didn't mean he couldn't represent the pub elsewhere? He had been part of the team once and their success was partly due to him, after all. Then again, it wasn't his professional behaviour Nessie had objected to, Sam thought, and she'd jump to all kinds of conclusions if she knew what Sam was considering. Maybe it was safer not to mention Joss until afterwards ...

'I've been stood up for the RAD awards this evening,' Sam said hurriedly, before she had a chance to change her mind. 'Fancy a night in London?'

Chapter Forty-Three

It had taken a while but, over the course of the long drive south, some of the tension between Sam and Joss had eased. He'd made her laugh with stories about the regulars from the pub he worked in now and she'd been careful to avoid any mention of Nick; no sense in rubbing salt into a healing wound. By the time they'd arrived at the Grosvenor House Hotel on Park Lane and checked in, Sam was hopeful that the evening ahead might continue to make things easier once they were back in Little Monkham.

The awards were being presented by a well-known comedian – Joss said he'd been their regular host for the previous few years and always went down well with the assembled crowd. 'Ruder than he is on the TV but never oversteps the mark.' He paused and winked. 'Well, hardly ever.'

Sam smiled. 'The champagne reception starts at 7 p.m.,'

she said as they made their way up to their rooms. 'Shall I knock for you and we can go down together?'

'Okay,' Joss said. 'It's probably better if we stick together, actually – things can get pretty rowdy as the night wears on, especially at the after party. People can sometimes be . . . inappropriate.'

Sam bit back a sigh, half irritated and half flattered by his concern. 'I've been to an after party or two, remember? Don't worry, I can look after myself.'

'It's not you I'm worried about,' Joss said, pulling a wry smile. 'It's me. There's a landlady from Uttoxeter who's determined to check my pipes, if you know what I mean.'

Sam couldn't help herself; she laughed. 'Got it. I'll see you at seven, then. Don't be late.'

When he opened the door an hour later, Sam could see why the landlady from Uttoxeter was so keen; Joss looked good in a tuxedo. Not in the same league as Nick, of course, but definitely handsome enough to turn heads. And she hated to admit it but the new clean-shaven look looked better with the crisp lines of the dinner jacket too. Sam squashed down a familiar flicker of interest as Joss fixed her with a direct, blue-eyed gaze.

'You look amazing,' he said, his eyes skimming her figure-hugging shimmering dress. 'Maybe I should be worried about you after all.'

'How about we look out for each other,' Sam said.

He smiled. 'It'll be just like old times.'

The champagne reception was being held in the hotel's

Red Bar and from the looks of things, some of the atten-
dees had started their celebrations early. Joss was greeted
with enthusiasm almost from the moment he and Sam
walked through the door; he was clearly among friends,
she realised. She spotted several women watching him and
wondered if one of them was the fan from Uttoxeter.

'Sam, this is George,' Joss said, drawing her into conversation. 'He's chair of the Midlands Real Ale division.'

She took the outstretched hand, gazing up at the heavily
bearded man with a practised PR smile. 'Sam Chapman,'
she said. 'From the Star and Sixpence in Little Monkham.'

'Lovely to meet you at last,' George said, his bushy black
beard twitching. 'I've heard a lot about you.'

Sam slid Joss a sideways look. 'Oh? Any of it good?'

George grinned. 'He's your biggest champion. In fact—'

'Don't let him get started,' Joss cut in easily. 'Before you
know it he'll be talking about the lesser-known micro-
breweries of Lima and you'll be wondering why you even
came.'

George gave him a look of mock outrage. 'I'll have you
know that there are some very fine micro-breweries in
Lima.'

Joss rolled his eyes. 'See?'

It was the same with almost everyone Joss introduced
Sam to; they all seemed to know much more about her than
she did about them. And it didn't take a genius to work
out the source of their knowledge – Joss. He'd clearly done
more than his share of bragging about the pub among his

industry mates before he'd quit. Sam couldn't decide quite how she felt about that.

After forty minutes or so of small talk, they were escorted into the Great Room, which had fifty or so round tables clustered around a red-carpeted stage.

'Table three,' Joss said, seemingly impressed. 'That's right up at the front. I've never been seated so far up the pecking order before – they must rate your chances.'

Sam glanced down at the seating plan; it looked like they were sitting with a few corporate sponsors and two other pubs from different regions of the UK. She spared a thought for Connor and Nessie; they should be sharing the glory here tonight instead of being stuck at home. Then again, Nessie should be enjoying the unexpected present Sam had arranged right about now. With a bit of luck spending an evening with Owen would help to reverse whatever damage Gweneth had inflicted on Nessie's already fragile confidence.

'Allow me,' Joss said, pulling Sam's seat out for her.

His gentlemanly manner made Sam smile – he really was making an effort. 'Thank you.'

The wine flowed during the three-course meal, although Sam limited herself to a single glass of Burgundy with the melt-in-the-mouth roast turkey main course, and she noticed Joss was being similarly restrained. By the time they got to the Christmas pudding crème brûlée, their table-mates were well on their way to being rowdy and the volume only increased as the coffee cups were cleared away in preparation for the award ceremony itself. Sam was feeling moderately sorry for their comedian host, who was due on stage any minute.

Joss leaned towards her. 'Feeling nervous?'

Sam shook her head. 'No. Winning the regional competition was enough – I don't expect to bag the top prize.'

'You never know,' he replied. 'There are other prizes too – Best Bitter, Landlord of the Year, Most Improved Pub and so on. Thirsty Bishop won the Best Bitter prize three years in a row while your dad was in charge.'

He said the last line in a matter-of-fact voice but Sam knew the awards would have been down to Joss, not her father. She'd come to accept that Andrew Chapman hadn't been as selfish and booze-raddled as she'd always thought, but she knew he would never have been capable of tending to the cellars of the Star and Sixpence in a way that would produce an award-winning ale. That was an achievement due entirely to Joss.

'I don't think I've ever thanked you for looking after Dad,' she said, keeping her voice low. 'I know there must have been times when you went way over and above the role of employee.'

His eyes met hers. 'It wasn't as bad as you think. He was a good man, Sam.'

An unexpected lump arose in Sam's throat. 'I know. You're a good man too.'

His blue eyes darkened as he gazed at her. He opened his mouth to speak but the PA system crackled into life.

'Ladies and gentlemen, please put your hands together for our host this evening, Archie Lewis!'

Reluctantly, Sam broke eye contact with Joss and glanced over at the stage as everyone began to applaud.

Archie Lewis was every bit as smooth as Joss had suggested. He slid into a well-observed comedy routine that poked fun at the audience and their trade but was also clever and witty in a way that ensured he'd be asked back again next year. Sam was impressed; if she'd still been in PR she would have added him to her list of bookable celebrities.

'But you're not here to listen to urinal gags,' Archie said, after a few more minutes of sly jokes and hilarious anecdotes. 'You're here to find out which landlord is the jolliest, which bitter is better and whose gaff is the one we all wish was our local. It's time to start handing out the silverware.'

Sam buried her hands in her lap, suddenly nervous. Up until that moment she hadn't been bothered about winning – landing the regional prize had been enough. But now her competitive side was kicking in and she'd be lying if she wasn't imagining how it would feel to collect the Pub of the Year award on behalf of the Star and Sixpence.

'Good luck,' Joss murmured as an expectant hush settled over the room.

The air of expectation grew as each winner was announced, although the noise levels increased too. But by the time Archie read out the nominations for the final category, even the rowdiest of tables were leaning forwards.

Sam composed herself and set her expression to neutral. She was sure they hadn't won. The winner had probably been notified in advance – that was the way award ceremonies usually worked. And yet she couldn't quite squash a tiny seed of hope ...

'The judges said each of the regional winners had all the hallmarks of the perfect pub,' Archie announced. 'A welcoming atmosphere, with friendly staff and great drink selection – the kind of place that represents the heart of their community. But there can be only one pub of the year and so, without further messing about, the winner of this year's Real Ale Drinkers' top prize is ...'

He paused and grinned at the expectant room. Sam felt her stomach contract even further as Joss reached under the table and gripped her hand.

'The Three Horseshoes in Hitchin!' Whoops of joy erupted from one of the tables. Archie raised his half-full glass in a toast. 'Let's hear it for landlord Neil and the rest of his team!'

Music began to play as the winners made their way up to the stage. Sam applauded warmly, beaming at the obvious delight on the faces of the Three Horseshoes' team. She'd met Neil and his wife earlier in the evening and had liked them both; from what she could tell they were worthy winners. And really it would have felt like too much for Sam and Nessie to have won the very first year that they'd opened – what else would they have to aim for? No, Sam thought as she clapped and cheered, it was better this way. But next year she was determined that the Pub of the Year trophy would have the Star and Sixpence engraved upon it.

Joss leaned in close to whisper in her ear. 'Well, I think you were robbed.' He paused. 'Fancy a tequila slammer?'

Nessie couldn't believe her ears when Owen presented himself at the busy bar and asked her what she wanted him to do.

'Do?' she echoed, hoping she didn't look as frazzled as she felt. 'What do you mean, do?'

'I'm your replacement barman for the evening,' he said. 'Although I'm surprised to see you here – I thought you'd be in London.'

'Change of plan,' Nessie said. 'I decided to stay here. That doesn't explain why *you're* here, though.'

'Sam said you were short-staffed and asked me to help out. Didn't she tell you?'

Sam, Nessie thought wryly. Why couldn't she stop meddling? 'But what about Gw—' she started to say, then stopped herself. There was no way she could ask about Gweneth without making Owen want to know why she was worried what his mother-in-law thought.

Rob waved an empty glass from further down the bar. 'A pint of Thirsty Bishop when you're ready, please, Nessie.'

Henry Fitzsimmons coughed. 'I think I've been waiting longer, old chap. Any chance of a whisky, do you think?'

Nessie nodded at both men to show she'd heard then gazed at Owen. 'I don't think this is a very good idea.'

He glanced around the pub. Nessie's eyes followed his, taking in the waiting customers, the uncleared tables and the waning fire. 'Let me help you,' he said softly. 'Friends help each other, right?'

Nessie swallowed a sigh; the truth was she was in no position to refuse. 'Okay, thank you. Do you want Henry or Rob?'

'Rob,' Owen said instantly. 'I think Henry has a soft spot for you and I wouldn't want to deprive him of a few minutes of your company.'

Nessie laughed. 'I hope you're wrong – I think Franny might arrange an unfortunate accident for me otherwise.'

She found herself mentally thanking Sam more and more as the evening wore on. The bar grew steadily busier; the village was clearly getting into the festive spirit and business was so brisk that Nessie soon forgot to worry what Gweneth thought about Owen helping her out. She enjoyed working with him; they seemed to have an unspoken understanding that meant they rarely got in each other's way and between them, the customers were happy, the tables were clear and the fire was roaring – exactly as it should be on a cold winter's evening.

It wasn't until the last customer had finished up and Owen was closing the front door that Nessie carefully asked how things were going with Gweneth.

Owen rubbed a weary hand across his face as he trudged

back towards the bar. 'Fine. She can be a bit overbearing sometimes, but people who live alone often are – they get used to pleasing themselves without having to think of others. She even tried to stop me coming over here tonight, can you believe it? Sometimes I think—' He caught himself and shook his head. 'Listen to me, sounding bloody ungrateful when all she's done is try to help.'

Nessie concentrated on cleaning the pumps, unable to think of anything to say. As far as she was concerned, Gweneth *wasn't* trying to help. 'It's bound to be a bit difficult,' she said after a moment. 'Especially when you haven't had much contact in the last few years.'

'I know,' Owen said as he loaded glasses into the dishwasher. 'But I feel like she doesn't trust me to do anything for Luke, as though she's the only one who knows how to raise a child, and I want to remind her that he's my son as well as her grandson.'

Nessie felt her heart beat faster: here it was, the perfect opportunity to tell Owen the truth about Gweneth and her threat to take Luke away. She swallowed hard, and took a long steadying breath.

'Maybe I'm being unfair,' Owen said, sighing. 'She means well, after all, and I would have struggled on my own with Luke without Kathryn. And it's hard for her, being reminded of Eliza at every turn.'

And just like that, the moment had vanished. Nessie straightened up and let the tension seep from her shoulders. 'Do you know when Kathryn will be back?'

'Christmas Eve,' Owen said. 'The plan is that Gweneth will stay for Christmas dinner and then take Luke home with her on Boxing Day for a few days.'

Nessie's stomach lurched. 'Oh? How does Luke feel about that?'

'He seems keen – she's promised to take him to the beach every day.'

Once again, Nessie steeled herself to tell Owen what Gweneth had said to her but somehow the words wouldn't come. She forced herself to sound light. 'I can see why he's keen. Who doesn't love the beach?'

'Exactly. And I might be calling on Gweneth again, if the band gets more work, so it seems like a good idea for the two of them to get to know each other.'

'You mean Gweneth might be here more often?' Nessie said slowly.

Owen nodded. 'It won't be easy but she seems to want to be part of Luke's life and it feels like another way for him to remember his mother.'

Nessie dipped her head and moved on to the next set of pumps. 'Yes, I can see that,' she murmured, seeing the temporary break she'd suggested to Owen stretching on and on into the future. 'Why don't you head off now? I can finish the clearing up.'

'Are you sure?' he asked, his forehead crinkling. 'I don't mind staying.'

'No, I can manage,' Nessie said, forcing herself to smile. 'Thanks for your help tonight.'

'My pleasure.' He paused, as though he was about to say something else, then stepped back. 'Night, Nessie.'

'Goodnight,' she called.

She watched until the door closed behind him and then slumped her head onto the bar. If Kathryn did start touring more – or worse, move out for good – then Gweneth might well become a permanent part of Owen and Luke's life. Which meant Nessie couldn't be. What was she going to do?

When Sam awoke the next morning, she could barely lift her head from the pillow. She lay still for a moment, squinting around the unfamiliar room and wondering where she was. Then it all came flooding back; she was in London for the RAD awards. The Star and Sixpence hadn't won. There'd been tequila, and a lot of champagne. The rest of the evening was something of a blur but she remembered laughing with Joss. He'd most definitely featured in the post-ceremony events . . .

Forcing her eyes open, Sam twisted around to check the other side of the king-size bed: to her relief, it was empty. She listened, straining to catch the sound of someone in the bathroom but the room was silent. Joss wasn't here. Whatever else had happened, they hadn't spent the night together.

Wishing she'd had the good sense to order breakfast in her room, Sam dragged herself reluctantly out of bed and into the shower. Fifteen minutes later, she was hurrying downstairs. She'd knocked for Joss and got no reply; either he was still sleeping things off or he'd spent the night elsewhere. Maybe the lady from Uttoxeter had finally got to him, Sam thought, trying to ignore a sudden tightness in her stomach.

There were several familiar, blurry-eyed faces as Sam entered the dining room, including George, who would not hear of her sitting alone.

'Come and join us,' he said, waving a hand at an empty chair beside one of his dining companions. 'Hangovers love company.'

'Hangovers love Prairie Oysters,' she corrected with a smile, thinking of Ruby's failsafe cure.

She sat down and George introduced Polly from Ginius, the independent gin distillery, and Raj, who ran a bar in Shoreditch. The conversation soon turned to gossip from the previous evening.

'Did you see Melanie from the Dog and Duck?' Raj said, his eyes twinkling with delight. 'She could hardly stand up.'

'She wasn't the only one,' George observed. He glanced sideways at Sam. 'Although Joss was probably pleased – she usually makes a bee-line for him.'

'Is the Dog and Duck in Uttoxeter, by any chance?'

George grinned. 'He's told you then. Yes, Melanie is his number-one fan but to be honest, he has quite a few admirers.'

'Unsurprisingly,' Polly said, with a wistful sigh. 'He's hot.'

Sam fought an unaccustomed stab of jealousy. 'He's also great at his job. He really goes the extra mile.'

Polly shook her head. 'He could go the extra mile with me any time. Is he single?'

She was pretty, Sam decided; raven-haired and petite with sparkling blue eyes and rosebud lips. Joss would be mad to turn her down. 'I believe so,' Sam replied, trying her hardest to keep her tone even. 'At the moment.'

'It's a shame you couldn't hang on to him, Sam,' George said, and for a split-second she thought he meant romantically. 'He really is one of the best in the business and I know how much he loved working at the Star and Sixpence.'

'Yes,' Sam managed, avoiding Polly's curious gaze. 'It is a shame.'

'Especially since he was the one who nominated the Star and Sixpence for Pub of the Year,' George went on. He layered a slice of bacon with ketchup. 'It came with a glowing recommendation, actually, made it sound quite irresistible.'

Sam stared at him. 'I didn't think you could nominate your own pub.'

'You can't,' George shrugged. 'This was after he'd left and had started at his new place — mid-June, I think. I remember because it was such a late nomination, only a day before we closed the list . . .'

He continued to talk but Sam barely heard the words. Joss had nominated the Star and Sixpence after they'd split up — in spite of all the bad blood between them? And he'd clearly done his best to make sure the pub was shown in the best possible light, too. It was such a lovely, thoughtful thing for him to have done that Sam felt her eyes swim with momentary tears.

George was frowning at her. 'I probably shouldn't have told you that — it's all meant to be confidential. Maybe I'm not quite sober yet after all.'

Sam summoned up a smile and reached for a slice of toast. 'Don't worry, George. Trust me, I know how to keep a secret.'

Chapter Forty-Four

A handwritten letter in unfamiliar writing arrived for Nessie on Friday morning.

She stared at it for a moment, taking in the Oxford post-mark, and then turned the envelope over and tore it open. As she'd hoped, it was from Ruby's son, Cal. She read it with breathless anticipation.

When she'd finished, she stood for a moment with her eyes closed in relief. Then she checked the time – forty-five minutes until opening time – and hurried upstairs to get her coat. She couldn't wait to see Ruby's expression when she gave her the good news.

'Really?' Ruby said, her face shining up at Nessie as she sat at the kitchen table. 'He really wants to see me?'

Nessie held out the letter. 'Read it for yourself. He sounds a tiny bit cautious but I expect that's understandable.'

Ruby read the letter through several times, running her fingers over the paper as though she could absorb the essence of her son through the ink. 'He suggests Monday in Birmingham for coffee.' She looked at Nessie anxiously. 'How am I going to get there? On the train?'

'Either Sam or I will take you,' Nessie soothed. 'Don't worry, we won't leave you to go on your own.'

Ruby clutched at her necklace and laughed, but it was high and nervous and nothing like her usual throaty laughter. 'Listen to me, I sound like a dithery old bat.'

'You do not. Anyway, it's okay to be nervous,' Nessie said. 'But try not to let it get the better of you. This is just the first step.'

The other woman stared at her for a moment, then seemed to pull herself together. 'You're right. And look, there's a mobile phone number – will you text him to say I'm looking forward to seeing him?'

Nessie gazed at her in puzzlement. 'Of course I will, but you can text him yourself if you'd rather?'

Ruby held out her hands and Nessie saw they were shaking. 'You know, I don't think I can,' she said. 'Be a darling and do it, please.'

Pulling out her phone, Nessie sent a message to Cal. Then she saw she'd somehow missed a call and a message from Sam. 'Oh,' she said, reading the message. 'Sam says we didn't win Pub of the Year.'

Ruby was reading the letter again. 'Hmmm?' she said, without looking up. 'Oh well, there's always next year.

Now, what do you wear to meet the son you thought you'd lost?'

Sam found herself seeing Joss through new eyes as they drove back from London. Thoughts swirled around her head; she'd wanted to ask him if he'd spent the night alone but couldn't think of a way to do it without sounding like a jealous ex. Thankfully, he'd eventually described dodging Melanie and escaping back to his room in a way that made Sam certain he'd been on his own. She'd also been tempted to ask him about the RAD nomination but something stopped her. Instead, she concentrated on the road, listening to him talk, and the closer she got to Little Monkham, the more relaxed and at ease she felt. As much as she enjoyed visiting London, it wasn't her home any more; the Star and Sixpence was. And that was going to be a problem when Nick arrived back from filming, expecting an answer. One of several problems, she thought, her gaze sliding briefly towards Joss.

She pulled up outside his flat and let the engine idle. 'Thanks for keeping me company,' she said. 'Losing was a lot easier with you there.'

Joss shrugged. 'You should never have lost at all. And you kept me safe from the dreaded Melanie so I reckon we're even.'

Sam studied him for a moment, then held out a hand. 'Friends?'

He hesitated, then took it. 'Friends.'

He stared into her eyes, his fingers still warm on hers,

then smiled and let go. He cranked the door handle to get out. 'See you soon, Sam.'

'See you,' she repeated as he slammed the door and walked to the entrance.

She sat there for a moment, waiting for her thudding heart rate to slow down. For a fraction of a second, she'd thought Joss would pull her close to kiss her. And for another fraction of a second, she'd really hoped he would.

Nessie greeted Sam with a hug.

'I'm so sorry you had to go through it on your own,' she said, taking her bag and leading her behind the bar. 'I wish I could have been there.'

Sam hesitated. 'Well, I wasn't exactly—'

Nessie shook her head. 'Maybe not technically but a room full of strangers doesn't count as company.'

'No, but—'

'Who did win?' Nessie asked.

Sam followed her up the stairs and into the living room. 'The Three Horseshoes in Hertfordshire,' she said. 'Joss said we were robbed.'

'Joss?' Nessie said, frowning. 'How would he know?'

Sam took a deep breath. 'He came with me. I bumped into him yesterday as I was leaving, and he said he wasn't busy, so we went together.'

'Sam!'

'I know what it sounds like but nothing happened,' Sam said, holding up her hands. 'It was all business-like and above board.'

Her sister stared at her, then shook her head. 'I can't believe you sometimes. After the way he treated you . . . Why didn't you tell me?'

'Because I knew you wouldn't approve.' Sam tipped her head. 'Would it help if I told you it was Joss who nominated us for the regional award?'

Nessie's eyebrows shot up again. 'Really? When?'

'After we split up, apparently.' She eyed her sister in satis-faction. 'So we have him to thank for our award-winning status. Not that he knows that I know, of course – nomin-ations are meant to be top secret.'

'I won't ask how you know,' Nessie said, rubbing her face. 'But it was a lovely thing for him to do, in the circum-stances. I didn't think he had the maturity, not after the way he flew off the handle over Will Pargeter.'

'Me either,' Sam admitted. 'Maybe we misjudged him.'

Nessie looked at her closely then, her eyes slightly nar-rowed. 'Is that affection I hear in your voice?'

'No, of course not,' Sam snapped. Then she relented. 'Maybe. A bit.'

Her sister groaned. 'Oh Sam, you do like to make things complicated. How does Joss feel?'

Sam sighed. 'I have absolutely no idea.'

'And what about Nick?'

'I don't know,' Sam said, slumping onto the sofa. 'We're talking tonight – maybe I'm just missing him.'

Nessie eyed her shrewdly. 'Or maybe you've never really got over Joss.' She took Sam's hand. 'Look, don't make any hasty decisions. Speak to Nick tonight and see how you feel tomorrow.'

It was good advice, Sam realised. And perhaps it was simply a case of missing Nick – six weeks was a long time to be apart, after all. One thing she was sure of was that she didn't want to move to London; her home was in Little Monkham now. If she and Nick were going to make a go of things, they'd have to do it at a distance.

'Okay,' she said to Nessie, managing a tired smile. 'How was your evening, anyway? Did you enjoy the surprise staff member I arranged for you?'

Nessie didn't smile back. 'He was very helpful, thanks.'

Sam waited, hoping for a sign that her sister and Owen had grown closer as they worked together, but Nessie remained tight-lipped.

'Oh,' Sam said, frowning. 'Well, that's good. And the two of you didn't . . .'

'We're still on a break, if that's what you mean?' Nessie replied stiffly. She stood up and headed for the door. 'One that looks very much like becoming permanent.'

She was gone before Sam could ask her what she meant. She stared after her sister, more certain than ever that the source of Owen and Nessie's problems was Gweneth. And she was even more determined to get to the bottom of it and put things right. Just as soon as she fixed her *own* love life.

It was eleven-thirty in the evening by the time Sam managed to video-call Nick.

471

'Hey,' he said, his face splitting into a trademark Borrowdale smile. 'How are you?'

'Tired,' she admitted. 'It was the Pub of the Year awards last night and it turned into a late one.'

'You don't look tired,' Nick said, 'you look gorgeous, as always. Tell me all about the awards – was it wall-to-wall beards?'

She laughed. 'Not exactly. It was surprisingly glamorous, actually. But boy, those guys can drink. They almost put City bankers to shame.'

'I bet. Did you win?'

'No, but that's okay.' She squinted at the screen of her phone. 'You're even more tanned than you were last time we spoke – if I didn't know better I'd say you were on holiday instead of working.'

He let out a dramatic sigh. 'What can I tell you – this role demands a tan. Obviously it's been a struggle . . .'

Sam listened as he described the scenes he'd been filming that day; for all his jokes, the schedule sounded gruelling. 'And there's still more to do. I'm sorry, Sam but it looks like I'll be stuck out here longer than I expected. I might not make it back in time for Christmas.'

'Don't worry,' Sam told him. 'I plan to spend most of Christmas Day asleep. You won't be missing anything.'

Nick frowned. 'Apart from being right next to you, obviously.' He paused. 'Have you thought any more about moving back to London?'

Here it is, Sam thought unhappily, the moment I've been dreading. 'Yes, I have, and I think I'm going to say no, Nick.'

His face fell and Sam pushed on. 'Things have been crazy busy here – business is booming and there's a lot to look forward to. I really think my future is at the Star and Sixpence with Ness, not in London. She needs me.'

'Duty isn't a good enough reason to turn your back on everything you know, Sam,' Nick replied.

'I'm not!' Sam said, stung by the words. 'In fact, I'm doing the opposite. Everything I know and love is in Little Monkham these days. I know you think I can rebuild my career in London but – well, I'm not sure I even want to. I like it here.'

There was a silence as Nick processed the information she'd just given him. 'Then we have a problem.'

'I know.'

'I don't think I can move to Little Monkham,' Nick went on. 'What if I get called to an audition at short notice, or need to call into the agency offices to sign some paperwork?'

Sam shook her head. 'I don't expect you to move here.'

'Then what do you expect, Sam?' There was a hint of frustration behind Nick's words. 'Because I've got to be honest, a long-distance relationship where we see each other once every six weeks isn't what I want.'

'But you said yourself, you're not going to be in London much,' Sam pointed out. 'So I'll be on my own, in a place I don't want to be, twiddling my thumbs until you come back. That's not going to work either.'

Nick was silent.

'Maybe this is a conversation we should have face to face,'

473

Sam said with a sigh. 'When do you think they'll wrap things up there?'

He puffed out his cheeks. 'I have no idea. Mum and Dad are complaining that I've forgotten where they live so if filming finishes before Christmas then I'll probably head straight to their house. Which means—'

'Which means I won't get to see you until New Year's Eve,' Sam finished. 'I don't mind that – really, I don't – but I would if we were living together.'

'You could come to see my parents with me,' Nick said, frowning. 'Then we'd be in the same place.'

Sam groaned. 'Which would mean I'd miss Christmas dinner with Nessie and Ruby. And there's the Festive Fayre on the village green on Christmas Eve – I need to be here for that.'

'Relationships are all about compromise, Sam.'

Something about his tone grated on Sam's nerves. 'But that compromise should be a mutual thing,' she said in exasperation. 'At the moment, it seems to be just me giving things up. And the thing that I can't – won't – give up is my sister and the Star and Sixpence.'

Nick gazed at her in silence, his expression every bit as brooding as his alter-ego on *Smugglers' Inn*. 'So we go back to how things were – fitting in visits where we can.'

Sam stared at the screen, hardly able to believe what she was about to say. 'No.'

His expression became still. 'No?'

Heart thudding with adrenaline, Sam forced herself to speak. 'I don't think we can go back – it's out there now.'

'Sam—' Nick began but she kept talking.

'No, don't interrupt. This is hard enough.' She took a deep breath. 'Look, we fell into this relationship because it was fun and it suited us both – I'll always be grateful to you for helping me to recover from what happened with Will. But it obviously doesn't suit us now – not if we're arguing over it. It's time to face the truth, Nick – we want different things.'

Nick watched her with miserable eyes. 'You're wrong. All I want is you.'

'No, you want the old Sam,' she said softly. 'The party girl who loved London – PR to the stars. I'm not that girl any more. I've outgrown her.'

His pain was almost palpable. 'So what – we're breaking up?'

The words hit Sam like a punch to the gut and she felt a hot ache in her throat. 'I – I suppose we are.'

Nick didn't reply immediately. His eyes were fixed on something Sam couldn't see, away from the camera. When he did speak, he sounded so sad that Sam wanted to reach through the screen to give him a hug. 'I knew it was too good to be true – us, I mean. I knew it couldn't last.'

She understood what he meant – it had been perfect as a fling, as long as they both kept things light-hearted. But as much as Sam loved being with Nick, she knew their relationship was never destined to become serious; as painful as breaking up was, it also felt right. 'You don't hate me, do you?'

He threw her an incredulous look. 'Hate you? How could I hate you – you're one of my best friends.'

Holly Hepburn

Tears filled Sam's eyes. 'Good,' she said. 'I couldn't bear it if you did.'

'I can't say that I'm happy and I might need a bit of time, but I'll get over it.' He sighed. 'This insane filming schedule should help with that.'

The lump in Sam's throat grew harder and more painful as she said goodbye and got ready for bed. Had she known, deep down, what was going to happen? She didn't think so; now that the adrenaline was wearing off, she felt empty and exhausted. It felt strange, knowing she was single again; no matter how much her head told her it was the right thing, her heart was harder to convince. It missed Nick already, even though he was on the other side of the world. But there was no going back – her head was certain of that. In time, they would be close again but they were no longer lovers.

Her eyes burned with the effort of not crying as she got ready for bed. It wasn't until she'd switched off the light and let the comforting darkness wrap around her that she let her tears begin to flow.

Sam knew something was wrong the moment she stepped into Weir Cottage on Monday morning. The air was usually filled with the scent of coffee – this morning it held the faint sour tang of juniper berries. At first glance, Ruby looked the same as ever, until Sam's suspicious gaze met hers and she saw the slight glaze.

'Ruby,' she said, fighting to keep her voice even. 'Have you been drinking?'

The older woman shook her head, a little too hard and a little too long. 'No.'

Sam stared at her. 'You have, haven't you?' She sniffed the air. 'Gin.'

Ruby glowered at her, raising her chin in defiance. 'Fine. If it makes you feel better then yes, I have had a small drink this morning. Just to calm my nerves about seeing Cal again.' She stepped back and stumbled into the table in the hallway. 'Whoops.'

Sam felt dismay wash over her; it didn't seem like a small drink to her. How could she take Ruby to meet her son – the son who'd cut all contact with his mother over her unhealthy relationship with alcohol – when she stank of gin? It was obvious she'd been drinking and once Cal realised she hadn't changed at all, Ruby's second chance would be over before it had begun.

'Oh, Ruby,' she said, pulling her phone out of her pocket and bringing up Nessie's number. 'You can't go and meet Cal like this. I'll ask Nessie to rearrange it.'

Ruby raised an unsteady finger and waved it in Sam's face. 'You've got no right.'

'I'm afraid I do,' Sam said, easing past Ruby to find the source of her downfall. 'Nessie and I are your cheerleaders – we might be tough but we care about you and that's why we want to help you.'

She soon found the tell-tale bottle of gin, hidden in the breadbasket. 'Where did you get this?' she demanded. 'I thought you'd given Nessie all the alcohol in the house?'

Ruby reached into her handbag and pulled out a shiny silver hipflask. 'That's my business, not yours.'

'Ruby!' Sam repeated, shocked. She snatched the flask from Ruby's hands. 'Have you forgotten what the doctors said? If you keep drinking, you'll die.'

The other woman pursed her scarlet lips. 'Nonsense – a little of what you fancy does you good. So give me my drink back.'

Sam refused. Instead, she marched into the kitchen and poured the contents of both the gin bottle and the hipflask down the sink. Then she sat at the kitchen table and stared meaningfully at Ruby. 'I know you're scared about seeing Cal again but alcohol isn't the answer.'

'Lighten up, Sam. It was just a small one to loosen my nerves.'

'I don't believe you,' Sam said. 'You're unsteady on your feet, which means you've had more than one, and you know how it works, anyway – one is never enough. How much have you really had?'

Ruby looked away. 'I don't need a lecture, darling. Cancel the meeting if you must but spare me the holier-than-thou attitude.'

Sam got up. 'Look at me, Ruby,' she said, taking the other woman's hands and waiting until her unfocused gaze drifted towards her. 'I don't mean to lecture you – I'm worried, that's all. You've worked so hard to stop drinking and I don't want you to slip back into its clutches.'

For a moment, Sam saw a flash of sober Ruby, the

woman who understood that alcohol was her enemy. She pressed home her advantage. 'Nessie and I love you, so do all your friends in Little Monkham – we want to help you. But if you want to see Cal then you have to do it sober.' She paused. 'You have to decide what's more important – seeing your son again, or having another drink.'

Ruby's gaze skittered away and Sam guessed she was battling an old adversary, one that was telling her Sam was lying; that alcohol only made her stronger, braver, smarter – a better version of herself. Seconds ticked by and turned into minutes. Sam waited, knowing the decision had to come from Ruby.

When Ruby spoke, her voice was subdued. 'Would you send Cal a message, please, darling? See if he can manage another day? I – I'm not quite myself this morning.'

Sam almost sagged with relief. 'Of course,' she said, taking both Ruby's hands and squeezing them with love. 'I'm sure he'll understand.'

Ruby looked at her then and Sam saw her eyes were bright with tears. 'I'm sorry.'

'Oh Ruby, there's nothing to be sorry for,' Sam said, gathering her into a hug. 'This is a hard path to walk. But you're not walking it alone – we're right beside you.'

The older woman shook in her arms. 'Thank you,' she whispered.

Sam smiled into her hair. 'It's okay. Now, let's rearrange that meeting.'

Chapter Forty-Five

It was just before five o'clock on Wednesday evening and the frost was already starting to bite as Nessie hurried across the village green towards the Star and Sixpence. Her breath formed clouds that sparkled beneath the multi-coloured lights strung between the trees and the grass crunched under her boots. She pulled her thick woollen scarf up to cover her chin and glanced at the Star and Sixpence, lit up and glowing against the navy-blue night. In three days' time it would be Christmas Eve and there would be a cluster of twinkling stalls in front of the pub, a whirling carousel and Santa's Grotto tucked away between the trees, but Nessie didn't feel in the least bit festive; she was too worried about Owen and Sam and Ruby for that. Her sister seemed to be coping in the aftermath of her break-up with Nick, and Ruby hadn't had another drink after her relapse, as far as anyone knew, but it felt like things were teetering on a knife edge, especially since Nessie hadn't worked out what to do about the situation with Gweneth. The thought of ending things permanently with Owen filled her with quiet desperation but she couldn't see any other way. She wouldn't put herself above Owen's relationship with his son.

She had almost reached the door of the pub when she heard Owen call her. Turning, she peered towards the forge and saw him heading her way. Her heart leapt and sank at the same time.

'I was hoping to catch you,' he said, once he'd reached the pub entrance. 'Are you around later – say seven o'clock?'

'Yes, I'll be here,' she said. 'Sam is going late-night shopping and it's Tilly's night off so I expect it will just be me. Why?'

Owen looked pleased. 'Good. I've got something for you. A little winter solstice gift.'

She stared at him in anxious confusion. 'What?'

'Don't worry, it's nothing big,' he said, noticing her bewilderment. 'Well, I suppose it is pretty big but it's not expensive.' He ran a hand through his hair. 'It's not even really a present, more a tradition. Anyway, I'll bring it over later if that's okay? At seven.'

'Okay, at seven,' Nessie echoed, even more confused. She didn't know much about the winter solstice, other than it heralded the shortest day of the year, and she had no idea what Owen's gift might be. Or what it meant.

'See you then,' Owen said. He hesitated for a moment, as though he was about to say something more, and then nodded in farewell before walking away.

'See you then,' Nessie called.

The pub was quiet, with only a couple of regulars nursing a pint as they flicked through the newspaper or chatted to each other. Nessie stoked the fire as she passed the huge fireplace that dominated the bar, enjoying the burst of heat from the leaping flames, then slipped upstairs to drop her coat off.

'Doing anything nice?' she asked Tilly as she let the barmaid go.

Tilly smiled wryly. 'Choir practice for the Christmas Eve carol service.'

'Ah,' Nessie said. The St Mary's Church choir was run by Franny and several village inhabitants were members, including Owen, Luke and Martha. Kathryn had resisted the recruitment process so far but it seemed Tilly hadn't escaped. 'Good luck.'

'Thanks. Frank the organist is on his second warning for freestyling during *Hark the Herald Angels*,' Tilly said cheerfully. 'It'll be a miracle if we make it to Christmas Day without bloodshed.'

By the time seven o'clock arrived, the regulars had finished their drinks and braved the cold to go home. Nessie cleared the tables and checked the stock levels behind the bar, then settled in one of the squashy armchairs beside the fire with a steaming mug of hot chocolate and her laptop to go over the accounts. These winter evenings when the pub was empty were secretly her favourite times, although Sam would be horrified to hear her say it: an unfilled pub was the last thing a landlord should wish for. But Nessie took a quiet pleasure in watching the fire burn. It was almost like meditation; a way to clear her mind, something she seemed to need more and more lately.

When the door opened again, it was Owen, carrying a wide, heavy-looking log complete with dangling roots at one end. The muscles in his arms bulged a little as he edged sideways through the doorway.

'Let me help,' Nessie said, jumping up.

'No need,' Owen said as he carried the log over to the fireplace and set it carefully down on the hearth. 'Yuletide greetings, Nessie.'

Understanding flooded through Nessie. 'It's a Yule log.'

Owen nodded. 'Traditionally burned on the shortest day of the year to welcome the return of the light and encourage prosperity for the months ahead. I used to bring one over to the pub every winter solstice.'

Nessie gazed down at the speckled bark and creamy wood. 'You didn't last year.'

'No,' he conceded. 'You'd only just arrived and I wasn't sure how you'd feel about the village blacksmith plying you with ancient pagan gifts. It might have sent you screaming back to London.'

She smiled as she imagined her sister's face. 'You could have a point. So, what do I do with it?'

Owen nodded towards the fireplace. 'You burn it slowly and think about the year that's gone and all the blessings you've received. Then, in the morning, you find a piece that hasn't burned and save it to light next year's log.'

Nessie frowned. 'But you didn't bring a log last year, so I don't have a piece to light this one.'

He reached into his pocket and pulled out a slightly charred chunk of wood. 'I saved you a bit from ours, hoping I'd know you well enough by this solstice to give it to you.'

His eyes met hers as he spoke and a shiver ran down Nessie's spine. They knew each other better than she'd dared to hope when they'd first met and yet there was still a lot she didn't know about Owen Rhys. But she might have suspected he'd observe some ancient traditions; he was a blacksmith, one of the oldest professions, and a Welshman. Old magic must run in his blood.

'Thank you,' she said. 'It's a lovely tradition.'

Using tongs, Owen dipped the fragment of the old log into the already-burning fire. It burst into yellow flames almost immediately. 'Old wood burns quickly,' he said, carefully passing Nessie the tongs and lifting the Yule log once again. 'Hold it beneath the root here, so that it catches alight.'

Nessie leaned forwards and did as she was told, trying not to notice how close she was to Owen or the warmth his body gave off. She concentrated on holding the crackling wood under the log, telling herself it was the heat from the flame that made her cheeks glow. Once the root was burning steadily, she stepped back and Owen lifted the log into the heart of the fireplace, his elbow-length leather gloves protecting him from the heat. He lowered it into the hearth with a flash of orange sparks. Amber and golden flames licked at the underside of the log and began to creep along the bark.

'It should last a few hours,' Owen said, straightening up and pulling off his protective gloves. 'I can pop in first thing tomorrow, if you like, to salvage a piece for next year.'

Nessie shook her head – she cleaned the fireplace every morning. 'You'll be busy with Luke. Don't trouble yourself.'

Owen's gaze was steady. 'It's no trouble. And it's part of the tradition – I'd like to.'

Again, Nessie felt a shiver of something – she liked the idea of creating a tradition with him that ran from year to year, even though she was growing more and more certain it would be as friends and neighbours, nothing more. 'Okay, thank you.' She glanced at the clock behind the bar. 'Have you got time for a drink or does Franny disapprove of drinking before choir practice?'

He nodded. 'She does but a drink around the Yule log is traditional too – the Romans used to celebrate with a feast that lasted for days. But I'll settle for a small Ardbeg.'

Nessie tipped a measure of peaty Scottish whisky into a glass and poured a ruby port for herself. She carried the drinks over to the armchairs facing the fire and set them on one of the low tables.

Owen waited until she was seated before raising his glass in the firelight, causing the tawny liquid to shimmer. 'To the year that's past,' he said, gazing deep into her eyes. 'I'm glad we've become friends.'

Nessie swallowed hard as the light from the fire danced and flickered across his face. There was definitely something of the old magic about Owen Rhys, she thought, her gaze drifting down to his gently curving lips and back to his dark eyes; he certainly seemed to have cast a spell on her, one that she couldn't shake no matter how hard she tried. Lifting her own drink, she touched it against his. 'And to the year ahead. I hope it brings you happiness.'

Glass chinked on glass. 'I hope it brings us both happiness,' Owen said quietly, holding her gaze. 'To new beginnings.'

Nessie was so caught up in a surge of bittersweet longing that she almost forgot to drink. It was only when Owen took a sip of his whisky that she remembered and mechanically lifted her own glass to her lips. The rich scent of fruit and the burst of warm spice that hit her tongue as she drank only served to heighten her feeling of intoxication. She swallowed, the ruby liquid burning all the way to her belly. If she put down her glass and closed the distance between her and Owen, she could kiss him. He'd taste of wood smoke and whisky. No one would need to know. No one would get hurt.

'I thought about bringing over some mistletoe,' Owen said, as though reading her mind. 'Another Yule tradition.'

Oh, I wish you had, Nessie thought.

He watched her over the top of his glass. 'But I wasn't sure I'd be able to resist the temptation.'

Nessie held her breath, trying to remember the reason she had for ending things between them. It seemed so ridiculous now; how could she let Gweneth come between them? 'Owen, I—'

The door swept open, bringing with it a blast of freezing air. Ruby stamped in, her cane thudding into the floor. 'Brrr, it's cold and dark out there. Everything the winter solstice should be.'

She paused in the act of taking off her coat, glancing first at Nessie's flushed cheeks and then across to a silent Owen. 'Bugger. I've interrupted something, haven't I?'

Owen drained his glass and flashed a smile at her. 'Not at all, Ruby. I was just on my way, to be honest. Choir practice waits for no man, especially not three days before Christmas.' He stood up and gazed down at Nessie. 'See you in the morning, then?'

She managed a smile. 'See you in the morning. And thanks for bringing the log. It was very thoughtful of you.'

Owen nodded once. 'Like I said, it's no trouble.'

His eyes lingered on her for a heartbeat, and then he was gone. Nessie busied herself with clearing the glasses as Ruby settled into the seat Owen had just left.

'I'm sorry for ruining the moment, darling,' the older woman said.

'You didn't,' Nessie assured her. 'We were just talking. And it's always lovely to see you.'

Ruby raised a perfect eyebrow. 'I've played more love scenes than you've had hot dinners, Nessie – I recognise a tryst when I see one, even if you apparently don't.'

Nessie felt herself blushing. 'Owen and I are just friends now.'

A peal of delighted laughter rolled across the bar. 'You keep telling yourself that, darling.'

'What can I get you to drink?' Nessie asked, determined to change the subject. 'An orange and cranberry spritzer?'

Ruby let out a delicate snort. 'I could have had orange juice at home and then you and Owen would be halfway up the stairs by now.' She sighed and shook her head. 'No, make me one of your gorgeously wicked salted caramel hot chocolates and entertain me while I drink it. And don't hold back with the flake.'

Sam stared at the Yule log smouldering in the grate at closing time that evening, then turned an accusing gaze on Nessie.

'Tell me again why you and Owen aren't together.'

Nessie wanted to groan. She recognised the determined look in Sam's eyes; it was the same one she'd had aged eight when she'd demanded to know where her baby teeth really went, and it meant business. Nessie wouldn't be able to fob her off with vague reasons and excuses. It was time to tell her sister the truth.

When she'd finished talking, Sam looked as though she'd like to hit something. 'That miserable, interfering bitch!' she stormed, getting to her feet and pacing the bar. 'I knew she'd done something to upset you, but this? This is beyond twisted.'

Nessie hung her head. 'I know.'

'So what are you going to do?' Sam stopped pacing to glare at Nessie. 'And don't say you're going to give in to this emotional blackmail crap because I won't let you. I'll go round there and have it out with her right now.'

'Sam!' Nessie cried in alarm. 'This needs careful handling. I can't just go and blurt it all out to Owen.'

'Why not? He deserves to know what a snake she is. In fact, I'm amazed he hasn't put two and two together already.'

'Yes, but—'

Sam gave a short sigh. 'Look, if there's one thing I know it's that you can't give in to blackmailers. You need to seize the initiative, take their power away, and the only way to do that in this case is to come clean with Owen.'

Nessie stared at her sister, feeling an all-too-familiar wave of panic and nausea. 'But what if Gweneth goes to Social Services?'

'Let her,' Sam replied promptly. 'I'm fairly sure it's an empty threat but let her try it. It's obvious Luke isn't neglected and there are plenty of people around the village who'll tell anyone who asks that Gweneth Morgan is a poisonous old witch who blames Owen for stealing her daughter away.'

Nessie froze. 'Does she? How do you know?'

'Franny told me,' Sam said. 'So I don't think any of this is really about you, Ness. I think she's punishing Owen. She can't bear the thought of him moving on when she can't.'

Could it be true? Nessie wondered. She thought back to the conversation she'd had with Gweneth in the graveyard; it certainly seemed to fit, although the older woman's words had been personal and cutting too. 'She told me I wasn't good enough for him,' she admitted to Sam. 'She said I'm half the woman Eliza was. She – she said I stink of beer.'

Sam's lips tightened. 'She's wrong on all three counts. And I doubt very much she knows the full story – Kathryn says Owen and Eliza were considering a divorce before she became ill. Maybe it's time Gweneth heard a few home truths about her precious daughter.'

'Sam, you can't!' Nessie felt a sickening lurch of alarm at the fury in her sister's voice. 'Think about Luke.'

'Okay, maybe I won't bring that up,' Sam relented. 'But this mess needs sorting out, Ness. You don't have to be there – in fact, it's better if you're not. I won't have to hold back then.'

'What are you going to do?'

'Tell Owen everything,' Sam said grimly. 'Then it will be up to him to put things right.'

Nessie's gaze travelled to the Yule log burning in the fireplace. What was it Owen had said? *To new beginnings.* And hadn't her Yuletide wish been that Gweneth would just vanish, leaving everything exactly as it had been before she arrived? Maybe it was time to make that wish come true.

'I'll tell him,' she said, taking a deep unsteady breath. 'First thing tomorrow morning.'

'Make sure you do,' Sam ground out. 'Because if you don't, I will.'

Nessie didn't expect to sleep much.

She expected to spend the night staring at the beamed

ceiling above her bed while her brain went into meltdown, worrying about Owen's reaction. But in reality, she fell straight into a dreamless sleep and didn't stir until her alarm went off just before six.

All the trepidation she'd managed to avoid the night before came crashing back as she prepared the guest breakfasts and printed off their bills, ready for them to check out. By the time Owen knocked on the door of the pub, Nessie's stomach was churning so much that she thought she might actually be sick.

She did her best to smile as she let him in. 'Good morning.'

'Good morning to you too,' he said, and Nessie saw the faint crease of a pillow still indented into his cheek. 'Did you sleep well?'

'I did,' Nessie admitted. 'Much better than I thought I would, actually.'

He nodded at the fireplace. 'That'll be the solstice working its magic. Sleep is a good way to spend the longest night.'

His eyes glittered at her for a moment, and then he crossed to the hearth and knelt beside it, rummaging among the cold ash until he found what he wanted. 'Ah, here it is.'

He held up a half-charred piece of wood. 'We need to keep this safe to light next year's log.'

Nessie felt her stomach turn over again. 'If there is a next year.'

Owen looked at her in surprise. 'Why wouldn't there be?'

She let out a short, hard breath. 'I think you'd better sit down, Owen. There's something I need to tell you. It's about Gweneth ...'

Owen didn't interrupt once. He grew more and more still, his expression becoming more stone-like with every word Nessie said. Finally, when she finished speaking and drifted into an uncomfortable silence, he stared at nothing for a long moment.

'I wasn't going to tell you,' Nessie said, when the silence became unbearable. 'But then you said Gweneth might be here more often and I—'

Owen stood up suddenly and Nessie stopped talking.

'I'm afraid you'll have to excuse me, Nessie,' he said, and she heard the cold ring of iron determination in his tone as he tucked the burned bit of Yule log into his pocket. 'There's something I need to do.'

Her heart pounded as she watched him leave. Was he angry that she hadn't told him right away? Or was he furious that she'd told him at all? 'Owen?'

He didn't reply, leaving her staring at the gently sighing door as it closed. The fact that he'd taken the fragment of Yule log was an encouraging sign, Nessie told herself as she slumped back into her seat and took in a shaky breath. Wasn't it?

Chapter Forty-Six

Christmas Eve dawned crisp and bright, with the kind of blue sky that seemed infinite.

Nessie awoke with a faint tingle of festive excitement, the same fizz she'd had as a child when school had broken up for the holidays and there was nothing ahead but fun and excitement and anticipation of a pile of brightly wrapped presents underneath the tree on Christmas morning. It was quite ridiculous, she told herself as she got out of bed; all she had to look forward to was a gift or two and the simple pleasure of roasting a turkey with all the trimmings. Her heart had felt heavy ever since she'd confessed the truth about Gweneth to Owen, probably because he had yet to speak a word to her after storming out. But the weight of keeping Gweneth's poison a secret was gone and with it some of the darkness she'd felt hanging over her. The arrival of her Decree Absolute had helped too – she was officially a single woman again. It was hard not to feel hopeful, Nessie decided.

She had no idea whether Owen had confronted his mother-in-law immediately or decided to wait until after Christmas. Sam had urged her to call into Snowdrop Cottage but her nerve had failed her – what if Gweneth opened the door? – so she'd concentrated on preparations for the Festive Fayre instead, determined to make it the most Christmassy night Little Monkham had ever seen. And maybe, if she was lucky, there would be a quiet moment when she might catch Owen alone . . .

The day flew by in a blur. She left Sam in charge of the pub and spent most of her time on the green, ensuring the carousel was in exactly the right spot, that Santa's Grotto had a comfortable seat and a sack full of presents. She also called into the butcher's and the baker's to pick up some last minute supplies for Christmas Day. Before she knew it, the skies were darkening and it was time for her to make her way to the candlelit carol service at St Mary's. Heavy grey clouds had gathered since the morning, obscuring the blue sky and giving the air a muffled, oppressive feel. Nessie pulled her hat down over her ears and hurried towards the brightly lit church.

Inside, it was packed. The entire village seemed to be there, apart from Sam, who had insisted someone needed to mind the bar even though they both knew no one would be stopping by for a drink – not when everyone was at the carol service. But as Sam pointed out, there was wine to be mulled and chestnuts to part-roast for the brazier on the green. Secretly, Nessie suspected her sister had yet to wrap a single present.

Nessie squeezed into an already full pew at the back. She spotted Owen and Luke immediately. They were near the front, with the rest of the choir, and Nessie's heart sped up at the sight of them. Luke said something to his father and as Owen leaned his black-haired head closer to answer, Nessie was reminded once again how different Luke looked; how like his mother he was. And she felt a momentary pang for Gweneth, stuck in her bitter mourning for Eliza. She hoped, in time, that the other woman's pain would be healed.

Father Goodluck beamed down at everyone from the pulpit. 'Good evening and welcome to St Mary's this blessed Christmas Eve,' he called. 'It is lovely to see so many of you here to fill our church with light and celebrate the miracle of Christ's birth.'

Nessie juggled her lit candle, with its collar of cardboard, and glanced down at the programme Henry had pushed into her hand as she'd entered the church. The first carol was *Hark, the Herald Angels Sing*, one of her favourites, followed by *Silent Night* and *Away in a Manger*. Nessie knew she wasn't much of a singer – she could carry a tune and not much else – but there was something special about carols that made her want to sing to the rafters. As the organ pounded out the first majestic chords, she lifted up the words and got ready to enjoy herself.

★   ★   ★

Sam had just written the last tag when she felt a blast of icy air. She looked up from her seat beside the fire to see Joss standing in the doorway, his gaze fixed on her.

'Hello, Sam,' he said. 'Merry Christmas.'

She stared at him in astonishment. 'Joss. I thought you'd be at the carol service.'

He shook his head. 'Not my thing.'

'Not mine, either,' Sam said, pulling a face. 'Although I love everything else about Christmas. So, what can I do for you?'

Joss started forward and stopped halfway between the door and the fire. Sam was amazed to see he looked nervous. 'What?' she said. 'What is it?'

'I thought—' He cleared his throat and started again. 'Listen, Sam, you can tell me I'm out of order if you want to but – well, there's something I have to say.'

She waited, steeling herself for another angry rant. 'Go on.'

He took a deep breath. 'I know you're with Nick now, and I honestly hope you're happy with him, but ... but it's Christmas and like that stupid bloody film says, at Christmas you tell the truth. So here it is, Sam.' He fixed her with an intense blue-eyed stare. 'I love you. I've always loved you. And I'm sorry I was an idiot – I should have listened to you when you tried to explain about that Pargeter bloke. Instead, I let my pride get in the way and it stopped me from seeing what was really important.'

Sam gaped at him; this was the last thing she'd expected him to say. 'Joss—'

'No, don't interrupt. First, I was jealous of Nick and then, when the news broke about you and Will, I got jealous of him too, even though all of that happened long before we met.' He let out a shaky laugh. 'I think ... I think you make me a bit crazy, Sam, and I'm sorry. I should have supported you instead of walking away and leaving the door open for Nick.'

Sam shut her eyes for the briefest of seconds, trying to take it all in. It was all such a gigantic mess. 'Oh, Joss.'

He threw her a wretched look. 'I know – I'm an idiot. And like I said, I know you're with Nick now and it's far too late for any of this but – well, I just needed to get it off my chest, that's all.'

Sam gazed down at the pile of presents by her feet, the shiny paper and ribbon blurring with tears. 'What if it wasn't too late?' she said in a low voice.

'What?' Joss said, frowning.

She blinked up at him. 'What if it wasn't too late? For us, I mean.'

'I don't understand,' he said, his frown deepening. 'What about Nick?'

'We broke up a week ago,' she said simply. 'When it happened, it felt like there were too many obstacles to over-come but now I can see there was just one.'

Joss watched her warily. 'Oh? What was that?'

Now it was Sam's turn to take a deep breath. 'You. I'm still in love with *you*, Joss.'

He stood frozen for a heartbeat, then stormed across the space between them and pulled her to her feet. A second later, his lips were on hers, not hard and crushing but gentle and searching. For Sam, it was as though something she'd been missing for months had suddenly returned. She wrapped her arms around him and kissed him back.

When they finally broke apart, Joss tenderly stroked Sam's cheek. 'Forgive me for being a moron. I promise never to do it again.'

Sam smiled and brushed his lips with hers. 'There's nothing to forgive.' She gazed up at him and felt something stir inside. 'I've missed you. Can you stay?'

He shook his head, glancing at the clock over the bar. 'I'm working tonight.'

'Then come here afterwards,' she said. 'Stay with me and have dinner with us tomorrow. Unless you have plans?'

'Nothing that can't be changed,' he said firmly, bending his head to kiss her again.

The choir sounded amazing, Nessie thought as they worked their way through all the traditional songs. Some carols were marked as choir only and she almost gasped in amazement when villagers she'd never suspected of being able to sing unveiled beautiful voices. Tilly had a delicate high soprano voice that somehow soared above everyone else's. Franny had a lower but no less pleasing tone to her voice and Ruby sounded good too, a few pews ahead of Nessie. But it was Owen and Luke who blew her away the most, as they duetted for *Good King Wenceslas*; Luke sang the page boy with heart-breaking clarity and Owen's deep Welsh baritone made the hair on the back of Nessie's neck stand on end. She found it hard to take her eyes off him after that. Why had he never told her he could sing?

It was with great reluctance that Nessie blew out her candle and slipped away just before *O Come All Ye Faithful*, the final carol, to make sure everything was all set for the Fayre. Something brushed her cheek as she walked and she looked up to see snow swirling down from the darkened sky, big fat flakes that caught the light from the streetlamps as they fell. She let out a gasp of disbelief – surely it wasn't going to be a white Christmas?

Nessie watched with bated breath as the snowflakes tumbled to the ground. Some melted as soon as they landed but others settled and more soon joined them. By the time she reached the village green there was a thin layer of white on the ground that thickened with every passing second and the tops of the stalls looked as though they'd been dusted with sugar.

'It's snowing, Sam,' she called as she pushed through the door into the pub. 'Come and see!'

She looked up to see Sam and Joss springing guiltily apart. 'Oh!' she exclaimed. 'Sorry!'

Joss seemed totally unfazed but Sam's cheeks turned cherry pink. 'We – uh . . . we kind of got back together.'

'So I see,' Nessie said, with dry amusement. 'Good for you.'

'I wondered whether Joss could come for Christmas dinner,' Sam said.

Nessie laughed, unable to do anything else – it was a

good thing she'd stocked up on extras. 'Of course – the more the merrier.'

Her sister smiled. 'Good, because I might have already invited him.'

Nessie glanced at the clock. 'I should warn you that the rest of the villagers are due to arrive any moment and they'll be expecting mulled wine and roast chestnuts and Martha's Rob as Father Christmas. Please tell me you didn't get side-tracked and forget, Sam.'

Sam threw her an indignant look. 'Of course I didn't forget – the Santa outfit is all laid out upstairs. Although now you mention it, I should probably go and check the oven. I got a bit distracted so the chestnuts might be a little more than part-baked.' She reached up to kiss Joss. 'See you later?'

He smiled. 'Definitely.'

'Don't say it,' Sam warned, once Joss had left and she'd rescued the chestnuts from the oven. 'I know you think I'm making a mistake.'

'I didn't say a word,' Nessie objected, halfway to the door with a tray of glasses for the mulled wine. 'In fact, I was going to say that you look happy for the first time in months and if it took Joss to do that, then I'm all in favour.'

'Really?' Sam asked, wide-eyed.

'Really,' Nessie said with a fond smile. 'Now, come on. I can hear the first revellers outside.'

The flurry of snow didn't dampen the Festive Fayre – if anything, it made the atmosphere even more Christmassy, especially once the choir started to sing more carols. The carousel whirled among the snowflakes, causing its riders to laugh in delight. Connor headed for the bar and started mixing up some Gingerbread Bellinis, his special Christmas cocktail, and outside, the mulled wine sent clouds of spice-scented steam into the freezing night air. Any children not riding the merry-go-round or queuing for Father Christmas raced around in circles, hurling handfuls of snow at each other. The adults clustered around the sizzling sausage stall or the brazier, where Sam was handing out hot roasted chestnuts and apologising for the burnt ones. Once the choir had finished, Sam cracked open her Christmas playlist and festive tunes spilled from a speaker beside one of the pub windows. Fairy lights twinkled through the trees on the green as they lit the way to Santa's Grotto and the dancing snowflakes made Nessie feel as though she had stepped straight into a Christmas film. It was one of the most magical sights she had ever seen.

Her gaze naturally gravitated towards Owen; he was policing the queue for Father Christmas and laughing at Luke, who was trying without much success to stuff a handful of snow down his father's neck. As she watched, Owen let out a roar of mock rage and scooped up some snow of his own to thrust under Luke's scarf. Nessie laughed. Owen was such a good dad – anyone could see he doted on his son and Luke clearly felt the same way about him. How Gweneth could have suggested otherwise was beyond Nessie.

A voice broke into Nessie's thoughts. 'No need to ask what your Christmas wish is.'

Blushing, she turned to see Franny, her eyes sparkling with mirth. 'Is it that obvious?'

Franny chuckled. 'I'm afraid it's like a big flashing sign over your head that says "I LOVE OWEN RHYS". But if it's any consolation, I think the only person who can't see it is Owen himself.'

'Or maybe he does see it and is pretending he doesn't,' Nessie said, sighing.

'Come now, Vanessa, you don't honestly believe that.' Franny's gaze grew suddenly severe over the top of her glasses. 'I've never seen a man more in love and, believe me, as chairwoman of the Village Preservation Society, I've made it my business to observe many over the years.'

'But—'

'But nothing,' Franny said briskly. 'Would he have sent Gweneth packing with a flea in her ear if he didn't care for you?'

Nessie's mouth fell open. 'Did he?'

Franny nodded. 'First thing yesterday morning. My sources tell me they had an almighty argument and he told her to never darken his doorstep again.' Her eyes narrowed. 'I thought he would have mentioned it.'

Nessie glanced over at Owen, who was laughing at something Martha had said. 'I haven't seen him, actually.'

'I imagine he's embarrassed,' Franny said. 'There's nothing worse than a meddling old biddy sticking her nose into other people's business, is there?'

There wasn't a trace of irony behind the words. Nessie

hesitated, unsure how much Franny knew about Gweneth, and then decided that Franny probably knew everything. 'He only did it to protect Luke—'

'Rubbish,' Franny snapped. 'I'm sure Luke's welfare played a part but the way I heard it, Owen went into battle for you, not his son.'

'What do you mean?'

'I mean that my sources also reported that Owen told Gweneth in no uncertain terms that he loves you.' Franny folded her arms. 'But for some reason, the fool thinks you're not interested and so he won't say the same thing to you. Honestly, I wish I could bang your heads together to make you see sense.'

Nessie felt her cheeks flame as she gaped at the postmistress. 'What?'

Franny's expression softened. 'It's really very simple, Vanessa,' she said in a slow and patient tone. 'You love Owen, but think he isn't interested. Owen loves you, and thinks you're not interested. Might I suggest you both stop acting like stubborn teenagers and actually tell each other how you feel? Or do I have to get Henry to hang about with some mistletoe until you get the idea?'

Could it be true? Nessie wondered, laying a cool hand against her too-warm cheeks. Had Owen really told Gweneth he loved her? She didn't have to ask whether she herself was in love with Owen; she'd realised with a jolt in the church that it was true, as she'd listened to him and Luke sing. If she was really honest with herself, she'd known for months.

'And Gweneth has really gone?' she asked.

'Really gone,' Franny confirmed. 'I watched her leave with my own eyes.'

Nessie blinked with heady relief and reached across to squeeze Franny's gloved hand. 'Thank you. I think I can take it from here.'

Franny graced her with a single nod. 'See that you do. I expect to hear good news when the pub re-opens on Boxing Day, do I make myself clear?'

Laughter bubbled up inside Nessie. 'Yes, Franny,' she said, doing her best not to break into hysterical giggles. 'Crystal clear.'

'Good. Now, if you'll excuse me, I need to track down Henry. Now that I think of it, I'm not sure I trust him around mistletoe.'

She bustled away, leaving Nessie alone. Once again, her gaze sought Owen across the green and this time, she discovered he was watching her already. Their eyes met. Seconds passed. And then Owen smiled and raised his glass of mulled wine in a toast. Nessie lifted her Gingerbread Bellini and it seemed to her that something unspoken passed between them. Then Luke landed a perfect snowball in his father's face and the moment was lost.

Nessie pulled out her phone. *Come for Christmas dinner*, she typed and sent it before she could change her mind. She watched Owen check his own phone and glance across at her, frowning.

A few seconds later, her screen lit up. *Are you sure?*

Her fingers flew in reply. *Of course – we have WAY too much food. Besides, I'd like you both to come – Kathryn too, if she's back.*

OK, we'd love to. What time?

Nessie hugged Franny's words to herself all evening: *Owen loves you.* And more than once, she remembered Owen's Yule wish that they would both be happy in the year ahead. Could she dare to hope that his wish might be about to come true?

Chapter Forty-Seven

It was Christmas Day.

Forcing her feet into her warm sheepskin slippers, Nessie padded across to the shutters that covered the windows and peered outside. She let out a squeal of delight when she saw the thick layers of crisp white snow that covered everything. Her very first white Christmas! She could hardly believe it.

Resisting the urge to knock on Sam's door, she headed to the kitchen to brew some coffee. Her sister was in charge of table setting and decorations and since Joss had arrived not long after closing time the night before, Nessie didn't really expect to see Sam much before ten o'clock. But there were vegetables to prepare, pigs in blankets to bake, an enormous turkey to roast and a mountain of expectation to manage — Nessie didn't have the luxury of a lie-in.

She was humming along to a carol service on the radio as she worked when Sam appeared an hour later.

'Good morning,' Nessie said in surprise. 'Merry Christmas.'

Hiding a yawn behind her hand, Sam reached for the coffee pot. 'Merry Christmas. Please tell me there's fresh coffee in here.'

Nessie pulled a face. 'There was, an hour ago. Why don't you make us some more? Unless you'd rather peel parsnips?'

'No, I'll do the coffee,' Sam said hurriedly, eyeing the vegetables in alarm. 'I'm pretty sure I read somewhere that life is too short to peel a parsnip.'

Nessie laughed. 'That's stuff a mushroom. But don't worry, I'll do it.'

Sam yawned again. 'Good. Anything else I can do?'

'I don't think so,' Nessie said, surveying the organised chaos that adorned every surface of the tiny kitchen. 'Everything is under control.'

'Great,' Sam said. 'I'll get Joss up in a minute and we'll make a start on downstairs.'

Nessie gave her a sidelong look. 'Are you going to tell me what happened between the two of you?'

Her sister shrugged. 'He apologised for being an unsupportive, jealous idiot and I accepted his apology. Then we kissed and made up.' She stretched and winced. 'All night.'

'I know,' Nessie said, grinning. 'I heard you.'

Sam seemed entirely unembarrassed. 'He says he loves me.'

'Well, duh,' Nessie teased. 'How do you feel about that?'

'Happy,' Sam said. 'I love him too.'

Nessie almost dropped the vegetable peeler. 'Really? Oh Sam, that's wonderful news!'

'Don't go buying a hat or anything,' Sam warned. 'It's still early days.'

'Even so . . .' Nessie beamed at her sister. 'Look at you, all grown up and admitting you're in love. I never thought I'd see the day.'

Sam tried to scowl but failed and smiled instead. 'Yeah, I know. Serial-dater Sam settles down.' She fired a meaningful look Nessie's way. 'Which just leaves your relationship to sort out. Please tell me you haven't dreamed up yet another reason not to be with Owen while you slept.'

Nessie's stomach swooped pleasurably at the mention of his name. 'No, I haven't. But today isn't the right time. It'll keep until after Christmas.'

Sam let out a groan. 'And then it will be New Year's Eve and you still won't have done anything. Nor will Owen. Honestly, Ness, can't you *carpe diem* or something?'

'I will,' Nessie promised, turning around to slide the turkey into the oven. 'As soon as Christmas is over.'

'You'd better,' Sam warned. 'Because I won't be held responsible for my actions if you don't. I want proper snogging and evidence of hot sex, do you hear me?'

Nessie felt her face flush in a way that had nothing to do with the heat from the oven. 'I'll do my best,' she managed.

Ruby was the first to arrive, shortly after midday. She swept Nessie and Sam into Chanel-scented hugs and insisted on giving them their presents there and then, rather than placing them under the tree in the bar.

'Wow,' Nessie gasped as she opened her gift. 'Is this a Mont Blanc fountain pen?'

Ruby nodded. 'Elizabeth Taylor used to swear by hers. "Ruby, darling, it's like the words just write themselves," she told me once. Happy Christmas, Nessie, I hope you like it.'

Nessie got up to plant a kiss on the other woman's cheek. 'I love it – thank you.'

Sam's present was a butter-soft Mulberry bag that made her whoop with delight.

'I'm sorry I don't have a present for you, Joss,' Ruby said, once Sam had thanked her. 'I didn't know you'd be joining us today.'

'Don't worry,' Joss said, reaching across to take Sam's hand. 'I think we managed to surprise everyone, including ourselves.'

Owen and Luke arrived next, and they had a surprise guest of their own.

'Kathryn!' Sam shrieked, wrapping Owen's sister in a warm hug. 'You made it!'

'I did,' Kathryn said, laughing. 'Although it was touch and go for a while – I thought I'd have to hitch a ride on Santa's sleigh.'

Luke rolled his eyes. 'Like that would ever happen. Everyone knows he doesn't carry passengers.'

Kathryn's eyes danced. 'But I did get chatting to

someone interesting while our train was stuck in the arse end of nowhere.' She smiled wickedly. 'I'm calling him an early Christmas present.'

Sam's eyes widened as she demanded more detail. Owen glanced across at Nessie and smiled. 'Merry Christmas.'

Nessie felt her heart thud as she returned his smile. 'Merry Christmas, Owen.'

Once Sam had heard all about Kathryn's mystery travelling companion, she got to work supplying everyone with drinks – for Ruby's sake, the bar was only serving mocktails. They were just settling into their places around the table when there was a resounding knock at the door.

Ruby looked around in bewilderment. 'Who could that be? We're all here, aren't we?'

Nessie exchanged a secret smile with Sam. 'Carol singers, probably. I'll just go and get rid of them.'

She crossed the bar to the front door and opened it. Framed against the pristine whiteness of the snow were three strangers. Nessie smiled at the man. 'Hello. You must be Cal.'

He shook her outstretched hand. 'And you must be Nessie. Thanks for inviting us today.'

She stepped back to let Cal and his wife and daughter in. 'It's my pleasure.'

Ruby had been regaling everyone with another of her wickedly funny theatre stories but she stopped the moment she saw Cal. Her eyes widened in shock and she almost dropped the glass of cranberry juice she was holding. 'It can't be . . .'

Cal smiled nervously. 'Hello, Mum. It's been a while.'

Clutching at her walking stick, Ruby hurried towards him. 'Darling,' she said, her eyes filling with tears. 'It's been too bloody long.'

Nessie felt her own eyes prickle with tears as the two embraced and she knew she wasn't the only one – Sam was blinking hard too.

'This is my wife, Merle,' Cal said, standing back to indicate the tall blonde woman at his side. Then he placed a hand on the shoulder of the shy little girl trying to hide behind his legs. 'And this ... this is little Ruby. Your granddaughter.'

It was all too much for grown-up Ruby: she burst into tears, which set Nessie off. Sam found a packet of tissues from somewhere and passed them round, dabbing at her own eyes as she supplied another round of drinks.

'I can't believe you're here,' Ruby said to Cal, for the fourth time. 'And I can't believe these wicked girls didn't tell me what they were plotting.'

Nessie and Sam exchanged smiles. 'It was all very last minute,' Nessie explained. 'We wanted to surprise you.'

Ruby dabbed at her eyes with a tissue. 'I am most definitely surprised. This is the best present I could have wished for.'

'All we need now is Micky,' Sam said.

'You haven't!' Ruby gasped, goggling at her.

Sam laughed. 'No, he's your New Year's Eve gift. But now that we *are* all here –' she tapped her glass with a fork to get everyone's attention, 'I'd like to propose a toast. To family.'

'To family,' they echoed, and there were plenty of warm glances.

Nessie stood up. 'And I'd like to propose that we *eat*.'

The meal was a roaring success. The turkey was golden and perfect, the roast potatoes were hot and crispy and the gravy was rich and, Nessie was grateful to see, lump-free. Laughter and groans filled the air as the crackers were pulled and jokes were told. And there were sympathetic squeals when Ruby revealed Cal was short for Caliban, from *The Tempest*.

'You have no idea how much I got teased once the kids found out at school,' he grumbled.

'It could have been worse,' Ruby said, her eyes sparkling with mischief. 'You could have been called Puck. Just think how much fun your classmates would have had with that!'

Nessie listened to the teasing and sat back, soaking up the happiness and basking in the glow of a job well done. Every now and then she sneaked a look at Owen, and dared to dream of Christmases yet to come.

Once everyone was so full that they couldn't eat another thing, she got to her feet and started to clear the plates.

'Let me help,' Owen said, standing up.

Nessie shook her head. 'You're a guest; you don't need to clear up.'

'And you cooked,' Owen countered. 'You definitely shouldn't do the dishes. So why don't we compromise and do it together?'

Nessie felt a shiver run through her as his eyes met hers. 'Okay.'

At the other end of the table, Merle started to get up too. 'Can I do anything?'

'Yes,' Sam said promptly. 'You can sit down. Nessie and Owen can manage on their own.'

Out of the corner of one eye, Nessie saw Ruby lean across and whisper something to Merle, who smiled.

'We'll just get on with it then, shall we?' Nessie said, casting an embarrassed glance around the room.

'I wish you would,' Sam muttered, raising her eyebrows.

Kathryn nodded. 'And don't come back down here until the job is done.'

Nessie cringed at their lack of subtlety. What must Cal and Merle think of them? Even worse than that, what must Owen think?

'Who wants to play Monopoly?' Luke asked, and a good-natured argument broke out over who was going to be the dog.

'That was a delicious meal, Nessie,' Owen said, once the plates had all been transferred to the kitchen upstairs. 'It must have taken you ages to prepare.'

'A few hours,' she said. 'Not that long. Most of it was already prepared – all I did was stick it in the oven.'

His brown eyes regarded her thoughtfully. 'I think you're downplaying things but thank you anyway, on behalf of the Rhys family.'

Flustered by his thanks, Nessie reached for a tea-towel. 'Do you want to wash or dry?'

His lips quirked into a smile. 'Dry, I think.'

They worked in silence for a few moments, then Owen cleared his throat. 'I think I owe you an apology.'

Nessie sent a wide-eyed look his way. 'You don't.'

'I do,' he said, sighing. 'Gweneth put you in an impossible situation and I should have guessed what she was about earlier. I'm sorry for that.'

She shook her head. 'Don't. You couldn't have known.'

'No, but I could have questioned why she was so desperate to take Luke back to Wales. I should have known that you had a very good reason to break things off between us.' He paused and pulled her hands from the hot soapy water, drying each one gently with the towel. 'And I should have told you how I feel about you long before today.'

Nessie's heart began to speed up. 'It really isn't your fault—'

He laid the tea-towel on the table and gazed at her solemnly. 'I didn't imagine saying this in a room full of dirty dishes but I don't want to wait any longer.' He took both her hands in his. 'Nessie Blake, I love you. I think I've loved you from the first moment I saw you, downstairs in the bar, looking like a startled hare who would run at any moment. And like a fool, it's taken me an age to admit it to myself – partly because I was scared of loving anyone again but partly because I couldn't be sure you loved me back.'

The breath caught in Nessie's throat. 'How could you think that?'

His forehead crinkled. 'Because you were always coming up with reasons why we couldn't be together, so I thought that maybe you just weren't that interested. And then you told me what you'd done, how you'd let Gweneth blackmail you to protect me and Luke, and I knew I'd been blind.'

Nessie was filled with a soaring swoop of delight. 'Of course I love you,' she whispered. 'I always have.'

He stared at her as though he didn't quite believe her. Then, after what felt like an age to Nessie, he smiled. 'That's all that matters, then,' he said, leaning down to kiss her.

Nessie thought she would burst with happiness as she wound her arms around his neck. They might have been kissing for one minute or five when Nessie realised they had an audience. She considered ignoring whoever it was but modesty prevailed and she pulled gently back to see Kathryn, Sam, Joss and Ruby beaming in the kitchen doorway.

'How long have you been standing there?' she asked, feeling embarrassment set fire to her face.

'Long enough,' Kathryn said, with considerable satisfaction. 'Do you have any idea how long the entirety of Little Monkham has been waiting for this moment to happen?'

Nessie's hands flew to her cheeks as she threw a mortified glance at Owen. 'Really?'

Sam nodded. 'Oh yes. There's even been a sweepstake.' She glanced at Ruby. 'Okay, who had Christmas Day?'

Ruby consulted a little notebook and then beamed. 'I believe that was young Luke.'

Luke poked his head around the door, grinning. 'All right – finally!'

* * *

It was much later.

Cal and his family were settled in one of the luxury guest rooms under the eaves of the pub and Luke was fast asleep in the other. Ruby had been escorted home with promises of a snowball fight with her granddaughter the next day. Kathryn, who was almost dead on her feet, had excused herself to fall into her own bed for the first time in weeks. Joss had gone upstairs to Sam's room and Owen had popped back home to collect some fresh clothes for the morning. Nessie could hardly breathe from anticipation as she stood in the doorway of the Star and Sixpence with Sam, gazing out at the star-filled sky over the snowy village.

'It's been quite a year,' she said.

Sam snorted. 'You can say that again. It's been crazy.'

Nessie wrapped her arms around herself and smiled. 'Crazy in a good way.'

'Yeah,' Sam allowed. 'Although if next year wanted to be less dramatic, I wouldn't mind.'

'And we owe it all to Dad,' Nessie said, with a slight shake of her head. 'Did you ever think you'd feel thankful to him for anything?'

'No,' Sam said after a moment. 'But I never thought I'd understand him, either, and I do. A bit, anyway. Enough.'

Nessie glanced back into the Star and Sixpence, aglow with light from the fireplace. 'Me too.'

Sam stared at her for a moment. 'I've got an idea. Stay here – don't move, even if Owen comes back and tries to sweep you off your feet.'

She vanished back inside the pub, leaving a blushing Nessie gazing after her in confusion. But everything became clear when she reappeared with two glasses of ruby red port.

Sam held one out to Nessie. 'A toast,' she said, lifting her glass. 'To Dad. Thanks for giving us exactly what we needed, even though we had no idea we needed it.'

Nessie raised her own glass and touched it against Sam's. 'To Dad,' she echoed, smiling. 'Here's to another year at the Star and Sixpence.'

Acknowledgments

My first tip of the hat goes to Special Agent Jo Williamson, of Antony Harwood Ltd, for believing in the Star and Sixpence and helping me to open the bar. Enormous thanks to the editorial dream team, Clare Hey and Emma Capron, for their patience and good humour: many deadlines whooshed by in the making of this book – sorry. A magnum of champagne to the legend that is SJ Virtue, and undying thanks to all the Simon & Schuster superstars – you make this so much fun.

A writer is nothing without her inspirational friends and so I owe a massive debt of gratitude to Kate Harrison (my go-to cocktail gal), plus Miranda Dickinson, Rowan Coleman, Julie Cohen and Cally Taylor for letting me share in their brilliance sometimes. Thanks to the Sisterhood, CAN and my sea-swimming mammal gals (you know who you are). A big sloppy kiss to all the reviewers and readers – thanks for your incredible support.

And lastly, thank you to T & E – my sunshine on a rainy day.

Bottoms up, everyone!

BANYAN TREE
~VABBINFARU~

WIN A HOLIDAY OF A LIFETIME AT BANYAN TREE VABBINFARU IN THE MALDIVES!

Included in the prize:

- A seven night stay at Banyan Tree Vabbinfaru in a Beachfront Pool villa for two people
- Full board basis, incl. soft drinks, excl. alcohol
- Return transfers from Male to Banyan Tree Vabbinfaru
- Two x return economy flights from London to Male up to a value of £700 per person
- Trip to be taken between 1 November 2017 and 30 April 2018. Blackout dates include 27th December 2017 – 05th January 2018

To enter the competition visit the website
www.simonandschuster.co.uk